*"I've wanted you . . . even before
you kissed me. Please,
Gresham . . . Charles—"*

His mouth was on hers before she finished
saying his name. This was Tessa, strong-
willed and confident and bold. It seemed as
though he had wanted her forever, and now
that she admitted she wanted him . . .

Tessa had known when she slipped out of
the inn that she was going to end up in Gresham's bed. The sensible worries that consumed
her before had been eroded and undermined
by that kiss, that breathless moment when it
seemed as though her soul had finally found
its mate.

He broke off the kiss with a groan, his
fingers working at the buttons of her dress.
"This dress has to go . . ."

Tessa nodded. "Yes, hurry."

"I've been waiting for this moment forever," he said in a dark voice.

Tessa licked her lips. "So have I."

D1053826

Romances by Caroline Linden

The Way to a Duke's Heart

❧ The Truth About the Duke ❧

CAROLINE LINDEN

AVON

An Imprint of HarperCollinsPublishers

AVON BOOKS
An Imprint of HarperCollins*Publishers*
10 East 53rd Street
New York, New York 10022-5299

Copyright © 2012 by P.F. Belsley
ISBN 978-0-06-202534-0
K.I.S.S. and Teal is a trademark of the Ovarian Cancer National Alliance.
www.avonromance.com

First Avon Books mass market printing: September 2012

Avon Trademark Reg. U.S. Pat. Off. and in Other Countries, Marca Registrada, Hecho en U.S.A.
HarperCollins® is a registered trademark of HarperCollins Publishers.

Printed in the U.S.A.

10 9 8 7 6 5 4 3 2 1

This one is for girlfriends, who know when to laugh, when to nod, when to be blunt and when to be kind, when to send chocolates and when to pass the wine.
You know who you are.

The Way to
a Duke's Heart

Prologue

He was born to be a great man.

At birth he was swaddled in the finest linens embroidered with the crest of the Earldom of Gresham—his father's second-highest title and therefore his, by courtesy of being the heir. The great estates of Durham and all his father's lesser properties, extensive and wealthy enough to be a small kingdom, would be his one day. His line could be traced back to the first Earl of Durham, ennobled by Richard the Lionheart himself, and on his mother's side he was descended from Edward IV. The blood of not just dukes, but kings, flowed in his veins.

He was expected to live up to it. One of his first memories was of his nurse scolding him for some misdeed and telling him how great he would be. "You'll be a duke one day, a great man like your father, and it doesn't become you to hit your brother," she'd told him as she spanked his hand with her wooden spoon. He squirmed in agony through the punishment, but there was nothing he could say in reply. His brother Edward wasn't the heir; he was not born to be great. Charles Cedric Spencer Fitzhenry de Lacey, eldest son of the Duke of Durham, felt the burden of his heritage from an early date.

When he was eight he was sent off to school. His mother cried, but Charlie was eager to go. Being the heir meant he was closely supervised, and school promised freedom. And first Eton, then Oxford, suited him; in their demanding halls and fields, where a boy's character as well as his body and mind endured trial by fire, he thrived. He made friends easily, and was big enough to hold his own against those he didn't befriend. His family's standing was among the highest in England, and he was usually elected head of any group of boys. He acquitted himself reasonably well in his lessons, and learned the trick of winning his tutors' favor to raise his standing even more. And his title made him irresistible to girls of all ages and shapes, which was just bloody brilliant in Charlie's opinion. Away from home, he felt quite up to the lordly destiny imposed on him at birth.

At home, though, was a different story. His father had always been a demanding parent, but his mother leavened the atmosphere at Lastings Park with laughter and love, teasing Durham out of his darker moods. When she died, the summer Charlie was eleven, it cast a shadow over the whole household but most especially over the duke. Durham grew stern and critical of everything his sons did. He constantly pushed them all to excel, but Charlie was held to a higher standard—impossibly high, it seemed. When he finished in the upper half of the form, Durham excoriated him for not being at the top. When he was reprimanded at school for some harebrained caper, Durham himself came to deliver a brutal lecture and suspend his pocket money for a full term, forcing Charlie to live like a pauper and borrow what he could from friends. Whatever he did, his father found fault with, citing his future position and duty as the bar he fell woefully short of. Charlie privately thought he wasn't quite as bad as all that, but he dutifully bore up under the lectures and thrashings. He was the heir, after all, and great men bore up under adversity.

And yet.

He came home from school at age sixteen to discover his father had begun talking about estate business with Edward—Edward, who was only thirteen. "The boy's uncommonly bright," the duke boasted to a neighbor, in hearing of all his sons. "Excellent sense in his head. Quite the brightest of my lads." Charlie shot an unhappily surprised look at his brother, who only gave a sheepish shrug. Edward couldn't help being clever with numbers. Charlie, who managed well enough at mathematics but didn't really care for it, knew he was beaten before he'd even realized there was a competition.

When he next came home on holiday from university, he discovered his youngest brother Gerard had shot up in height and now topped him by two inches. Charlie, accustomed to seeing Gerard's eager face turned up to him in admiration, found this unsettling. Gerard had inherited the de Lacey streak of fearlessness, and when he rode the unbroken colts, Durham roared with approval. Charlie, who had been forbidden since birth to touch those raw colts, watched in grim silence. While not precisely longing to risk his neck on Durham's wildest horseflesh, he rather resented his father's obvious approval of his youngest brother's abilities and daring.

But all this, too, one might endure. As infuriating as it was to suffer in comparison to younger brothers, Charlie still had the consolation of knowing he was the heir. Edward might be cleverer at managing the estates, but they would be *his* estates. Gerard might cover himself in glory on the battlefield, but *he* would have the seat in Parliament, where the direction of the nation was decided. He might never be renowned for his brilliance or lauded for his courage, but he would *matter*. He told himself the rest was immaterial; he didn't hate his brothers for their talents, even if his father clearly preferred them. Lord knew he wasn't the only heir to chafe under a strict and demanding father's hand.

But then he met Maria.

He had gone to the local assembly rooms on a lark with Rance and Longhurst, two mates from university. All three were whiling away a few weeks of freedom before departing on the Grand Tour; Durham had finally decided he might travel abroad, so long as he stayed clear of any lingering madness in France. In a room filled with gentleman farmers and a handful of gentry, Charlie and his titled friends stood out like candles in the darkness. Every female in the room sighed in rapture at their entrance, from the blushing young ladies to their suddenly alert grandmamas. So many females were presented to him that night, Charlie lost count. He danced until his feet were sore, and was in search of liquid refreshments when he caught sight of the ravishing creature who would turn his world upside down.

She was almost ethereally beautiful, with sky blue eyes in a perfect pale oval face. Her dark curls were tied with a simple white ribbon, and her pink dress displayed a plump, luscious figure. Even so, it was the toe of her slipper, peeking from beneath her skirt and tapping in time with the music, that really caught his eye. Why was such a lovely girl not dancing? And who the devil was she?

A few discreet questions supplied the answers. "Maria Gronow," Rance reported. "Family's a bit dodgy, if you believe the gossip. Still—by gad, Gresham, she's a sweet piece."

"Yes," said Charlie, staring at her openly. "Find someone to introduce me."

It was nearly love at first sight. She blushed very prettily when he bowed to her, but her smile was almost coy. She agreed to one dance, which sadly turned out to be an old-fashioned pavane that prevented any significant conversation, and then refused to grant him another.

"A lady must be so careful of her reputation, my lord," she murmured, looking up at him through her eyelashes and flashing an enigmatic smile. "And a gentleman must mind his intentions."

"Of course, Miss Gronow." He returned her smile, already anticipating the pursuit.

When he called to pay his compliments, she smiled in her coquettish way and said she hoped he would come again. He did, with flowers, and was rewarded with her agreement to go riding with him. Mrs. Gronow, her mother, granted permission with a smile, but it was nothing to the smile Maria gave him later, after he stole his first kiss on that first ride together. From that moment, he was lost.

It was an intoxicating month. Charlie called on her every day, taking her riding and driving and even just walking. He grew drunk on the taste of her, the scent of her, the touch of her lips. She understood him; for hours they talked, and she never failed to take his side and roundly malign anyone who slighted him. She looked at him as if no one else in the world existed, and he didn't know how he could survive without her. He couldn't sleep for thinking of her. He could barely carry on conversations for thinking of when he would see her next. Every kiss drove him mad, every touch made him burn, and her tempting little smile only fueled the inferno of desire inside him. Quite rapidly his world divided in two, where there was only the bright heaven containing Maria and the cold dark hinterland containing everyone else.

His friends noticed. They teased him about his luck in securing the prettiest piece of muslin in Sussex, and Charlie just smiled. His love for Maria, he knew, was a tricky thing. He couldn't bear the thought of leaving her for several months to take a Grand Tour. Not because he feared falling in love with someone else, as she sometimes teased him, but because he was mad for her. If anything, she would find another fellow while he was gone, someone polished and older and independent. He was sure Maria could tempt a royal prince himself, if she happened across His Highness's path. The more Rance and Longhurst talked of the tour looming before them, the more resistant Charlie grew. Italy and Greece would always be there; Maria, young and beautiful and almost his, would not. By the time his friends departed for their family homes to prepare for the journey, he had made up his mind. He was not going. He was going to stay in Sussex and marry Maria.

He just had to tell his father.

"I don't think I shall leave for Italy next month after all." He fired his opening shot at dinner one night. Opportunely, he was dining alone with the duke; Gerard was at university and Edward was in Wales, studying sheep farming with their uncle, the Earl of Dowling.

Durham didn't say anything. He looked at Charlie for a long moment over the rim of his glass, then waved one hand, sending the footmen from the room. "Why not?"

"I haven't been home much. I ought to learn the estate."

Durham just focused a hawklike stare on him.

"I thought you'd be pleased," Charlie forged onward. "Shouldering my duty, and all that."

"It wouldn't have anything to do with that girl, would it?"

The question caught him off guard. He hadn't said a word about Maria to his father, and Rance and Longhurst were too cowed by His Grace to betray him. "She's not just any girl," he snapped back before he could think better of it.

His father grunted. "No, indeed. She's the very

worst sort of adventuress, trying to entrap a boy barely out of short coats."

"I'm twenty-two years old," he replied, flushing with humiliation. "I'm not a boy, Father, I'm a man."

"Then act like one." Durham turned his attention back to his plate. "Don't be led by your prick, lad."

"I'm in love with her." He was trying to be calm and firm about this, but his father knew just how to provoke him.

"No, you're not," said Durham, unmoved. "You want to bed her."

That was true—desperately, painfully true—but Charlie bristled in the face of such bald accusation. "I haven't! I wish to behave honorably toward her."

His father raised an eyebrow. "Indeed? Then you're giving her far better coin than she gives you. The Gronows are unparalleled leeches."

"She's as decent and modest as any young lady in England!"

Durham put down his knife and fork and leveled a stern finger at him. "I don't care how badly she teases you or how desperately you want her. You're not going to marry her. Talk your way under her skirts if you will, but no son of mine is going to marry into a scheming family of charlatans. She may have some finer qualities, but mark my words: she wants to be a duchess, with ready access to Durham's funds to support her worthless father. Don't fall for her pretense of affection, Charles."

He took a deep breath, his hands in fists. "I'm bringing her to call," he announced. "You'll reconsider when you meet her."

Durham stared at him. "Very well," he said at

last. He reached for his wine as if peace had been restored. "Invite her parents if you like."

The Gronows were delighted to accept the invitation. Charlie suffered a pang of hesitation when Mrs. Gronow almost crowed in triumph as she stepped into the house, and he didn't miss the way Mr. Gronow eyed the furnishings and paintings with a calculating, hungry look. His father was wrong, damned wrong, about Maria, but perhaps Durham knew something about her parents Charlie did not. His fears evaporated when Maria caught his eye and gave him a rueful smile as her parents exclaimed a little too loudly about Lastings Park. He managed to take her hand as they followed the butler to the drawing room, and she squeezed his fingers back, setting his heart at peace again.

Durham made his appearance half an hour later. At first he was the very model of an aristocrat, polite but chilly. Charlie began to relax, despite the gleeful glances Mrs. Gronow kept giving Maria; he hoped his father couldn't see those. To himself, Charlie admitted the Gronows were rather grasping and avaricious, but he wasn't marrying them, he was marrying Maria, and she was enduring this endless visit with the same serene assurance she always had.

"So," said Durham abruptly, fastening his dark gaze on Maria. "I understand there is talk of an alliance."

"Indeed, sir." Mrs. Gronow sat up a little straighter and beamed at her daughter. "We hear nothing at home except of Lord Gresham—and I daresay my daughter is too modest in her praise of him!"

"I daresay," murmured the duke. "Has an offer been made?"

"Yes, sir." Charlie met his father's eyes evenly and confidently. Despite his father's warning the other night, he had asked for Maria's hand in marriage. He couldn't resist a fond glance at his betrothed. "Happily she has consented, and Mr. Gronow has given his blessing." Maria blushed a pretty shade of pink and modestly lowered her eyes.

"With great pleasure," declared Mr. Gronow. "I couldn't hope for a better match for my child. We are all honored by the connection."

Durham shot an unreadable look at him. "No doubt." He turned back to Maria, his eyes narrowed almost as if he were studying her for flaws. Charlie was sure even his father, demanding and particular, could find nothing false in her. She was so beautiful, perfectly at home in the elegant drawing room. He flashed her another confident glance, and was rewarded with her little smile, the intimate look she reserved just for him.

"I do not approve," said Durham quietly. "He is too young to marry."

Mrs. Gronow made a shocked gasp. Her husband's chin dropped. Charlie could barely see for the haze of humiliation that sprang up before him. "I am old enough, sir—" he began, but his father wasn't finished.

"He is much too young," repeated the duke. "I cannot consent to this, and I will not bless it. He has not reached his majority, and if he were to contravene my wishes, he would be cut off without a farthing for the rest of my life."

There was a frozen silence in the room. Maria's

blush faded to stark pallor as she stared at the duke with burning eyes. Mrs. Gronow looked fearfully at her husband, who seemed to be struggling for speech. Charlie could hardly breathe. How humiliating, to be treated like—and called!—a child, in front of his beloved and her parents. It was bad enough to hear his father praise Edward's intelligence over his, or applaud Gerard's bravery, but this . . . All he asked of his father was permission to marry the girl he loved, and Durham had cut him down in the cruelest way possible.

Unruffled by the tension in the room, the duke got to his feet. "Good day." He was out the door before anyone else moved.

"Well!" Mrs. Gronow sucked in a deep breath, and then another. "Well!"

"I'm very sorry," said Charlie in a low, tight voice. "I never dreamt—"

"It wasn't your fault," Maria said woodenly.

"Of course not," added Mr. Gronow. He gave Charlie a distracted pat on the shoulder. "Maria, Mrs. Gronow, let us go."

Charlie followed them through the house. "Don't despair, darling," he whispered to Maria as the footmen fetched their things. "It's not the end."

She looked at him with skeptical hope. "How can it not be? He refused to give his consent—he appeared quite implacable!"

"I don't need his bloody consent," growled Charlie. He touched one finger to the corner of her mouth, desperate to see her smile again. "I won't be bound by his arbitrary pronouncements."

Maria shook her head. The hopeful light in her face faded. "How? How can you persuade him?"

He couldn't, and he knew it, but Charlie didn't give a damn right now. "Can you get away tomorrow?" Her parents were ready to go; he had only a moment left with her. "Meet me at the bridge, tomorrow morning. Please, Maria," he begged as she glanced uncertainly toward her father. "For just a few minutes."

"I cannot . . ."

"The day after," he urged. "Three days from now. Any time. *Please*, darling."

She bit her lip, but nodded. "Ten o'clock, Friday."

Four days from now. An eternity, but he was desperately grateful for the chance. "Until then." He pressed her fingertips to his lips, disregarding their companions.

"Good-bye," she whispered, and then the Gronows were gone, Maria hurrying in her mother's wake, her head down. Charlie watched until their carriage was gone, but she never looked back at him.

A sharp ache speared his chest. How dare his father do that to him? He knew Durham didn't approve, but to denigrate his heir that way, in front of others, was intolerable. He stormed off to vent his humiliation and hurt at his father, but it was unsatisfying. Durham absorbed his fury without responding to it. He listened and said nothing when Charlie wanted him to erupt in fury. He wanted his father to feel the same pain he felt now, the same panic. Maria was doubting him. Mr. Gronow might withdraw his consent. And still his father refused to engage, merely repeating that Charlie was too young to know his own mind and the decision was irrevocable.

For three days he brooded about it, avoiding his father. On the day he was to meet Maria, Charlie rose with his mind made up: he would make one last effort to persuade his father, and failing that, he would elope. He would be cut off from his allowance, true; but what was money when weighed against losing the love of his life? Durham couldn't disinherit him. Sooner or later Charlie would ascend to the dukedom and its trappings, and probably sooner than later. His father was nearing seventy, albeit without any real sign of infirmity. His heart hardened with resolution, he went into the breakfast room and bowed.

"Sir," he said. "I implore you one last time to reconsider."

Durham didn't ask about what. His face set, he slowly shook his head. "No."

As he had expected. Charlie bowed again. "Good day, then."

Maria was waiting by the time he reached the bridge in the woods, her blue cloak a bright spot amid the greenery. His heart jumped as always at the sight of her; he was off his horse and rushing toward her before she even turned to face him. But her expression stopped him in his tracks.

Her eyes were grave. Her porcelain skin was frighteningly pale, and her mouth trembled at the sight of him. Renewed fury bloomed inside him, that his father had done this to her—to them. He clasped her in his arms, and she clung to him as if her life depended on it, soft and fragile in his embrace.

"Run away with me," he whispered. "I can't bear to lose you. Elope with me."

She raised her face to him. "We can't. Your father—"

"Damn him," Charlie growled. "I love you."

"We'd be *poor*," she cried in anguish. "Cut off. Cast out."

"Only until he dies." It was cold and heartless to say it that way, but Charlie thought those words described the duke's action perfectly. "Maria, darling, we can manage."

"How? Do you really mean to be destitute for years and years?" She stepped back out of his hold. "Did you know he called on my father?"

Charlie stared, thunderstruck. "No."

"He said you wouldn't have a farthing from him if we married against his wishes. Papa was quite indignant on your behalf—how could a father cast out his eldest son?—but His Grace was adamant. He declared the previous Duke of Durham lived past age ninety, and he meant to do the same. Don't you see, we *can't* run off!"

"I'll take care of you," he promised recklessly. "Somehow."

A tear rolled down her cheek. "No," she whispered. "I wish I could, but I can't. My parents told me this morning I'm not to see you again, because His Grace threatened them if they did not separate us. Mama wants me to go to her cousin in Bath—a change of scene, she says. My heart is breaking. I love you. I always will. But I cannot marry you, not like this."

She went up on her toes to kiss him. In agony, Charlie seized her and held her close, trying to persuade her with his kiss if not with his words. She wound her arms around his neck and kissed him back, but in the end she pulled away from him. "Good-bye, my love," she said, her voice quaking. "Good-bye." She turned and hurried off, leaving him alone.

She hadn't exaggerated. He heard through neighborhood gossip Maria left the day after their farewell; in fact, all the Gronows went to Bath. But if Charlie thought that was the harshest blow to bear, he was mistaken: barely a fortnight later news reached his ears that she was being courted by an older, more sophisticated man. By the time he heard whispers that Maria Gronow had snared herself an earl—a proper earl, in full possession of his estates and income—Charlie was past the point of feeling the pain.

His father found him in the garden the night he heard the heartbreaking news, staring off in the direction of the bridge where they had parted that last time—forever. For several minutes Durham just sat silently beside him on the cold stone bench.

"She fooled you," the duke said at last. "It hurts, but better now than later, when you would be irrevocably tied to her."

"She loves me." Charlie's voice sounded flat and dead to his own ears. "And I love her."

"She wanted to be a duchess," countered his father. "And her family schemed to make her one. Did you never wonder why a mother would allow her sixteen-year-old daughter so much freedom with a young man?"

He had wondered, briefly, but Maria told him her mother suffered headaches and was often confined to bed, not noticing where her daughter went.

Because it suited his wishes so perfectly, he accepted it. Had she lied to him? He shook his head slightly; it didn't matter now.

"Gronow made no effort to hide it. He hinted you had compromised the girl, thinking to force my hand." Durham glanced at him. "I know my son. You're too honorable." Charlie just sat, stony-faced, remembering every little liberty Maria had allowed him, and every one she had denied him. He *had* been too honorable. If he'd taken advantage of her innocence, just once, to make love to her and get his child on her, Durham would have had no choice but to agree.

"But I'm not a fool, and I didn't let him mistake me for one," his father went on. "Gronow was born a viscount's son, but he's a scoundrel and a liar, looking to twist everything to his advantage." Durham paused, shooting a contemplative glance at him. "He had the temerity to suggest my opinion of the match counted for little, when I said you would never marry his daughter, and to point out I could not disinherit you. He asked if I would allow my grandchildren to be raised in penury."

"I *would* marry his daughter," replied Charlie.

"I told him I would not be blackmailed into supporting his family," went on his father, as ruthless as ever. "He wanted money, Charles. As soon as I called his bluff about the girl's virtue, he asked for recompense for her broken heart, first ten thousand pounds, then five, then one. He's awash in debts. His pretty daughter is the only asset he's got."

"She's not like that."

"Perhaps not, but I see she wouldn't elope with you. And now she's engaged to marry another

man, barely three weeks after professing her love
for you."

Charlie shuddered.

"She got what she wanted, and it wasn't you; it
was a title and a fortune." The duke's tone grew a
shade softer. "Surely you see that now."

"What choice did she have, after being humiliated here? You're not the only one with pride,
Father, although not everyone exercises it so
cruelly."

Durham stiffened and looked away. "You'll understand some day," he said at last, his face grim
and shadowed. "And you'll thank me for it."

Slowly, Charlie turned to stare at his father, feeling hollow and numb. He could endure being the
least favorite son; he could endure being criticized
on every point, made to feel inferior and useless.
In some corner of his mind, he had known his
father wouldn't approve of his match with Maria,
but never had he guessed the old man would go to
such lengths to prevent it, to drive her away so she
would be forever beyond his reach. And to say he
would some day *thank him* for ruining his every
hope of happiness, without even a word of sympathy or regret . . .

"No, sir." He could almost see the wall between
him and his father now, invisible but impenetrable
all the same. "I will never thank you for it. I can
barely look at you."

Durham's jaw twitched. "I am saving you from
a fate far worse than you can imagine."

Rage poured through him, so sharp he was suddenly trembling with it. "What is that? The fate of
being married to the woman I love?" He lurched

to his feet and flung his arms out wide. "What's so terrible about that?"

His father hesitated. He started to speak, then closed his mouth into a firm line.

"I'm leaving," said Charlie, his voice taut with fury. "I'm not coming back. I've disappointed you for years, so I expect it will be a relief for you as well as for me. Good-bye, Father." He swept a mocking bow and turned to go.

"Charles," said the duke behind him as he walked away. Charlie paused, waiting, but his father didn't say another word, so he walked on. He packed his things that night and left at dawn the next morning. He didn't see his father again. No one tried to stop him; in fact, the stable boy had his horse ready and waiting in the morning. He took the road north, toward London, not certain what he would do there but absolutely determined not to be controlled and manipulated like a puppet on a string.

His father thought he was reckless and foolish; so be it. His father thought him a boy, thinking only of pleasures and nothing at all of responsibility; very well. His father thought he wasn't quite good enough, no matter what he did, so Charlie had had enough of trying. Perhaps the duke deserved to see how very, very right he was. What was the point in striving for something if one was doomed to fall short forever? He might not be a great man, but he could certainly be the greatest libertine in England.

When Charlie reached London, it didn't take long to lose himself in myriad pleasures and vices. He spent wildly, drank copiously, gambled to excess, and carried on with women of every rank. Within a few years he was established as the most scandalous of rakes, the wildest of rogues, the very embodiment of a scoundrel.

His father disapproved, vehemently—but his excoriating letters never contained a single hint of apology or regret.

And Charlie kept his word never to return.

Chapter 1

1810

Tessa Neville had never met the Earl of Gresham, but she hated him just the same.

She was not normally given to hating people. It was a waste of time and a rather indulgent emotion, in her opinion, and Lord knew there was enough indulgence and emotion in her family already. Had she encountered Lord Gresham under different circumstances, chances were she would have thought little of the gentleman, if she even noticed him at all. Earls, especially of his status and notoriety, were far out of her normal circles, and she was quite happy that way.

Awareness of him, however, was forced upon her, and not in the best way. She supposed there might be a good reason one could be forcibly aware of someone, but generally it was a bad reason. And at this particular moment, in this particular way, Lord Gresham managed to leave her annoyed, impatient, and disgusted with him and herself.

His first offense was not a personal failing. By

simple bad luck, she arrived at the York Hotel, Bath's finest, only a few minutes before the Gresham entourage. And to be fair, her mood was already on edge. Eugenie Bates, her elderly companion, had been in such a state of nerves over the journey she hadn't been ready to leave on time, and so had made them later than Tessa wished. It was a very warm day, making travel even more uncomfortable than usual as the heat and brilliant sun seemed to wilt everything but Eugenie's ability to worry aloud. By the time they reached Bath in the late afternoon, Tessa was already tired, hungry, and heartily wishing she had defied her sister and left Eugenie at home. She'd told herself all would be better once they reached the hotel and she could change out of her wool traveling dress, have a refreshing cool drink, and stretch her legs. She'd all but leaped down from the hired travel chaise, anxious to settle Eugenie into the hotel.

But no sooner had she walked through the doors and given her name than there came the rattle of harness and a clatter of wheels in the street, and almost immediately a hue and a cry rose. The hotelier, who had come forward to welcome her, excused himself in a rush and hurried out to see what was the matter. The arrival's title reached her ears in a whisper both delighted and alarmed: the Earl of Gresham!

When Eugenie, straggling in Tessa's wake, heard the name, she gasped. "Oh, my dear! I did not know this hotel catered to such an *elegant* crowd!"

"It is a hotel, Eugenie," replied Tessa, watching the hotel staff rush past her without a second glance. "It caters to whoever can pay the bill."

"Lady Woodall will be so dismayed she missed such a sight!" Eugenie's fatigue vanished. She watched in open fascination as servants bustled back and forth, bringing in luggage and carrying it away up the stairs.

"I am sure she will be nearly as delighted when she reads your account of his arrival." Tessa thought her sister would have stationed herself in the hall to look fetching, hoping to secure an introduction. Louise was looking forward to her life in London with almost feverish eagerness, and being acquainted with an earl would have made her faint with joy. At least Eugenie was too shy to thrust herself forward that way.

"Oh, my dear, we must wait and catch a glimpse of the gentleman!" Eugenie caught sight of Tessa's wry smile and blushed. She was such a pink and white creature, Eugenie Bates. Tessa had been making her blush since she was a schoolgirl of ten, when Eugenie, a poor but beloved distant cousin of her mother's, had come to live with them. All it took now was a certain look, because Eugenie had a vast experience of what Tessa's looks might mean. "So I might relate it to Lady Woodall," she protested. "Not to be rude, of course."

"Naturally," agreed Tessa. "It wouldn't be rude to stand here to see him at all, as we were standing here before he arrived, and because we simply have no choice but to wait until the hotel staff remember we exist."

"Oh, I'm sure they haven't forgotten us! Mr. Lucas will surely return at any moment. Are you tired, Tessa dear? Should we sit down in the lounge over there?" Eugenie's disappointment was clear, but she dutifully gestured to the small sofa on the other side of the room.

Tessa, who *was* tired, patted her hand. "I'm perfectly fine. And here comes the earl now." She was glad of that last part. Eugenie could have her glimpse of the noble personage, the hotel staff could grovel at his feet, and the sooner that was done, the sooner she would have her own peaceful room. She obligingly stepped back to allow her companion an unimpeded view of His Lordship's entrance.

"Good heavens, an earl!" Eugenie leaned forward, her face alight. "I encountered a marquess once, but it was quite by accident—I expect he thought I was a woman of low morals, for he was *very* forward! For my own part, I was so amazed he spoke to me, I'm sure I gave no very good account of myself, either. And of course I was acquainted with your dear papa, and now your brother, but otherwise I've never seen anyone of such rank!"

"Not true; you once saw one of the royal princesses in Wells, taking the waters."

Eugenie waved it off. "That was from afar, dear! This is very near, only a few feet apart. I shall be able to see every detail of his dress, and whether he has a kind face, and what sort of gloves he wears. Lady Woodall will be so anxious to know what is fashionable for gentlemen in London, so she might order accordingly for young Lord Woodall . . ."

Tessa stopped listening whenever issues of fashion arose, especially anything to do with Louise's idea of fashion. It wasn't that she didn't care about her own appearance, or didn't wish to look smart. She just had no patience for endless dithering over the merits of ivory gloves versus fawn gloves, or whether a blue gown should have white ribbons or blond lace or perhaps seed pearls for embellishment. She had been born with an unfortunately firm and decisive personality, much to the dismay of her frivolous sister. In the time it took Tessa to change her dress and arrange her hair, Louise could scarcely choose a handkerchief. Eugenie fell much too easily under Louise's spell, although she did improve when away from her. And since Tessa had been persuaded that she had little choice but to bring Eugenie with her on this trip, she could only pray the lingering influence of her sister faded quickly.

Her mind drifted as Eugenie breathlessly narrated the earl's infuriatingly slow progress into the hotel. She had a great deal to accomplish this week, and she did hope for a few days of seeing the sights before leaving. Tessa might be immune to the lure of a milliner's shop, but she loved to spend a pleasant hour in a bookshop, and the coffeehouses of Bath occupied a special place in her heart. Eugenie was looking forward to visiting the famous Pump Room, with strict instructions from Louise to take note of what all the ladies wore. If Tessa could have left her companion behind in Bath, she would have done so, to the greater happiness of both of them. Eugenie would enjoy herself here a great deal more than out in a small town in the country, but Louise had insisted Tessa couldn't possibly go alone. And once Louise set her mind on something, it was best just to admit defeat. Pyrrhus himself would have conceded the battle was not worth fighting.

"My dear!" Eugenie's voice went up a register in excitement. "My dear, he is coming!"

So much the better, thought Tessa, since no one would serve them until he came through; but she obligingly stepped forward to see what sort of man could upend the entire York Hotel.

Mr. Lucas, the hotel proprietor, ushered the earl to the door himself. Lord Gresham was moderately tall and wore clothing of unmistakable elegance and quality. He turned on the doorstep to speak to someone still outside, and she studied his profile. A high forehead, square jaw, perfect nose. His dark hair curled against his collar, just a bit longer than fashionable. From the tips of his polished boots to the crown of his fashionable beaver hat, he exuded wealth and privilege.

"Such a handsome gentleman!" breathed Eugenie beside her, clinging to Tessa's arm as if she would faint. "I've never *seen* the like!"

"I would like him a great deal better if he hadn't been responsible for everyone deserting us to carry up his luggage," she replied.

"And his carriage is so elegant! Everything a gentleman's should be, I'm sure," went on Eugenie, either ignoring or not hearing Tessa's comment. "How fortunate we should be in Bath at the same time, at the very same hotel! I do believe Lady Woodall mentioned his name recently—oh, she shall be in transports that we have seen him! What was it she was saying about him?" Her brow knitted anxiously. "I'm sure it was some *bon mot* that would amuse you, my dear . . ."

Tessa suppressed a sigh. She didn't listen to Louise's gossip, and Eugenie didn't remember it. What a pair they made. She shifted her weight; her shoes were beginning to pinch her feet.

Lord Gresham smiled, then laughed at whatever was said outside the hotel, and finally walked through the door. He moved like a man who knew others would pause to make room for him to walk by. It was the bold, unhurried stride of someone with the world in his pocket, with a whiff of predatory grace, as if he knew just how arresting his appearance was and meant to use it to his best advantage. Because Eugenie was right: he was a blindingly attractive man.

Tessa had learned the hard way to be wary of attractive men. They often thought it counted for too much, and in her experience, a handsome man was not a man to be trusted. And this man, who not only had the face of a minor deity but an earldom and, from the looks of his clothing, a substantial income, was nearly everything she had come to mistrust and dislike. That was all without considering how he had inconvenienced her, however unknowingly. Together, it pushed her strained temper to the breaking point. She arched her brows critically and murmured to Eugenie, "He looks indolent to me."

Here the earl committed his second grievous offense. He was several feet away from her, with Mr. Lucas hovering beside him and a servant—probably his valet—trailing close behind, and yet when she spoke the peevish words in a hushed whisper, Lord Gresham paused. His head came up and he turned to look directly at her with startling dark eyes, and she knew, with a wincing certainty, that he had heard her.

Eugenie sucked in her breath on a long, whistling wheeze. She sank into a deep curtsy, dragging

Tessa down with her. Chagrined at being so careless, Tessa ducked her head and obediently curtsied. She fervently wished she had arrived half an hour earlier, so she and Eugenie could have been comfortably ensconced in their rooms before he arrived, or even half an hour later. Now she would have to be very certain she never ran into the earl again; if he remembered her face, or heaven forbid, learned her name and connected her to Louise, her sister would quite possibly murder her.

For a moment the earl just looked at her, his gaze somehow piercing even though she still thought he looked like a languid, lazy sort. Then, incredibly, one corner of his mouth twitched, and slowly a sinful smile spread over his face. As if he knew every disdainful thought she'd had about him, and was amused—or even challenged—by them. Tessa could hear Eugenie gasping for air beside her, and she could feel the heat of the blood rushing to her cheeks, but she couldn't look away. Still smiling in that enigmatic, wicked way, Lord Gresham bowed his head to her, and then finally—*finally*—walked away.

"Oh, my," moaned Eugenie. Her fingers still dug into Tessa's arm, and it took some effort to pry her off and lead her to a chair in the corner. "Oh, my . . ."

"I'm sorry," said Tessa, abashed. "I never dreamed he would overhear, but I was wrong to say it out loud. But Eugenie, he won't remember. Or if he does, it will be some amusing story he tells his friends about the shrewish lady at the York Hotel."

"What if we see him again?" whispered Eugenie in anguish. "He might remember, Tessa, he *might*!

And your sister, so hopeful about her new life in London! He's quite an established member of the haut ton; he could ruin her!"

"I will hide my face if he approaches," she promised. "You know I would never deliberately upset Louise—and you shouldn't either. Telling her about this will only send her into a spell and cause her to worry needlessly." It would also unleash a flurry of letters to Tessa, full of despair and blame. She prayed Eugenie wouldn't set her sister off. "And really, I am very, very sorry. It was badly done of me, and I won't make the same mistake again." She did so hate it when her temper got away from her, and this time it could leave Eugenie on the verge of a fainting fit for the duration of their stay in Bath. Seen in that light, the coming week seemed endless, and she applied herself to reassuring her companion.

Once the earl's retinue had proceeded up the stairs, someone finally remembered them and came to conduct them to their rooms. Tessa helped Eugenie up the stairs, still patting her hand as the porter led them to a lovely suite and carried in their luggage. When she finally coaxed Eugenie to lie down with a cool cloth on her forehead, her first instinct was to leave. She could slip out of the room and soothe her cross mood with a short walk before dinner. If she happened across a new novel or delicious confection in Milsom Street, so much the better. Eugenie would be immensely cheered by a small gift, and a novel would keep her occupied for several days. Tessa hadn't wanted anyone other than Mary, her maid, to come with her, and already she was chafing at Eugenie's presence.

She pulled the door of the bedroom gently closed and quietly crossed the sitting room. "I'm going out for a walk," she told Mary softly, throwing her shawl around her shoulders and picking up her reticule. "See to Mrs. Bates; she'll likely have a headache." Eugenie was very prone to having headaches when Tessa had done something she disapproved of. Mary might as well be forewarned to have her favored remedy, a good bottle of sherry, at hand.

Some instinct made her pause at the door. Instead of just leaving, she opened the door a few inches and took a quick look out. The first person she saw was Mr. Lucas, the hotelier. The second person was the Earl of Gresham. He had shed his long greatcoat and hat by now, displaying a figure that didn't look the slightest bit soft or lazy. His dark hair fell in thick waves to his collar, and somehow up close he didn't look like a languid fop at all. Tessa froze, hoping to remain invisible by virtue of holding very, very still. Mindful of her recent promise to Eugenie, she all but held her breath as the men came nearer, just a few feet away from her door. Her prayers seemed to be answered as they passed without looking her way, but only for a moment. When she cautiously inched the door open a bit more and peered around it to see that they were gone, she beheld a door only a few feet down the corridor—almost opposite her own— standing open, with Mr. Lucas ushering the odiously keen-eared earl through it.

Tessa closed the door without a sound. Well. This was a dilemma. How could she leave her rooms if he might be passing in the corridor at any moment? She could ask for a new suite, perhaps, in another part of the hotel, but that would be a terrible bother. On the other hand, having to sneak in and out of her own hotel room was the height of inconvenience. What was she to do now?

She shook her head at her own dithering. "Mary, did you pack a veil?" she asked her maid, who was bustling about the room unpacking the valises.

"Yes, ma'am." Mary produced the veil, draping it over her bonnet, and Tessa picked up her parasol as well. She would not be held prisoner in her own room, but neither did she want to break her promise to Eugenie. Not that he was bound to recognize her, even if he did see her. Eugenie was worried over nothing. She was well beneath the notice of any earl, particularly a vain, arrogant, indolent one. On her guard this time, she let herself out of the room, and safely escaped the hotel.

Charlie was having a hard time ridding himself of Mr. Lucas, the smooth and somewhat oily hotel proprietor. He had no objection to being personally greeted, nor to being shown to his rooms, and then to a larger, better suite when the first was unacceptable. But then he wanted the man to leave, and instead Mr. Lucas stayed, blathering on about his hotel's service. Mostly Charlie was tired and longed to prop up his stiff leg, nearly healed by now though still ungainly, but Mr. Lucas was undeniably annoying as well.

"Yes, that will be all," he said at last, resorting to a lofty, bored voice. "Thank you, Mr. Lucas." He motioned to Barnes, his valet, who obediently whisked the obsequious hotelier out the door.

"Fetch something to eat, Barnes."

"Yes, Your Grace." Without being asked, Barnes offered the cane he had just removed from the trunk. With a grimace, Charlie took it, inhaling deeply as he shifted his weight off the injured limb. He was trying to wean himself off the cane, but by evening it was still welcome, much to his disgust. What a bloody nuisance a broken leg was. He'd fallen down the stairs after too much brandy almost two months ago and broken it in two places. It no longer throbbed as though a red-hot poker had been rammed into it, but after a long day in the carriage, it was stiff and sore. He hobbled across the room and settled himself in the chair by the window overlooking George Street.

"Shall I procure some laudanum?" Barnes murmured when he had arranged a tray with dinner and a bottle of claret at Charlie's elbow.

He scowled and eased his aching foot onto a stool, surreptitiously placed by Barnes. He still wore his boots, and it would hurt like the devil to take them off. Of course, he probably deserved the pain. It was a good substitute for the sorrow he ought to feel at his father's death. "No."

He dismissed his valet and picked up the glass of wine. It was still incredible to him that the duke was dead. Durham had been eighty, but remained vigorous and vital in his memory; Charlie had been sure, when he got Edward's first letter detailing their father's failing health, that the duke would survive on force of will alone. Edward had written a dozen more letters, first hinting and then outright asking him to return home, but Charlie hadn't gone. Partly because of his broken leg— the doctor had strictly warned him to stay in bed or be crippled for life—but partly because he just couldn't. In the eleven years since he left home, he'd had a letter from his father every few months, letting him know how splendid things were without him at Lastings: how brilliant and capable Edward was at business, how clever and heroic Gerard was in the army. Those letters never intimated the slightest hint of reconciliation, and now it was too late.

For a few maudlin moments he tried to remember what life had been like, years ago, when his mother still lived and made his father smile. The memories were dusty and dim, and mostly of just his mother, as if he had deliberately cut the duke out of them. He remembered the way the joy went out of his father after her death, like a candle snuffed out. But he couldn't remember a moment since then when he and Durham had gotten along.

And Charlie couldn't see how that would have changed had he obeyed his father's dying wish and returned home in time to hear Durham's confession. His father, that unforgiving paragon of ruthlessness and keen judgment, had had a scandalous past. No, not simply scandalous; Charlie knew scandal, and what his father had done was something much worse. As a young man, Durham had entered into a secret marriage with an inappropriate young woman—an actress!—and then simply parted ways from her when they ceased to get along. There was no divorce, and until the day of his death, Durham had no idea if she still lived or had died years ago.

Quite aside from the element of hypocrisy, it was nearly the worst sort of thing he could have done, in every respect. The vast majority of the Durham holdings were entailed on the next duke; most of the money was also tied to the estate, although Charlie's mother's dowry funds had been held separately and become a handsome sum under first Durham's and then Edward's management. As long as Charlie became the next duke, all three brothers had a secure future. If he didn't inherit, though, because he was an illegitimate son of a bigamous marriage, he and his brothers would each only be left with his share of their mother's dowry and a single property his father had won in a bet.

As if all that weren't bad enough, someone had discovered this clandestine marriage and begun sending Durham blackmail letters a year before his death. For that year, the duke had known his past was a boil about to burst, and instead of confessing it then, he'd hidden it. He had betrayed his sons in the worst way, not only with an illicit marriage but with his utter inability to humble himself and admit fault.

Whatever bitter irony Charlie might have appreciated about the situation—at least the old devil had known what he was talking about when he railed about unwise attachments to inappropriate females—was lost in the enraging realization that this could ruin all three of them, and the deep alarm that they wouldn't be able to stop it. Hell, they couldn't even agree on a plan to solve the problem. Edward favored a legal battle, and Gerard announced his intention to find and shoot the blackmailer. Charlie, to his private horror, had no ideas at all, which made him almost resent his brothers for being so certain they did. It seemed

the best thing he could do was stay out of the way
of their plans, to avoid mucking things up.

Not that either of them had been proved right.
Edward, against advice, told his fiancée of the trouble, and she faithlessly sold the story to a scandal
sheet and then jilted him. If things had been grim
before, they became positively beastly after that,
when all London began scrutinizing their every
move and whispering about the Durham Dilemma,
as the gossip rags had dubbed the disaster. Charlie
endured it with his usual front of careless disregard
for anything unpleasant, but inside he seethed.
He still thought Edward's plan to mount a bold,
swift legal action was eminently reasonable and
the most likely to succeed, but the gossip compli-
cated things. The courts moved slowly. And when
he called on Edward after a few weeks to see how
they were progressing, his brother not only said it
wasn't over but sent him a dispatch case filled with
all the documents and told him he must fight for
Durham himself. For the first time Charlie could
ever recall, Edward was leaving a task unfinished
and turning it to him. That was shocking enough,
to say nothing of alarming. It got even worse when
Edward threw all his usual caution and reserve
to the wind to marry an outspoken widow who
had bewitched him—there was no other explanation for such shockingly unusual behavior on his
brother's part.

And now it appeared Gerard's plan to bring the
blackmailer to a swift and brutal end had also run
off track. After disappearing for weeks, the first
word they had from their youngest brother was a
desperate letter for help. Edward actually refused

to go, which thoroughly quashed all Charlie's amusement at his head-over-heels tumble into love. Edward handed the letter to him and wished him luck, then retired to make love to his new wife in shameful, callous, blatant disregard of his duty to family. Or so Charlie imagined, as he told Barnes to pack his things.

So now he was in Bath. Tomorrow he would call on Gerard, discover what sort of trouble his brother was in, and then . . . He had no idea. Chase down the blackmailer, he supposed, since that should provide a link to the truth. Either the villain had proof of his charges and meant to demand something for it, or he didn't, in which case his actions would all come to nothing when Charlie was declared the rightful duke. Charlie couldn't decide which seemed more unlikely. Hopefully Gerard had learned something useful, but he had also somehow acquired a wife, according to his letter, and Charlie had seen how marriage changed Edward. It still amazed him that ruthlessly logical and practical Edward had thrown over his family for a woman; Gerard, always more prone to emotion and impulse, was likely to do even worse, if he'd also fallen in love with his bride. And that would leave only Charlie to find the blackmailer, discover the truth about Durham's long-lost first wife, prove his claim to the dukedom, and save them all from disgrace.

He caught sight of the leather satchel on the writing desk across the room. In it were all the documents and correspondence from the investigators and the solicitors relating to that damned Durham Dilemma, as well as his father's confessional letter.

He turned his head away, not wanting to look at it. He'd forced himself to bring it all to Bath, but just thinking about it left him angry at his father, irked at his brothers, and deeply, privately, alarmed that his entire life now hung by a thread. If rumors in London—and Edward's expensive solicitor—could be believed, Durham's distant cousin Augustus was about to file a competing claim to the dukedom, alleging that Charlie could not prove he was the sole legitimate heir. If the House of Lords upheld that claim, the title and all its trappings would be lost—at best, held in abeyance until proof was found, or at worst, irrevocably awarded to Augustus. Either outcome would effectively ruin him.

Charlie hoped to high heaven the answer to all their troubles could be found in Bath. And even more, he hoped he was capable of finding it before the House of Lords heard his petition.

He let his head drop back against the chair and closed his eyes. How ironic that the first time anyone expected great things of him, the stakes were so high. Right now he didn't want to think of anything beyond his dinner and the glass of wine in his hand. If the lady from downstairs could see him now, she would surely think him the most indolent, useless fellow on earth.

A smile touched his lips, picturing her defiant expression when she realized he'd heard her disdainful remark. She was sorry he'd overheard, but not sorry at all for saying it. What a prudish bit of skirt. No doubt she had a collection of prayer books and doted on her brood of small dogs. Charlie was accustomed to people making up their minds about him before they ever met him, but for some reason she amused him. It was always so unfortunate when a woman with a mouth like hers turned out to be a judgmental harridan. In fact, if she looked less cross, he might have said she was attractive, but it was hard to call any woman a beauty when she was looking down her nose at him. He wondered if she'd formed her opinion of him from the London gossip sheets or if his infamy had preceded him to Bath.

He raised his glass in silent toast to her. For tonight at least he would be utterly, happily indolent. And he hoped the thought rankled her deeply.

Chapter 2

Tessa's luck held for the first couple of days. Only twice did she hear Lord Gresham's name, and both times she was able to turn aside or slip away without seeing the man himself. From one exchange overheard in the corridor, she gathered he had left town, and although he kept his room at the York, the staff wasn't sure he would return. She breathed a sigh of relief at the news. It had been a near miss, but now that worry was over and she could carry on with her business.

Eugenie slowly recovered from her paralyzing fear that Tessa would humiliate them all and became her old self—which is to say she was a bit silly and inclined to fancy herself on the verge of illness, but sweet-tempered and anxious not to hinder Tessa. A visit to Molland's sweet shop did a great deal to restore Eugenie's humor, and an expedition to the Pump Room set her thoroughly to rights.

"Such healing waters," she exclaimed, even though she grimaced as she sipped them. "Tessa dear, you really should take a glass. One never knows what terrible maladies might await you in the countryside."

"I shall endure as best I can, without benefit of the waters." Tessa had tasted the Bath waters before, and had no desire to repeat the experience. Eugenie, on the other hand, would try any remedy suggested to her. "I vow, that lady's pelisse is a full six inches longer than last season. Do you think my sister would like it?" And the mineral waters were forgotten, as her companion was successfully diverted into a close study of every fashion in the room.

After two days of shopping Tessa went down to the tearoom at the hotel. This was the real reason she had come to Bath; a canal was to be built some fifteen miles to the south, conveying coal from the mines between Mells and Coleford to Bath and then onward to London and other markets. There was already a prosperous canal in place, which would serve as a starting point for this new branch. The path was surveyed, the plans were drawn, and Tessa—or rather, her brother, Viscount Marchmont—had been invited to purchase shares in the new branch. William, as usual, was unsure. He was capable of seeing every side of every issue, and would never decide on anything if left to his own devices. Everyone agreed it was better to send Tessa to meet Hiram Scott, who was part owner of an ironworks near the proposed path of the canal and was heavily recruiting new investors. Tessa was never swayed by the exquisite cut of someone's waistcoat, or even by a convincing prospectus; she had the practical—almost ruthless, her sister called it—turn of mind necessary to make wise investments, and the forthright demeanor vital to getting the truth.

"Mrs. Neville." Mr. Scott was waiting for her with a smile. They had met before, at her brother's home, and Mr. Scott had displayed no reluctance to deal with a woman at that time. Of course, a very large investment hung on her decision, and he was under no illusions about that.

"Mr. Scott." She bobbed a brief curtsy in response to his bow, then took the seat he pulled out for her. "It is very good of you to meet me in Bath."

"I hope I might answer all your questions, ma'am, and spare you the trip south." He seated himself opposite Tessa and laid a portfolio of plans in front of her. "The canal works are truly no place for a lady."

Tessa paused, glancing up at him through her eyelashes. "Do you object to a lady visiting, then?" William had been quite explicit that he was relying solely on her report to decide whether to purchase shares. If Mr. Scott had any qualms about opening his books to a woman, he might as well let her know now and spare them both the aggravation.

"Not at all," replied the man promptly— smoothly. "I wish only to spare my investors any inconvenience. It's also my job to give a fair and accurate report of the works. I hope to do it well enough that not everyone feels the need to visit personally." He lifted one shoulder, still smiling. "I daresay your visit would be far pleasanter for us, who are used to the rough conditions and bemoan the lack of fair company."

She allowed a small smile. "You flatter me, sir. I

am only trying to give my brother a full view of the project before he commits so much money to it."

They were both lying to each other, she knew, but at least Mr. Scott was willing to engage in the pretense. Many men treated her as if she hadn't a thought in her brain. She had learned long ago to arm herself with strongly worded letters from her brother, emphatically stating that he would give great weight to her recommendation. It tended to adjust men's view of her, she had found, if they knew she could turn aside their requests with one word. In this case, William was contemplating a rather large investment, six thousand pounds, and he was very anxious over it. Investors in the Somerset Coal Canal had reaped healthy returns on their investments, which argued in favor of it. But it was a great deal of money—nearly a year's income—and William's overriding fear in life was of losing his income. Like his father before him, he had been born without an ounce of business sense. Fortunately for him, Tessa, like her mother before her, had been born with enough of that for three people. Fortunately for everyone, her brother did have enough sense to realize this and to make her a part of everything he did.

Mr. Scott further endeared himself to her when he ordered a tea tray, then sat back and let her read in peace when the refreshments arrived. Tessa skimmed through the surveyor's reports and studied the maps and plots of the countryside, speckled with coal mines marked in red. She flipped through the documents outlining the construction, including the estimated costs. She looked at the list of subscribers, because there was no point investing William's money if the whole enterprise was doomed to fail. She asked a few questions for clarity, and Mr. Scott gave reasonable answers. Finally she closed the portfolio and slid it back across the table to him.

"It looks to be in order, sir. Since I must be my brother's eyes and ears in this, I still would like to see the works myself."

He accepted it with good grace, assuring her he would be prepared to give her a thorough viewing of the site. "I beg pardon I cannot escort you there myself," he added, "but I must return on the morrow. I've been away over a month now."

Tessa waved aside his apology. "I quite understand. My companion and I shall follow by the end of the week."

"Might I take the liberty of arranging lodging for you? Frome isn't nearly as elegant as Bath, but I shall find something suitable, if you wish. I will send word as soon as I secure rooms in your name."

"That would be very good of you, sir."

He shook her hand, another point in his favor, and departed. Tessa went upstairs to find Eugenie, who was reading a novel from the lending library. It must have been a Gothic one, from the way she had a handkerchief pressed to her lips as she read and the start she gave when Tessa came into the room. "Goodness!"

"It must be a good book." She smiled as she took the chair across from Eugenie. "You're flushed."

"Heavens, yes!" Eugenie fanned her pink face with her handkerchief as she set the book aside. "It's ever so dramatic—a young girl thrust upon a family of strangers in the dark of night, a perilous journal through a mysterious forest . . . I expect brigands and murderers are waiting around every corner."

"No doubt. But I expect Mrs. Radcliff will bring it all out well in the end."

"Of course she will." Eugenie gave a stout nod. "She's one of my favorites. I would never read her again if she didn't make it all come right in the end."

Tessa laughed. It never failed to amuse her that Eugenie, who fretted over the slightest breeze or cough, loved Gothic novels where the heroine endured a hundred dire dangers.

"How did you find Mr. Scott, dear?"

"Very well. Informative and polite."

"I think he fancies you." Eugenie turned to the tea tray beside her and touched the side of the pot. "Would you like some tea?"

"Fancies me?" Tessa raised her eyebrows, trying not to laugh again. Eugenie was an incurable romantic. "You flatter me, Eugenie."

"Oh, no, I don't think so. He's not a gentleman, of course, but he's a prosperous man, and he understands you." The old lady gave her an almost sly smile. "And he's not blind, dear."

"Nor is he a fool," Tessa retorted. "I've given him no encouragement of that sort."

"Nor should you. Your brother would not approve, I'm sure, although it would lift dear Lady Woodall's spirits if she thought you were finally taking an interest—"

"I'm not." Tessa got to her feet. Heaven save her from Louise's raptures if she ever gave any sign of wanting to marry anyone. She had made that mistake once, and had her heart not just broken but crushed beyond repair. "I am decidedly not interested in Mr. Scott, and if you tell my sister so—"

"Oh, never! I never would!" cried Eugenie, blushing again. "I merely remarked how happy she would be if you did relent on your *vow* against men."

Tessa pressed her lips together. She hadn't made any vow against men, just a vow never to be misled by a man's flattery and attention again. Once was bad enough. Trust Eugenie to cast her self-preserving instincts in such a melodramatic light. "I am only interested in the shares Mr. Scott has offered William," she said evenly. "You'll see soon enough."

"Oh." Eugenie visibly deflated. "We're going to Frome, then?"

Tessa had said from the beginning she intended to visit the canal works between Frome and Mells. It defied her comprehension how everyone around her constantly doubted her words. "Yes, we leave the day after tomorrow. I have a few more commissions before we go. You might wish to procure some more novels, as I understand the countryside is a good deal less refined than Bath."

Her companion sighed. "Yes, dear."

Tessa spent the next day making arrangements and preparations to spend as long as a fortnight in Frome. Louise had asked her to purchase several things, and although she tried to get her companion to tend to her sister's fashion needs, Eugenie would have needed a month to make the decisions required of her. Tessa, on the other hand, was able to place the orders in a single day and arrange for it all to be shipped to her sister. Her own purchases took a bit longer, but by tea time she returned to the hotel, a little footsore but pleased with her day's work. Eugenie had flagged by midday, so she had returned to the York earlier. Tessa walked through the lounge and untied her bonnet as she peered into the tearoom in search of her companion.

She had completely forgotten about the Earl of Gresham and her bad-tempered assessment of him. She hadn't seen him or his servants about the hotel in three days or more, nor heard his name. It was a rude shock, therefore, to come around the corner and see him sitting at a table in the center of the room, his long legs crossed before him in a pose of elegant ease.

It was an even greater shock to see Eugenie sitting on the other side of the table, smiling brightly at him.

Chapter 3

Charlie was beginning to think he had used up his store of luck in life. He'd had a rather good streak of it over the last thirty-odd years, but now it all appeared to be coming to a crashing end.

He arrived in Bath only to find his brother had left. More than a little put out, he had to cool his heels for the better part of two days, waiting. He had no idea what this meant for the trouble Gerard's letter had mentioned, and even more curiously, there was no sign of the wife his youngest brother had mentioned. Gerard, married? He'd left London a contented bachelor, set on tracking a blackmailer. Now he had a wife? Following so soon after Edward's whirlwind courtship and wedding, it felt almost like a desertion to Charlie. Obviously his brothers weren't nearly as worried about losing Durham as they claimed to be, if they had time to fall in love and marry.

When Gerard did return to Bath, he hardly cared at all for solving the Durham Dilemma. Some quarrel had sent his wife off, and Gerard could think of nothing but following her. Half amused, half concerned, Charlie went with him. By the time he met his newest sister-in-law, he knew Gerard would abandon him as Edward had done. Edward at least made a little speech pricking him with guilt, telling him the dukedom was his to pursue or lose; Gerard effectively said he cared more for his wife and it was Charlie's duty to find the blackmailer. This was all well and good for Gerard, whose new bride had brought him a large fortune that would insulate him from the consequences of failure. Charlie, on the other hand, was astonished that both his brothers were turning everything over to him after they'd barely consulted him on what to do. Now they thought he was suited to handle the entire problem on his own?

The sad truth was, he feared he wouldn't be up to this challenge. His brothers had been unable to solve it. Gerard had uncovered the blackmailer's name, Hiram Scott, but then passed up an opportunity to pursue him in favor of haring off to reconcile with his wife. Instead Gerard handed over the original blackmail letters and eight ancient notebooks from the Fleet minister who had married Durham to his first wife all those decades ago, and wished Charlie luck.

The very thing he seemed to have run out of.

Charlie had no experience in locating someone, especially someone who wished to remain unknown. Gerard at least had some military training, and Edward had the patience to plod through hundreds of possibilities, but Charlie had never had to exert himself; people came to him. He tried to make sense of the minister's notebooks, but there were a dozen entries per page, all in faded, cramped handwriting. The thought of combing through all eight books made his eyes water, but he squared his shoulders and made himself open the first book.

After an hour of frustration, Charlie set it aside. He wasn't giving up, but this would require some fortification.

Instead of having something sent up to his rooms, he went downstairs, away from the ledgers and documents and other proof of his present morass. He should have brought his chef with him, so he could have a proper pot of coffee instead of tea. He should probably send out inquiries about Hiram Scott; the man had been in Bath just a few days ago, according to the postal clerk who had recognized him and reported his presence to Gerard. In fact, he had just caught Mr. Lucas's eye, intending to ask where he might hire a man to ask some discreet questions, when the very name he was seeking floated by his ear.

"From Mr. Hiram Scott! You must take it right up for Mrs. Neville, Mary; she'll be expecting this letter." The speaker was a petite older lady swathed in a lavender shawl, her white curls clustered under a lace cap. She handed over a sealed letter to a younger woman, obviously a maid from the way she curtsied and hurried off with it, a number of parcels in her other arm. Charlie watched the letter go with hungry eyes. Then he turned toward the woman who had received it. Perhaps his luck hadn't deserted him after all.

"Are you well, madam?"

At his query, she looked up from digging in her reticule. Her eyes traveled up his figure, growing wider and wider until she met his gaze. Her mouth dropped open and her cheeks flushed bright pink before she stammered, "Oh—Oh, indeed, sir!"

"Forgive me," he said with a penitent, though charming, smile. "You looked a trifle unsteady. May I escort you to a chair?"

"Oh—well—I'm sure I'm perfectly . . ." Her flustered protests died away as Charlie offered his arm. For a moment she simply looked at it, before a slow awe dawned across her face. "Now that you ask, perhaps I am just a *shade* unwell. It is too kind of you to trouble yourself." Gingerly she placed her hand on his arm.

"It is no trouble at all," he replied. Charlie had spent ages sitting with his aunt, the Countess of Dowling, and her friends, and he knew just how to appeal to older ladies.

"Is everything all right, my lord?" Mr. Lucas appeared beside him, his oily, fawning expression in place.

"No, indeed not," said Charlie as his unwitting captive started to nod her head. "This lady is feeling unwell. Allow me to escort you to a table in the tearoom, Mrs. . . . ?"

"B-B-Bates," she stammered. "Eugenie Bates, my lord." She bobbed a sort of curtsy, looking every bit as unsteady as he had declared her to be. And no wonder; he wasn't giving her a chance to demur, holding her hand lightly but firmly on his arm.

"How delightful to make your acquaintance," he replied. "I am Gresham. Bring tea at once, and something to eat," he directed Mr. Lucas, urging Mrs. Bates toward the tearoom. "And some sherry, just in case."

"Oh," squeaked the lady, pinker than ever. "My lord, you are too, *too* kind!"

"Any gentleman would do the same for a lady," he assured her. "But here—I am presuming! Do you require your maid? Shall I send someone after her, or escort you to your room to rest?"

They had reached the table. A waiter whisked up to them with a tray of delicate sandwiches, no doubt intended for someone else but diverted at Charlie's imperious demand. Mrs. Bates cast a dazed look over the table—the best in the room—and sighing in longing. Charlie eased out a chair. "Be seated, madam," he said gently. "Just for a moment, until you recover."

As expected, no older lady of strained means could resist that invitation. She wet her lips, then fell into his trap, sinking down in the chair he held. Hiding his satisfaction under a concerned mien, Charlie seated himself opposite her. "Please, Mrs. Bates, eat something. I cannot rest easy until you do. Ah, Mr. Lucas," he said, turning to find the hotelier leaping forward. "You have the sherry?"

"Oh, sir, I'm sure I don't need that . . ." Her protest died away as Mr. Lucas presented a pair of glasses and a bottle of fine, pale sherry. The expression on her face argued very much against her words.

"Just a drop." Charlie leaned forward and poured a small glass, giving her a sly wink as he placed it in front of her. "To allay my fears."

"Well . . ." She smiled, blushing again, and took a tiny sip.

It was child's play from there. Under the influence of the sherry, fresh tea, and a plate of pastries in addition to the sandwiches, Charlie learned all he wanted to know from Eugenie Bates. She was in town with her dear, late cousin's daughter, a widow named Mrs. Neville. They were from Wiltshire, where they lived with Mrs. Neville's brother, Viscount Marchmont, at the very lovely family estate called Rushwood. The siblings' widowed sister, Lady Woodall, was soon to take up residence in London, and she had charged Mrs. Bates with discovering the latest in fashions. Charlie equably answered all her hesitant questions, divining that Lady Woodall's young son, Thomas, would be the prime beneficiary of his sartorial wisdom. Mrs. Bates was not sorry she wouldn't be moving permanently to London herself, as the city seemed too intimidating and taxing, although she did so look forward to visiting her dear relations there and seeing the sights.

Between her words, Charlie read more detail: she was a poor relation, shuttled from home to home as convenient for her hosts. She considered herself utterly beneath his notice, and his continued attentions acted as the most efficient lubricant on her reserve. The sherry, no doubt, helped as well.

Slowly he began to steer the conversation toward his object. A decade of enforced sloth and idleness had some benefits; Charlie had learned well the trick of listening to someone with only one ear while still making the proper responses. As she chattered along, increasingly voluble after he poured a second glass of sherry, he tried to guess what brought Hiram Scott, blackmailer, into contact with this apparently innocent elderly lady. She had sent the letter upstairs, and said his whole name; Scott wasn't likely well-known to her, or she would have referred to him more familiarly. Her young friend, Mrs. Neville, must know the man well, since she was expecting his letter, but how?

The first time he mentioned Mrs. Neville, though, Mrs. Bates grew suddenly quiet. She continued to smile and blush at him, but uneasily. Charlie exerted every ounce of charm he possessed, but still learned little. Mrs. Neville had business in town, and she was out shopping. That was all Mrs. Bates would share. What about Mrs. Neville did Mrs. Bates not want him to know? There was something, he could tell. He was just about to invite both women to dine with him that evening when his companion's expression broke with relief.

"Why, look at the time! I really must be going, my lord. It was too, *too* kind of you to be so solicitous of me, but I'm *quite* refreshed now."

Charlie turned his head, certain the mysterious Mrs. Neville had arrived. As suspected, a woman hovered in the doorway, fluttering her hand at Mrs. Bates. She quickly lowered her arm when she noticed him looking, and something like a grimace flashed across her face.

He could guess why. Mrs. Neville was the woman who had called him indolent the night he arrived in Bath. Now, as then, a slow grin spread over his face. Oh, this was too perfect. Somehow he'd been hoping to meet the beautiful shrew face-to-face, just once. He rose to his feet, already looking forward to the coming clash.

She crossed the room as if someone were shoving her in the back. By the time she reached the table, she had arranged her face into a stiff, polite smile, but he didn't miss the wariness in her eyes. "My lord, this is my dear friend, Mrs. Neville," said Mrs. Bates, tittering nervously. "Tessa dear, Lord Gresham has been *so* attentive to me since I became unwell a little while ago."

Her gaze touched the sherry glass for a moment, as if she suspected he had plied the older woman with wine. "How very kind, sir." At last she looked directly at him. Her eyes were the most unusual color of green, pale and clear like a polished peridot. For a moment he stared, set off-balance by their shade and depth. "I hope you weren't inconvenienced."

"Not in the slightest." He recovered his most charming smile. "It was entirely my pleasure. In fact, I was about to invite Mrs. Bates, and you, to dine with me this evening, as we are both travelers without friends in town."

"Oh!" Delight pinkened Mrs. Bates's face, but it was quickly snuffed by worry. "Oh, how very kind of you, sir! But we are . . . that is . . ." Her voice trailed off as she looked anxiously to the younger woman.

"That is excessively kind, but we must, unfortunately, refuse, my lord," Mrs. Neville said smoothly. She had a lovely voice, clear and ringing with confidence. From her voice, at least, she managed to keep all trace of dislike. "We must retire early, as we depart in the morning."

"Ah," he replied. "A sad disappointment, to part so soon after meeting. I understand you are to be in London later this year; perhaps our paths will intersect there."

Mrs. Neville's eyes went to her companion, who

blanched and tried to smile. How interesting; she wasn't pleased Mrs. Bates had told him about their trip to London. "Perhaps," was all she said. "If you are unwell, Eugenie, we should return to our rooms so you can rest."

"Yes." Mrs. Bates gave herself a small shake. "Yes, of course. The time . . . and my head . . . Thank you ever so much, Lord Gresham. It was perfectly delightful, sitting with you."

"The pleasure was all mine," he assured her, bowing over her hand as he helped her rise from her chair. "Might I walk you to your room, in case you should feel faint again?"

Mrs. Neville didn't approve of that, he could tell. Her mouth pressed into a flat line and the little pendant on the chain around her neck twitched in time with her rapid pulse. It convinced Charlie there was something here to root out, something she didn't want him to learn about her. Did she know anything about Dorothy Cope, Durham's long-missing first wife? She was nervous, and he was determined to know why.

"Well . . . now that you mention it, I do feel a bit weak in the knees . . ." Mrs. Bates let her hand linger in his, and cast a pleading look at her young friend. "It wouldn't be improper, would it, Tessa dear?"

Mrs. Neville fixed her penetrating gaze on her companion. It was clear she thought it highly improper, or at least undesirable. Whatever she wished to hide, though, it was clear Mrs. Bates had no inkling of it. "Of course not."

"I promise to behave myself with the utmost circumspection," he said gravely, but letting his eyes twinkle at Mrs. Bates. She turned pink and smiled back, softening again. "Just to your door, where I will deliver you to your maid's care." To drive home his advantage, he looked up, over the old lady's head, to Mr. Lucas. "Deliver the sherry to Mrs. Bates's room, Mr. Lucas. It restored her so wonderfully."

Mrs. Bates gave a faint gasp of delight. Mrs. Neville's eyes frosted over. "You are kindness itself!" cried the older lady, now clinging to his arm. "Tessa dear, isn't he the most charming gentleman?"

"Without question." Her stiff smile back in place, Mrs. Neville turned and headed for the door. Charlie followed, in no rush to pursue her since he had her companion well and truly snared. Mrs. Bates hung on his arm, enthusing about his kindness and gentlemanly nature and how very glad she was that he had been around in her moment of need, for she was quite fearful she would have needed a doctor if he hadn't come to her rescue. Charlie murmured the appropriate reassurances and flattering replies, but half his mind was turning over Mrs. Neville's reaction. Mrs. Bates knew to be wary of him, though not strongly enough to resist when he tempted her with pastries and sherry. She seemed anxious for the younger woman's approval, but she didn't appear to be in great fear of her disapproval.

Perhaps that was natural. A blackmailer would be a fool to trust a chatty old lady like Mrs. Bates. Charlie was sure he could tease just about any secret from Mrs. Bates, given enough time and sherry. Tessa Neville, though, was made of stronger stuff. In fact, she seemed determined to hate him, even after he'd been cordial to her. Could that mean she knew Scott was a blackmailer? Or even that she was party to it, as unlikely as that seemed? Perhaps she was just a bit shrewish by nature . . . but it provoked him like nothing else could have.

Mrs. Bates directed him to turn down a corridor leading toward his own rooms. He almost laughed out loud when she stopped in front of a door nearly directly across from his. What a fine joke on him, if the person he sought had been mere feet away since he arrived in Bath. "Why, how near we are!" he exclaimed, not hiding his pleased surprise. "My own suite is right there. Should you require more assistance, you must send your maid to knock."

"Oh!" Mrs. Bates blushed again. "How—How delightful, my lord! But really, I have been enough nuisance to you . . ."

"Not a bit," he assured her.

"Well, and yes, we are leaving tomorrow," she went on, sounding increasingly relieved. "It has been such a pleasure; I am sure it was the *finest* afternoon I spent in Bath!"

"I shall hope we meet again in London." He bowed and kissed her hand as the young maid opened the door. "Farewell, Mrs. Bates."

"Farewell, my lord," she replied breathlessly, fluttering her fingers as she went into her room. Beyond her Charlie could see no sign of Mrs. Neville, who had rushed ahead of them. He wondered what sort of scolding she would give her companion once he was safely away. The maid bobbed an uncertain curtsy and closed the door.

He went to his own rooms, where his valet

looked up from polishing a boot. "There are a pair of ladies in this hotel, Barnes, lodged directly across the corridor," Charlie told him. "Mrs. Tessa Neville and her companion, Mrs. Eugenie Bates. They are leaving tomorrow. Find out where they are going, and pack my things. We're going to follow them."

Chapter 4

Tessa stayed out of sight until the door closed on Lord Gresham's charming smile and perfect manners. Then she pounced on her companion. "Eugenie! What were you thinking?"

Eugenie gave a great start. Her dreamy little smile vanished, turning into alarm. "Oh, my dear, was it really so bad of me? He was *so* polite and *so* kind and *so* solicitous—"

Tessa waved it away impatiently. "After you made me promise to avoid him at every turn! What possessed you to speak to him?"

"Well," replied the older woman cautiously, "he spoke to me first. Mary and I had just returned to the hotel—that reminds me, dear, Mr. Scott left a letter for you. Mary, where is the letter for Mrs. Neville?"

"Here, ma'am." The maid fetched it from the mantel.

Tessa accepted the letter without looking at it, still focused on Eugenie. "Thank you, Mary. You may go for now."

"I'm sorry, dear." Eugenie twisted her hands,

looking penitent. "But don't you see? He wasn't angry about what you said, not at all. And now I can safely tell Lady Woodall we have formed an acquaintance with His Lordship, and you know how pleased she will be about that." She hesitated. "Was it really so awful? Surely your opinion of him must have improved, due to his gracious behavior today."

Tessa sighed and pressed the back of her wrist to her forehead. Everything Eugenie said made sense, and if Lord Gresham remembered them with any regard at all, it would completely disarm any fears Louise might raise when she learned of her own earlier, rash remark. There was no chance Eugenie would keep silent about that now, as it fed into the delightful story of how she met the earl. Sooner or later she would tell Louise, and Tessa knew her only hope of avoiding a storm of reproach was a newly cordial, or at least civil, relationship with the gentleman.

Still, there was something that made her uncomfortable. "How did you meet him?" she asked Eugenie. "You looked quite well, only a little tired, when we parted. I'd no idea you were unwell."

"Ah . . ." Her companion's brow wrinkled in thought as she sank into a chair. "I don't remember. We came back to the hotel, and I did plan to take tea, but no sooner had Mary gone upstairs than he appeared beside me, inquiring after my health. I must have looked unwell—perhaps I swayed on my feet? I *was* very tired, and you know my left ankle has been tender since we left Rushwood. But Lord Gresham escorted me to the tearoom, and ordered an *excellent* sherry—delivered by Mr. Lucas himself, my dear!—and we had a very amiable conversation."

"What did he want to talk about?" asked Tessa, suspicious again.

"Why . . ." Eugenie's face blanked. "Nothing of import, dear. He made the most polite inquiries about what brought us to Bath, and where we were from. When I mentioned we would be in London in a fortnight's time, he answered my every meek query about the city with kindness and great charm. Lady Woodall shall be so very pleased to know all I learned from His Lordship about London."

That sounded very innocent. Tessa couldn't quite put her finger on why she still felt uneasy about Eugenie's tête-à-tête with the earl, but she most certainly did. "That was all? He didn't ask about me?"

"He did ask, a little, although it made me recall . . ." She cleared her throat primly. "Well, I did become more reticent, not wishing to remind him of what you said, in case he had forgotten, but he showed no sign of any displeasure! Why, when you came into the room, I thought his expression looked . . . well . . . rather *intrigued*, dear . . ." Her voice, having become almost hopeful, petered out as Tessa stared at her incredulously.

"Eugenie, I'm shocked at you. Persuade me if you will that he acted out of excessive solicitude for you and your health, but you're mad to think he—" She stopped short. "It's rubbish. Don't be ridiculous."

"But you're a very attractive lady," persisted Eugenie timidly. "And he's such a handsome gentleman . . ."

"He's an earl," she snapped. "A titled nobleman leagues above a woman of my position. You're indulging in fantasy, Eugenie, and I beg you stop."

"Yes, of course. I didn't mean to upset you." The older woman subsided, looking small and woebegone in the large armchair.

Tessa drew a deep breath. There was nothing to be gained by snapping off Eugenie's head over this. If Lord Gresham didn't remember or didn't care about her imprudent remark, she should count herself very fortunate. If he found anything at all to like about her, so much the better, at least with regard to keeping Louise in good spirits. But what Eugenie intimated was complete farce, almost frighteningly so. The Earl of Gresham was the very last sort of man whose attention she wished to attract. There had been a flash of something in his eyes when he turned to see her trying to catch Eugenie's attention from the tearoom doorway. She couldn't even say what it was; he looked . . . well, almost pleased to see her, which was a puzzle. Their only connection was her rude remark, but he hadn't said or done anything to indicate offense.

He had in fact been the picture of charm. Up close, the earl was even more attractive, with black hair that had just a hint of wave and dancing eyes as dark as sin. His mouth seemed permanently curved with a devilish hint of smile. It was really no surprise Eugenie had melted under the brilliance of his attention. Even Tessa, whose heart had grown a hard, protective shell years ago, felt the warmth of his smile right to her bones. Of course, that allure was also the reason she was so distrustful of him. Such a charming fellow must have some purpose in plying Eugenie with sherry and flattery. But what?

She gave her head a small shake to refocus her thoughts. How unfair it was that she could never meet a handsome man without suspecting him of every sort of vice and treachery. Just because one handsome, charming fellow had proven himself a lying snake, intent on deceiving her and using her, didn't mean every such man was equally horrible. "I'm not angry. I was alarmed when I saw you sitting with him, but it sounds as though he acted honorably and decently, for which I am very grateful to him. I cannot believe he would notice me in any significant way, but as you say, it's always flattering to be admired, and I would far rather be in his good graces than suffer his ill will." Did that cover everything? Nearly. "And since we are leaving in the morning, there's very little chance we shall see him again, which quite allays any last worries I had. Forgive me for being snappish with you."

"Oh, but in London, we might—" Eugenie stopped as Tessa gave a small shake of her head. "You think not, dear? Would he snub us?"

"Likely not," she said gently, "but you must remember, London is a far larger place than Bath. I doubt we shall move in the same circles, even if all my sister's hopes are realized. It's unlikely he would seek us out, and it would be most improper of us to seek out him. You mustn't depend on seeing him in London."

"You're right," murmured Eugenie after a moment. "I know you are. Still . . ." She sighed and plucked at her shawl.

Tessa felt a little sorry for her companion. No one as elegant and urbane as the Earl of Gresham had ever paid Eugenie any heed, and it was clear to see the experience had been utterly bewitching. She felt terrible for squashing all the lingering delight of her companion's tea with the earl, but it would be harder if Eugenie lived in constant hope of meeting him again in London—or even worse, filled Louise with false expectations of an acquaintance. "Is he as charming as he appears?" she asked, trying to atone for the disappointment. "I don't think we've seen a handsomer man in Bath."

Eugenie's face lit up. "Indeed! I knew even you could not deny how very attractive he is. And he is even more charming! He said I reminded him of his aunt, the Countess of Dowling. My dear, can you imagine? I reminded him of a *countess*!"

Tessa smiled. "I like him a little better now." A very little, but she did. Not every man would pay so much kind attention to a lady like Eugenie. It shocked her that the earl would do so out of nothing more than Christian charity, but perhaps she was judging him too harshly. She had a tendency to do that, according to her sister.

"And he spoke of his brother, who has been living this summer in Bath. He's a decorated army captain, newly married and very dashing. And— Oh!" She tittered with laughter. "Here is something that will amuse you: he is a passionate coffee drinker, like you! Although he has a low opinion of the coffeehouses here in Bath. What was the one you particularly liked? I tried to remember to recommend it to him."

"Gardner's," said Tessa.

"Oh, yes, now I remember. But he said they were all dreadful, so he only drinks tea in Bath."

"How very principled of him. Who could possibly dislike such a paragon?" She rose and went to kiss Eugenie on the cheek. "I'm sorry I arrived to cut short your visit with him. If only something half so pleasant would happen to me!"

"Oh, but it would, dear, if only you wouldn't—" Her companion stopped suddenly, her fingers on her lips.

"If only I wouldn't lose my temper and insult perfect strangers?" Tessa gave a wry, guilty smile. "How fortunate I am to have you along to smooth the way after my wayward tongue."

Eugenie sighed wistfully. "And he wished us to dine with him! Dinner with an earl, could you imagine it? If only we weren't leaving tomorrow."

"If only." But inside Tessa was glad. The earl might be as handsome as the devil, and even more charming, but the way he looked at her made her skin prickle. The sooner they were away from him, the better.

Charlie was mildly shocked at how resourceful his valet turned out to be. He expected Barnes to discover a few mundane details about Mrs. Neville, but his man came back after dinner with far more.

"They arrived the same day Your Grace arrived, from near Malmesbury. Mrs. Neville paid the bill in advance, and she got a very pretty price, too."

"How do you know that?"

Barnes glanced up from the trunk he was packing. "I nipped into Mr. Lucas's office and read the account books."

"Oh, indeed?" Charlie raised an eyebrow.

His valet didn't look abashed in the slightest. "As Your Grace's man, I expect I could go anywhere in this hotel and not be said nay."

"Right. Go on."

"The lady left word she was expecting a gentleman, a Mr. Hiram Scott." Barnes paused at Charlie's sudden stillness. "Your Grace?"

"Nothing," murmured Charlie. "Who, pray, is this Mr. Scott?"

"A businessman of some sort. The waiter who served them in the tearoom said Mr. Scott had brought a number of ledger books and plans with him, and Mrs. Neville read them with great attention. He thought he heard them talking of canals."

Charlie's eyes narrowed. Canals were all the rage. He vaguely remembered vigorous debates over their efficacy, but he didn't know much about them. Somehow he'd pictured the blackmailer as a scoundrel with expensive tastes, gambling debts or loose women or something equally ordinary. A canal must be accounted a very expensive endeavor—so expensive, in fact, five thousand pounds would hardly suffice to build it.

But what did that make Hiram Scott? Was he an innocent businessman, wrongly identified by a postal clerk as the man who sent those blackmail letters to Durham? Or was he a rank opportunist, with his fingers in a variety of pockets? For a moment Charlie wished he could quiz Mrs. Neville about the man, but he didn't dare. Either she knew nothing about the blackmail, and therefore could tell him nothing, or she knew she was associating with an unscrupulous fellow, perhaps even approved of his actions, and was just as unlikely to reveal anything helpful.

"That fits with what the lad in the stable said," Barnes went on. "Mrs. Neville engaged a travel chaise to take them toward Frome tomorrow, where they're building a canal. Mrs. Bates is uneasy about the journey, and sent down a half-dozen requests for hot bricks and the like."

That was no surprise. "Frome," he said thoughtfully. "That's rather near, isn't it?"

"Close on a dozen miles."

Charlie rose. "Excellent work, Barnes. Be sure to pack some good sherry. And hire a travel chaise, to depart tomorrow." He had worn his horses into the ground lately, first coming to Bath from London and then helping Gerard retrieve his wife. As much as he preferred the luxury of the Durham coach, it was best to leave it in Bath, for many reasons. He caught up his hat and let Barnes help him into his coat, and left the hotel.

It was only a short walk to his brother's town house, where he found Gerard fortunately at home. "Come in, come in," Gerard said. "Bragg, bring the port," he called to his batman, who nodded once and vanished.

"I trust I haven't interrupted anything." Charlie glanced from side to side. "Where is my charming sister-in-law?"

"Lying down. She felt a bit faint."

Charlie drew a breath and waited, bracing himself for an announcement of impending offspring. It was clear to see his brother was utterly besotted with his new wife, and Charlie was sure he would be an uncle inside a year. But Gerard merely waved him toward a seat. "Have you learned something?"

"Hiram Scott is involved with the canals," he told his brother. "It seems he was in town to meet with someone, armed with ledgers and maps."

Gerard's eyebrows went up. "So that's it. I wonder why none of my queries turned him up?"

Charlie shrugged. "He didn't seem overtly mysterious in his visit; he visited the post office and called upon a lady at the York, then left her a letter. He's not staying at the hotel."

"Hmm." Gerard leaned back and kicked his feet out in front of him, crossed at the ankle. He frowned thoughtfully, his arms folded. "There are speculators around every corner in these parts. The coal fields, I suppose; that's mostly what the canals transport through Bath. Still, I never heard of him."

"You didn't know you were looking for Hiram Scott," said Charlie. "Perhaps you heard the name but had no reason to remember it."

Gerard hesitated, but admitted, "That's possible."

"Or since he was blackmailing Durham, perhaps he wished to stay out of sight. Perhaps he wanted the money to purchase shares of his own and grew more desperate—or brazen—after Father died without paying him a penny. Who knows?" Charlie waved one hand, as though swishing away his own doubts about Scott's motives. "Perhaps he's gulling half of Parliament, and thinks himself too clever to be caught."

His brother shot him a narrow-eyed look. "You haven't forgotten what I said, about Scott wanting to torment us more than to profit from Father's indiscretion?"

Charlie hadn't, although he still didn't know what to make of the idea. Gerard had suggested that

Scott didn't really care about the money he'd tried to extort from Durham, that his true purpose was merely to torment and harass his sons. That would explain why the demand for money was made only once, months ago, and never repeated, but otherwise it made little sense. Why had Scott sent the letters only to Durham, not to any of them, if his aim was to rattle them and not Durham? And why hadn't he sent more, once the scandal broke? It had been several weeks since a gossip sheet ignited the furor over his father's clandestine first marriage, but not a single scurrilous letter had arrived in over two months. Of all the people Charlie could think of who might wish to torment him—and he allowed there were some—he couldn't think of one who had the restraint not to.

"He hasn't sent another letter," he reminded his brother. "If he wished to torment us, wouldn't he have tried to draw a little more blood, once his threats blossomed into public scandal? Edward would have paid a small fortune to end the rumors, if Scott had approached him at the right moment. If his sole purpose was to torment us, he must have great discipline in savoring his triumph in silence, without even a single word of gloating."

"True." Gerard thought a moment. "What lady at the York Hotel did Scott meet?"

Charlie's smile was slight. "An interesting creature. She despises me."

"What did you do?" asked his brother, half in interest, half in suspicion.

"I believe I inconvenienced her," he said mildly. "Without any forethought or intention, but it roused her ire."

"Is she part of the blackmail scheme?"

"I've no idea." But he thought it still possible. Such hostility must spring from something more than a dislike of his appearance. Indolent! Surely it would take more than a passing glance to determine that.

"What are you going to do?" Gerard, as ever, leapt right to action. "Shall I send out inquiries about her as well? I know an excellent fellow here in Bath who would be glad to take up the task, Lieutenant Carter from my regiment."

"I've already learned a good deal about her, thank you." Charlie raised one eyebrow at his brother's expression of surprise. "Do try not to look astonished. It required nothing more than sitting in the tearoom, chatting with her elderly companion."

"The tearoom?" Gerard repeated incredulously, a tinge of horror in his voice. And no wonder; sitting with Mrs. Bates would be truly awful to Gerard, who never had been able to sit still for long, especially not to converse about fashions with elderly ladies. He was very like their father in that.

Charlie chose to accept it as a compliment to his superior patience. "Indeed. It is a fine place to meet ladies."

"I suppose it must be." Gerard grimaced. "What did you learn?"

There was no reason not to tell his brother everything, but for some reason he hesitated. He could see no connection between his family and Tessa Neville apart from Hiram Scott, and no idea why Hiram Scott had begun blackmailing their father. It was possible the postal clerk had mistaken Scott for the true blackmailer as well. It was really a slender thread of possibility that he was on the right track by following Mrs. Neville, but he was still determined to pursue her. Besides, he had nothing else to go on. "Nothing of any obvious import," he said slowly. "But she leaves Bath tomorrow—to follow Scott, I believe—and I intend to follow her."

Chapter 5

The trip south to Frome was every bit as trying as Tessa had feared.

Eugenie had nothing to do with it. Contrary to her usual fretting over the inconveniences and discomforts of travel, she was quiet the entire journey. Tessa enjoyed the peace at first, but then grew concerned. It was so unlike Eugenie to be silent, she began to fear her companion had taken ill.

"Eugenie, are you feeling well?" she finally asked.

"Yes, dear, I'm very well." The older woman summoned a rueful smile. "I shall miss Bath, though."

"Of course. But we will be in London within the month, and that must cheer you," Tessa cajoled her.

"It does! Most certainly." She sighed, flicking at the fringe of her shawl. "I do hope I shan't be a bother to you until then."

"What nonsense," said Tessa in surprise. "You're not a bother to me. I'm delighted to have your company." Which was generally true; the moments when Eugenie made her want to tear out her own hair were infrequent and brief. But it was very uncharacteristic for Eugenie to be so melancholy. "If anything, I'm sorry I cannot offer you a more diverting trip than through the backways of Somerset. I know you would rather have remained in Bath."

Eugenie's face lightened a bit. "Indeed," she said wistfully. "But it was not to be." She looked at Tessa's face and blushed. "Don't worry, dear, about me. I'll be cheerful, I promise."

Tessa suspected her companion was still mourning the loss of Lord Gresham's company more than anything else. She felt sorry for depriving Eugenie of something so wonderful and thrilling, but at the same time, she couldn't shake her relief to be away from the earl. It seemed odd for a dazzlingly handsome, wealthy nobleman to pay attention to any woman unless he wanted something from her, and there was precious little an earl could hope to gain from Eugenie, who had neither money nor rank nor influence. She was simply a sweet, kindhearted older lady who liked her novels and gossip about the latest fashion.

So why was he interested in her? Eugenie declared Lord Gresham didn't care a whit for Tessa's impertinent remark about him, which only doubled the mystery. What other connection was there between them that he would care about? Tessa hadn't been to London in years, and she was sure she would have remembered if she'd ever met Lord Gresham. Heaven knew she hadn't been able to get his face out of her mind, nor forget how his voice sounded, which was almost as unnerving as the mere fact of his interest in her. She told herself she should be more concerned about that than about whatever he might want from her or Eugenie. And now that they'd left him behind in Bath, it was highly unlikely she even needed to worry about it. Chances were, he wouldn't remember her even if they came face-to-face in London.

Frome was barely a dozen miles from Bath, but the countryside underwent a complete change as they drove south. The rolling verdant hills around Bath degenerated into a harsher, wilder landscape punctured by rocky outcrops that gave a forbidding look to the land. The elegant cream stone of Bath's buildings gave way to small towns garbed in brick and thatch, the houses smaller and meaner. At times the workings of the coal seams could be glimpsed from the road, the shouts and calls of the miners audible over the rattle of the carriage wheels. The roads were terrible, hardly more than rutted tracks; no wonder there was keen interest in a canal to bring the coal to market. It took almost the entire day to reach Frome, and Tessa stepped down from the carriage feeling as battered and tired as if they'd traveled forty miles or more.

As promised in the letter he'd left her in Bath, Mr. Scott had arranged lodging for them at a small inn. After the luxury of the York Hotel, it seemed rather plain and almost shabby. Tessa saw Eugenie's face fall at the sight of their small rooms, and tried not to sigh. First she had to disappoint Eugenie's hopes regarding Lord Gresham, and now she would feel guilty for having dragged the poor lady away from the comfortable York for this lodging. Curse Louise for making such a fuss over this trip. Tessa couldn't think of anyone who would care if she came to see the canal alone—not anyone whose opinion she valued, at any rate. She still suspected Louise had wanted Eugenie out of the way as she prepared for her move to London. Louise loved the older lady dearly, but she also knew Eugenie's endless worries would wear away her most exuberant plans. After fourteen years of marriage to doughty Lord Woodall, Louise was ready to embrace widowhood and the delights of London at the same time.

Still, Tessa had to breathe deeply to fight back her indignation. It wasn't that she didn't love Eugenie; rather the contrary, in fact. Eugenie had lived with them for almost as long as she could remember, as devoted to the three children as their own mother had been. Tessa never wanted to hurt Eugenie, no matter how trying her little vagaries could be at times. She hadn't wanted to bring the older lady along on this trip precisely because it would be dull and uncomfortable and only Louise would care if anyone commented on Tessa traveling with only her maid, Mary, for company. She was eight-and-twenty years old, for heaven's sake, and capable of taking care of herself. There was no need to fear ruining her marital prospects, because she had none and wanted none, and if someone decided to attack and rob her on the road, the presence of Eugenie was hardly likely to serve as any deterrent. If only Louise had been rational and logical, she would have seen that it made far more sense for Eugenie to stay home at Rushwood, or even to remain in Bath while she visited the canal works herself.

But that was all pointless wishing now. She had given in, after all, when Louise grew hysterical and dramatic, and Eugenie was with her. They would all have to make the best of things.

"Shall we step out to tea?" Tessa asked as Mary began unpacking their things. It was too late in the day to do much more, and after hours in the travel chaise, she wanted a bit of exercise.

"Yes, dear, if you like." Eugenie smiled valiantly, although without any of the wide-eyed enthusiasm she'd displayed on their arrival in Bath. Of course, it was highly unlikely they'd meet anyone as illustrious as the Earl of Gresham in Frome—and thank goodness for that, Tessa reminded herself.

She gave her companion her arm as they left the inn. Another week or so and they would be on their way to London, where there would be plenty to brighten Eugenie's eyes again.

Once Charlie knew where his quarry was headed, he saw no point in rushing out of Bath at an uncivilized hour. He enjoyed his breakfast and then settled into the hired coach for the journey. At his instruction, Barnes put the leather satchel from Edward in the carriage instead of packed away in a trunk, and finally, reluctantly, Charlie opened it.

The first item he removed was a copy of the petition filed with the Home Office, requesting the writ of summons that would establish Charles de Lacey as the eighteenth Duke of Durham. The pages of dense, neat script made his eyes cross. His brother Edward had hired the best legal minds in London to produce this; there was nothing he could add to it, even if he'd had the first idea about what it said. Gingerly, Charlie set it aside.

Next he pulled out a packet of letters, bound with string, which proved to be from Mr. Pierce, Durham's country solicitor. These went back over a year and included letters from Durham in reply to Pierce's. Charlie stared at his father's handwriting, no longer as sharp and bold as it had once been but shaky, almost scrawling, at times. He knew Edward had handled the vast majority of Durham business for eight years or more. Mr. Pierce must have written to Edward at least every week during the span of these letters, and yet the solicitor had never breathed a word about them. Durham had commanded him not to. Charlie read one letter from Pierce, reporting almost miserably on the lack of progress by the hired investigators; they had exhausted all clues of Dorothy, and begged for any scintilla of information that might guide them to more fruitful inquiries. But Durham could remember none. He had told them all he knew, and their inability to find any trace of the woman left him displeased and skeptical of their competence. His writing had deteriorated, but Charlie could hear the duke's impatience as if his father were reading the reply aloud.

He sighed and put the packet aside. There was another stack of letters, from the London solicitor recently engaged by Edward to try again where Durham's earlier investigators had failed. Charlie could see no substantial difference between them, nor did he have any wish to try. Those investigators had been looking for Dorothy Cope, the long-lost Fleet wife. Charlie was looking for Hiram Scott, who had tried to blackmail them. Find Scott, he reasoned, and he would find a link to Dorothy.

Dorothy was the key to the whole puzzle, and it wouldn't be solved until he found her, but Scott was apparently the only one who knew anything about her.

He took out the blackmail letters themselves, obligingly handed over by Gerard, and the stack of thin, battered notebooks Gerard had unearthed from a country farmer's stable in Somerset. They were the records of one William Ogilvie, who had allegedly performed the marriage ceremony between Durham and Dorothy in the shadow of Fleet Prison. Charlie's first attempt at reading them, in Bath, hadn't gone well, but then he'd chanced to meet Mrs. Bates and Mrs. Neville. With any luck, he wouldn't need to read these registers after all. He set them aside with a great deal of relief.

And then there was Durham's letter, his last confession. It was the last letter in his own hand, recounting his ill-fated amour and begging forgiveness. It was dated only five days before he died, when he must have known he wouldn't live to see the matter resolved—when he knew he had failed. Charlie had read it when Edward and Gerard brought it to London weeks ago, and the sight of it still filled him with fury. It was the coward's way, to confess in a letter that wouldn't be read until after his death, when he would be forever removed from any condemnation or questions.

For a few minutes Charlie thought about the woman who had so bewitched his father sixty years ago. Durham's letter had said surprisingly little about her, only that she was a spirited beauty who shared his taste in revels. What sort of revels had his father enjoyed? What sort of passion had he conceived for the alluring Dorothy, and how had she managed to resist him at all? The duke was in his forties when Charlie was born, a matured man with a will of iron who brooked no refusals. But if he'd ever been frivolous and devoted to revelry, Charlie never saw a sign of it.

He sighed and put all the papers back into the satchel. Clearly he hadn't known his father well at all. As much as he feared coming up short in this quest to root out the truth about the duke, he couldn't deny a certain amount of morbid curiosity. What had his father been like as a young man? Had his heart broken over his first love, as his own had? Perhaps it had been this misadventure that shaped Durham into the demanding man he became. Had he viewed that early humiliation as a lesson—and if so, what lesson? As far as Charlie could see, the main thing his father seemed to have learned was to keep it secret at all costs, and that hadn't turned out terribly well in the end. And the one time Durham might have put the lesson to good use and admitted his youthful indiscretion, when he opposed Charlie's long-ago desire to marry Maria Gronow, the duke had instead acted with all the compassion and sympathy of a boulder.

Despite the late start, he reached the village of Frome in good time. The afternoon sun was sinking over the crooked silhouette of the roofs, and the carriage creaked as the roads sloped upward into town. A glance out the window put him in mind of the wooden blocks he and his brothers had played with as boys. Frome had the same appearance as their imagined towns, built for the sole purpose of being destroyed, a haphazard arrangement of wooden buildings on the side of the hill. The idea of knocking the whole town down with a cricket bat, as Gerard had once done with their blocks, was mildly amusing.

When the carriage stopped at an inn, Charlie stepped down and cast a more critical eye about him. He had no qualms admitting he liked comfort— even luxury—and the inn before him appeared to offer little of either. It was neat enough, but on the shabby side, and fairly small. He reminded himself he could endure some rough living for a few days, and went inside to take rooms.

After seeing the alleged best room, though, he promptly decided he couldn't bear it after all. The bed was thin and uninviting, the window wouldn't close all the way, and through the wall he could hear the sounds of a couple arguing. He told Barnes to go out the next morning in search of something better, preferably a cottage or house where he would have some privacy.

"Somewhere quiet," he told his valet, as the argument next door grew more heated. "As near Frome as possible, though."

"Yes, Your Grace," murmured his man.

"And none of that title in Frome," Charlie added. Barnes and his other servants had begun addressing him as the duke from the day he learned that his father died, but he was not formally the Duke of Durham, and had only used the title among family. It occurred to him now that it might be best to keep all mention of the dukedom quiet, especially until he learned more about Scott. "I'm still Gresham while we're here."

"As you wish, sir." Barnes bowed.

He crossed the room and pushed open the warped window. A brisk breeze blew in from the direction of the river. Somewhere nearby, Hiram Scott was waiting for him, knowingly or not. Charlie wanted to get the maximum benefit from their first meeting. The only question was . . . how?

After thinking about it overnight, he got up early the next morning to strike the first blow. It was surprisingly easy; a few desultory inquiries in the inn's taproom were enough to discover Hiram Scott owned an ironworks in Mells, a small village nearby. It appeared to be a prosperous enterprise, from the respect in people's voices when they spoke of Scott. Charlie murmured something about canals, and again received an easy acknowledgment. There was a canal branch being dug to Frome, intended to run westward through the coal fields and, of course, Mells. Mr. Scott was an enthusiastic promoter of the canal and was well-known in Frome for trying to drum up investments. One gentleman said Scott must hardly know where his own bed was anymore, he traveled so far and so often in search of new investors for his project.

Charlie thanked them and went out for a walk. A canal promoter. That explained the travels, although this near Bath, one would think it might make Scott well-known there. Gerard said he'd made extensive inquiries, although perhaps his brother had gone about it from the wrong angle. Gerard would have been looking for someone who hated Durham, someone thwarted or affronted by the duke in some way. He told Charlie all he'd heard was polite condolences concerning their father's death, and barely veiled curiosity about the scandal. They hadn't learned Scott's name until very recently, however, so perhaps Gerard had been asking the wrong questions, or asking the wrong people. It was unlikely Gerard, an army man who took little interest in business, would have sought out the businessmen and tradesmen who might have known Scott as an iron manufactory owner.

Of course, Charlie felt even less qualified to do that.

He turned into a wider street, considering his options, and beheld his very best one. Eugenie Bates stood a hundred yards in front of him, fanning herself weakly. Her short, plump figure was unmistakable, from the fluffy lavender shawl she clutched with one hand at her neck to the woe-begone expression on her flushed face. He headed right for her.

"Mrs. Bates!" he exclaimed. "How astonishing to meet you here!"

She looked up at him with the same startled look as the first time he'd accosted her, in the York, but this time it brightened at once into joy. "Why, Lord Gresham! What a lovely surprise!"

"And it appears I have come across you in distress, yet again." He frowned in concern. Unlike last time, when he'd wholly invented her illness, the older lady did look unwell today. "May I fetch a doctor?"

"Oh, no, no, I was merely a bit overheated." She fluttered her fan more vigorously. "I feel *much* better now. And very happy to have met you again. I shall never forget your kindness in Bath, *never*."

He waved one hand. "It was a pleasure to make your acquaintance, and one of the few I enjoyed in

Bath." He glanced around. "Have you come alone? I thought you were traveling with Mrs. Neville."

"Oh, my, yes! She's just in the apothecary's shop, I'm sure she'll be right out. I grew a bit faint—the odors, you know . . ." She stopped and blushed. "But now I count it quite fortunate, for it drove me outside at a most opportune moment!"

Charlie smiled at her, not mentioning that he would have walked every street in town in search of the two of them. "Fortunate indeed."

"And there is Mrs. Neville now," said Mrs. Bates, beaming. "Tessa dear, see whom I met!"

The lady emerging from the apothecary's shop turned at Mrs. Bates's call. With the advantage of surprise on his side this time, Charlie could take in her full reaction. She stopped dead in her tracks, her lovely mouth open and her startling pale green eyes wide with surprise. In that moment, without a trace of frost or disdain in her face, Mrs. Neville was rather beautiful, Charlie realized. He was not accustomed to beautiful women disliking him, and for some reason her antipathy struck him as especially unfair—and gave him the sudden urge to charm her mercilessly. How dare she think him indolent, when he had just chased her across Somersetshire?

"Mrs. Neville." He removed his hat and bowed very properly. "How delightful to see you again."

"And how surprising, my lord." Her curtsy was a bit stiff. "Mrs. Bates didn't mention you were also traveling to Frome."

He smiled. "We hardly had time to become acquainted in Bath—though I am thoroughly pleased to rectify that failing. But I've come to Frome on rather dull business, and wouldn't wish to bore either of you with it."

Her mouth flattened and she looked positively grim for a moment. "Of course not," she muttered. "We wouldn't dream of keeping you from your important business, sir."

He barely kept back his grin at her faint stress on the word "important." Mrs. Neville felt slighted. "On the contrary," he replied easily. "It is my most fervent hope you and Mrs. Bates will grace me with your company a time or two. I assure you it would brighten my visit immeasurably."

"Oh, Tessa dear," gasped Mrs. Bates. She turned and looked up at Charlie with shining eyes. "How very, *very* kind of you, my lord!"

He inclined his head graciously without taking his eyes from Mrs. Neville. She watched him back, a faint line between her brows. Her gaze was sharp and a little bit puzzled, as if she couldn't make him out. He had the feeling he was being measured against some invisible standard, and for a moment he wondered how he'd be found, worthy or lacking. But she didn't look nervous or guarded anymore, which strongly indicated she knew nothing about Scott's blackmail.

Quite by surprise Charlie found that he strongly hoped that was the case. He wasn't sure why it mattered to him that she be innocent of any particular sin. Mrs. Neville obviously found him indolent, vexing, and tiresome. He told himself it was for Mrs. Bates's sake he cared; the elderly lady would be very hurt if her young friend turned out to be complicit in blackmail, and Charlie liked Mrs. Bates enough to wish her no harm. But he couldn't deny there was something about Mrs. Neville herself that caught at him. Even though he hoped his doubts about her would prove baseless, he wasn't at all sorry he had to examine her more closely. To tell the truth, he was looking forward to unraveling her, far more than he should be.

"May I offer you my arm?" He did so as he asked the question, and this time Mrs. Bates didn't waste a moment. She gave him her hand and beamed at him as he folded it around his arm. "Mrs. Neville?" He turned to the other woman, who still hadn't moved, and offered his other arm.

"Thank you, no," she said. "I am perfectly capable of walking down the street unaided."

Charlie just bowed his head. "Indeed. It was merely to gratify my own desires I inquired."

She gave him a sideways look of suspicion, but fell in step beside him and Mrs. Bates as they set off.

"Do you plan to stay long in Frome, my lord?" asked Mrs. Bates.

"A little while," he said vaguely. He could see Mrs. Neville's reticule swing forward on her arm with every step she took, a bright blotch of red against her dark blue skirt. Her gown was stylish but simple, and a bit on the sturdy side. She dressed practically, it seemed. "I've come to see a gentleman about some business matters."

"Just as we've done," exclaimed Mrs. Bates. "Or rather, just as Mrs. Neville has done; she's quite the cleverest young lady I've ever met, my lord."

"Eugenie," said Mrs. Neville.

"Lord Marchmont relies upon her for investment guidance," Mrs. Bates chattered on, ignoring the look from the younger woman. "Although I do hope we shan't have to visit the coal mines. I've heard they're very dirty, dangerous, *disagreeable* places, and I fear so much for dear Tessa when she ventures off."

"Eugenie," said Mrs. Neville again, the note of warning clearer this time.

"I'm sure Mrs. Neville is sensible enough not to venture too dangerously," said Charlie. "Although I quite agree about coal mines." He made a face. "I've come to see a fellow about the canals, though, not the mines."

"But so has Mrs. Neville!" Mrs. Bates seemed immune to the increasingly aggravated glances Mrs. Neville was giving her. Charlie could feel each of them; they practically singed his chest as the lovely widow glared around him at her companion. "She's considering Mr. Scott's canal, is that the same one you're looking at?"

"Mr. Hiram Scott?" repeated Charlie as if in amazed disbelief. "That's just the fellow I've come to see! My, what a remarkable coincidence."

Mrs. Bates almost crowed in delight, her cheeks pink. "Why, Tessa dear, isn't that amazing? Who would have guessed, when we met in Bath, we were both on the same errand?"

Mrs. Neville cast an aggrieved glance at him. Charlie didn't say anything, just met her gaze with an expression of pleased discovery. Here at last was the connection he wished to explore. To his relief, she didn't appear excessively upset that her companion had betrayed her connection to Scott. If she really feared what Mrs. Bates would say, she wasn't very firm in forestalling the older lady. "Yes, Eugenie, it is amazing," she said at last, in the same tone she might have agreed that smallpox was just as bad as consumption. "But I hope you won't prattle Lord Gresham's ear off about coal mines and canals and other dull things."

"On the contrary," said Charlie quickly, staring hard at Mrs. Neville. How did he manage to irritate her so completely? It was very nearly a gauntlet thrown in his face. "I should like to hear all about the canals. No doubt your view would be most helpful to me, since"—he smiled at her—"it appears we are interested in the same thing."

Tessa's hands were in fists and she longed to hit him, just to wipe that smile off his face. It was a sly little quirk to his lips, coaxing and secretive all at once. The way he said "we are interested in the same thing" sounded more like a seduction than any sort of intelligent discussion between equals. Not that he viewed her as an equal, of course. Until Eugenie had mentioned the canals, he hadn't wished to *bore* her with *dull* details about business. Temper warmed her face. She'd wager a guinea she could keep—and read—an account ledger better than His Pampered Lordship could, but like most men, he assumed she had the brains of a pigeon and would feel light-headed at the mention of debentures or bonds. She longed to ask his opinion of the engineer's plotted route, or if he had any doubts about the projected dividends. If he agreed with the demands of the landowners who were insisting the canal weave from mine to mine to lessen their own costs, or with the investors who wanted the most efficient route and the most economical construction.

"I wouldn't wish to bore you," she said before she could stop herself. "I'm sure my opinions would be quite inconsequential to you, my lord."

His steps slowed and his expression turned keen and thoughtful. Tessa jerked her eyes away from him and refused to look back, even though she could feel his scrutiny like the heat of a fire. She had overdone it again, no doubt. Oh, why had he decided to take an interest in Eugenie? She honestly couldn't fathom what possessed him. Surely her single rude remark, well over a week ago, wasn't enough to inspire this much attention, and if his purpose was to make her squirm in regret, he had already achieved that. Eugenie was still clinging to his arm like a happy barnacle, so Tessa didn't walk away as she wanted to, but she wished mightily that Lord Gresham would go away at the end of the street.

But Eugenie seemed to have cast off any care or awareness of what she wished, because at the end of the street, Lord Gresham asked if he might escort them on their errands and then back to their lodging, and Eugenie accepted before Tessa could demur. She couldn't keep back a sigh, and then gritted her teeth at the inquiring—though highly satisfied—look Lord Gresham gave her.

She tried to clear her mind as they walked. Eugenie was talking enough for both of them, idle chatter that flowed past Tessa without sinking in, although Gresham's replies scraped across her nerves like a bow over a violin string. What could he want with them? There weren't many possibilities, she decided. First, he might have some honest affection for Eugenie, although whence it sprang she couldn't imagine. Second, he could wish to torment her in revenge for her remark, but this seemed far-fetched. Why would he care what a woman of no real social standing thought of him? It made no sense, so logically she discounted it.

But that cleared away the most likely reasons. Had he perhaps some connection to William? Tessa oversaw her brother's books and knew there was no mention of any business with the Earl of Gresham. In addition, William was happily married and rarely left Wiltshire, so it was unlikely they had argued over a woman or cards. Unlike Louise, William had no desire to join the whirl of London and was only making a short visit to the city to see her settled. And if Louise had any connection to Lord Gresham, Tessa—along with the rest of the shire—would have known of it in great detail. Louise was incapable of keeping a secret, especially not one involving so delicious a person as the Earl of Gresham. From what Eugenie had recalled of the gossip about him, he was a very dashing rake, living on his charm and title and money, with a long trail of mistresses and lovers.

Tessa could easily see why—women must fall left and right for his lazy, knowing grin, when his dark eyes glittered with amusement and interest— but that only provided less connection between them. Rakes liked women of easy virtue. Scoundrels had no interest in people who were on guard against their deception. Tessa was sure she fit into neither category.

The only other possibility she could think of involved Mr. Scott's canal, but she didn't even know what that might be. If Eugenie's gossip was right, he had far more money to do with as he pleased than William did. If Gresham wished to invest in the canal, Tessa knew she'd be fortunate to secure even an hour of Mr. Scott's time again; she was already well aware that Hiram Scott's first loyalty was to his shareholders, and securing Lord Gresham's backing, either in pounds sterling or in a Parliamentary vote, would obscure whatever investment Tessa might counsel William to make. Mr. Scott would trample her into the dust in his haste to curry favor with an earl. The shares were effectively unlimited, so Gresham couldn't possibly fear losing the chance to invest if she bought the shares instead. None of it made any sense at all.

"Oh look, dear," piped up Eugenie. "Here is the coffeehouse. We ventured forth in search of it, in fact," she told Lord Gresham. "Mrs. Neville is *so* fond of a cup of coffee."

"Indeed." He turned the full force of his dark-eyed smile on her. Unthinkingly, Tessa looked up and met it head on, almost tripping over her own feet at the warmth in his gaze. Quick as a wink, his hand was on her arm to steady her. "We share a passion, Mrs. Neville."

The touch of his hand was a shock. His fingers curved under her elbow, strong and firm although his grip was light. For a moment she felt stunned, dazzled and weakened by the glare of his attention. Good heavens; no wonder he was a rake. Her heart skipped and her breath caught and her thoughts scattered as he smiled at her. She had only felt that way once before in her life, and it had ended so badly . . .

But this time she wasn't a naïve young girl, reduced to speechless wonder by a man's attention.

Richard had once held her arm and smiled at her almost as warmly as Gresham did, and it was only because he wanted something from her. It was a harsh lesson, and she hadn't forgotten it.

"I don't want coffee anymore," she blurted. She didn't want anything except to get away from him. "I'm going back to the inn."

"Oh, dear!" gasped Eugenie in comical despair.

"I hope you're not unwell," said Lord Gresham, a note of concern adding an extra resonance to his voice. He was still holding her arm.

Tessa jerked free. "I'm perfectly well. Good day," she snapped, then turned and hurried off before he could do anything else, like insist on accompanying her.

The breeze was cool on her hot face as she stalked away. How dare he make sport of her? It was all fine and good for him to charm Eugenie; Eugenie was in heaven over his attentions, and Tessa felt cruel and heartless every time she denied the older woman some innocent pleasure, even from a well-born rogue of nebulous intentions. But Lord Gresham had no business trying the same flummery on her. She didn't like him, didn't see what he wanted from her, and she absolutely loathed that he managed to make her cross and uneasy just by turning that provocative smile on her.

There was simply no reason he should be interested in them, and it was all quite infuriating.

Chapter 6

Mrs. Bates was in despair over Mrs. Neville's departure. "Perhaps I should go with her," she said before the lady in question had marched more than a dozen paces away. "She may be unwell. Mrs. Neville does have such a difficult time asking for help, she's really so *very* capable and clever, my lord."

Charlie was fairly certain Mrs. Neville wanted away from him more than anything else, although he still couldn't say why. It was animosity she displayed toward him, not unease or dismay. It was beginning to eat at his mind. What was behind it? Women *always* liked him. He finally threw craftiness to the wind. "I can't help but think she's taken me in dislike," he said, watching her wend her way through the crowd. Her dark blue skirts swung briskly as she walked, and her straw bonnet never turned even the littlest bit to the side. If they were in London, he would have said she just gave him the cut. "Have I offended her in some way? I certainly did not intend to."

"Why, no," cried Mrs. Bates. "You've been

the *most* proper gentleman, my lord! No, no, she merely . . ."

"Yes?" He tore his gaze from the departing figure when Mrs. Bates hesitated too long.

"She isn't . . . quite . . . at ease in . . . society," his companion finally said, struggling with each word. "She is too . . . forward."

That, he could see. Mrs. Neville would be wise to practice some reserve in London, if she wished to have any standing. Especially if she planned to take many earls or similar personages into such extreme and obvious dislike. "Have my actions contributed to her unease?" he persisted. "You know her much better than I, Mrs. Bates. I should hate to have unsettled her, even without intending to."

"Oh, I'm sure I can't think of anything you've done that might have offended her!" But the older lady's cheeks were bright pink and she wouldn't look at him.

So there was something. "You're being too kind, madam," he said in gentle reproach. "I would rather hear of my failing than continue in ignorance, alienating Mrs. Neville forever."

Mrs. Bates bit her lip and tipped her head from side to side, her face a mask of guilt and indecision. "I should not tell you this, my lord, but really— Mrs. Neville is best pleased when gentlemen treat her as they would another gentleman. She does not like flattery, or any suggestion she needs protecting. She is so enormously clever, but because she is also so lovely, gentlemen sometimes mistake her for a typical female. I'm sure I cannot understand her interest in investments and canal shares, but then I haven't nearly the head for figures she's got.

Lord Marchmont quite depends upon her; why, I expect she knows more about running Rushwood than he does! Not that she lacks a woman's heart," she added quickly, as if fearing she had tarred her friend too badly. "But . . . finding a husband is far from paramount in her mind. She said she was done with that after—"

Charlie guessed from her vivid blush and sudden silence that Mrs. Bates regretted saying that last part, which only inflamed his curiosity. He wondered exactly what sort of blow Mrs. Neville had sustained to make her content to be a widow. Heartbreak? Scandal? Something worse? It really was a pity for such a beautiful woman to be alone . . .

With a start he realized he was unconsciously wondering what it would take to tempt her. No. He was not here to seduce Mrs. Neville—who might, he reminded himself sternly, be part of the plot to ruin him. No doubt her sharp tongue had warded off any man tempted to approach her, and any heartbreak she suffered had been as much her own doing as any man's. If she thought him—Earl of Gresham, heir to the ancient and wealthy dukedom of Durham—indolent and unworthy, she obviously had different standards of worth than every other woman in Britain. Even if she had a luscious mouth and a lovely figure, he was not interested—intrigued and challenged, yes, but not foolhardy enough to pursue her.

Still, there was no reason not to use what he had learned. "I quite understand," he murmured. "I shall bear your words in mind when next I meet Mrs. Neville, and treat her as I would any gentleman of my acquaintance." He wasn't sure how on earth he would do it—his aunt's scolding would ring in his ears if he behaved too informally with any respectable lady—but it was an interesting thought.

Mrs. Bates beamed at him gratefully. "You are so good, my lord! Most gentlemen cannot bring themselves to do it. I am certain you shall see her thaw immeasurably."

"May we put it to a test?" he asked, pressing his advantage. "May I call upon you tomorrow morning?"

Delight fairly bubbled out of her. "We would be honored, sir!"

Charlie smiled. "The honor would be mine, madam." He didn't want to act too quickly. Gerard would have already been on his horse, pistols loaded, heading for Mells to confront Scott over the blackmail letters, but somehow Charlie felt that would be the wrong approach. He wanted to know more about the man, and perhaps, if he played his hand right, Mrs. Neville would tell him. He also wanted to know more about her, for a variety of reasons. She confounded him. She intrigued him. And blast it all, he did find her attractive. Again he hoped she had nothing to do with the blackmail, because if she did . . .

There would be no reason to heed his manners regarding her.

By the time Eugenie returned to the inn, still blushing pink with pleasure, Tessa's temper had calmed. She had told herself she was being silly and rash as she stormed up and down Frome's crooked streets. There must be a reason for Lord Gresham's interest, even if it was a foolish reason like boredom. It was surprising to hear him declare he had come to see Mr. Scott, when Mr. Scott hadn't mentioned him; the man was very fond of mentioning his well-connected investors at every opportunity. Surely the Earl of Gresham would have rated at least a passing word, but perhaps his interest was new.

She had no idea what had brought him to Frome and whatever it was about her or Eugenie that had caught his eye, but she grudgingly admitted she was making a mess of things with her behavior. She had begun badly by calling him indolent. Was it better now to apologize, or to pretend it never happened? If only he wouldn't look at her with those laughing black eyes of his. It was too much like Richard had once looked at her, before he made a complete fool of her and she ruined her life by rashly retaliating. Just as she was doing now, to her vexation. Even if Lord Gresham had some similar design upon her—and she couldn't think of any reason why he would—she was forewarned this time, and had no intention of making the same mistake twice.

So from now on she would treat the earl, whenever they might meet again, with cool propriety and perfect manners. If he wished to escort Eugenie about town, she would not object. If he wished to call on them, she would sit quietly in the corner during his visit. If he decided to tease her again, she would simply smile and ignore it. By being prickly she was only throwing out a challenge, and he, being an idle rake and scoundrel, was naturally unable to resist needling her in turn. It was the only logical answer she could think of.

After making this resolution, she pushed the earl from her mind and sat down to write her letters. William had asked for an account of every part of the canal plan, and Tessa had dragged Eugenie out to walk along the proposed junction in Frome, where the construction was already in progress. Then Eugenie felt one of her headaches coming on, so Tessa stepped into an apothecary shop to buy some headache powder, only to emerge to find that Lord Gresham had somehow appeared in Frome, every bit as unsettling as he'd been in Bath.

No—she was falling into the same trap. She pushed the enigmatic earl from her thoughts and wrote only of the canal to William, finishing just as Eugenie let herself in. Tessa put down her pen and looked up with a smile, determined not to bedevil the older woman anymore. But her companion surprised her.

"Teresa Neville," said Eugenie sternly, "where are your manners? Your mother would be horrified by the way you have treated Lord Gresham."

Tessa's mouth dropped open. "Eugenie!"

"Lord Gresham has been a perfect gentleman, and you have been abrupt and cold to him," her companion barreled onward. "What are you thinking? I don't expect you to delight in his attentions if you don't care for him, but be sensible! He is a prominent, well-connected nobleman in London! Think of the reflection on your brother and your sister, and how you endanger their standing." Eugenie paused, her sweet round face set in uncharacteristic disapproval. "What on earth do you dislike about Lord Gresham?"

Tessa sat in speechless surprise. Every word of

condemnation was true, but she was shocked to hear it so vehemently from Eugenie. "I'm sorry," she said quietly. "I will do better."

"I hope so!" The older lady flung off her shawl and fumbled with her bonnet. Her fingers shook, another sign of how distraught she was. "He asked to call tomorrow, and I accepted with pleasure. If you do not see the value in an amiable connection with him, I do!"

"You're right," said Tessa after a long hesitation.

"I am!" Eugenie's chin went up and she looked almost fierce for a moment, but then her expression softened into confusion. She came and sat down in a nearby chair. "What did he do to make you dislike him, dear? For he has noticed your disdain, I assure you."

Tessa rolled the pen between her fingers, feeling guilty and mortified. "It's not really disdain. At first I thought he meant to torment me, for my impertinent remark in Bath—and well I would have earned it," she added penitently. "I don't disclaim that. But he doesn't appear to be set upon that. I cannot for the life of me think why he's so interested in us, two women far below his social standing and outside his usual circles."

"But does it matter?" For a moment Eugenie sounded almost pleading. "He helped me when I was unwell—"

"Which was very kind of him, but he seems far more devoted than one might expect."

"He said he was also traveling alone . . ."

"And the only company he could find was the pair of us?" Tessa raised her eyebrows. "Really; a wealthy, well-connected, eligible earl cannot find anyone to have at his table but two ladies he's never met before?"

Eugenie bit her lip. "Then what do you suspect him of?" she asked mournfully. "For I cannot think what he hopes to gain from our acquaintance if not simple pleasure . . ."

Tessa hesitated, tapping her fingers on the tabletop. "I don't know," she said at last. "He didn't mention he was leaving Bath when we did; he gave every appearance of remaining in town. Now suddenly he turns up here, in the same small town we're visiting. It just seems . . . odd. He is *so* attentive, Eugenie."

"Yes," agreed her companion, although with a faint air of being pleased instead of puzzled. "But you can find no *absolute* objection to him, I hope?"

She sighed. Aside from her own wary suspicions and antipathy toward all handsome, glib men, no. "I had already resolved to be more tactful. I don't wish to antagonize him, truly I don't, and I don't mean to ruin your pleasure in his company."

Eugenie beamed at her. "He's to call tomorrow morning. I think you would find him charming, Tessa dear, as I do, if only you won't think him the same sort as *that vile man we don't mention*." She whispered the last, as she always did when mentioning Richard Wilbur. Tessa managed a tight smile. Trust Eugenie to say it out loud, as if confirming the similarities.

"I'm sure Lord Gresham couldn't possibly be that odious." No one could be, really, in her opinion. "And in the future I shall be faultlessly polite to him," she promised.

And she was. When Lord Gresham appeared the

next day, she smiled and curtsied and made all the correct responses. Then she sat back to listen quietly and politely as Eugenie chattered his ears off. To her relief, Lord Gresham did not turn his provocative half smile upon her; in fact he hardly looked at her at all, and when he did so it was with a direct, open gaze that she found impossible to dislike. Gradually, she found herself drawn into the conversation, especially when it turned toward the canal.

The earl, it turned out, had much the same purpose she had. "I plan to drive out soon and see Mr. Scott," said Lord Gresham. "Someone put his name to me as the man to see about the canal."

"Why, Mrs. Neville has an appointment with him this very day," exclaimed Eugenie. "What a coincidence!"

"Today!" He looked at her in surprise.

"Yes," said Tessa politely. "This afternoon."

"Perhaps we can drive together," he said. "It seems ridiculous for each of us to hire a carriage and negotiate these beastly roads."

"Oh yes," burst out Eugenie as Tessa hesitated. "How very kind of you, sir! I was so worried about her driving to Mells, with the roads the way they are in this country. Shameful, that's what they are! It would be *such* a relief to me to know she wasn't alone."

He grinned. "Now, Mrs. Bates, you're fretting over nothing. It's only a few miles to Mells. Even if the carriage came completely apart, one could walk to either town for help."

"Not if she were thrown from the carriage and seriously injured!" She turned to Tessa. "Do say you will allow His Lordship to accompany you."

"You have found me out," said Tessa dryly. "I did plan to drive like a manic to Mells and risk death and dismemberment, but now I shall have to reconsider."

"That sort of driving is no fun at all unless you are racing someone else, in any event," murmured Lord Gresham.

"Perhaps we should each hire a carriage and see," she replied before she could stop herself.

But Gresham only laughed and turned back to Eugenie, who was looking uncertainly between them. "Are you also going to Mells, Mrs. Bates?"

Eugenie hesitated. "I prefer not to," she said carefully, glancing sideways at Tessa as she spoke. "I worry about Mrs. Neville going alone, and it is my duty to look after her, but I confess . . . I do not look forward to it."

No, Eugenie didn't want to go, and had only agreed to go because Louise became hysterical at the thought of her sister driving around Somerset alone. Tessa gave a mental sigh and surrendered. Let this be part of her penance for being rude. "There is no need," she told her companion. "Since Lord Gresham has so kindly offered to go with me, you needn't come along. Perhaps you might enjoy that new novel you brought from Bath."

"Yes, indeed!" Eugenie smiled in gratitude. "You will drive safely, won't you, my lord?"

"As safely as Mrs. Neville desires," he said with a grin. He turned back to her. "Would an hour from now suit you?"

Tessa agreed, and soon after Lord Gresham left. Eugenie could barely speak, she was so pleased. "Do you see, dear, how very *charming* he can be?"

she cried, fluttering her fan in front of her pink face.

"Yes."

"And how kind! How very convenient it was that he planned to go to Mells today, just as you did, and then offer to escort you!"

"He is not escorting me," Tessa reminded her. "We are going on the same business, at the same time. I know what you're thinking, Eugenie, and you must stop."

The other woman gaped at her, then assumed a pious expression. "I'm sure I don't know what you mean, dear. I worried for your safety, that's all."

Tessa shook her head. She knew how Eugenie's mind worked, and could almost hear the hopeful thoughts racing through her head at the possible outcomes of her drive with the earl. Eugenie was very fond of novels and fairy tales, where the lonely maiden fell in love with a handsome hero. If there existed a more perfectly handsome hero than the Earl of Gresham, Tessa couldn't imagine him, but she was no helpless maiden in search of a hero. "Then we are all satisfied. I shan't be alone, and you shall have a peaceful day of reading." What Lord Gresham would gain, she didn't know, but he also seemed pleased by the arrangement.

Eugenie's smile was proof she held out very high hopes indeed, whatever Tessa said. "Yes, dear. I am *quite* satisfied."

Charlie thought his morning's visit couldn't have gone better. By careful effort he managed not to look at Mrs. Neville, and to pretend she was not a beautiful woman he wanted something from. It seemed to work, since she spoke to him without any of her previous frosty manner. Even better, she agreed to drive with him to Mells, which meant he could tackle two problems at once.

First, he would have his introduction to Hiram Scott. Without the slightest idea what connected him to Durham or Dorothy, Charlie had decided a straight-on approach would be best. The man's reaction to his sudden appearance would tell him a great deal, if not betray him altogether. It would also drive home to Scott that his secret was out, and perhaps lead him to negotiate a deal where he handed over any proof he had about Dorothy Cope, and in exchange Charlie would keep Gerard from killing him.

But second, he would have Mrs. Neville to himself for the drive each way. Charlie couldn't deny an unwarranted thrill of anticipation. He could try to tease more information about Scott from her. And even if those efforts failed, he would still have almost two hours to wheedle his way into her good graces, where he was increasingly interested in being. Tessa Neville was uncommonly attractive when she smiled.

He called for her at the appointed time, pleased to find her ready and waiting. Her dark green pelisse highlighted her unusual eyes, and Charlie barely stopped himself from complimenting her. With a brief touch of hands, she stepped up into the gig he'd hired, and they were off, bowling down the road toward Mells.

"Thank you for offering to accompany me," she said. Her gloved hands were folded in her lap, and she stayed primly at her end of the seat.

"No trouble at all," he said, reminding himself again not to engage in empty pleasantries. "In fact, I hoped I might ask a favor of you in return."

"Oh?" He felt her glance, and hoped Mrs. Bates's advice was worthwhile.

"I've only recently begun inquiring into canals," he said, raising his voice as the wheels rattled over loose stone on the road. It was a miracle any commerce at all was conducted around here, with the roads as they were. Mrs. Bates had been right to be concerned about the drive to Mells, but he kept the thought to himself. "I've come to see Mr. Scott, but have never met the man. Might I ask your impression of him?"

She had a way of pursing her lips that was very appealing. Charlie could see it from the corner of his eye, and had to concentrate very hard on the horse's ears to keep from turning to admire it more openly. "He is very clever at choosing the best way to present his plans," she said after a moment. "I don't wonder that he's been so successful in recruiting investors."

"Is he an honest man?" He wondered if she would tell him the truth. He wondered if she knew it.

"I've no reason to think otherwise," she said in some surprise.

"And yet you've come all the way into Somerset to see for yourself." He dared a quick glance at her. "What doubts do you have?"

"He wants a great deal of money," she said tartly. "I don't want my brother to be taken advantage of."

How interesting that she was here to protect

her brother; normally it would be the other way around. Charlie began to see why Mrs. Bates had advised him to treat her like a man. "I see. But what precisely in Scott's plans do you question?"

"Everything."

"Everything," he repeated in astonishment. "You must have quite a store of knowledge to question every last detail of the canal."

"Not every last detail," she said with an exasperated glance at him. "A canal is a complex project. There are landowners who must be appeased by the track of the canal. Investors don't always make their contributions. There are engineering difficulties to overcome, with tunnels and aqueducts. This canal traverses quite a drop, and will depend on reliable locks. Then there are problems with money, wages, workers . . . There are quite a lot of ways it could run into trouble."

Good Lord. Charlie had no desire to engage in a point by point analysis. He didn't give a damn about the canal or its engineering, only about Hiram Scott. And, in a different way, about Tessa Neville. "Yet canals have been very rewarding in this shire." It hadn't been hard to learn that much. "Surely they've learned ways around the difficulties."

"That is precisely why I'm wary. It's become almost accepted fact that canals are prosperous, therefore investing in a canal, any canal, is a wise decision."

"You don't agree." He didn't need to ask.

"I don't accept everyone else's opinion as fact, no."

"What is your inclination in this case?"

"I wouldn't have come this far if I were inclined against it," she replied.

"So you expect to make the investment," he persisted.

She hesitated. "Yes, I believe it will turn out to be prudent. Mr. Scott's numbers are compelling and impressive. I just need to be sure." There was no waver in her voice, just plain confidence.

"Because you don't quite trust him," said Charlie, to provoke her.

"I don't completely trust anyone who wants money from me, my lord."

He glanced at her before he could stop himself. She sat facing forward, a composed, neatly contained woman. Her pale green eyes surveyed the road in front of them; she didn't look at him. But with the sun on her face, gleaming on the dark curls that escaped her bonnet, Charlie wondered that any man could think of money when looking at her.

"I think you don't completely trust anyone," he said on impulse.

Her gaze flew to meet his, flashing fire. Her lovely mouth compressed, then eased. "Why should I?" she replied evenly. "Do you trust everyone, sir?"

He laughed. "Not everyone, no. But I don't immediately assume every man I meet is untrustworthy."

She turned away, facing forward once more. "Nor do I."

Charlie looked at her serene profile for a moment. "Yes, you do."

Instead of becoming indignant, she merely sighed and gave a slight shake of her head. "As you like."

"You are the wariest woman I've ever met," he went on. "And I cannot decide if you merely dislike me, or if you fear I have nefarious designs upon Mrs. Bates."

A faint pink suffused her cheeks, but her expression didn't change. "You heard what I said at the hotel in Bath, when you arrived, for which I am very sorry. I can only plead a short temper, made worse by the discomforts of travel, and offer a humble apology."

"You should," he told her. "Normally it takes people at least a half hour's conversation to decide how indolent I am."

"Yes." She slanted him a look. "So I see."

He grinned. "Precisely! Now at least I haven't been convicted on prejudice, but on my own failings."

Her lips pursed up again, and finally a reluctant smile broke through. "Hardly, my lord."

"Perhaps, with diligent effort and enough time, I can improve my standing in your eyes," he went on, enjoying himself now. "Next week I might appear merely shiftless, and the week after that lackadaisical. Why, dare I hope to rise so far as . . . benign?"

This time she laughed, just a little. "You're a silver-tongued serpent, aren't you?"

"Nonsense. I'm as harmless as a lamb," he said solemnly.

Those bright green eyes narrowed on him. "I doubt that very much."

Charlie affected great shock. "Indeed! On what evidence, madam?"

He thought he had her there. He'd been the soul of propriety and good manners—exquisite manners, even—toward her and her companion. She looked at him, hesitating, and he grinned in triumph.

"You're too charming," she said at last.

"Flattery, madam!" he exclaimed in glee. "First indolence, now charm! You mustn't accuse me of such things, I may expire of the shock and drive us off the road."

"I am ready to take the reins at any sign of infirmity." She smiled as she said it, and Charlie almost did drive off the road. Tessa Neville's eyes glowed with sly mirth and her lips curved in a wholly bewitching way when she was in the right humor. And by God, he liked it.

"Which, I gather, you consider an excess of charm."

"In some cases, yes."

"And is that my chief failing, Mrs. Neville?" He kept his eyes trained forward, on the twitching left ear of the horse, but he could see his companion still. "You may tell me honestly—in fact, I hope you will."

The mirth faded from her face. She studied him for a moment, her gaze direct and clear. Mrs. Bates had one thing right: he certainly shouldn't treat Mrs. Neville as he would any other woman. No one else looked at him so frankly. Charlie was used to a variety of female expressions—coyness, calculation, adoration, seduction—but he'd never felt as though he was being assessed as he was now. Not for the value of his title or the size of his income, not for his physical appearance or even for his reputation among the ton, but for something more. He had the sense Mrs. Neville was trying to decide if she could trust him, at least enough to answer his question honestly.

"You puzzle me, my lord," she said after a

minute. Charlie kept his face bland but curious even as his heart sped up. "I cannot think of any connection between our families, but you've taken so strongly to Mrs. Bates."

"She reminds me of my aunt, whom I love very dearly."

"Do you not see your aunt often?"

"Every other week, during the Season."

One corner of her mouth puckered in bemusement. "Then you're not expiring from the lack of company. What can you possibly mean by lavishing attention on Mrs. Bates?"

"May I not enjoy her company? She seems to welcome it," he parried, beginning to wish she would turn that incisive gaze away. He could feel it cutting into him even without facing it head-on.

"She could not possibly be more delighted by it," said Mrs. Neville, a bit dryly. "I don't wish to be rude, but it festers in my mind. Why us? What about her, or about me, attracted your attention and keeps it fixed on us?"

"Do you think yourself not worth my attention?" he asked.

"No," she said frankly. "Not at all. My family doesn't know yours. We've never met. I have nothing you could want, no advantage I could offer you, and Eugenie has even less—unless you are perishing for want of someone to debate the latest style in bonnets or the newest Minerva Press novel. And yet you wait on us as if you desperately need something from us."

Charlie thought a moment, then took the risk. Either this woman was the most accomplished actress since Sarah Siddons or she knew nothing

about any blackmail. "Perhaps I do, Mrs. Neville."
He glanced at her sideways as he spoke, and caught
the spark of satisfaction in her eyes at his words,
followed closely by suspicion. "No great thing. It's
mere happenstance you're the one I must ask it of."
They had reached Mells, and Charlie slowed the
horse, turning toward the ironworks. Scott's factory was obvious, the tall chimneys rising above
the thatched roofs of the little village.

"Well, what is it?" asked the woman beside him
as they circled through the wrought-iron gates into
the yard of the factory. It was a gracious but solid
stone edifice, obviously prosperous, with a wide
arched door and lines of clean windows. A carved
wooden sign swung on an arm, bearing the title
SCOTT & SWYNNE, IRON MANUFACTORS. It didn't
look at all like a blackmailer's lair.

He pulled up the horse in front of the entrance
and set the brake. Distant clangs of metal on metal
echoed from within, although they seemed out of
place with the offices in front of them. He turned
to look at her. Mrs. Bates had been right; flummery would get him nowhere with this woman.
She was still watching him with the same direct,
almost probing gaze as before. She'd never forgive
him if he tried to manipulate her or lied to her,
and inexplicably, undeniably, Charlie wanted her
to like him. And as for what he wanted from her
. . . "All I ask is an introduction to Hiram Scott."

Chapter 7

Tessa's mouth dropped open. "An introduction?" she repeated stupidly. Of all the things she might have expected him to say, that wasn't one of them. It was ridiculous. He was a wealthy earl. He didn't need her to introduce him to anyone, let alone a factory owner.

"Yes." Lord Gresham jumped down from the gig and gave her a faint smile. "Too demanding?"

It made her suspicious all over again, which was too bad. She'd almost begun to like the man. Tessa smoothed her face and let him help her down. "Not at all," she said. "I would be happy to introduce you to him." It would add more to her stock with Mr. Scott than it would to Lord Gresham's, but if he thought this was a favor she did him, so be it.

Mr. Scott was waiting. Tessa smiled as he came across the clerk's office to take her hand. "Mrs. Neville," he said. "I trust your drive out was pleasant?"

"Yes," she said. Until Lord Gresham's last, puzzling, request, she'd enjoyed the drive more than expected. "In fact, I was fortunate enough to meet a gentleman who also wishes to see your plans, and he kindly drove with me. May I introduce you to him?"

Mr. Scott's eyebrows went up, but he was pleased. "Capital! By all means. Is this the gentleman?"

Tessa turned, thinking the earl was still outside, and started when she realized he'd been right behind her, silent as a shadow. How odd. She would have expected him to step forward at once, not wait for her to speak. "Yes," she said. "My lord, may I present Mr. Scott. Mr. Scott, this is the Earl of Gresham."

As Tessa had known it would, Scott's attention swung from her to Lord Gresham and didn't swing back. "An honor to make your acquaintance, my lord," he said cordially, making a crisp bow.

Gresham, she couldn't help noticing, barely bowed his head in reply. "And I, yours," he said, in a different voice than she had ever heard from him. He sounded harder, colder, and not charming at all. There wasn't a trace of his wicked grin, and he was looking at Mr. Scott as if he wished to bore a hole in the man.

What had happened? A few minutes ago he'd been smiling and teasing her, and now he looked every inch the merciless aristocrat. Tessa frowned a little. Which was the true man? Perhaps they were all part of him. She stole another peek at him, and wondered why he chose to show her his charming, persistently friendly side.

"Why, I daresay I don't deserve the honor!" Scott was so pleased, he seemed not to notice how grim Lord Gresham's face had become. "Have you heard of our canal works, or do you have a need for iron?"

Lord Gresham didn't speak for a moment, just stared hard at Scott. "The canal," he finally said in the same wintry tone. "But I won't interrupt your appointment with Mrs. Neville."

From the expression that flickered over his face, Mr. Scott would gladly have ignored Tessa for the rest of the day in favor of an earl, but he recovered well. "Of course not." He swept out one hand. "Mrs. Neville has come for a tour, to ensure I don't swindle her." He chuckled. "You are very welcome to accompany us, my lord."

Lord Gresham's dark eyes turned to her. Tessa made herself smile although Scott's invitation irked her. She had made this appointment and come all the way from Malmesbury, and didn't appreciate being shunted aside so carelessly. It wasn't Lord Gresham's fault, directly, but she'd known this would happen as soon as he asked to come with her today.

"No," said the earl. "Mrs. Neville doubtless has come prepared with many questions, and I would only impede her. I shall wait here while you show her about."

Scott cleared his throat. "Of course. As you wish."

"No," Tessa heard herself say. She stared at Lord Gresham. He stared back, his expression inscrutable. He wanted to meet Mr. Scott, he wanted to see the canal works, and then he declared he would sit in the office and wait while she asked her questions? Her brother William would not have hesitated to take precedence over her, even though he wouldn't have the first idea what to ask about the canal. Lord Gresham, who didn't know her and who outranked William by a league or more, deferred to her. It was startling and disarming.

It was also rather silly to ask Mr. Scott to lead two tours, especially since hers would be rushed and short if Mr. Scott was eager to return to the earl. "I certainly have no objection, if you wish to accompany us," she said. "You have come to see the canal, and there is no reason for Mr. Scott to show us each separately."

He bowed his head. "That's very kind of you. Thank you."

The following tour was decidedly odd. Mr. Scott was intent on currying Lord Gresham's favor, which had the benefit of drawing fulsome answers from him in response to her questions, accompanied by frequent asides to His Lordship. Scott didn't forget himself so far as to overlook her entirely, but Tessa was well aware he was addressing himself to Lord Gresham at least as much as to her. It annoyed her, but she conceded it was making things easier for her, so she tried to ignore it.

As for Lord Gresham, he strolled along a step behind and barely said a word. Every time Tessa stole a glance at him, he was watching Mr. Scott with the same hard expression. He didn't ask a single question, and if he examined any part of the canal plans in detail, she didn't see it.

It was possible that he, like William, didn't really know anything about canals and shares, but then why would he come to see for himself? William hadn't even suggested such a thing; everyone just assumed she would go for him. It would be easier for Lord Gresham to send an estate agent in his stead, or his solicitor. She would have suspected the earl came for some other reason entirely, except he had clearly said he was interested in the canal. She didn't understand it, but then, she didn't understand most things men did, and this particular man was particularly puzzling.

"Have I satisfied all your worries, madam?" asked Scott jovially as they returned to the front of the ironworks. "And yours, my lord?"

"For the moment," murmured Lord Gresham.

"I shall still want to see the latest accounts," Tessa said, reminding Mr. Scott of what she told him weeks earlier. What he had shown her today was exactly what she'd expected to see: a small section of canal already built, all neat lines and solid stone. Since it would service his very own factory, she would have been shocked to see anything out of order with it. The success of the canal would depend on more than the three mile stretch from Mells to Frome, however. This branch was intended to run out into the coal fields, carrying lucrative shipments of coal straight into the established canal running through Bath. Scott also predicted grains and other cargoes, including iron from his own factory, would make the canal a thriving enterprise. The pamphlets and list of shareholders he'd brought to persuade William had made it sound as though money would be streaming in from passage fees, paying dividends of ten to fifteen percent or more on shares. In Bath, Mr. Scott had produced more documentation, but it wasn't enough to justify fifteen percent.

"Of course," Mr. Scott replied, his smooth smile back in place. "I've been trying to gather everything you asked for; perhaps in a few more days all will be ready."

The earl gave a single nod and walked away toward the carriage without another word. Tessa thanked Mr. Scott and shook his hand before following. She waited until they had driven out the gates again before saying anything to Lord Gresham, as he still wore the closed-down expression that seemed to forbid approach.

"Was Mr. Scott not what you expected?" she asked at last.

He didn't look at her, but kept his eyes on the road. "No," he said after a moment's pause.

"How so?" As soon as she said it, she realized she probably shouldn't ask. It was none of her business, and he was obviously deep in thought about something. "I'm sorry," she added quickly. "That was impertinent."

He took a deep breath and glanced at her. Some of the lighthearted look came back into his expression. "Impertinent? Not at all. Inquisitive, perhaps, or at worse prying, but not rude."

She blinked in consternation. "Well . . . well, good. I didn't want to be rude again."

Charlie grinned, easily slipping back into his former mood, before they had reached the factory. It was a relief to put aside his thoughts about Scott and think about Mrs. Neville instead. "No, he was not at all what I expected, but I'm exceedingly grateful to you for the introduction."

She looked baffled. "It was nothing. If anyone is in my debt for that introduction, it appears to be Mr. Scott."

"Will you return to the ironworks?" he asked. He had barely paid any attention to the details of what Scott said, but he'd heard every word from Tessa Neville's mouth. "He didn't answer all your doubts today, I presume."

"No, he didn't. Canals are notorious for costing more than anticipated, and although Mr. Scott assures me this canal is being built with great economy, he hasn't produced any accounting for it, only the initial projections. I won't throw Marchmont's money into a company that will waste it."

"I see." Charlie realized he was feeling a measure of scorn for Lord Marchmont, who sent his sister out to invest his money for him. But wasn't he the same? He hadn't made any effort to take control of his estate, or even prepare to do so, from his brother Edward. Telling himself it wasn't really his estate yet was only an excuse, and he gave himself a mental slap for being so . . . *indolent* about it.

When they were within a mile of Frome, he slowed the carriage and gestured to a neat little house set back from the road. "My new lodging. Should you or Mrs. Bates ever need to contact me, you may send word to Mill Cottage."

"You plan to stay in Frome a while, then," she said in surprise.

"No," said Charlie. Only as long as it took to sort out Hiram Scott. He'd sooner sleep in a stable than listen through the thin walls of the inn to the couple next door argue all night again. Fortunately for him, he didn't need to settle for a stable. It had taken his valet exactly one hour to find an estate agent very keen to let any house in Somerset to His Lordship. Barnes should have already removed his belongings to the cottage by now.

"Ah." She was quiet a moment. "Mrs. Bates and I plan to leave for London within a fortnight, if not within the week."

"Commendable." Charlie hoped he was as lucky. "You will be staying with your sister, I believe?"

"Yes," she murmured. Some of the light went out of her face, and he realized she wasn't looking forward to it with much pleasure. Every response he thought of, though, seemed inadequate or insensitive, so he said nothing, and they drove into Frome in silence.

He reached The Golden Hind, where she was staying, and stopped the carriage. "My thanks again for your company, and for the introduction to Mr. Scott," he said as she stepped down.

She smiled uncertainly and bobbed a curtsy. "Thank you for driving."

"It was my honor," he said, and meant it.

"You're too kind." She was looking up at him with a vaguely quizzical air; he wondered what her agile mind was thinking now. It was rather amusing that she thought he'd been following her because she called him indolent. Of course, telling her he only wanted an introduction to Hiram Scott made only a small bit more sense. This woman wasn't fooled by any prevarication or flattery. He'd have to think faster the next time he saw her.

That thought put a real smile on his lips. He would definitely see her again. "Good day, Mrs. Neville." He touched his fingers to his hat, and watched her turn and walk inside the inn before he lifted the reins.

He had only begun to order his thoughts by the time he reached his new residence. To his consternation, Hiram Scott hadn't displayed a blink of recognition when Mrs. Neville introduced him. It was possible Scott wouldn't know to connect the Gresham name with Durham, but that wasn't very good research for a man who hoped to make five thousand pounds in blackmail money. It would have taken nothing more than a quick perusal of any London newspaper to discover the connection, thanks to the recent scandal. It was possible that Scott had learned someone was looking for him—subtlety was not Gerard's strength, and word might have circulated in Bath—and prepared himself for the encounter so well that he could react without any alarm. But Scott had expected Mrs. Neville alone today. Charlie had watched Scott from the moment the man came out of his office to greet her and hadn't seen even a flicker of surprise or unease. If anything, Scott's eyes had lit up in delight, which he only amplified during the tour.

Charlie had been counting on learning something from the confrontation, and was a bit confounded by the results. Scott made no mention, not even a hint, of the Durham Dilemma, even though it was probably the most infamous story in Britain right now. The man seemed pleased to see him, and appeared bent on winning his favor. Perhaps Scott thought his chances for blackmail had died with Durham, and now hoped to wring the money from him by more direct means. He had all but begged Charlie to buy some shares in the canal company. If Scott had any purpose in life, it was that damned canal.

But what did that imply about the blackmail? Perhaps there was a different Hiram Scott who traveled through Bath . . . but this fellow fit the description, and he was in obvious pursuit of funds. Charlie would be absolutely certain of him if only he could find a single thread connecting Scott to Dorothy Cope.

On the other hand, Mrs. Neville and Mrs. Bates

also seemed unaware of the Durham Dilemma. He was rather certain Mrs. Bates at least would have been unable to resist saying something, if she'd known. Her memory wasn't all it used to be, though, she'd told him, and Charlie thought he'd made such an impression on her, she might have overlooked it anyway. Mrs. Bates was utterly dazzled by his attentions.

Not so Mrs. Neville, although Charlie hoped she was thawing toward him, now that he had learned the trick of how to talk to her. It was just his luck to run up against a logical, intelligent woman who was clearly not dazzled by anything about him, when it would have suited him so much better to have her entirely under his sway. Which wasn't to say he didn't fancy her as she was; in an odd way, it was part of her allure. He had never had to work for a woman's regard before, and even as it frustrated him, he found it somehow invigorating. He had to be in top form around her. He no longer suspected she had any part in Hiram Scott's scheme, but he certainly wasn't ready to give up the advantages of her acquaintance with Scott. And he really didn't want her to know he had ever suspected her at all.

He handed the reins to the groom who came running when he stopped in front of the cottage. The front door stood open, and he found Barnes in the sitting room supervising a handful of servants, all dusting and sweeping and polishing. Charlie gave him a brief nod and walked through the rest of the house. It was small, dark, and sparsely furnished, but isolated and private, and there were no neighbors to argue loudly at nights. And he only had to endure it for a few days, so it was perfect.

Barnes found him in the main bedroom, looking out over the ruins of the mill on the nearby stream. "Will it do, my lord?" he asked.

"Perfectly." Charlie nodded. "Well done."

"Thank you, sir."

"Carry out a table and chair over there," Charlie added, indicating a sunny spot near the old mill. "And fetch something to eat and drink. No, I don't need that anymore," he added as Barnes made a motion toward the cane, propped in the corner. His valet nodded and slipped from the room.

Charlie flexed his foot, stretching his healing leg. It was a bit stiff from driving back and forth to Mells, but not beyond what he could bear. He was done with the cane, just as he was done avoiding his duty. With one last deep breath, he turned. The leather dispatch case Edward had given him was sitting on the dressing table, waiting. It had been waiting for a while now, and finally he was ready to face it. Confronting Hiram Scott had revealed nothing—yet. It was time to read the Fleet minister's wedding registers.

Chapter 8

The next few days seemed to drag by. Tessa was normally quite capable of occupying herself, but for some reason she felt out of sorts and restless. It might be Frome itself; the village was small and dull, with only a few shops and a lone, rather dismal coffeehouse. She wrote to William, took her usual brisk morning walks for exercise, and found herself with nothing to do by midday. Even Eugenie had a novel to savor.

She wished Mr. Scott had gathered the materials she wanted in good time. The day after her trip to Mells, he sent a brief note, apologizing for not having the books ready but explaining he had to make a trip to Poole and would be away for a day or two. Since he wanted to be at hand to answer any questions she might have, he hoped she would forgive him another delay. There was nothing Tessa could reply but that she understood completely, even though she wanted to browbeat him. Really, how hard was it to bring out the canal company account books and let her read them? He was the treasurer of the company and as such maintained the accounts himself. They were probably kept in his very own factory. He professed complete understanding of her desire to see them, but he certainly wasn't making it quick or easy for her to do so. If she were a man, Scott wouldn't be so cavalier about putting her off repeatedly. Tessa wondered in aggravation if she'd have more luck getting to see the books if she persuaded Lord Gresham to ask for them.

Well—there was no question she would. Scott would trip over himself to fetch the books for the earl. If only there were a way to ask Lord Gresham without seeming too forward and presumptuous. Or even any way at all to ask him, because after he accompanied her to the ironworks, His Lordship hadn't called on them once.

Eugenie blamed her for this, Tessa knew. When he didn't call the day after their visit to Mells, Eugenie asked timidly if there had been any disagreements between them. She said no, but rather too quickly, and saw the disappointment on her companion's face. She tried to tell herself it was the truth, but as another day dragged on without him, she began to wonder, uncomfortably, if he'd been more offended than he appeared to be. She had apologized for calling him indolent, and invited him to come along on her tour, but there was no question Lord Gresham had come away in a dark temper, and hadn't spoken half as much on the drive home as on the drive out. It made her uneasy and annoyed all at once. She knew she had less social grace than everyone else, and that she was often too blunt for her own good. But Lord Gresham, with his provoking little smiles and devil-may-care laugh, hardly seemed the sort of take deep offense so easily. If he had put on some easygoing pose just to lure her into greater indiscretion . . .

She caught herself and wondered what had come over her. She was too insignificant to have such an effect on Lord Gresham. He claimed he'd only wanted an introduction to Mr. Scott, which he had duly gotten, so perhaps he was just done with her—and with Eugenie by extension. It would decimate her opinion of him if that were true, but she didn't know him, and heaven knew, most aristocrats wouldn't hesitate to act that way. In fact, it would only confirm her original feeling about him, which ought to have added the prospect of some vindication, but somehow she felt more betrayed than anything. She had wanted to hate him, and now that he'd made her like him instead, she didn't want to hate him again.

This tortured thought sent her to her feet. It was a warm, sunny day, and she was going mad in this small inn. "I shall go for a walk," she told Eugenie, who was embroidering listlessly by the window. "Would you like to come along?"

"No, dear," sighed her companion. She poked her needle through the cloth again and glanced out into the street. "I shall stay here. My ankle is feeling very tender again."

Left unspoken was Eugenie's lingering hope Lord Gresham might call. It hadn't escaped Tessa's notice that Eugenie stationed herself by the window overlooking the street every day, with her book or her sewing in hand. It only increased her own guilt, that she had driven the earl away without even knowing how.

She put on her lightest pelisse and went out, determined to quiet her nerves with vigorous exercise. She struck out away from town, wanting more peace than the streets of Frome offered. The Somerset countryside lacked the idyllic serenity of Wiltshire, where she had grown up, but there was a kind of beauty in the wildness of the land, and she occupied herself with studying the unfamiliar flora as she strode briskly along the rutted roads. Anything to get Lord Gresham's wicked grin out of her mind . . .

After a while she began to feel more herself. It was the inactivity, she decided; at home she had plenty to do and therefore little time for her mind to wander to inconsequential questions, like why Lord Gresham had paid her any attention in the first place or why he had abruptly stopped. Tessa preferred things that way. She didn't want to be cross and bewildered over the actions of that man, or any man. In a few days she would be done here in Frome and would go on to London, returning to her family, where everything was normal and no handsome earls would bedevil her sensible, well-ordered life.

Of course, London would hold a new host of trials. It wouldn't be so bad if only William and his wife, Emily, would be there. William respected her desire to forge her own way, and Emily would never dream of coercing her into attending balls and soirees where the ladies would discuss nothing more important than how one was ever to learn the latest fashions from Paris, given the rude impositions of war. But this time Louise would be there, full of determination to establish herself among the ton. Louise would insist that she go to balls and masquerades and Venetian breakfasts; her sister couldn't fathom how any female could be utterly indifferent to fashions and gossip. Tessa had tried to explain that she chose her clothing based on what appealed to her own eye, not what other women were wearing, and that she only cared about gossip if the scandals involved would impinge on her life, but she might as well have been speaking some African tongue. Louise waved her hands and said she understood perfectly, and then went right on trying to coax her into new dresses and hinting that certain gentlemen didn't mind a lady well past her youth.

That last thought always made Tessa scowl. A patch of bluebells caught her eye and she waded into the field to pick some. She didn't feel old, except when Louise started with her hints. Why must a woman be old when she wasn't yet thirty? It wasn't even half of her life, most likely. Her great-grandmother had lived to the glorious age of eighty-three, hardly allowing that she was old then. Tessa picked her flowers, tugging firmly to get them up by the roots so they would stay fresher longer when she put them in water. And what did it matter to Louise if she married or not? It would be one thing, she supposed, if Louise had been happily married and merely wanted the same joy for her sister, but no; rarely had a day gone by during Lord Woodall's life when Louise didn't complain about him in some way. Tessa thought many of her sister's complaints were valid, but then, that was also Louise's fault for marrying a boring, unintelligent man whose main interest in life was shooting whatever bird happened to be in season. Far better to be unmarried than wed to someone wretchedly dull, in Tessa's opinion. At times, in her darker humors, she thought Louise wanted her to get married just so she wouldn't be the only one unhappy.

But now Louise *was* happy. She was moving her family to London, free at last of Lord Woodall's parsimonious drudgery and away from William's rather nervous oversight. She was a widow with a plump jointure, still attractive and relatively young. She would have all the fashions she could afford and all the gossip she could stand, and Tessa hoped she enjoyed every minute of both. She was only sorry Louise had decreed she must go, too. The one true disadvantage of being unwed was her dependence on her family. Louise usually managed to wear William down when she set her mind to something, which meant he had eventually agreed that Tessa *could* be spared from Rushwood for a few months; that Tessa *ought* to make an effort to widen her circle of acquaintances beyond their small village in Wiltshire; and that Tessa *would* find a husband if she only made herself look for one, preferably in London where she might have a clean slate with eligible gentlemen and no one would remember that terrible business with Richard Wilbur. With no money of her own, Tessa had little choice but to give in, just as she'd had to give in and bring Eugenie with her to Somerset, even though Eugenie didn't want to come. In many ways she and Eugenie were in much the same boat. They were both dependent on William's support, and both of them must abide by his wishes. The fact that she was his sister, while Eugenie was only a distant cousin, didn't change the fact that William's word was the final one.

She stood and stretched her back, clutching her wild bouquet in one dirty glove. The sunlight was beginning to slant; it was growing late in the afternoon, time to return to the inn. She looked around to get her bearings, and realized with a start she was just down the road from Mill Cottage, where Lord Gresham had said he was staying.

For a moment she stood there, the wind ruffling the grass and wildflowers around her. She had no reason to go to Mill Cottage, and it was improper for a lady to call on a gentleman anyway. Not that she wanted to call on him; no, she wanted him out of her mind. She repeated this to herself as she tramped out of the field, climbed up the bank to the road, and headed back toward Frome . . . past Mill Cottage. It was the most direct route, after all, and merely walking past his house meant nothing.

In spite of herself, she couldn't help slowing for a cautious look at the house as she passed. It was a rustic but charming cottage, built of weathered stone with a gravel drive leading to it. As she walked, an old mill came into view, set behind the house on the stream that burbled along parallel to the road. It was peaceful and quaint, and for a moment she envied Lord Gresham his retreat. Being able to sit in the sunshine by the stream must be very pleasant on a day like this.

Which, she told herself a moment later in embarrassment, was probably why he was doing just that. A slight rise had blocked her view, but out on the sun-drenched lawn by the old mill sat the Earl of Gresham. He was lounging in a chair, one booted foot propped on another chair as he read a book. He wore no coat or hat, and as she watched, he ran one hand through the dark waves of his hair and tossed his book on the table beside him. He put up both his feet, and reclined even farther in his chair, letting his head drop back as if he wanted the sun on his face. Tessa stood rooted to the spot. He was blindingly handsome even when being arrogant and proper; lounging in his chair, relaxed and easy, he was irresistible. Even she, who was never blinded by men's looks, couldn't look away. And some small part of her heart wondered again, with a pang, what she'd done that ended his interest and attentions.

Another man came from the house, carrying a tray with a pitcher. A servant, she guessed. He placed the tray on the table and stacked up several books alongside it. He must have said something to Lord Gresham, because Tessa caught the impression of a grin on the earl's face, and a whisper of his laugh drifted to her on the breeze. But then Gresham lifted his head and looked right at her, and she jerked around, flushing at being caught staring. She started walking again, clutching her bluebells and fixing her eyes on the road in front of her.

"Mrs. Neville," he called. "Mrs. Neville!"

She stole a sideways glance from under her eyelashes and grimaced. He was coming toward her, striding across the grass at such a clip, he'd be upon her before she could scurry around the spinney of trees ahead. She was caught. She forced herself to stop instead of breaking into a run, as her instinct urged. "Lord Gresham. How do you do?"

"Very well, now." He grinned at her and made a brief bow. "Are you out walking?"

"Yes," she said. "I have circled Frome three times and finally needed a new vista."

He laughed. "How delightful you came this way! Won't you sit down and rest a moment? My man Barnes has just brought out some fresh lemonade."

Tessa hesitated. Louise would probably say it was improper, but Eugenie would say the earl could do no wrong. Sitting outdoors in full view of the road was hardly a scandalous tête-à-tête. And she was very fond of lemonade, which was quite a luxury in so rustic an area. "Thank you, sir. Fresh lemonade is too tempting to refuse."

"I knew I would find something," he murmured. "Come—Barnes, fetch another glass," he called to the servant, who had followed him halfway across the drive. Barnes nodded and went back into the house.

Tessa ignored his comment and walked beside him, a careful distance apart. "A very peaceful spot," she said. "And such a lovely day to enjoy it."

"Indeed. If only I were free to indulge in a walk, as you did." Tessa snuck a glance at the books on the table as they reached it—rather musty looking journals of some sort—but he didn't mention them. "I see you are taking some of Nature home with you."

"Oh." Tessa looked down at her bluebells, already beginning to wilt. "Mrs. Bates is fond of bluebells."

"Is she well?" He pulled out the chair he'd been lounging in and gestured to it. Tessa sat, feeling awkward and self-conscious. She really oughtn't to be here. Now she would have to talk to him.

"She is well," she replied to his question. "Frome doesn't offer many entertainments, though. I fear we are both beginning to languish."

"Oh?" He raised his eyebrows. "You've found *any* entertainments in Frome?"

Tessa smiled ruefully. "I didn't expect to."

"Ah, yes; you came on business." The servant brought out a tray with glasses, and Lord Gresham said nothing while the man poured lemonade for them. "Has Mr. Scott answered your questions?"

"No." Tessa ran one finger down the side of her glass, then picked it up and took a small sip. It was bracingly tart and cool, exactly as she liked it. She closed her eyes and took another, longer sip. "Not yet."

Lord Gresham didn't reply, and she looked up to see him staring at her, his eyes dark and intense. She sat a little forward in her chair, beginning to fear he was in the same grim mood he'd fallen into at the ironworks. "Has he satisfied your doubts, sir?"

He blinked, and a vaguely bitter smile curved his mouth. "Not at all."

She shot him a puzzled glance—it sounded almost ominous, when he said it that way—but he didn't say anything else. She sipped more lemonade, wishing for once that she could chatter as easily as Eugenie did with him. "Have you really come to see the canal?" she said, unable to hold back the curiosity any longer.

His eyes brightened and he leaned back in his chair. The sun was full in his face, gleaming on his dark hair and flashing off the signet ring on his finger as he propped his chin in one hand. "Of course. As you yourself noted, Frome has few other attractions."

She nodded. "You didn't seem deeply interested when we visited Mells."

He shrugged. "I didn't expect him to show me any troublesome parts."

"So you think there are some?"

"I've never built a canal," he said, stretching out his long legs in front of him, "but I've yet to hear of any large engineering project that didn't have troublesome spots."

That confirmed her own feeling. She put down her glass of lemonade and turned her full attention on him. "Where do you think the problems lie?"

He took his time replying, but for the first time Tessa didn't feel uncomfortable at his regard. His dark eyes moved over her face thoughtfully, without teasing or laughing. "I expect the money is a problem," he said at last. "Scott wouldn't travel so widely in search of investors if he had plenty of funds. And more than one canal company has brought bills before Parliament seeking more funding authority."

"Yes." She frowned. "They're usually successful, aren't they? Has this canal applied for a new act?"

Again he hesitated. "Not that I know of."

"Nor have I." That was reassuring. Lord Gresham, with a seat in Parliament, would surely know if this canal had lobbied for a new act to raise more funds, or even if there had been rumblings of it. And he wouldn't be here at all, considering an investment himself, if he knew of serious shortfalls. She ought to have thought of that sooner. "Other canals have been built with the original authorization. Mr. Scott assures me this one will be as well."

"It would be in his interest to say so, wouldn't

it?" murmured the earl. "He wants to persuade you his canal is a sound investment."

"Which is why I won't agree until I see the account books," she pointed out.

He nodded. "One wonders why Mr. Scott hasn't produced them promptly, then. I presume he knew before your visit you wished to see the books."

"Yes, I told him at Rushwood when he came to see my brother, and I told him again in Bath a week ago." Her mouth tightened as she thought about it. "It's a trifle annoying he hasn't got them ready yet."

"Yes. It might make one wonder what he has to do to make them ready."

She tipped her head to one side and studied him. He lounged very easily and informally in his chair, but with none of the lurking laughter she was accustomed to seeing in his face. He was regarding her as curiously as she was watching him, she realized. Of course, they were having a remarkably serious conversation. "Do you think I'm odd to want to see the books?" she asked on impulse.

"Odd?" His eyebrows flew up.

"Yes, for a woman to care so much about money."

He took a deep breath and let it out slowly. "I think we are all born with our own talents and interests, male and female. If you have the intellect and the interest for investing, I see no reason why you wouldn't wish to see the account books. I presume Scott wants a handsome sum from your brother."

"Yes, six thousand pounds."

Gresham inclined his head. "There you are."

"Most men find it odd that I have either the interest or the intellect," she said, then wondered why she'd told him that. She might as well have embroidered the words "prosy bluestocking" across her bodice. She forced a smile. "Most women find it odd, as well."

"Most people have frivolous interests, and intellects to match, as my father used to say." A faint smile touched his mouth. "I doubt he would have said it of you, though."

Tessa warmed, feeling as though he'd just paid her a true compliment. "Thank you, sir."

He chuckled. "At last! A compliment paid, and no charges of flummery."

She opened her mouth to protest, then thought better of it. "Thank you," she said again, just as Louise had instructed her to reply to any kind word.

Something changed in his eyes as he looked, becoming more contemplative, almost as if he had just realized something about her. Uneasily, Tessa picked up her lemonade and drank some more. It was warm now, not as cool and refreshing as before, but still delicious. She set the glass down with some regret when it was gone. "I should return to town. Mrs. Bates will wonder what's become of me."

His gaze dropped. "Alas, your wildflowers have wilted."

Tessa looked down at the clutch of bluebells, lying limply in her lap. "Oh. And I picked them all. What a waste."

With a quick motion, Lord Gresham dashed the lemonade remaining in his glass onto the ground. "We can put them in water and revive them." He got to his feet. "Come."

Tessa obeyed, trailing behind him as he strode to the stream, glass in hand. She watched in mild surprise as he stepped onto a rock jutting out of the bank, then to another large rock amid the swiftly running water, and carefully stooped down to fill the glass. He glanced up at her and grinned. "You must jump in and save me if I slip," he called. "This water is freezing cold."

Dumbly she nodded. Balanced on a rock amid the rushing water, paying no heed to the water spraying his white shirtsleeves and spotless breeches as he filled a glass with water for a bunch of wilted bluebells, the Earl of Gresham was mesmerizing. He didn't look indolent or arrogant at all, but rather . . . gallant. He rose and cast a measuring eye toward the bank.

"Stand back," he said.

"What?" She wrenched her gaze from his shirt, thoroughly dampened to his skin. "Why?"

"In case I fall," he said, bouncing on the balls of his feet a moment before taking one giant, lunging step toward the bank. His polished boot hit the stone he had originally stepped from, but it was slick with water and Tessa realized with horror that he was about to take an ignominious plunge into the stream.

"Oh!" She leaped forward and flung out her hand. He grabbed it just in time, balanced precariously for a moment, then leapt nimbly onto the bank, not seeming to care that his polished boot landed ankle-deep in the mud.

"You saved me!" He grinned at her, giving her hand a light press before letting go. "Did I injure your arm?"

"No." Her fingers tingled. Had she really leaped out and grabbed him? "Not at all."

"Good. Put the flowers in," he said, holding out the glass. Tessa held out the bluebells, and he took them, poking the roots down into the water and draping the drooping stems over the rim. "They'll revive in a bit," he predicted. "I shall send them into Frome when they do."

She looked up at him in wonder. Dark hair tumbled forward over his brow after his jaunt into the brook. Up close she could see the faint shadow of stubble beginning on his jaw, and smell the crisp scent of his shirtsleeves. That signet ring on his right hand flashed as he pushed the stems deeper into the glass. Her hand felt warm, remembering the clasp of his fingers around hers. "That's quite a lot of effort for wildflowers," she said before her brain could rein in her tongue.

He looked up from the flowers. "Not if they are dear to you."

She forced her gaze back to the bluebells. "They are just wildflowers," she said softly. "Small and insignificant and common."

He was quiet, and she stole a glance at his face. He had that probing look again, as if he were trying to make out something essential about her. She was accustomed to seeing that sort of look on people's faces, but Lord Gresham's expression was . . . different. He didn't seem confounded or alarmed or even dismayed by what he saw in her, but curious. Surprised. Almost . . . intrigued.

"No bit of beauty is small or insignificant," he murmured. "And as for common . . . I've never seen the like." He touched one dainty flower head, less wilted than the rest, and turned it up toward her. "Don't belittle it. Marvel, instead, that such a creation sprang up out of a common field, with no one around to appreciate it until you walked by."

"And now I have pulled it out by the roots," she said.

He grinned, and the air between them lightened noticeably. "Only to share it with others. The bluebells would have wilted anyway, in a day or two. Now they will have brought joy and beauty to others before they do."

She couldn't help smiling. "A lovely way of putting it." She tipped her face up to him again. "Thank you for the lemonade."

"It was my pleasure."

Heavens above. She made the mistake of meeting his eyes when he smiled at her, and she was sure the earth moved beneath her feet. It should have sent her scurrying away; she'd fallen for a handsome man who paid her attention before. But somehow she didn't feel the same wariness she'd worn like a second skin ever since. Somehow she liked the way this man smiled at her.

"I had the right of you the other day," she said impulsively. "You are a silver-tongued devil."

He chuckled. "I knew I would improve upon you."

Tessa just pursed her lips. They walked to the end of the gravel drive, where a low stone wall separated Mill Cottage's grounds from the road. "I would be glad to walk you back into Frome," he said, but she shook her head.

"There is no need. It's not even a mile, and the sun is still bright."

He bowed his head and didn't argue, which she found refreshing. "Give my regards to Mrs. Bates."

"I will." Tessa hesitated. "She will be so pleased to hear you are well."

The earl grinned ruefully. "Yes, I've neglected her, haven't I? I should like to call again, if I am welcome."

"Very welcome," she said, then blushed at her unintentionally quick reply.

Lord Gresham stopped by the stone gatepost and gave a very civil little bow. "And you are very welcome for more lemonade, any time your wanderings bring you this way, Mrs. Neville."

She ducked her head. It would be harder than she thought to stay away now. "Thank you. Good day." She set off at a brisk stroll, restraining herself from looking back. He was a gentleman, with the exquisite manners to match; that was all. But she liked him more and more every time she saw him. It wasn't every man who would care for wild bluebells.

When the road bent around the clump of oaks, she dared a quick peek over her shoulder. He was still watching her, leaning against the stone post, one muddy boot propped over the other. She could just make out the smile on his face as he lifted the glass of wildflowers in salute. Tessa raised her hand in reply, then hurried onward.

She smiled all the way back into Frome.

Chapter 9

Mrs. Neville's surprise visit brightened Charlie's mood considerably. Two days of disciplined hard work had been even more taxing than he'd expected, and he certainly hadn't thought it would be simple. But this was his duty, his cross to bear, and he was determined not to shirk it any longer. Edward had shouldered the daunting and tedious task of hiring a lawyer. Gerard had gone off to risk his life and liberty for the family. Charlie told himself he was more than capable of reading some dusty old ledgers in search of his father's ill-fated marriage. All he had to do was read through each page, one faint, illegible line at a time. There was no possible reason he couldn't complete this task successfully. He just had to be disciplined.

So he had buckled down and painstakingly begun working his way through the marriage registers, and it made him want to race back to London as fast as possible. The registers told tales of desperation, poverty, and questionable morality that left him grim and gloomy. A forty-two-year-old man wedding a girl of sixteen, in the front parlor of a brothel. Charlie would bet anything the signature of the bride's "mother" was really the brothel's madam, foisting an unwanted girl off her hands. A couple married in a tavern for a shilling and a chicken, with another shilling to be paid later. This was the way his father had married? He tried to picture the duke and some mysterious but alluring girl waiting their turn in the tavern while the couple with the chicken plighted their troths, and utterly failed. How could Durham not have known that was a bad omen? Charlie had been about to tell Barnes to bring drink far stronger than lemonade when his valet remarked there was a lady lingering on the road, looking his way.

He told himself he was desperate for any respite from the registers as he rushed to intercept her. But there was no denying the thrill that shot through his veins when she looked up at him with those crystal clear eyes and professed to have walked this way by chance. Tessa Neville was not a flighty female who wandered the countryside obliviously. He knew she would never admit it, but he wondered—even hoped—if she might have passed his cottage with the thought of meeting him again. And the possibility was inordinately pleasing.

He still wasn't quite sure what about her drew him. There were her eyes, no question, and the frank way she looked at him. The rest of her was lovely as well, from her sleek dark curls to a curved, supple figure he had to work hard not to admire openly. She wasn't like any other woman he'd ever met, and in the end Charlie simply gave up trying to puzzle it out. Whatever it was, he liked it. He was used to women who batted their eyelashes and simpered, or boldly murmured propositions in his ear. It kept a man on guard, ready to deflect any unwanted offers with charm and speed, constantly vigilant for any traps laid by hopeful duchesses-to-be. If Tessa Neville saw anything appealing about his person or was laying a matrimonial trap, she concealed it well. And the attraction of proving himself worthy of her good opinion was too much for him to resist.

Of course, he still had to mind his tongue around her. He knew she hadn't quite believed him when he claimed he only wanted an introduction to Hiram Scott, and he barely managed to deflect her question about why he paid attention to her and Mrs. Bates at all. What he'd told her was the truth—now—but it hadn't always been true, and he didn't want to think what she would say if she ever learned he'd once suspected her, even slightly, of blackmail. That was the sort of secret he planned to carry to his grave. Now that he'd gained some ground in Mrs. Neville's affections, he meant to keep it.

Charlie dressed with care the next day. The cheerful pot of bluebells sat on a table in his bedroom, his excuse for calling on her. He thought he'd killed them at first; it had been a long time since he'd done any gardening. He was more likely to send a footman to order flowers from a London florist when he wanted to impress a lady. But it seemed he'd done a decent enough job, after almost falling into the brook, for the wildflowers had perked up after being planted in an earthen pot, and he was disgustingly eager to give them back to Mrs. Neville.

The sound of a carriage outside caught his attention. A quick glance out the window made him curse under his breath. Hiram Scott was stepping down from a gig, handing the reins to one of the lads from the stable.

Charlie paced away from the window, thinking hard. Perhaps Scott had come to press his demands in private. Perhaps he thought himself still concealed and wanted to take a new tactic to get the money. The man had gall, coming here.

When Barnes brought in the card, Charlie let his visitor wait awhile before he went down. He would say as little as possible and give Scott every opportunity to place the noose around his own neck. After letting the man sit for over a quarter hour, he went down to the small parlor. "Mr. Scott," he said, affecting the bored, imperious tones he'd used at the ironworks. "This is a surprise."

The other man swept a bow. He didn't seem at all put out by being left waiting. "I hope you will forgive the liberty, sir. If I've called at an inconvenient time . . ."

Charlie waved one hand. "Here in the country, there are no convenient hours." He took a seat and indicated his guest should do the same. "What brings you to Frome?"

Scott seated himself, looking very pleased. "I come to issue an invitation, my lord. As a prospective investor, you would be very welcome to join me for a dinner with a few other shareholders and committee members."

Charlie gave him a heavy-lidded stare. "Dinner."

"Yes." Scott nodded, still smiling genially as if he hadn't schemed and plotted to disrupt Charlie's entire life. "Tomorrow evening in Frome. It isn't a full meeting of the committee, so not much business will be discussed, but we would be delighted to have you join us."

Charlie made a noncommittal noise in his throat. The idea of dining with a canal committee held very little appeal, but it was another opportunity to take Scott's measure. So far the man had him utterly puzzled; was he a conniving swindler, a man desperately trying to conceal his attempt at blackmail, or a hopeless sycophant mistaken for a villain? Charlie couldn't tell, and he was hesitant to act until he could sort it out.

"Normally we would dine on board the company's yacht," Scott went on at Charlie's silence. "The *Saville* is in dock for repairs at the moment, though, so we shall gather at The Bear in Frome. The innkeeper's wife, Mrs. Lewis, is renowned for her cooking, and they keep a very good table."

"Yes," said Charlie. "I lodged at The Bear until recently." The food had been the only attraction, in his opinion, although any renown must be considered relative.

Scott bowed his head with another gratified smile. "Mr. Lewis did mention it to me, when I spoke with him. It was he who told me where I might call upon you to extend the invitation."

"Will Mrs. Neville be attending?" he asked, still delaying. He hoped not. She was too distracting.

Scott hesitated only a moment, but Charlie saw it. "I do not know, sir," said the man carefully. "But I would be pleased to invite her, if that would be agreeable to you."

Damn. Now Scott thought he wanted her there.

And worse, Charlie realized he couldn't say no. Mrs. Neville would want to be there, and truth be told, she had more right to be there than he did, if they really meant to discuss canal business. She might actually wish to invest, while he wouldn't be giving Scott one bloody farthing, not even if his canal mined gold sovereigns straight from the earth. And if Scott ever told her that he hadn't wanted her to be there . . .

He made himself lift one shoulder. "I presumed she would be as welcome as I, since she is also a prospective shareholder."

"Of course, of course," said Scott heartily. "I hesitated only because it won't be a purely business affair, my lord. And as the only lady, she might feel out of place."

"Perhaps she is already otherwise engaged," replied Charlie, knowing it was unlikely. There was nothing to do in Frome, and this canal was her whole reason for coming into Somerset. Even if she'd had other plans, she would change them to meet the canal committee. But he had a feeling Scott had planned a gentlemen's dinner, and she *would* be out of place, whether she knew it or not. Scott wanted money, badly enough to blackmail a duke for it; letting a woman attend a meeting shouldn't bother him, if six thousand pounds hung on her approval. Charlie wondered if the other men of the committee would feel the same.

"That shall be for Mrs. Neville to decide," said Scott with a look that indicated his feelings about the subject. "I shall invite her directly. May I count you among our dinner companions, sir?"

He nodded once. "You may." If he said no, Scott

might not care to invite Mrs. Neville after all, and Charlie didn't want that. She would be furious to learn she had been excluded, and to be honest, it smacked of unfairness. If she attended the dinner, he would rather be there than not. Just in case the other gentlemen weren't so gentlemanly after all.

"Excellent!" Scott beamed at him. "It was a great delight to learn of your interest in our canal, sir. If there is any way I might help you decide to make an investment, I would be delighted to do so. Perhaps you would care to see the prospectus?"

Mrs. Neville had already seen it and called it useless. "By all means," said Charlie languidly, guessing that the appearance of indifference would spur Scott to greater efforts. "Send it if you like."

He guessed correctly. "I would be pleased to conduct you to any part of the works you wished to see," Scott went on, an eager gleam in his eye. "Or correspond with your man of business, should you have cargoes suitable for shipping on the canal. Shareholders are preferred in shipments, you know, and pay very reasonable rates."

Charlie lifted one shoulder again, and decided to rattle Scott a bit. "Perhaps. But you may deal with me directly; my man is occupied in London." By which he meant his brother Edward, the one with a head for business. Not that the de Laceys would be conducting any legitimate business with Hiram Scott.

"Of—Of course," said Scott. He hesitated, then forced a smile, looking discomfited for the first time. "I confess it is rare to deal with a man of your standing directly, Lord Gresham."

He raised his brows. "Is it?"

"Yes. Naturally, I called upon each shareholder, in case any should take a deeper interest, but . . ." He paused, then cleared his throat. "Although, may I inquire how you learned of our canal? I don't believe your name was on our original list of gentlemen whose support we solicited."

Charlie didn't move a muscle although his heart skipped a beat. Was this the opening he'd been waiting for? "I first heard of it in Bath," he said evenly. "From my brother, Captain de Lacey."

Gerard's name produced no flicker of recognition, even though Gerard had been prominently in Bath for some time. "Of course," Scott said. "I travel through Bath quite frequently, although I can't recall the pleasure of your brother's acquaintance . . ."

"He took up residence only recently," said Charlie. "After the death of our father."

He expected to see something; some twitch of the jaw, a blink of the eye, a stiff smile. Scott showed none of that. His face instantly became grave. "My condolences, my lord," he murmured.

Charlie stared at him. His pulse beat like a drum in his ears. For a moment he forgot all about stealth and cold revenge, and thought of nothing more than thrashing Scott within an inch of his life. How dare the man sit there and offer his sympathy on Durham's death, as if he hadn't darkened the duke's final months with his threats and demands? What the bloody hell was this man's game?

With difficulty he brought his breathing back under control, and unclenched his fist. He had to untangle this mystery all the way. "Thank you," he said when he was able to speak calmly.

Scott looked uncertain at Charlie's frigid tone. He shifted in his chair. "Indeed. Well, however you became interested in the canal, I am delighted by it. I pride myself on being most attentive to my shareholders; if there is anything I can do—"

"Yes, yes," said Charlie, getting to his feet. "Thank you for your visit today, Mr. Scott. I shall see you tomorrow evening."

Scott smiled in relief. "Very good, my lord. Eight o'clock, if that suits—"

"Yes. Good day, Mr. Scott." He had to get the fellow out of his house before he punched him.

Charlie waited until the canal promoter was out the door before cursing a blue streak. By God, he hated that man, for everything from starting the trouble in the first place to not showing any proper sign of terror at the approaching retribution. But he didn't merely want to confront Scott; he wanted to ruin the man, for all that he'd done. And if he had to endure a shareholder dinner to destroy Scott completely, so be it.

And Mrs. Neville would be there. He took a slow, calming breath and told himself that didn't matter. His purpose here was Scott, not her. It didn't work; he was still looking forward to seeing her, despite his serious misgivings about her presence. In fact, all the more reason he should be there. He certainly didn't want Scott to win her over now. This way he could keep an eye on her and try to steer her away from Scott's clutches.

But otherwise . . . he had no idea what to make of Scott's behavior. The man didn't show the slightest trace of shame or uneasiness at facing him, nor even opportunistic greed. It was as if Scott had no

idea that he had any relation at all to Durham—
which simply couldn't be true. Gerard had been
utterly right: the threat of exposing Dorothy
Cope's marriage to Durham really wouldn't have
hurt Durham, except through his children. Scott
had to know that. Wouldn't he have taken even
passing notice of who those children were? It was
quite likely Durham's death had been reported in
every ha'penny gossip paper in Britain, thanks to
the scandal.

This unexpected cordiality was upending Charlie's plans. He had anticipated a confrontation, but
Scott wasn't rising to it. It was making him unsure
of himself, unsure of Gerard's report, unsure of the
postal clerk's identification. If he had the wrong
man, all this would have been wasted effort. Charlie did not want to leave a single point to chance;
he couldn't afford to. The Committee for Privileges
would require absolute verification of his right
to the dukedom in light of the salacious rumors
about his father. He was scouring the registers for
any proof, one way or another, of a marriage ceremony, before he struck his final blow. It was slow,
miserable work, and so far he'd found nothing. It
was entirely likely he'd find nothing in the remaining registers, leaving him right where he was now:
unable to prove or disprove anything in his father's
final confessional letter, and uncertain enough of
Scott that he dared not do anything to him.

He tried not to think again that he was the
brother least likely to solve this tangle. Perhaps he
should hand it back to Edward or Gerard, or at
least show them how weak their clues were. Grind-
ing his teeth, he went to the writing table and drew

out a piece of paper. He wrote a summary of his meetings with Hiram Scott, detailing how blithely unaware the man seemed to be. He wrote of the canal and the ironworks, looking again for any connection to Durham; Edward would know if their father had ever dealt with Scott financially. He asked how likely it was that the postal clerk in Bath had remembered the right man who sent the blackmail letters after so many months. And he inquired how the legal proceedings in London were faring.

That last point made him hesitate. Edward had claimed he gave Charlie everything about it. He could probably read for himself how strong his case was and how well the solicitor had prepared it. All those documents were also in the leather satchel, but he hadn't read them. He hadn't finished reading the marriage registers, not even after the last two days of rather conscientious work. They still sat on the side of the writing desk, taunting him.

Charlie looked at his letter. He was the heir. He shouldn't need his younger brothers' help— and for the first time, he realized he didn't want it. He wished he understood Scott's connection to Durham, and he wished the man had acted in a more illuminating manner, but these were his riddles to solve. How could he ask Edward, who was in London, and Gerard, who was in Bath, to know and do more than he himself, when he was the one in Frome, able to face down Scott at any time? Decisively, he scooped up the letter and tore it in half, then again. He hadn't achieved anything; therefore, there was nothing to tell his brothers. He would write to them later, once he knew something definite. Whenever that might be.

His good spirits flattened, he debated not going into Frome after all. He wouldn't be good company. But then he spied the bluebells Mrs. Neville had picked, and remembered how she'd looked at him when he put them in water, and he sent for the gig to be hitched up and brought around.

He knew he was avoiding those infernal registers yet again, but he needed to think of something else, and thinking of Tessa Neville unquestionably raised his spirits. He kept picturing her face as he drove into Frome, her pale green eyes soft and unguarded as she thanked him for a glass of lemonade. As certain as he was that she was warming to him, he knew even more that he was warming to her. He'd never met such a direct woman. When she talked of canals and investment, all wariness and distance dropped from her face. Her eyes grew bright and her voice grew confident and warm. Charlie found himself thinking furiously about canal bills, and wondered what had come over him; he was Charles de Lacey, devil-may-care, good-for-nothing, indolent rake and scoundrel . . . wishing madly he already had his writ to sit in Parliament just so he could tell Tessa Neville with certainty what bills were being promoted this session. His father would be shocked. His brothers wouldn't recognize him.

He stopped in front of the inn where she was staying and jumped down, taking with him the revived bluebells. His heart skipped as he tossed a coin to the boy who came out to hold his horse and he went inside.

The ladies greeted him with pleasure, and in Mrs. Bates's case, a glad cry of welcome. Even Mrs. Neville was pleased to see him, giving him her sparkling, direct smile, which had an unwarranted effect on his mood. He handed her the earthen pot with a small flourish.

She shook her head, looking surprised and impressed. "You saved them. Thank you, sir." She brushed her fingertips over the small blue-violet flowers, setting them swaying on the stalk. "I hope you didn't go to much trouble."

Out of nowhere, Charlie wondered how she'd thank him if he ever did her a true service. Something about her bare fingers running through the wildflowers caught his attention and struck him almost dumb. "It was well worth it, for a thing of such beauty," he said in belated answer to her question. "And not much effort at all. A pot, some dirt . . ." He made a bored face, and after a moment she smiled back, her lips trembling.

"What is this?" chimed in Mrs. Bates, who had watched the exchange with alert, lively eyes. "Oh my, what lovely flowers, Tessa dear!"

It broke the spell. "Yes," said Mrs. Neville, turning to carry them to the windowsill. "I picked them yesterday and Lord Gresham was kind enough to save them from wilting."

"Oh," said Mrs. Bates. "How very kind of you, my lord."

Charlie grinned. He heard the thread of disappointment in her words. Unless he misread everything about her, Mrs. Bates was encouraging his interest in her young friend.

Good God. Interest? The thought had slid through his mind without any preamble or warning, and now Charlie found it impossible to dislodge. He admitted he found Mrs. Neville fascinating and unusual. And beautiful. And . . . very appealing. She leaned over in front of the window to set the pot in a sunny spot, and the reflected light illuminated her face for a moment. Charlie's gaze moved helplessly over the glossy chestnut curl that had escaped its knot and teased the nape of her neck, over the firm but delicate line of her jaw, over the ripe curves of her bosom. She stood straighter, and the sunlight streamed in around her, limning her figure in sharp, clear relief. She gave the pot a little push and glanced up, spearing him with that clear green gaze. "They should do well here."

He cleared his throat, which had gone rather dry. "Yes."

"I expect they'll thrive," said Mrs. Bates softly, with an adoring smile. "Tessa will see to it."

Mrs. Neville waved one hand as she came back to sit beside her on the small settee. "I'll water them. They are wild bluebells, Eugenie, and will fade in a few days no matter what I do."

"Nonsense," cried the older lady, blushing pink. "They will last as long as you tend them!"

She shot her companion an odd look. "You know I'm hopeless with plants."

"I'm afraid Mrs. Neville is correct, ma'am," said Charlie. "The bluebells will be gone in a few days." Mrs. Bates's face fell. "Of course, they are wild, and will bloom again next spring. Plant them in your garden and they will eventually spread to cover the whole garden."

This time she looked almost proud. "You have a gardener's soul, my lord."

He chuckled. "I am a gardener's son. My mother was very keen on roses, in particular. My earliest memories, in fact, are of digging in the garden with her." He paused. "I wonder if I ever dug a hole in the right place, though . . ."

"Likely not," said Mrs. Neville with a smile. "Boys tend to dig with abandon, if my nephew is any guide."

"All the better to create a mountain," he replied. "I remember one enterprise, when another boy and I tried to build a mountain so high we could jump from it into the horse chestnut tree by the pasture . . ." He shook his head and sighed as Mrs. Neville laughed. "We were both thrashed and sent to read the story of the Tower of Babel, after we filled in the giant pit we'd dug."

"Punishment, indeed," murmured Mrs. Neville.

"Filling in that hole was *cruel* punishment," he replied, and she laughed, as he'd intended, but Charlie still found himself unprepared for its effect on him. He was more than interested. To tell the truth, he was well on his way to being entranced.

He cleared his throat. "Mr. Scott called upon me," he said, not caring that he was changing the subject abruptly and almost crassly. "Have you spoken to him?"

Her expression grew serious and alert. "No. Why?"

Charlie made a careless gesture. "There is to be a meeting of the canal company, and he invited me to dine with them." Pique flashed across her face for a moment, before he added, "He said he would issue the same invitation to you. Since the dinner is to be held in Frome, I would be pleased to escort you."

"That is very kind of you, sir," said Mrs. Bates quickly.

"Yes." Mrs. Neville smiled at him, without any trace of her former prickliness. As if she were pleased he had offered, and pleased to accept. "Thank you."

God help me, thought Charlie, even as his own grin threatened to split his face. "It will be my pleasure."

Chapter 10

When Lord Gresham was gone, Tessa felt lighter than she had in days. She told herself it was a relief that his goodwill hadn't faded, removing any fear that Eugenie, or worse, Louise, would hold her accountable for losing it. And he had brought undeniably interesting tidings of the canal committee dinner. But every time she caught sight of the pot of cheerful bluebells, her lips turned up of their own accord and she had to find something else to occupy her thoughts before she devolved into too deep a contemplation of the man who'd brought them.

"It was ever so lovely of His Lordship to care so tenderly for your flowers," Eugenie said unhelpfully.

Tessa wiped her smile away, knowing the impression it would give. "Yes, but they are your flowers. I picked them for you."

"Pish," the other woman declared. "You picked them, and he brought them to you. They are yours."

"They are ours, then." Tessa couldn't believe she was arguing over a pot of weeds. "Have you got a new nib? Mine broke, and I must write to William."

"You've been writing too many letters to him.

What news have you got to report since yesterday?"

Tessa glared at her. The answer was nothing, since she was just cooling her heels until Scott provided the account books. But she needed something to save her from Eugenie's hints about Lord Gresham. "I didn't finish my letter of yesterday. The nib broke, you see."

"He's likely left for London already," said Eugenie, sorting through her embroidery silks. "I believe he only cares to hear your final opinion on the canal in any event: yea, or nay. If he had any sort of head for the details you send him, he would be here himself."

That was true. Tessa fidgeted in her chair, unable to argue even though she wanted to. "It cannot hurt to give him a full view of the project."

Eugenie snipped a length of bright blue silk. "Nor can it hurt to encourage Lord Gresham's good opinion of you."

Tessa froze in place. "Of course not. I never disagreed with that."

"He seems determined to cultivate *your* good opinion." Eugenie didn't look up as she threaded her needle.

"He's been very kind," she said stiffly. "But I think he's mostly fond of you."

Now Eugenie looked up with an expression of open incredulity. "My dear, you are far more intelligent than that. Handsome young men don't call on elderly ladies unless there is a lovely young lady to be found nearby."

"Don't be ridiculous!"

Eugenie raised her eyebrows. "I'm not the one suggesting Lord Gresham is blind."

Tessa shot out of her chair, tucking her hands

under her elbows to hide the way they clenched into fists. "I don't know what he wants, Eugenie, but it isn't me," she said harshly. It *couldn't* be. Could it? No, it could not, and even if he did want her, he certainly wouldn't if he ever heard her history. "You're imagining things because you feel sorry for me. Don't. I'm perfectly happy without a husband, and you know why."

Her companion didn't buckle and apologize, as expected. She lowered her embroidery to her lap and gave Tessa a long searching look. "Oh my dear," she said gently, even sadly. "I don't feel sorry for you. You're one of the strongest people I know! But can you really be happy as your brother's steward for the rest of your life? You're still young enough to marry, to know the joy of loving someone and being loved." Her lip trembled, and Tessa remembered that Eugenie's husband had died after only a few years of marriage. "And Lord Gresham is nothing like *that vile man*. Will you really punish yourself for the rest of your life over him?"

She wasn't punishing herself. She was guarding herself. Once she had fallen all-too-easily for a man's charm and attention, and she was bound and determined that it would never happen again. Richard had also seemed to want her. When she discovered his true intentions, she lashed out in anger and revenge, damaging her family's and her own reputation. Only by devoting herself to the family estate had she repaired their trust in her. Being William's steward, as Eugenie put it, was safe; it calmed her parents' fears that she was mad, it relieved William's worries that supporting her would be a burden, and it offered an excuse for why she had never married. The only men she met were tradesmen and merchants, bankers and solicitors, none of whom were suitable matches for a viscount's sister. Louise was the only one who ever suggested that she might find a husband, and Tessa was sure that desire was solely rooted in Louise's passion for shopping and spectacle. Planning a wedding for anyone would make Louise ecstatic, and Tessa was the only unwed person of marriage age in the family.

And as long as Lord Gresham was someone to be wary of, she was still safe. As long as he thought of her as a shrew, she was safe from his laughing dark eyes and devilish little smile and chivalrous concern for wilted bluebells. As long as he only wanted an introduction to Hiram Scott from her, she could ignore the little jump in her pulse when he grinned at her, and the way he looked lounging in the sunlight without his coat on. He was an earl—too good for a country viscount's sister. He was a London gentleman, too elegant for a blunt-spoken, managing female. He might tease her now, marooned in the wilds of Somerset for a few weeks, but when he went back to his real life, he wouldn't notice her among the beautiful women who must surround him in town.

"He's not like that vile man," she agreed at last. Even saying her former fiancé's name would set Eugenie into a fluttering temper. "I never said he was."

Eugenie turned her embroidery over a few times, as if debating something. "Would it be such a terrible thing if he did admire you? Because I assure you he does."

Tessa longed to deny it, just to turn away Eugenie's questions. But even she, who seemed to have been born without the usual feminine instincts regarding men, had to acknowledge that Lord Gresham paid her a great deal of attention. He was relentlessly polite and good-natured even when she was rude and short with him. He went to great lengths to make her smile, from laughing at himself to delivering wildflowers he planted himself. Tessa's chest felt tight as she thought of all his actions and what they might mean.

"I'm going to buy a new nib," she said abruptly, and went to get her pelisse and bonnet before Eugenie could protest.

But walking didn't help. Tessa strode along as briskly as she could, until her shins burned and there was a stitch in her side, and still Eugenie's words circled her brain, like smoke trapped in a room until it was suffocating. *He admires you . . . the joy of loving someone and being loved . . . he's nothing like that vile man . . .* Finally she stopped, out of breath, when she got to the river, and tried to think logically.

Gresham was a handsome man. Excessively handsome, in fact. That was not a fault, or at least not one she could hate him for. Nor was being charming and well-mannered, even if it made her suspicious of his motives. So far, his motives were unexceptional, as far as she could tell. He had done nothing whatsoever to earn her enmity, and had gone out of his way to be charming and kind to her. Eugenie, who despite her frequent silliness was rather good at reading people, thought him the finest man of her acquaintance. And if Eugenie thought he was looking at her with more than mere polite interest . . . he probably was.

Tessa took an unsteady breath and allowed herself to think about it. He might well admire her, even find her attractive, but that didn't mean he would act upon it. If he did, though . . . she wondered what he would do. In her one previous, disastrous experience with love, Richard had been direct; he told her she was lovely and he kissed her. She hadn't had to say anything except yes, and then he guided her—right down the road to hell, as it turned out. Lord Gresham, on the other hand, was markedly different from Richard. She'd thought Richard was like her, deep down, while Gresham couldn't be more different. Unlike Richard, there couldn't be anything Gresham wanted from her except . . . her. When Richard courted her, she'd been a young lady of good reputation and modest dowry. Now she was older, with a clouded past, and all mention of her dowry had quietly faded. But she was also wiser now, confident of herself in everything except matters of the heart, and this time she would not be so foolishly swayed by a few pretty words. Not even from Lord Gresham.

She found a grassy place to sit, even though the day was cool and breezy. The bracing chill felt good on her face as she thought about the earl. She did like the way he cocked his head in sly amusement. His voice seemed to resonate in her blood, and his laugh made her want to smile even in her crossest temper. There had been that moment the other day in Frome, when he took her arm, and then his gentle words about bluebells. Tessa closed her eyes and shivered. It would be so easy to fall for a man like that, if she could let herself believe it real . . .

But there was the trouble. No matter how charming he seemed, or how attentive he was to her or to hapless wildflowers, Tessa could never get that nagging little voice out of her head. What if his interest sprang from boredom, or some sort of fascination with her unusual manner? What if he was merely a consummate rake and seducer, with a knack for finding every woman's weakness? What if he was everything decent and honorable, but they were simply too unsuited to each other for any future together? It did little good—and even a great deal of harm—for her to fall in love with a man with whom she had no chance of lasting happiness. Tessa feared, deep down, this was the most likely problem. Lust would fade; fascination would dull; and all that would be left was her unfashionable interests, her lack of elegance, her tendency to speak too bluntly. This was the reason she hadn't bothered looking at men in that light for several years; not looking was safe. Eugenie had made her look at the earl, but that didn't mean she had to be foolish about it.

A while later she got to her feet and turned back toward the inn. She had considered the possibility, and found it more appealing than she should, but it was still just supposition on Eugenie's part. Until Lord Gresham gave some inarguable sign of deeper interest, she would do best to keep on as she was. She could enjoy his company, and even welcome it, but absent anything else, she would guard herself just as carefully as always.

Chapter 11

The dinner went off almost entirely as Charlie expected it would, with a few notable exceptions.

The first exception was the way Tessa Neville looked when he called for her at The Golden Hind. He'd become accustomed to her rather practical dress, and it was a shock—an alarmingly pleasurable shock—to set eyes on her in a rich gold gown that displayed her bosom in ways he'd only dreamed about. Her dark curls were pinned up in a smooth coiffure that exposed the lobes of her ears. Charlie was momentarily mesmerized by the sight, and had the sudden, though not new, temptation to press his lips to the soft skin at the corner of her jaw and nip her earlobe.

"How lovely you look," gushed Mrs. Bates. "Oh, Tessa dear, I am *so* glad you heeded Lady Woodall's advice to bring one evening gown."

"Yes," said the lady with a wry smile, pulling on the cloak her maid brought out. "My sister was right; I admit it. A lady must be ever prepared for a dinner party, no matter where she roams. Are you ready, sir?" She turned to Charlie, who had to plaster a quick smile on his face to conceal any sign of his lascivious thoughts.

"To offer you my arm? Of course."

Her lips parted and she gave him a sideways look before her smile reappeared. "I meant for dinner with Mr. Scott."

"I am prepared for that as one prepares for an examination by the tooth drawer," he replied. "With stoic valor and fierce determination not to weep."

She choked on a laugh. "You're ridiculous."

"No, merely unserious. But I am greatly looking forward to escorting you to the banquet." He put his hat back on and made a show of offering his arm. "Shall we?"

"Good-bye," said Mrs. Bates, beaming at them as they went out the door. "Have a pleasant evening!"

"Thank you for coming for me," said Mrs. Neville as they walked. It was only a short distance to The Bear, and it was a very fine evening. The last of twilight still lit the sky, and patches of light from doors and windows checkered the pavement ahead of them. Other people hurried past, going home or ducking into pubs or heading to the playhouse. Frome was a small town but by no means a sleepy one.

"I didn't wish to arrive alone," Charlie replied. "You have done me the favor."

She laughed. "Flummery!"

He grinned, as he always did when he made her laugh. "Truth! The mere thought of facing the bankers alone . . ." He shuddered. "Instead I shall arrive with a lovely lady on my arm, and she shall likely be the most informed person in the room to boot."

He spoke lightly, but the glance Tessa Neville gave him was not. It was hesitant, curious, a bit wary—as if she wanted to take his words seriously and wondered if he had meant them so. "How very unusual you are, my lord, to say such a thing."

Charlie bent his head toward hers. "I gather I'm not like most men you know, Mrs. Neville."

"Indeed not," she replied with such wry fervor he couldn't help a grin.

"Indeed not," he repeated in delight. "Good heavens, how you do torment me."

"Oh? How so?" She looked braced for a rebuke.

"How shall I know exactly what you meant? 'Oh, no, Lord Gresham, you're not like any other man of my acquaintance. No one else is quite as impertinent.'"

"Oh, Lord, no," she said at once, with a relieved little laugh. "If I'd thought that, I would have merely smiled and murmured something politely vague."

"Then it was a compliment." He let a bit of swagger creep into his stride. "Thank you, madam, for recognizing my superiority to other men."

Her eyebrows went up but she only smiled. "As you wish, my lord."

"Ah," he murmured. "I knew a compliment was too much to hope for."

"I suggest you not hope for compliments, sir," she answered as they reached The Bear. "Expect none, and then each will seem a lovely surprise."

Charlie paused, his hand on the door, and looked at her. She was serious. He didn't know a woman in London society who didn't expect compliments, or who didn't thrive on them. Tessa Neville not only grew a shade uncomfortable when complimented, she clearly preferred a more egalitarian relationship. She owned her faults, and made no effort to hide her weaknesses—and she required the same of him, puncturing his pride with glee but also crediting him with the same level of meticulous interest in Scott's canal that she had, when the rest of the world would have laughed uproariously at the thought of Charles de Lacey buying his own canal shares, or even knowing what one was.

"You're a most unusual woman, Mrs. Neville."

"I'm well aware of it," she said with a faintly weary smile. "I hope you can overlook it."

"On the contrary," said Charlie, still staring at her in fascination. The light from the inn shone on her face, turned toward him with an open, frank expression. Any other woman would have clung to his arm and either teased him or played coy all night. There was nothing coy about Tessa Neville. "I believe I like it."

Her eyes widened in surprise, and he swept the door open for her. With the tiniest frown at him, she walked into the inn, where the landlord hurried forward to show them to the parlor where dinner would be served.

Charlie followed, somewhat surprised by how that thought had become so clear to him of late. Tessa Neville was unlike every other woman he'd ever met, and he did like it. He liked her, in fact, a great deal. This was not new. Charlie had liked a number of women. The part that was new was his intense interest in her feeling for him: initially chilly, gradually thawing, and finally—he hoped—a state of growing regard. It made him want to laugh at himself; if the ladies in London had ever guessed that forcing him to work for their regard would have tantalized him so, he'd have been the most disdained man in London.

Scott came forward at once to greet them. "Welcome, my lord," he said with a bow. "Mrs. Neville. How good of you to join us this evening."

Charlie just bowed his head. At his side, Mrs. Neville dipped a curtsy. "Good evening, sir."

"Let me introduce you." Scott offered her his arm and led her to the gentleman standing before the fireplace. "This is Mr. Tallboys, from Norswick and Gregg, in Poole. Mr. Tallboys is our banker." A slim man with thinning brown hair bowed. He was as nondescript as every other banker and solicitor Charlie had ever met. "Sir Gregory Attwood, whose property lies along the canal line. As you know, all our shareholders are welcome to attend any meeting of our directors, even such a small one as this." Scott smiled, but Charlie got the feeling Attwood wasn't actually welcome, but rather tolerated. Attwood was a rotund figure of a man, with pale blue eyes set rather far apart in a round face. Drops of wine already marred his waistcoat, and he gave Mrs. Neville a glance that was almost a leer.

"And tonight I've invited Mr. Lester, our resident engineer, as well," Scott finished, indicating the last man, who stood behind the other two. He was a strapping fellow about Charlie's own age, but with a weathered face and somber air. He bowed very courteously as Scott introduced them. "We're a small group, but I believe that will be beneficial tonight." Scott beamed at them all, looking very pleased with himself.

Tallboys, the banker, stepped up to Charlie as Scott led Mrs. Neville aside. "A great pleasure to make your acquaintance, my lord. Mr. Scott's mentioned your name and said you've an interest in our enterprise."

Charlie tore his eyes off Mrs. Neville, who was exchanging pleasantries with Scott and the engineer. "Yes—or rather, perhaps. I've not decided yet."

Tallboys smiled. "I would be delighted to answer any queries you might have. How can I persuade you?"

Good Lord. Would he actually have to speak of the canal? He should never have let Tessa Neville leave his side. "It's behind schedule," Charlie said, plucking one recollection from his brain. "When will it be completed?"

"Only a few months behind," said Tallboys, launching into a detailed description of a troublesome aqueduct, the difficulties of hiring competent workers during the war, and so on. Charlie made no pretense of attending. He watched Mrs. Neville nod and converse, very soberly, with Mr. Scott and Mr. Lester. How could she bear this? he wondered. Tallboys's voice was like the drone of an insect in his ear. Who cared for the bloody price of iron, or how many bricklayers a canal needed? Charlie wanted to know what Tessa Neville had meant when she said he wasn't like other men.

For her part, Tessa couldn't stop thinking about Lord Gresham's last remark, that she was unusual and he liked it. He liked it? That was a step above tolerating her, or finding her oddly fascinating like some sort of museum specimen. She knew Eugenie would sigh and smile in delight if she had heard that, which made her doubly glad he'd only murmured it to her in passing, and at a moment when she couldn't drive herself mad wondering what he'd really meant.

"Mr. Lester is our resident engineer," Mr. Scott said after he'd introduced her to the man in question. "Any particular questions you have, he is the man to ask."

Mr. Lester ducked his head. "Honored to make your acquaintance, ma'am."

"How good of you to join us this evening," she replied. "Thank you for making time to come. I'm sure the canal must keep you very busy."

A flush stained his face and he dropped his gaze. " 'Tis part of my job, ma'am. I shall try to explain anything you wish to know."

The poor man looked so uncomfortable, Tessa was almost glad when Mr. Scott clapped him on the back. "There, Lester! No need to worry. I doubt Mrs. Neville plans to scrutinize your drawings and check your figures."

"Of course not," said Tessa with a smile. "I merely wish to evaluate the canal as a business proposition, not as an engineering marvel."

Lester gave an awkward smile and darted a glance at Mr. Scott. "I'm sure I never thought so, ma'am."

Scott cleared his throat. "Lester, would you be so good as to ring for dinner?" Looking vastly relieved, the other man ducked his head again and hurried away. "He's a very capable engineer," Mr.

Scott said quietly to Tessa. "Started as a mill-wright's boy when he was small, and knows his way around anything you want to build. But these dinners make him uncomfortable. He's a solitary sort, I suppose."

"I understand." And she did, all too well—except that it was fine society parties that made her uncomfortable, not business dinners.

"And I must apologize—one of our chief share-holders was expected tonight, but I had a note from him just this morning with his regrets. Lord Worley would have been able to discuss every part of the enterprise with you at great length; he's been one of our most important proponents from the beginning, both in Parliament and in local circles."

"He is a landowner?"

Scott nodded. "His estate is west of here, in some rather rugged, though beautiful, hills, but he owns a large tract of coal-producing land further west, along the canal route. Naturally he has a high interest in the canal, but I assure you, he is an exacting man who requires the best of us." Scott chuckled. "I daresay he's as attentive to detail as you are yourself, madam."

"How unfortunate he was unable to come." Tessa would have liked to meet someone who knew the project from the beginning, especially someone with a critical interest in it. Scott wouldn't dodge her questions in the presence of one of his chief shareholders.

"Yes, indeed." Scott hesitated. "I particularly wished him to meet Lord Gresham as well. I've been unable thus far to determine how deep His Lordship's interest runs; dare I presume to ask if . . . well, if you might have a word with him? Only after I've satisfied all your own questions, of course."

Tessa's eyes narrowed. "I'm sure Lord Gresham can decide on his own. I was quite as surprised as you to discover he contemplated investing."

"Of course," murmured Scott. "Of course. Naturally, should you counsel Lord Marchmont to purchase shares, it would be in his interest as well for Lord Gresham to purchase shares. Any question of money running short would be detrimental to the canal."

She raised her eyebrows. "Is there any question of money running short?"

"No," he said quickly. "None! But as I'm sure you know, no engineering project can ever be too flush with funds." He gave her a rueful smile.

Tessa returned it. "Yes, I do know." She wasn't about to promise anything regarding Lord Gresham, though.

"Ah, here is Lester," said Mr. Scott, looking up as the engineer slipped back into the room, followed by a parade of servants carrying covered trays. "Madam, gentlemen," he said to the room at large, "shall we dine?"

Mr. Scott took the head of the table, ushering her to the seat at his right hand. Sir Gregory Attwood took the seat beside her, leaving Lord Gresham across from them with Mr. Tallboys at his side. Mr. Lester silently went to the chair at the foot of the table. Scott beamed at them all as the wine was poured. "This isn't a true meeting of shareholders, but on behalf of the South Somerset Coal Canal, welcome!"

"Welcome, indeed," added Mr. Tallboys, raising his glass. "We are delighted to have such company, and hope it is a portent of meetings to come."

"Aye, I daresay," muttered Sir Gregory, raising his glass and tossing back the entire contents. "Let us eat, Tallboys! No one will buy your shares if they faint from hunger."

Mr. Scott gave him a pained look but nodded, and they all sat down to eat. For a while the conversation wandered down dull and trivial paths; the weather, local politics, nothing of use. Tessa tried from time to time to bring up something related to the canal, but Mr. Scott or Mr. Tallboys always answered her question lightly and changed the subject. Mr. Lester, whom she would have liked to speak to, kept his head down and said little.

Charlie would have been content to exchange empty niceties all night long. He wasn't paying much heed to it anyway as he wracked his brains for a way to draw Scott out in some betraying fashion. There was nothing to the man; he had no wife and no children, no passions or interests beyond his iron factory and this cursed canal. Was this what ambition looked like? He had the damnedest self-possession Charlie had ever thought to see in a blackmailer, never losing his equable smile, no matter how snide or pointed a comment at the table. It began to annoy him, in fact, almost as much as Mr. Tallboys did. While Scott held court like some genial host, Tallboys seemed bent on worming his way into Charlie's good graces. It was only by steadily eating and drinking that he was able to avoid speaking to the man. Even listening to Mrs. Neville ask about the water sources was preferable to Tallboys's voice.

At one point, when Charlie had adamantly ignored his overtures for some time, the banker leaned closer and murmured, "I perceive you are a man who prefers to listen, and form your own conclusions. Very admirable, my lord."

"Yes." Charlie tipped his glass to his lips again to avoid saying more.

"Mr. Scott can be a trifle carried away in his enthusiasm at times," Tallboys went on with a sympathetic look. "But then, I daresay a man of his rank and profession must be more prone to emotion and ambition. He is a merchant, and has been selling something or other since he was a boy."

"You make him sound a charlatan." A servant appeared to refill his glass the instant he set it down. Charlie broodingly watched the burgundy stream into his goblet. Decent wine was the sole salvation of the evening, in his opinion.

"That was not my intent," replied Tallboys hastily. "Merely that he hasn't got the same reserve and decorum a gentleman might."

Charlie knew several gentlemen without reserve or decorum; in truth, he was often one of them. If he kept drinking this way, and Tallboys continued annoying him, he might yet lapse into his usual ways.

Somehow that thought led his mind to another point, and then another. "You're the banker," he said abruptly. "You must keep the account books."

Tallboys blinked, but nodded politely. "I do indeed, sir. Mr. Scott also maintains a set of books. Do you wish to see them?"

"Mrs. Neville does." Charlie gestured at her with his wineglass. "Scott hasn't produced them for her. I wonder why."

"Ah—yes, yes, he did tell me the lady wished to

review the books. I believe the delay has been mischance; I said Mr. Scott maintains a set of books, true, but they are not complete. I understand Mrs. Neville wishes to see the complete accounting, which I have brought with me from Poole. I expect he shall make them available to her very soon, as they would be to any prospective investor." Tallboys's gaze went to the woman across from them. "Perhaps you wish to view them with her, my lord."

One corner of Charlie's mouth bent upward. He'd rarely had to read a ledger in his life, and didn't plan to start with a canal ledger he had no interest in, not even for the pleasure of reading it with Tessa Neville. "No. I prefer to make my judgments based on other criteria."

Tallboys's mouth pursed in minute frustration, but he merely bowed his head. "Of course, my lord. I remain ready to answer any criteria you have."

"Excellent." Charlie raised one finger, and the servant with the wine promptly stepped back up to fill his glass yet again. "Sir Gregory," he said into a momentary lull in the conversation, "what is your opinion of this canal?"

Sir Gregory looked up from his plate, casting a critical eye on Charlie. He had hardly said a word thus far, the dribbles and spots on his waistcoat showing his true interest: the roast joint of beef. If Scott intended to lure investors with fine food and drink, he was doing an excellent job. Attwood leaned back in his chair and swiped the trickle of juice from his chin. " 'Tis a damned fraud, sir."

Charlie raised one eyebrow. Hiram Scott made a sound like a sigh before smiling stiffly. "Now, Sir Gregory, we've addressed your complaints."

"Not all of 'em," retorted the older man. He caught up his wineglass and fixed his gaze on Charlie. "You're a fool if you give these gentlemen your money, Gresham."

"And yet you allowed them to build across your land," said Mrs. Neville. "Why has your opinion changed, sir?"

Attwood's eyes bulged a little, and he turned to glare at her in indignation. "And what business is it of yours, madam? I changed my mind, and that's that."

"I didn't mean to offend," she said evenly. "I merely meant that something dramatic must have happened to change your opinion of the canal so completely."

Attwood huffed and snapped his fingers at the servant with the wine. "I daresay it wouldn't concern you much, if it had."

Charlie saw the flush of color come up in her face. She was quite a beauty when she blushed, even though it meant she was working up a head of fury. "On the contrary, sir," he said lazily. "The lady is considering a rather large investment in the canal. Surely it behooves you to explain your statement, particularly since you made it in the presence of two of the canal's directors. You must admit it's curious."

Attwood's eyes narrowed on Charlie. "Ladies don't invest! God's breath, man, you can't say you support this?"

"Now, Sir Gregory," interjected Scott. "Mrs. Neville is here on behalf of her brother, Lord Marchmont."

Attwood remained sullen. "Then he ought to be

here himself. What sort of man sends a woman to make his decisions for him?"

Mrs. Neville was staring at him with loathing in her gaze. The flush had confined itself to two bright spots in her cheeks. "My brother values my judgment of such things, sir."

"Damned fool him." Attwood poked his finger at Scott. "And you, too, Scott, for encouraging this nonsense."

"You haven't said what changed your mind about the canal," said Charlie. He leaned back in his chair and tossed back some more wine. "Was it just a whim, Sir Gregory? You seem inclined to quick judgments."

The older man's face turned purple. "As if you would know the first thing about canals, you London popinjay!"

Charlie bared his teeth in a smile. "Instruct me, then. I've already learned far more from Mrs. Neville than from anything Mr. Scott has told me." He waved one hand as Scott drew breath to speak. "Not now, Scott."

Attwood glanced from man to man. His lips pressed together. "I don't have to explain myself."

"No, you have every right to make yourself out to be impulsive and bad-tempered," said Mrs. Neville under her breath, yet loudly enough to be heard by everyone.

"Impulsive!" Attwood sputtered. "How dare you!"

"Was it carefully considered, then?" Her eyes flashed with that fury Charlie had sensed earlier, but she kept her frosty calm steady. "I wonder you could stand to sit at the same table with men who mislead you into a foolish investment." Attwood gaped at her in shocked fury, but she just raised her eyebrows. "Either you were duped in the first place, you took the money for the cut across your land out of pure greed, or you've discovered new information about the canal that reasonably changed your mind and made you regret your investment. Which is it?"

"Oh, Mrs. Neville!" Scott cried.

"This is unseemly," said Tallboys through thin lips.

"Where is the fault in my logic?" she fired back. Charlie could only watch in awe, his mind blunted by the rather large quantity of wine he'd consumed. She was magnificent, like the Archangel Uriel. If she'd had a flaming sword in her hand, he had no doubt Attwood, and perhaps Tallboys as well, would be missing his head by now.

"This was not intended to be a business meeting," pleaded Scott. "Can we not return to more cordial topics?"

She turned on him. "I would only dine with you upon business matters, Mr. Scott."

The man flushed under the rebuke, but Tallboys was the one who replied. "Madam, we have been most accommodating. I wonder at your insistence on pursuing all hints of displeasure. Perhaps your interest in the canal isn't genuine."

"So you fear what Sir Gregory might say?" she asked. "You must wonder why he just told Lord Gresham not to invest—unless you already know his complaint."

"Sir Gregory spoke in jest," said Mr. Scott hastily. "He keeps us on our toes, don't you, sir?" He bent a significant look on the man in question.

Attwood scowled in reply, but grumbled something vaguely agreeable.

Belatedly Charlie realized Scott was right. Attwood was a bit of a troublemaker, but he was also an important part of Scott's plans. The canal ran through his property, which made him a shareholder and thus gave him power over Scott. Attwood could wheedle what he wanted from Scott by being a constant burr in the man's side, even denigrating the canal to potential investors. Chances were, Attwood was merely trying the same tonight, and in a company of gentlemen, over a great deal more wine and cigars, he would have backed off his charge, mentioned his petty grievance, and Scott would have been pleased to demonstrate his efficiency—for Charlie's benefit—by solving it.

But Tessa Neville didn't think that way. She was logical and focused, and the glass at her place was largely untouched.

"No doubt Sir Gregory will find a way that Mr. Scott can help him," Charlie said. "That's what you do, isn't it, Scott?" He got to his feet. The room swung rather wildly for a moment, and he leaned one hand on the table, regretting the last few glasses of wine. He'd lost his head for liquor out here in the wilderness. "I feel in need of some fresh air. Mrs. Neville, may I escort you back to your inn?"

Hiram Scott was already nodding, leaping to his feet as if he, too, was anxious to leave. "Indeed! The hour's grown quite late, I must be off. Tallboys, are you staying the night here?"

The flush had suffused Tessa Neville's face. "Is

that your answer to me, sir? You doubt my interest in this canal?"

"I'm sure Tallboys doesn't know what he doubts now, after this excellent Madeira," said Charlie. Tallboys was looking at her with dislike, and he might have been drunk enough to say something even ruder than he already had. "Scott, thank you for the illuminating evening. Attwood, Tallboys, a pleasure." He made a vague bow toward them. "And Mr. Lester," he added, catching sight of the engineer, sitting with his shoulders hunched in misery. "Good night, sir."

"Good evening, sir," called Scott with obvious relief as Charlie took Mrs. Neville by the arm before forcefully escorting her from the room. She didn't protest until they reached the main hall of the inn, while the servant rushed off to gather her cloak and Charlie's coat.

"How dare they," she finally said through her teeth. "I am not a child to be bullied about! They should go bankrupt for treating any investor that way!"

Charlie glanced at the eavesdropping crowd in the taproom. "Of course they should." He pushed open the door of the small parlor behind him and pulled her into the room. "But they're idiots, Tessa."

"I have every right to ask questions, especially when Sir Gregory says such provoking things!" she continued in a lather. "What did you call me?"

"Tessa," he answered. "But look here—Attwood's being an ass in order to get something from Scott. He wasn't trying to insult you, he just . . ."

"Belittles women out of habit?" She made a

sharp motion with one hand. "I didn't give you leave to call me by name."

"But I like your name," he said softly, the wine flowing warm and hazy through his blood and trampling all caution into oblivion. "Ignore Attwood."

She took a deep breath. "I could," she said. "But I cannot ignore Mr. Tallboys's complete dismissal of my concerns! And you should not call me by name."

Charlie nodded. Part of his brain acknowledged she was right, and justifiably irate. The other part of him had already forgotten Scott and Tallboys and Attwood, and could only see how very luminous her skin was in the low light of the single lamp. How her hair seemed to be tempting his fingers to touch it. How strongly he wanted to feel her arms around his neck, and discover what sort of sigh she would make if she were kissed. If *he* kissed her.

"You see, it's like this," he began, and then he stopped, mesmerized by the way her eyes flashed and her chin tipped up so boldly toward him. When had he fallen so hard for her?

"Yes?" she prompted.

"Oh, hell," he muttered, and leaned down and kissed her.

She jumped and made a muffled squeak, but Charlie already had his arm around her waist, drawing her against him. He threaded one hand into her gleaming curls and brushed his lips against hers, "Tessa," he murmured. "*Darling.* My God, Tessa . . ."

For a heartbeat she was still. Then, with a soft

sigh of capitulation, she wound her arms around his neck and pressed against him, kissing him back as hungrily as she did in his dreams. For the span of a few minutes time seemed to stop for Charlie. She was heat and passion and perfectly female in his arms, not a prudish, cold creature, not a dried-up widow, but a woman who felt the same desires he did. And for those few minutes nothing else in the world mattered but her.

The tap at the door broke the spell. He lifted his head and looked down at Tessa, feeling oddly as though he'd been knocked in the head and yet now thought more clearly than ever. She blinked at him, her eyes soft and starry for a moment, before the servant with their cloaks tapped again. With a gasp she stepped back, out of his arms, and turned away. "Yes," she said in a strained voice. "Come."

The serving wench brought in her cloak. Tessa swirled it around her shoulders before he could take it, and she wouldn't look at him as she tied the fastenings. Feeling more sober by the moment, Charlie put on his own coat and motioned the wench from the room.

"Well, this has been an exceptional evening," Tessa said unevenly. She pulled up her hood, hiding her expression from him. "Mrs. Bates will be waiting up for me. Good night, sir."

"Yes," he murmured. He wanted to kiss her again. "I'll call on you tomorrow . . ."

"No!" She recoiled from his extended hand. "I'm going now. Good night."

"Let me escort you to your door, at least," he tried to say, but she gave him a single alarmed glance.

"*No.* Leave me in peace!" She turned and hurried out the door and out of the inn, her head held valiantly high even though she was almost running.

Charlie cursed under his breath. He couldn't let her walk back alone. Keeping well back, he followed her through the streets just until he saw her duck safely back into The Golden Hind.

Grimly, he turned back toward The Bear, where his horse and gig were stabled. He wished he'd never agreed to attend that miserable dinner. He wished he hadn't drunk half a barrel of wine. He wished he'd shot Hiram Scott the first day he arrived in Frome. He wished he'd kept his head and not kissed her. He wished he hadn't let her go, no matter who knocked upon the door.

He stalked around another corner, and almost collided with a man coming the other way.

"Beg pardon, my lord," mumbled the man, stepping aside and snatching off his cap. It was Lester, the engineer who had been tense and quiet all evening.

On some impulse, Charlie stopped. "What the devil is Scott hiding?"

Lester said nothing. The guilt stamped on his face told all. Charlie gave a predatory smile, casting off restraint and scruples. "Let me buy you a drink, Mr. Lester."

Chapter 12

Early next morning Tessa gathered her mortified dignity around her like a suit of chain mail and sent off a peremptory letter to Mr. Scott, telling him that if he didn't have the account books ready for her examination by the next day, she would understand that he did not mean to show them to her and she would return to London to tell her brother not to invest. It was the sort of note that would send Louise into the vapors, brutally direct and abrupt without the slightest hint of tact, but Tessa was beyond caring. She almost hoped Scott put her off again; it would give her an excuse to leave Frome without admitting defeat of any kind.

But this unvarnished demand worked wonders on the man. Within an hour she received his reply, apologizing profusely for the delay and inviting her to visit the ironworks at her convenience, where the books lay ready and waiting. Somewhat mollified, Tessa decided to take him up on it and instead of sending her answer, dressed to go to Mells herself.

"Ought you to tell His Lordship?" ventured Eugenie, watching her tie on her bonnet.

"Why?" Tessa kept her eyes on the mirror. She'd told Eugenie almost nothing of the horrible dinner, just that it had been unpleasant and a waste of time. Then she'd gone straight to bed to forestall any more questions, especially about Lord Gresham or why he hadn't walked her back. No one needed to hear about that. If she could have purged it from her memory, she would have, especially that last intoxicating, treacherous moment.

"Well, dear, he might accompany you . . ." The older woman's voice died away as Tessa turned a sharp look on her.

"I don't need an escort. I don't need to be driven when I can drive myself, at my own convenience. And if he wishes to examine the books himself," she added as Eugenie's face brightened and her mouth opened, "he is welcome to visit at any time." Welcome indeed; Hiram Scott would leap from his bed in the dead of night to show Lord Gresham anything he wanted to see at the canal, from the account books to the privy pits.

Eugenie's face fell. "Whatever happened, Tessa dear? You made no effort to keep your actions from him earlier."

Her face burned. "Nor did I rely on him to nursemaid me from Frome to Mells! I'm surprised at you, Eugenie, urging me to impose upon the kindness of a busy man."

Now Eugenie blushed. "It's only because I worry about you so," she argued, following Tessa across the room. "The roads here are so dreadful, you know—you admitted it yourself—and for a woman traveling alone—"

"Yes, perhaps you are right." Tessa went into

the bedroom and came back out with her loaded
pistol in one hand. "I should take this as well."

Eugenie made a gasping chirp, recoiling from
the weapon. "Oh, dear! Could you really shoot
someone?"

"I could indeed." She put the pistol into her reticule; the handle stuck out, but in her current mood,
she didn't care. Let everyone in Frome know she
was armed. She was a good shot, and felt very capable of shooting someone at the moment.

Eugenie made a few more despairing noises but
didn't try to stop her. Tessa went downstairs and
hired a gig. The innkeeper's eyes strayed to her
pistol but he said nothing. This was the country,
after all, not London, and women were generally
judged more capable in the country. Or perhaps
her expression was warning enough to hold his
tongue. The gig was brought around quickly, and
she set off.

Her drive to Mells was uneventful, although
it did seem longer than when she had gone with
Lord Gresham. As she concentrated on navigating
the wretched roads, she tried not to think about
His Lordship, but it was impossible. Why must
everything remind her of him? Tessa scowled as
she reached a particularly twisted length of road,
trying not to recall how he had driven so capably
over the same stretch just a few days earlier, and
how he'd been so charmingly deprecating, telling
her he hoped she might eventually consider him
merely benign. Benign! As if he weren't the most
dangerous man she'd ever met.

First she tried to tell herself he'd been drunk,
and that was why he kissed her. She had noticed

that all the gentlemen last night seemed to drink a good deal, but Gresham outdid them all. It had reminded her that he was a London gentleman, with more decadent tastes and habits than she was used to. But she also had to admit he hadn't seemed drunk until that last moment, when he looked down at her with that oddest expression—dazed? spellbound? She didn't even know how to describe it—right before he kissed her.

Then, Tessa was ashamed to say, the fault had ceased to be his alone. Even though he was drunk and she was shaking with fury at Attwood, the kiss had felt so right, so necessary, she lost all grip on reason and kissed him back. Not chastely, as a decent lady might have excused, but wildly, passionately, even desperately. As if something restrained and pent up inside her had finally burst its banks and overwhelmed her, leaving her drowning in nothing but the sharp awareness of his arms around her and his mouth on hers and the way he whispered her name. And once she started kissing him, she didn't know how she would have ever stopped, if the girl hadn't knocked on the door.

No, he was not benign. She had sensed from the beginning that if she ever let him get too close, she would go up in flames for him. She had just never thought immolation would feel so wonderful.

Mr. Scott seemed to grasp at once that she was not in any temper to be trifled with. He came out to meet her as soon as she arrived, and made no mention of the dinner as he led her inside. "I've got the accounts waiting, just as you asked," he said cordially, as if he hadn't delayed producing them for over a fortnight. "I've had them brought to a quiet room over here; take as long as you need to examine them."

"Thank you, sir." She even smiled at him, although it was probably a frosty smile. It certainly felt stiff and frozen on her lips.

Then Mr. Scott left her, bowing out of the room with a promise to answer any questions she might have. Tessa settled herself in the chair and opened the first account book, taking a deep breath as the smell of fresh ink and paper hit her. Her nerves began to calm down at last. This was what she was good at; the neat columns of numbers soothed something inside her, and she began to feel more like herself as she studied them. With numbers, she was confident and sure of her competence. The numbers never made her feel a fool. The numbers were steady and sure, telling their story plainly. Numbers could be made to lie and twist the truth, of course, but unlike with men, a close eye could divine the lies and tease out the truth. Numbers, at least, were perfectly benign.

She spent the rest of the day there, occasionally catching a minor arithmetical error and noting it in the margins. Scott's clerks weren't quite as meticulous as they might have been, and the cost of wages had risen slightly more than projected, but overall the picture was very much in line with the prospectus. Scott had even written off the cost of some of the lock gates, which were being made in his own factory; there were small notes indicating they had been late, and so he absorbed their cost. Tessa approved of this show of compromise; one thing she had been particularly alert to was any sign of profiteering. When she closed the books at last, it was with a refreshed spirit of satisfaction. Scott's canal looked to be as sound as he claimed, and she was relieved that this trip hadn't been a complete waste of time.

He met her himself when she came out, somewhat surprised to see how late in the day it was. Unraveling a complex ledger was like a puzzle to Tessa, thrilling but engrossing, and she looked ruefully at Mr. Scott.

"I see the day is gone, sir. Thank you for allowing me to monopolize your books all day."

"Nonsense." He bowed his head with a smile. "Have you any questions? Any other requirements?"

Tessa shook her head. "I believe I have quite enough information to advise my brother. The final decision, of course, will be entirely his." Not that William had ever gone against her advice, but she always said it anyway.

"Yes, yes, I understand. Please convey my very best regards to Lord Marchmont." Scott's smile remained fixed on his face as he walked out to her waiting gig with her. "I hope your trip to Somerset has been worthwhile, Mrs. Neville."

Tessa stepped up and took the reins. "Yes, I believe it has been." She gave him a nod. "Good day, Mr. Scott."

She drove home feeling as though the world, which had rocked precariously off balance under the unsettling Lord Gresham's attention and influence, had been set back to rights. She had achieved her purpose here. Anything else was immaterial. It didn't matter whether Mr. Tallboys thought well of her; it didn't matter what Sir Gregory Attwood thought of her at all. In the end all they cared about

was William's money, just as in the end she was
sure Gresham only cared for seducing her on his
jaunt in the country. He was a rake and a scoundrel and she'd never really trusted him anyway, not
completely. All Eugenie's hints that he was in love
with her were just wishful thinking, and she was
glad she'd realized it before doing anything truly
stupid. Again.

She reached The Golden Hind just as the sun was
dipping below the rooftops, and handed the hired
gig over to a stable boy. Now that her purpose was
done, she could leave Frome. The thought put a
spring in her step, even though it meant going to
London. At least in London, Lord Gresham would
be so occupied with other women he wouldn't
spare time to torment her anymore.

Pausing only to ask for a tray with dinner to be
sent up, she hurried to her rooms. Eugenie would
be disappointed, no doubt, to leave the earl behind,
but she would have to bear it. Tessa supposed it
was possible he would call on them in London,
out of obligation to Eugenie, but she could con-
trive to be out then and avoid him. After that, she
told herself, it would be simple never to see him
again; after a few weeks in London, Louise would
let her go home and she could return to her life of
ledgers and accounts and never once feel sorry for
herself because she'd almost fallen for a handsome
scoundrel.

She let herself into their small sitting room, pulling
off her gloves. To her astonishment, Eugenie leaped
at her as soon as she was through the door. "Oh,
there you are, at last," she cried with an outsized air
of relief. "Lord Gresham must see you at once!"

Chapter 13

Charlie's temper was perilously close to snapping. The day had not begun well, with a ringing headache from his previous evening's overindulgence. Despite the strong temptation to remain motionless until the room stopped revolving around him, he dragged himself out of bed. Barnes, his unsympathetic valet, offered cold cloths and headache powders until Charlie snarled at him to go away. As much as it felt like he'd been rolled down a hill head first, he needed to think. Naturally, it took some time for his thoughts to settle down into order again

The inescapable conclusion was that he had to tell Tessa what he'd learned. Lester's revelations hadn't helped him very much, but they would make an enormous difference to her. He had told himself originally he didn't want to interfere with her at all; the canal was more than Hiram Scott, and if it was a profitable investment, who was he to stop her from making it? It hadn't pleased him, but he'd deliberately kept his business with Scott separate from hers. Still, he'd become increasingly disenchanted with that stance, and now that he knew crucial information about the canal, he was bound to tell her, and not just because he wanted to keep her away from Scott—even if she didn't want to see his face at the moment.

But the lady was not in when he called. Mrs. Bates wrinkled up her face and wrung her hands when he reached the inn. "Oh, dear," she cried. "I'm dreadfully sorry! She's gone to Mells, my lord."

"To Mells?" he exclaimed, jolted by the news. ... Had Lester confessed? Had Scott drawn Tessa out to Mells to pressure her?

"Mr. Scott wrote and said he'd got the books ready for her to look at," explained Mrs. Bates. "And she'd been waiting so long to see them, she would not be deterred from driving out straightaway, Lord Gresham, even though I *begged* her to wait . . ."

"She went alone?"

"She insisted," she said, looking cowed by his sharp tone. "I did suggest she ask you, my lord . . . but she would not impose, even though it makes me *dreadfully* uneasy to think of her driving all that way alone . . ."

Charlie took a deep breath. It was no surprise she hadn't wanted to ask him; he deserved that. And she had been waiting to see those books. He didn't like the coincidence of it, but after last night, he didn't like anything connected to Scott and his bloody canal. Odds were it was entirely ordinary. It wasn't far to Mells, the road was straight enough, and Tessa knew the way.

"My lord?"

He blinked out of his thoughts at Mrs. Bates's timid query. "Yes?"

"Did . . . Did something happen last night? At the dinner, I mean."

He hesitated. "I expect Mrs. Neville was not in the best humor when she returned."

"No," she murmured, looking as though she was bracing herself. "She was not herself."

"Some gentlemen of the party proved themselves unworthy of a lady's company," Charlie said, choosing not to mention that perhaps he himself had been one of those unworthy gentlemen. "It was rather uncomfortable, and not, I gather, what Mrs. Neville expected."

"Oh, dear." Mrs. Bates sighed. "I feared as much. She was so tense this morning, and so abrupt—almost as if she wanted to provoke Mr. Scott into refusing again to show her the books, which, you will understand, was quite shocking to me. Of course she's been growing impatient with him for his rather inconsiderate delays, but when she got out her pistol—"

"Her pistol!" Charlie stared.

Mrs. Bates blushed bright pink. "She's quite able to handle it, my lord, *quite* able! She insisted Lord Marchmont teach her, and she's likely as good a shot as most men in Wiltshire—"

"Why did she take a pistol to see Mr. Scott?"

"Oh!" The older lady started. "Oh, she didn't mean to shoot Mr. Scott—at least, I can't think why she would do that. I protested when she said she would drive herself, and that's when she got out her pistol and said she could shoot someone indeed." Mrs. Bates gazed up at him fearfully. "You don't think she intended to use it on Mr. Scott, do you? I thought she meant it for protection, if someone should stop her—"

"Yes, I'm sure that's it," said Charlie to reassure her. "It's wise for her to have it, if she meant to go alone. I presume . . . That is, I expect she welcomed the chance of some solitude." He remembered the way Tessa had all but run from him the previous night, crying that she wanted peace.

"Yes, I'm sure she did." Mrs. Bates's face filled with relief. "Of course you're right, my lord. She's always needed her privacy and time to think. Why, we used to think she would prefer to be a hermit!" She laughed, then choked off abruptly, looking horrified. "But that was long ago," she added anxiously. "After—After a rather difficult time . . ."

"We all of us have moments when our own company is all we can bear." Charlie sighed. "I'm sure she is in no danger, but I must speak to her. Have you any idea when she'll return?" Mrs. Bates shook her head. "Will you send word to me when she does? What I have to say to her cannot wait."

"Would you like to leave a note for her?"

He shook his head. He suspected she might tear it up, if she still bore him ill will over last night, and he couldn't let her ignore this. "Will you send to me even if she professes she doesn't want to see me?"

Her expression fell. "Oh dear," she murmured. "Will she not wish to, my lord?"

"I don't know," he said honestly. "But I must speak to her immediately."

Mrs. Bates bit her lip but nodded. Charlie thanked her and left, even though it was past midday and Tessa must be returning soon. But he sensed she would be in a better temper if he didn't drive out and intercept her on the road from Mells, and he also remembered she'd taken her pistol. An angry woman was one thing, but an armed angry woman was another. He'd have to make use of the delay as best he could.

True to her word, Mrs. Bates sent word when Tessa returned. Unfortunately, it didn't come until after dinner, and it included a warning. *She was very adamant that she didn't wish to speak to you, sir, even after I told her it was urgent,* wrote Mrs. Bates. *And now she says we shall leave for London the day after next, so I beg you will make haste if you wish to see her in Frome.*

The last part made him curse quietly. Of course she was leaving Frome, if she had gotten the information she needed from Scott's books, but he sensed she was in such haste to leave because he had kissed her.

He hoped to God that wasn't the case.

He balled up the note and dropped it into the fire. Very well, then; he would find Tessa in the morning and make her listen to him, even if it ruined him forever in her eyes.

As expected, she was not at the inn when he called the next morning at a truly unfashionable hour. Mrs. Bates, still in her morning gown and cap, met him with a worried look. "She's gone out already," she said. "She said she wanted coffee and a walk."

He gave a short nod. "Thank you. I'll find her."

It took almost half an hour to do so. He visited the coffeeshop, the book shop, even the millinery, without catching sight of her slim, determined figure. When he finally did spy her staring pensively at a shop window, his heart leaped and a tiny smile curved his lips even after he remembered she was purposely trying to avoid meeting him. There was just something about her that drew him.

She was still at the window when he reached her.

Charlie took that as a hopeful sign, since he hadn't tried to disguise his approach. He stopped beside her, a careful arm's length away, and joined her in contemplation for a moment.

"Are you considering the pipe, or the snuff boxes?" he asked. They were staring at a tobacconist's display.

"The grinder," she said. Charlie looked, and realized the shop also sold coffee. "One cannot find a decent cup of coffee in this whole shire."

"It's not fit for bilge," he agreed.

"Fortunately Mrs. Bates and I are leaving tomorrow for London," she went on. Her voice was poised and cool, but she hadn't looked at him. "I expect they have decent coffee there."

"Buy the grinder, if you're holding out that hope. The best coffee isn't found in any coffeehouse, you must grind it fresh and brew it at once. My chef in London won't serve coffee more than half an hour after he's made it."

"My sister thinks it is common," she returned. "She won't allow it in her house. It's my private vice."

He glanced at her. "How very decadent."

Her eyelashes flickered. "If you say it is so, I must believe it."

Charlie laughed. "Yes, I have a far greater acquaintance with vice than you do!"

"And decadence," she added.

He smiled. He wouldn't mind lavishing a little decadence on her. "I've been looking for you."

"Mrs. Bates said you would be." She turned and walked away, and Charlie followed.

"I understand if you prefer to avoid me. I should apologize for the other night."

"Why?" Her face was serene, but he heard the

slight edge in her tone. "You were not responsible for other gentlemen's behavior."

"I wasn't apologizing for that."

She was silent for a few steps. "I don't recall anything else worthy of note."

He looked at her. She had her mouth pursed up in that way he found so maddeningly enticing. "Very good. I wasn't, in fact, very sorry for doing it, and if you feel you are owed no apology for it, I shan't bother to issue one."

She took a deep breath and stopped, turning to face him. "It is not necessary, my lord, to apologize for actions of no significance. I daresay our acquaintance is nearing an end in any event, and I should hate to part on bad terms. Thank you for all your kindness to Mrs. Bates, and all your assistance to me. It has been a great pleasure." And she put out her hand, as if in farewell.

Charlie took her hand but he didn't let it go. "A very great pleasure, indeed. Will you come for a drive with me? I have something to show you."

She tugged. "Certainly not. I must pack—prepare to leave—"

"And yet you have time to shop for coffee grinders. It won't take but an hour or two. Mrs. Bates will oversee the packing quite competently."

She pulled again, harder this time. "Let me go. I don't want to go anywhere with you."

"If it were only my own wicked pleasures at stake, I would release you, however much it pained me to do so." Still holding her hand, he pulled her arm around his despite her resistance. "But sadly, my purpose is far more mundane, and I must insist."

"Let me go, Gresham," she said through her teeth as he towed her back down the street to where he had left his horse and gig.

"Not yet."

"Please," she said in murderous tones.

"No. We're going for a short drive—I have the purest intentions, Tessa," he added at her glare. "But if you try to run from me, I shall chase you down and carry you back."

"Fine," she spat. "Where do you want to drive?"

"Just north of Vobster." He handed her up into the carriage, and she went without protest.

"Vobster! What is in Vobster?"

He stepped up and settled on the seat, feeling an unhealthy rush of elation at being so close to her. Her knee bumped his as she shifted on the narrow seat, and he had to fight off the urge to slide his arm around her waist and pull her close, just for a moment, and press his lips to the curve of her throat, right below her jaw. "I gather you aren't willing to take my word for anything," he said in response to her question. "So I shall show you."

She stared at him with that thin line between her brows before facing forward with a faint huff. "Drive quickly."

He grinned and said nothing. It took almost no time to navigate the crooked streets of Frome and then they were on another rutted country lane heading west. For a long time neither said anything. Charlie caught her glancing at him a few times, but she never spoke. He longed to know why she was so alarmed by his kiss, and finally just asked. "Was it really of no significance?" he said softly. "When I kissed you?"

She averted her face, so the bonnet brim hid it. "It meant nothing to me, and even less to you, I suspect."

He nodded. "You've got me all puzzled out, haven't you? Indolent, ignorant, arrogant, good-for-nothing scoundrel."

She slanted a challenging glance at him. "I never said that. Is that how most people see you?"

The question surprised him. "I suppose some do. Of course, most people see what they want to see. A title, a fortune, a handsome face . . ." He shrugged. "It's enough to render any man a rogue in search of scandal."

"A handsome face," she repeated tartly. "I understand where the charge of arrogance originates."

He gave her a lazy smile. "It's not arrogance to speak the truth."

Her eyes flashed and her cheeks pinkened. "Handsome is so subjective, one might hesitate even to use the word 'truth' near it."

"Very well, I misspoke; I should have said 'a face widely considered among the handsomest in England.' Does that please you?"

The color in her face deepened. Good Lord, it was thrilling to argue with her. "I don't care what other people think of your face at all."

"No, of course you wouldn't." Charlie knew he should stop teasing her—and it was beginning to feel very arrogant, arguing his own attractiveness—but she was irresistible. And at least she was speaking to him again. "What do you think of my face?"

She blinked. Something like alarm flashed in her clear green gaze before it narrowed on him. "Searching for compliments, sir? How very crass—

even arrogant. One might call it ignorant of all good manners, worthy only of a scoundrel who is up to no good!"

Charlie burst out laughing. She had managed to use each and every slur in one sweeping condemnation. "Pax! I am vanquished, completely unstrung. I confess to arrogance, indolence, and all the rest, along with a sad, misshapen face that sends children running in fright."

She stared at him, open-mouthed, then jerked around in her seat to face forward. "I hate it when you do that," she muttered.

"What?"

"When you make me want to laugh in the middle of an argument."

He couldn't see her face, but the nape of her neck was pink. "I like to hear you laugh."

"I'm very . . ." She hesitated, as if loath to speak the word. "I'm a very dull person, too serious for my own good. My sister says I was born without enough good humor."

"My father said I was born with too much."

"Enough for two people at least," she replied.

The road dipped and twisted, and Charlie slowed the horse. "I didn't kiss you merely out of excessive humor. Nor because I drank too much wine."

"I wish you hadn't done it at all."

He shouldn't ask, but he had to know. He had never in all his life been so twisted up over a woman, nor so driven to know what she felt for him. Until that kiss, he would have laid even odds she found his interest flattering at best; but that kiss . . . No woman could kiss a man like that if she felt nothing for him. "Then why did you kiss me back?"

She didn't move. "Too much wine."

"You had one glass."

"I shouldn't have had any."

"Leave a kiss within the cup, and I'll not ask for wine," he murmured.

"It was madness," she said, almost wistfully. "As well you know. A moment of weakness. Heaven knows a week in Frome might drive anyone mad, at least temporarily. Had we been ourselves, in London, it never would have happened."

Charlie was silent. She might be right; if the Durham Dilemma hadn't sent him out into the countryside, he probably would never have crossed paths with an outspoken widow who cared more for account books than contemplating his—or any other gentleman's—handsome face. It was somewhat shocking how sobering he found that possibility. "Then I am glad for Frome, because I don't regret it, madness or not."

She heaved a faintly sad sigh. "Where are we going?"

"Just a little farther."

"Is this about—about that kiss?" Her voice wobbled on the last word.

"Ah—no." He cleared his throat. "Did you see the account books yesterday? Mrs. Bates said you went to Mells."

"Yes," she said slowly. "Mr. Scott produced them at last."

"And did they persuade you to invest?"

"Yes," she said again, beginning to sound annoyed again. "The canal is quite sound, and only slightly exceeding its projected costs. Is that what this is all about? You wanted to know my opinion of the canal?"

They were almost where he wanted to go. Charlie turned the horse off the road at a clearing, slowing the animal to a cautious walk. "Have you written to Lord Marchmont yet?"

"No, he's already left for London—as Mrs. Bates and I intend to do tomorrow morning," she added defiantly.

"Good." Charlie brought the carriage to a halt and jumped down, tying the reins to a nearby sapling. "Come with me."

"Why?" she demanded. "What are you up to? Can you not tell me anything?"

"I want to show you," he said. "Get down."

Scowling, she reluctantly held out her hand. Charlie took it, then hauled her down bodily, ignoring her startled exclamation. "I've already seen the canal works," she said as he pulled her along by the hand. "What are we doing here?"

He led her through the trees and stopped on the edge of a little knoll, looking down over the canal where a lock was being built. He had learned yesterday that this was the linchpin of the canal, in more ways than one. "Down there is the problem," he said, waving one hand over the scene. It looked much like the rest of the unbuilt canal, with towering mounds of displaced dirt above deep pits, crawling with men and horses and carts. "That lock should lead to the aqueduct toward Vobster."

"What is the problem?" She was frowning as she scanned the landscape. "Are they stealing? Not building it properly?"

"No," said Charlie. "The locks. They aren't working, especially not this one."

"They trialed one and it performed well!" she protested. "Mr. Scott designed them himself, and custom-built the iron gates!"

"Perhaps that's why he won't admit they're failing—but they are. And you yourself told me this canal depends on efficient locks, given the drop."

She said nothing, her face pale and set.

"The canal is going to fail, Tessa," he said gently. "Scott's been hiding quite a bit from you because he's in desperate need of more funds."

"How did you discover it?" she asked numbly.

"I got the chief engineer drunk. He's in despair because he thinks he'll be blamed for it."

She jerked as if he'd struck her. "Perhaps they can be fixed—"

"With a great deal more money, perhaps," Charlie agreed. "Will you risk your brother's funds on it? With a man who's already kept the truth from you?"

"Why?" she asked after a moment. Her face hadn't altered much, still stony and leached of color. Charlie guessed she was reviewing everything Scott had told her, every promise he had made, every accounting he had shown her.

"He's treasurer of the canal company, with a personal bond of ten thousand pounds. I believe he's hoping, as you suggested, to get in enough new money to repair and improve the locks so the canal can be finished. If he can finish the canal, it might yet be made profitable, even if not for several years. If he can't, shareholders will demand their money back and the company will collapse, taking his bond with it. And he'll have no canal to ship his iron, either."

She swayed on her feet, and for a moment he feared she would faint. He made a motion toward her, and she put her hand on his arm, her fingers digging into his flesh. "How did you learn that?" she demanded. "How? I asked every question, examined every ledger—"

He didn't tell her it was because men like Scott and Tallboys found it easy to lie to a woman. He didn't tell her Scott had put her off for days while Tallboys created a fresh ledger that didn't show the costs of the failing locks or include Mr. Lester's warnings about them. He didn't tell her he had spent yesterday bribing a clerk and a crew foreman to hear their unvarnished thoughts once the engineer poured out his anxiety, or that they confirmed Lester's charges. "I wanted you to know," he said instead. "Before you wrote to Marchmont to send the funds."

She shoved him away. "How can that be right?" she cried. "How? I don't—" She put her hands on the sides of her head and paced away from him. "It can't be right," she insisted. "There are models of successful locks—all they need to do is build ones like those! Why would they persist with unworkable designs? It makes no sense!"

"I agree—" he started to say, but she shook her head.

"Take me home." She turned and stormed toward the carriage. "I can't believe it."

"Very well." He followed her to the carriage, where she threw herself into the seat and turned

away from him, her face set in fury and indignation. She didn't say a word as he drove back into
Frome, even when he handed her down at the
inn. "Should I walk you up?" he asked, thinking
he could have a quick word with Mrs. Bates. The
news had hit Tessa hard.

"Why?" She looked at him with dead eyes and
turned to walk away. "I'm perfectly well."

He caught her arm. "I can see you are not," he
said quietly. "I'm sorry—"

"For what?" She didn't tell him to release her,
but her tone conveyed it fully. "What have you
done wrong?"

He was sorry she'd been lied to, and sorrier still
that she had believed it. He wasn't sorry she knew,
and he wasn't even sorry he'd had to tell her. But
he knew Tessa. *She is so enormously clever,* Mrs.
Bates had said, and she was right. Tessa was perhaps the most intelligent person he'd ever met, man
or woman, and she had made it her shining virtue,
her point of pride. But he had never known a clever
person who liked to be proved wrong, even less
when they had been deceived and not spotted the
deception. Tessa didn't trust lightly, but even the
keenest mind had to accept some things on faith.
Scott had treated her with apparent respect, as if
he esteemed her as much as any man, and all along
he'd been playing her for a fool. Charlie allowed
her every right to be angry and humiliated and
shaken.

He let go of her arm and she walked away without a backward glance.

Chapter 14

He couldn't sleep that night. It had begun to rain after dinner, first a gentle drizzle that steadily grew harder until it drummed on the slate roof and rattled against the windows. Charlie sent Barnes and the other servants to their beds and sat in front of his sitting room fire, drinking brandy and brooding.

What the hell was he doing? He'd come into Somerset to catch a blackmailer, find Dorothy Cope, and eliminate any threat to his inheritance. So far he'd located Hiram Scott but done nothing to confront him, heard not one word of Dorothy, and learned nothing of any help in saving his brothers and himself from penury and disgrace. Instead he'd cultivated an old lady's devotion, gone out drinking with engineers and laborers, and fallen head over heels for a direct, confident woman who thought him a bit of an idiot. Which, all things considered, he most likely was.

He let his head fall back against the hard sofa and sighed. If only Tessa Neville had been a jolly, middle-aged woman. If only Scott had been the calculating thief he'd pictured. If only Edward or

Gerard had come instead, and left him to continue his useless but happy life in London.

That last thought floated away as soon as it drifted through his mind. Edward and Gerard wouldn't have known the first thing to say to Tessa. She would have astounded Edward, horrified Gerard, and neither would have ever truly appreciated the first thing about her. He raised the brandy glass to his lips. He wasn't sorry Tessa was as she was, either. That was his entire trouble—he liked her too damned much just as she was, and he didn't know what to do about it. That was why he was sitting in the dark, drinking alone, trying to think how he could raise her spirits after the devastating blow of this afternoon. Perhaps he could go pound Hiram Scott into a bloody mess; that would satisfy two inclinations at once, and he had almost convinced himself it was a brilliant idea when there was a faint knock on the front door.

Tessa Neville stood on his doorstep, soaking wet. Her dark curls had escaped her bedraggled bonnet and hung in sodden ropes around her neck. Rain dripped off the tip of her nose. She looked up at him with those magnificent green eyes and said, "You were right."

"It shocks me as much as it shocks you," he said. "Come in out of the rain."

"How did you know?"

"A lucky guess," he said. "Did you walk here?" There was no carriage or horse behind her. It was a miracle she hadn't gotten lost or been swept into the stream by the gusting rain.

"I don't believe you. It wasn't a guess at all," she said.

"Come inside," he said again. "It's raining, you see."

"How did you know to ask?" She stayed on the doorstep as if she hadn't heard him. When he reached out and took her arm to pull her through the doorway, she didn't resist. "To get the engineer drunk? To—" She paused, then sneezed loudly.

"That's what wastrels do, my dear; we get drunk with anyone who cares to lift a pint with us." He peeled the cloak from her shoulders and tossed it back outside before closing the door. It couldn't get any more wet than it already was, lying out on the steps. He rooted in his pocket and pulled out a handkerchief. "Here."

"You sought out the engineer," she said, letting him fold her hand around the handkerchief when she made no move to take it. "Why?"

Charlie shrugged, unknotting her bonnet ribbons as she just stood there, pale and soaked and stunned. "Chance." He hadn't been looking for fault in the canal; he didn't care one way or the other about that. His hope had been to learn something about Scott, anything that would hint at why he sent Durham the blackmail letters. It was really nothing but chance that the engineer, thinking him a skeptical investor, had poured out his doubts and guilt instead.

"You're not a wastrel," she said in a low voice. Her eyes were unearthly in the low light. "You're not a scoundrel."

"I knew I would improve your opinion of me, given enough time." He got the bonnet off and smoothed a strand of wet hair from her forehead. Her skin was cool and damp under his hand. "You should get dry," he murmured, but his fingers stayed where they were, moving over her skin, touching her hair.

"Why did you come to Frome?" Her voice had dropped even further, into a husky register that did terrible things to his already faltering restraint. "Was it because of the canal?"

"Yes," he lied without hesitation. "Let—Let me ring for Barnes. You should have some tea . . . or coffee . . ."

"I don't want tea." She stared up at him with those stunning green eyes. Water dripped from her sodden clothes in a steady plip-plop on the floor, but neither one of them moved. "What would you do if I kissed you?" she whispered.

He looked at her for a long, long moment. Even dripping wet and almost blue with cold, she was beautiful. She was magnificent, in every way. "I would kiss you back," he replied. "And take you to my bed to ravish you for the rest of the night and most of tomorrow." Her lips parted, and he took a painful breath. "Which is why I should drive you back to The Golden Hind and put you safely into Mrs. Bates's hands. You need a hot bath and dry clothes and a cup of tea, and if you stay here . . ."

"Make love to me," she whispered. "Ravish me."

He held very still. "I don't believe it counts as ravishment if the victim requests it."

She looked up at him and touched his chest, her fingers light but steady on his waistcoat buttons. "I don't care what you call it. I want you."

His heart slammed into his ribs. His hands shook as he stroked her jaw, the side of her neck, the smooth slope of her collarbone. "Christ, Tessa.

A woman shouldn't say such things to a man . . ."

She blinked. Her fingers moved down his chest. "You want me, too." Charlie inhaled so hard his eyes closed.

"Mrs. Bates told me you weren't like other women," he said between his teeth. "I didn't know how right she was . . ."

She leaned into him, her breasts soft against his chest. "You don't want to bed me?"

He wanted her so badly, bed be damned. There was a sofa ten feet away, and a wall right behind her. He sucked in a deep, fortifying breath, trying not to push his hips forward, against hers, even though his pulse was screaming for just that. "You're upset. In the morning—"

She brushed her lips along his jaw. "Do you think I'm not myself?"

"You've just had a terrible shock," he tried to say. Holy Mother of God, her hand was still moving, lower across his stomach, and he wasn't a decent enough man to move away. "Don't . . . ah . . . regret . . ."

"I wanted you," she went on, sounding remarkably lucid and damnably certain, "even before you kissed me the other night. Please, Gresham . . . Charles—"

His mouth was on hers before she finished saying his name. This was Tessa, strong-willed and confident and bold. It seemed as though he had wanted her forever, and now that she admitted she wanted him . . . there wasn't a moment to be wasted in hollow protests.

Tessa had known when she slipped out of the inn in Frome that she was going to end up in

Gresham's bed. He wanted her, and she couldn't deny any longer that she wanted him. The sensible worries that had consumed her before had been eroded and undermined by that kiss, that breathless moment when it seemed as though her soul had finally found its mate. For two days she had tried not to think of it; souls did not have mates, and even if hers did, it certainly wouldn't be the wealthy, impossibly handsome, silver-tongued Earl of Gresham. Her soul's mate was far more likely to be a practical village merchant intent on stretching his every farthing. Instead, for reasons she didn't understand, she was falling, helplessly, deeper in love with Gresham every day. Every argument her head made, her heart ignored. She didn't want to fall in love. She hadn't even wanted to like him. And yet here she was, soaked to the skin, winding her arms around his neck and kissing him back as if her life depended on it.

He broke off the kiss with a groan. "You're soaking wet," he breathed, his fingers working at the buttons of her dress. "This dress has to go . . ."

Tessa nodded. "Yes, hurry." She began working at the lower buttons. She only dimly felt the chill of the rain now. It was desire, not cold, that made her fingers shake as she forced one button after another free of the fabric. His fingers were slower than hers, but he was also still kissing her neck and jaw, and when all the fastenings of the dress finally parted, there was no hesitation at all in the way he stripped the bodice from her.

"Even your shift is soaked," he muttered. Tessa nodded, struggling out of the clinging wet fabric as he peeled it down her body and went to work on her petticoat. Now she felt the chill again, in just her undergarments. His arm went around her waist as she shivered, but then he stopped. Tessa looked up into his face and felt her stomach knot up at the focused desire she saw there. Gently, almost reverently, he traced his fingertips down her throat to the curve of her breast, circling her erect nipple through the wet lawn of her shift.

"I've been waiting for this moment forever," he said in a dark voice.

Tessa licked her lips. "So have I." Her back arched involuntarily as he scraped his thumb over her flesh.

His gaze flew to meet hers. She had never seen him so intent and serious, and touched his cheek. "Are you that surprised?" she asked, trying to smile. "I was certain you knew . . ."

"That's it." He stopped stroking her breast only to sweep her into his arms, lifting her right out of the crumpled pile of her wet dress and petticoat. "I want you"—he kissed her as he strode through the hall—"naked"—and again at the foot of the stairs—"in my bed"—Tessa laughed, clinging to his neck as he paused, pressing her against the wall for a moment so he could nip her earlobe between his teeth before continuing up the stairs—"for many hours to come."

"I'm not leaving," she said as he opened a door upstairs and then kicked it closed behind them.

"Not for a very long time," he agreed, letting her feet down and spinning her around to unlace her corset. When it came loose, Tessa pulled it off but backed away.

"Take off the shift," he commanded.

She shook her head, winding her finger in the ribbon that held it closed. The fabric of her shift was plastered to her skin, so wet it was almost transparent. "Take off your coat. And waistcoat."

His grin flashed, dangerous and promising rather than lighthearted and easy, and he stripped off the garments.

"Now the boots," she said, backing toward the bed.

His dark gaze fixed on her, he complied, advancing on her all the while.

"The shirt," she whispered, her heart pounding in her ears. "The trousers."

"The shift," he retorted, whipping the shirt over his head.

She bumped into the bedpost, and reached behind her to curl her fingers around it for strength. He was beautiful, broad-shouldered and lean-waisted, his skin golden in the light of the lone lamp. His hair fell loose around his temples, ruffled by her own hands, but didn't hide the heat in his eyes. Without the elegant trappings of crisp cravat and tailored waistcoat, he wasn't the imposing earl, but just a man . . . who wanted her as desperately as she wanted him. With shaking hands, Tessa reached for the hem of her shift and tugged it off, casting it aside with a faint plop as it hit the floor.

His gaze sharpened into ravenous hunger. All trace of laughter and geniality vanished from his expression. "I should have brought another lamp."

She shifted her weight. "I could go get it."

That devil's grin touched his lips, and he looked at her with gleaming eyes. "You wouldn't make it to the door."

"Oh?" She made a motion as if to try it, but he caught her before she'd gone two steps.

"Do you really want to leave?" he whispered, brushing aside the wet tangle of her hair so he could skim his lips along the back of her neck. His hand moved down her arm to cup lightly around her breast. "Don't tease me any longer, Tessa . . ."

She shivered, as much from his words as from the way he was playing with her nipple again. "I haven't teased you at all."

He laughed softly, still touching her gently, his fingers tracing her hip bones, the edge of her ribs, the faint swell of her belly. His chest was broad and solid against her back. "You've driven me half mad."

"No, I meant I wasn't trying . . ." Her words scattered in a sigh as he wrapped both arms around her. He was still nuzzling the back of her neck, and every slight scrape of teeth on her skin made her quiver. "I didn't *mean* to tease you," she tried to explain.

"That's undoubtedly why it worked so well." He was kissing her shoulder now, his breath hot on her skin.

Tessa bit back a moan and wet her lips. "Charles," she said. It felt daring and intimate, using his name. Of course, she was naked, pressed up against his nearly naked body, eyeing his bed with longing. Intimacy felt right.

"Charlie," he whispered. "I despise the name Charles. It sounds so pompous."

Tessa laughed in spite of herself. "You are hardly pompous."

"I certainly hope not now." He flattened his palms on her waist and slid them down over her

hips, then leisurely back up the front of her body.
This time she couldn't hide the moan. "You're be-
witching," he said in a voice both soft and dark.
"Simply exquisite."

"Charlie . . ." Her knees were giving out as he
stroked his wicked, beautiful hands over her skin.
She managed to turn in his arms to face him,
touching his face with an unsteady hand. "Make
love to me . . ."

"Yes," he said as if roused from a dream. With
shocking ease he picked her up and carried her to
the bed. "Absolutely."

Restraint faded quickly in bed. Tessa had a
fleeting thought that he must be the very wick-
edest of rakes, because no man should be able to
wring such feelings from a woman. Every inch of
her skin seemed to grow more sensitive, as if her
nerves were straining toward him. It confounded
her. She was no virgin, and she'd thought she
knew what to expect. But with Charlie . . . He
turned her onto her back at one point, and she
realized she hadn't even noticed she was on her
stomach. He surrounded her, engulfed her, until
she had no capacity for thoughts or feelings that
didn't center on him, and her, and the way they
moved together.

When he rolled away from her abruptly, Tessa
struggled onto her side and raised her head.
"What's wrong?"

"Not a thing." He was sitting on the edge of
the bed, head bent, then stood and peeled off his
trousers. She'd almost forgotten he still wore them.
"Not one bloody thing."

Tessa stared. "No, I see not," she said without

thinking. The visual proof of his arousal made her more intensely aware of her own.

He caught hold of her knee and lifted her leg as he rejoined her on the bed. He knelt straddling her thigh, catching her knee under his elbow. "Yes, you should see," he murmured, devouring her, pinned beneath him. "If I just told you how much I want you, you wouldn't believe it . . ."

She blushed, although not with much shame. "I would."

Slowly he shook his head. His expression taut, he flicked a stray lock of hair from her temple, then traced a scorching path from her cheek, down her throat, over one breast, across the hollow of her waist, back to the dusky bit of curls between her legs. His gaze followed his fingers as he stroked her there. Tessa arched off the bed, the pleasure all the sharper after having ceased for a few minutes.

"Yes, that's how I want you," he said in a growl. "Writhing . . . begging . . . wild with wanting . . ."

"Please," she gasped, knowing she was all those things, and more: desperate for him to feel the same.

"Good God, yes." He shifted his weight and drove his full length inside her in one smooth stroke.

She gave a long gasping sigh. He inhaled deeply and rolled his head back. For a moment neither moved, as if too caught in the sensation of joining, of connection. When he opened his eyes and looked at her, Tessa saw her own lust and longing reflected in his eyes, as if his facade had fallen away to reveal his soul to her.

"Again," she said, her voice vibrating with desire. His mouth quirked, and he slowly flexed his hips, withdrawing before surging forward again. This time she gave a little cry. "Yes," she panted. "Again."

He pressed a hard kiss on her mouth. "And again." He planted his hands beside her shoulders and loomed over her. "And again . . . and again—my God." His voice grew rough and raspy as he matched his actions to his words. There was an agony, and a desperation, and at the same time an awed joy to his tone—or perhaps that was her own feelings again, swamping her senses. She groped for him, gripping his shoulder in wordless urging. Her heartbeat drowned out all thought as her blood flowed hotter, faster, seeming to sing in her veins. She hiked her leg over his hip, shamelessly opening herself even further, begging him to take more, reveling in the way his breath hitched as he did so, his strokes becoming longer and harder.

She opened her eyes, swimming in tears. Her skin felt taut over her bones, pulled tight by nerves and anticipation. With shaking hands she touched his cheek. His eyes met hers, black and deep like the night sky. "Charlie," she said with hardly a sound.

He lifted one hand and brought it to his mouth, swirling one fingertip between his lips. Then he slid that hand over her trembling belly, and touched her where their bodies joined.

Tessa sucked in air. She dug her heels into the mattress. One heartbeat—two—and it broke, that unbearably delicious tension inside her, in a pulsing wave. Charlie seized her knee where it curled around his waist, as if for balance. His breath huffed as he thrust twice more, and then he gasped and groaned as his body joined hers in climax.

For a while neither moved, Tessa because she had no desire to, and Charlie because . . . well, probably because she was clinging so tightly to him he couldn't. She didn't want to let go of him. Slowly, gingerly, he lowered himself, taking care not to crush her with his weight as he folded his arms around her. His breath was hot and fast on her shoulder when he pressed his lips to her collarbone, and she could see his pulse, as rapid as hers, in his throat. It was bliss. She let her eyes fall closed and a smile curved her mouth.

She must have dozed off, although little had changed when she opened her eyes again. Charlie still held her close, his head beside her shoulder. With his free hand he was lightly tracing delicate patterns over her skin, his touch as soft as a feather. From the hollow at the base of her throat, over the sensitive swell of her breast, across the lines of her ribs, into the dent of her navel. It was bold yet reverent, and so tender she felt another piece of her heart slip away.

Tessa knew she had no delicacy, no coyness in her. It wasn't in her to be artful. She didn't pretend that making love presaged a betrothal, or even a lengthy affair. She didn't know if tonight had affected him as if had her; but whatever her other failings, she didn't lie to herself, and she couldn't lie to him, not now.

"I'm not a widow," she whispered.

The man in her arms went still, his fingers pausing mid-stroke along the sensitive curve of her waist. "I see," he said after a moment. "Is Mr. Neville more accomplished with his pistols, or should I send Barnes to fetch a sword?"

A half-hysterical, half-despairing bubble of laughter lodged in her throat. "Neither." She wet her lips. "There is no Mr. Neville. There never was. I invented him. I've never been married."

He let out his breath. "That is a great relief. I swore off married women years ago."

She turned her head away, not wanting to know about the women he'd had before. She waited for him to ask why she'd lied, but he didn't. His fingers resumed playing along her skin, a caress so artless it grated on her conscience. "Don't you want to know why?"

He was quiet for a moment. "Do you want to tell me?"

No. She didn't want to talk about it ever again, but it wasn't really fair not to tell him. Not when they lay tangled in each other's naked arms in bed. The more the haze of hunger and lust cleared, the more uneasy she felt misleading him. "I was almost married," she began haltingly. "Once. Long ago. He seemed to understand me—my odd, unfeminine ways, as my family called them—and wasn't bothered by my manner."

"It has some perverse appeal," he murmured.

Tessa frowned. "Don't tease me now."

"Sorry," he said, kissing her shoulder. "Go on."

That kiss unnerved her. He was taking this very well; perhaps he wasn't paying attention. Or perhaps he didn't really care so much after all. "I believed his promises. He said we would have a per-

fect marriage, that we were made for each other.
I—and everyone else—believed him. Eugenie was
the only one who didn't warm to him, not that it
mattered to me then. Eugenie is very dear to me,
but she can be so silly at times, and I ignored all her
worrying and warnings because I thought he loved
me. I have always been rather determined . . ." She
faltered, feeling again the weight of her stupidity. "I
daresay even headstrong—"

"Surely not," he said.

She flushed, thinking again that he was laughing at her. "But I overheard him the night before
our wedding, talking with his brother. His brother
called me the oddest woman he'd ever met, and
instead of protesting, he laughed and agreed, and
said he would never have offered for me if not for a
few redeeming qualities. He said I had a shopkeep-
er's brain that would make his fortune, sufficient
connections to establish him in society, and just
enough beauty that he could tolerate bedding me."
To her disgusted horror, her voice began to tremble at the memory, and she ruthlessly quelled the
unexpected surge of hurt. "Within a year, he assured his brother, he would have trained me when
to speak and when not to, and keep me quietly at
home, where he might get a couple of brats on me
while he put my dowry and business sense to good
use in London. He, naturally, would keep his mistress in town, because no woman who thought as
much as I did could be satisfactory in bed."

For a long moment he said nothing. Tessa kept
her eyes resolutely fixed on the shadowy outline
of the closet door, slightly ajar. It cast a long
slender shadow over the wall toward the bed, a

dagger of darkness pointing right at her. All over again she felt like a naïve nineteen-year-old girl, fancying herself in love with a gentleman who understood her forward ways and respected her intelligence. She felt again the thrill of spouting off her thoughts on investments and money, not just household economies women were expected to learn but ideas about bank stocks and lease agreements. She remembered the attention Richard had paid her, and how blindly she had reveled in it. And most of all she felt the stabbing humiliation that she hadn't seen he didn't really care for her; he'd been using her all along, and she had been grateful to him for it.

"At least he recognized you were his superior, intellectually," said Charlie at last.

She frowned, then snapped her head around to see him. His face was ghostly pale in the moonlight, but his expression was enough to make her heart twist. "I wasn't," she whispered. "I let him seduce me. I thought I loved him."

His jaw hardened. "Don't mistake my next question; I'm ferociously glad you rid yourself of him. But . . . did your father or brother do nothing?"

"I didn't tell them. Only Eugenie knew—I told her about his plans for me, not my foolishness with him—and I swore her to secrecy. I was young, and I was hurt, and I wanted to hurt him back. I waited until we reached the church." She paused. "I wanted to make sure he never came back. My greatest fear, if I merely broke it off with him, was that my parents would attempt to persuade me to reconsider; no one else had ever shown the slightest interest in marrying me, and they had been so pleased . . . But I was so *angry*, Charlie. I wanted to humiliate him, as he had done to me, and so I waited until we stood at the altar, before my family and his, and when the vicar asked if I took him to be my husband, I said, very loudly and clearly, 'Never, for he is a whining boor without the wits of a sheep.' "

Charlie ducked his head. He cleared his throat. Then his shoulders began to shake. Alarmed, Tessa gripped his shoulder. "What?"

He rolled onto his back, laughing openly. He threw one arm around her and pulled her close to press a smacking kiss on her forehead. "If only I'd been there! I would have stood up and applauded!"

"No, you wouldn't have," she protested. "The vicar gasped out loud, and my mother screamed."

"I most certainly would have," he said, still shaking with laughter. "Good God! I trust that put him in his proper place."

"He turned as purple as a turnip," she said in a small voice. "But I was proud of myself. I handed my sister my prayer book and walked right out of the church, leaving my horrified family to deal with him. It was awful of me, don't you see?"

After a moment he got himself under control again. His fingers began stroking through her hair, and Tessa's eyes almost rolled back in her head. She'd never realized how much she liked being touched—or perhaps it was just the way he touched her. "Nonsense. Awful? I think it highly appropriate. He hadn't the wits of a sheep, if he thought you could be deposited quietly in the country and left to yourself."

"No, Richard really was quite intelligent. I'd

never have considered him if he'd been a fool . . ."

He laid a finger on her lips. "He was a damned fool," he said, his voice dark and hard. "Don't ever believe otherwise. Mathematical ability or a studious nature has no impact on whether one is foolish or not." His touch softened, and his fingertip trailed down the side of her jaw, lifting her face gently toward him. "Do you regret jilting him?"

She paused. "No, not really." She had never admitted that; she often wished she had thought of a cleverer way to do it, sparing her family the pain she had caused them, but deep down she still thought Richard deserved every iota of humiliation.

"Then you did the right thing. And I say he was an idiot," he whispered, brushing his lips over hers. "I would have applauded your telling him so."

Tessa kissed him back. She was the fool, not recognizing Richard Wilbur as the vain, arrogant arse he was. She had been fooled by his obvious intelligence, his handsome face, his flattering interest in her thoughts on business matters but never on anything else. If she hadn't been so naïve, she would have noticed that he cared very little for her feelings, or hopes, or even what sort of entertainments she preferred. He, rightly, had seen at once that she was an awkward young lady, not likely to attract other gentlemen's attention. Hadn't her mother all but said so, in her delight over his offer for Tessa's hand? *We thought you'd never find someone to suit you,* she'd said after Richard had spoken to her father. And Tessa, relieved beyond measure that she wouldn't be a spinster all her life as Louise used to tease her, had agreed. She'd been a complete fool, blinding herself to his faults because she wanted so desperately to be like other young ladies and not disappoint her parents.

And she clearly hadn't grown wiser. She'd thought Charles de Lacey was an idle, arrogant aristocrat who cared only for the fashionable cut of his coat. Would she never learn anything about men? He had seen the truth in Mr. Scott's canal scheme when she, with all her careful examination of account books and engineering plans, had not. He had saved her from making a terrible mistake—she, who'd always had such pride in her own judgment and perception. He made her feel admired and respected and even beautiful—the way she'd always imagined—dreamed—a woman should feel.

"Tell me about the fictitious Mr. Neville," he murmured. "I hope he was kinder to you."

She smiled. "Far better. He was serious and quiet, and never vexed me at all. And then he tragically died. He was my great-aunt's idea. My parents sent me to her to recover my nerves after—"

"Very wise of them," he said when her words abruptly ran out. "My father merely imposed his will, when I wished to marry a girl he didn't approve of." He paused, and Tessa darted a surprised glance at him. It was too dark to see his expression clearly, but she sensed his light tone was contrived. "He was right in the end, of course, but I didn't realize it until long after I'd taken myself off to London in high dudgeon."

"To recover your nerves?" she said, and he laughed, a bit ruefully.

"My pride, at least."

Tessa thought about that. Being sent to Scotland

to her great-aunt had allowed her to do the same.
A year away from her family and the gossip had
given her time to recover her confidence and dull
her rage at Richard, and then she had rebuilt her
life as she wished it to be: she had left a girl in
disgrace, and came back a free woman, even if the
widowhood had been a lie. "Pride is important,
too," she said softly.

He was quiet for a long moment. "It can be," he
finally replied, almost too quietly for her to hear.

They lay for a while, touching each other, content to be together, watching the moonlit shadows
sway and wave across the ceiling. The rainstorm
had died out, leaving behind the peaceful fresh air
that follows a storm. She felt the same way, as if a
storm had blown through her and left a refreshed
calm in its place. She couldn't recall the last time
she'd ever felt this way—if, indeed, she ever had.

"How long can this last?" she whispered. "I fear
I will wake at any moment, and find it was just a
dream."

" 'Tis not a dream." He kissed her shoulder.

"No." She turned her head to face him, silver-
gilded in the moonlight. "But I fear it cannot last."

His face grew still. "Why not?"

Tessa opened her mouth, then turned away. "I've
finished what I came to do in Frome. I'm expected
in London—as are you, I expect, eventually."

"Ah." The bed ropes creaked as he rolled over.
"Yes, I suppose I am." For a long moment he was
silent, then went on. "I've not been candid with
you. I, too, had a particular reason for coming to
Frome."

"Of course," she said, puzzled. "The canal."

"Not precisely." He heaved a sigh, and then sat up as if he would get out of bed. "My father died recently."

"Oh," she mouthed in soft regret. "I'm sorry . . ."

He waved one hand. "I hadn't spoken to him in over a decade. We didn't . . . get on well." He hesitated and she didn't know what to say. Tessa knew she'd been a puzzle to her parents, especially to her father—*What sort of girl thinks about money more than gowns?* Papa had wondered in bewilderment—but she'd never doubted they loved her and cared for her well-being, even after her lunatic behavior on her wedding day. What sort of man had Charlie's father been, not to speak to his son for ten years?

"When he died, my brothers and I learned he'd had a secret." Again he paused, his jaw hard. "A terrible secret, actually, as it could cost us our inheritance, and me, the title."

Tessa sucked her lower lip between her teeth. That was a terrible secret indeed, if it could cost him his earldom. Instinctively she began thinking of ways to solve the problem. "Can it be fixed? Or perhaps hidden? If no one knows this secret, how can it harm you?"

He glanced at her, wryly amused. "You really don't read the gossip papers, do you?" She shook her head, and he sighed. "My father was the Duke of Durham, Tessa. I'm the eldest, the heir to it all . . . except that my father had a clandestine marriage sixty years ago, and no one knows what happened to the woman. If she still lived when my father married my mother, I could be pronounced a bastard, and heir to nothing."

Her mouth had fallen open halfway through this explanation. "A duke?" she repeated. "You're a duke?"

"If all goes well, yes. I've got to prove it before a hearing of the Committee for Privileges in Parliament before the Crown will grant the title." He looked at her expression and gave a short laugh. "Good Lord, it's not as bad as that."

"No, no," she said, scrambling to adjust her thoughts. "I never said it was bad—"

"Your expression said it all."

"Well, why are you calling yourself the Earl of Gresham if you're really a duke?" she retorted, aggrieved. "If I'd known you were a duke . . ."

"What then?" he prompted when she stopped speaking and scowled. "You would have been kinder to me? Been dazzled by my superior status and curtsied in polite awe when we met?"

"Don't be silly," she said, flustered, and he laughed.

"I'm not sorry, and I refuse to apologize if it would have meant any changes in the way you behaved toward me." His gaze grew hot and wicked as it dropped, lingering over her exposed breasts. "In any way," he repeated in that low, dark voice that made her heart leap.

Tessa looked away, trying to hide her brilliant blush and resist the urge to throw herself at him again. When he looked at her that way, he wasn't the vexing Lord Gresham—or Duke of Durham—but Charlie, sinfully attractive and maddening and so endearing it made her chest hurt.

"I haven't got the dukedom yet," he went on in a less seductive tone. "I suppose I haven't really got the earldom, either, but I've been called Gresham since I was born. A year ago someone began sending my father letters, first claiming knowledge of this long-missing first wife and then demanding five thousand pounds in exchange for his silence. My father reacted in his usual manner: he sent a horde of investigators to find the miserable swindler and put a swift and bitter end to him. Unfortunately for Durham, they failed, and even more unfortunately for me and my brothers, my father never told us about any of it. We didn't learn of it until he was dead, and now it's on our heads to prove ourselves legitimate, or lose everything."

She thought for a moment. "Was the woman from Frome?"

Approval flashed in his eyes. "I have no idea."

"No?" She frowned. "Then why did you come here? It's hardly a scenic sort of place . . ." She looked up. "Mr. Scott."

Charlie nodded once. "I knew you would deduce that. He's the blackmailer."

Tessa's mouth dropped open. "No! He is? How do you know?"

"My brother Gerard tracked the blackmail letters to Bath, where two were posted. A clerk in the post office positively identified Hiram Scott as the man who sent them."

"It's incredible," she protested. "Why on earth would he do that—in public view, where anyone might observe him? Even my brother William, who is the mildest of gentlemen, would have killed him for such a thing."

"Durham would have retaliated, yes," he said with an odd, twisted little smile, making her think he meant his father would have unleashed the wrath of God upon Mr. Scott.

"Well! I never expected that. I thought he must have some information about the missing woman, or . . ." Her voice trailed off as she thought hard. "Oh," she whispered as the truth dawned on her. "Of *course* . . ."

"What?"

"And I met Mr. Scott in Bath," she went on, thinking aloud. "At the York Hotel, right where you were staying—did you expect that, or was it happy coincidence?" She waved one hand as Charlie said nothing, looking suddenly wary. "I wonder you didn't think I was involved, once you saw me meeting him. And all this time I thought you were merely annoyed by what I said!" She glanced at him and smiled broadly at his disbelieving expression. "I've wondered for so long, but it all makes sense—finally! I see why you took to Eugenie so quickly! And you came to Frome to find Mr. Scott, but you really did only want an introduction from me," she went on, putting all the pieces together with great satisfaction. "I knew there was something, some reason why you'd singled us out for your attentions, and I was right!"

He began to laugh, harder and harder until she thought he would be sick.

"Oh, really, I don't think it's as amusing as that," she said in reproof. "Why are you laughing?"

Quick as a cat, he rolled over, pinning her under him. "You," he said, still chuckling. "You." He kissed her, a deep stirring kiss that ended with her arms around his neck and his hands roving beneath the bed linens twisted around her.

"Tessa darling, you amaze me," he murmured. "I've spent hours plotting how to keep you from discovering I suspected you of being involved in blackmail and that I followed you to Frome for the sole purpose of unmasking Scott. I should have known you would puzzle it out no matter what I did."

"I'm not offended," she explained, very reasonably, although her breathing hitched as his wicked hands stroked more slowly over her skin. "It makes perfect sense; of course you should have suspected us. I suppose I didn't help, did I, by trying to avoid you?"

"Not at all." He was kissing her neck. "It was very unsporting of you to avoid me."

"Of course, if I had decided to blackmail you, you wouldn't have found me out as easily as that," she pointed out. "I wouldn't have been so foolish as to let anyone see *me* posting the letters, and I certainly would have collected the funds. Five thousand pounds is a large sum, and if you put it into the right investments—"

"You would have taken me for everything I had," he agreed. "And my only revenge . . ." He tugged the twisted sheet out of the way and raised her knee. " . . . is this." He lowered his head, pressing soft kisses against her throat, slipping slowly down the length of her body.

Tessa sucked in an unsteady breath. She was wrong. He was taking *her* for all she had: all her sense, all her reason, every ounce of her justified restraint. With one wicked kiss he stole them all and locked them out of her reach, leaving her defenseless against his sly smile and knowing touch and the scorching look in his eyes when he told her he wanted her without saying a word. And the frightening part was, she liked it. It thrilled her. She didn't feel odd or awkward when he looked at her with that smile, and when he kissed her like this . . . His tongue swirled over her navel and she quivered, grasping at the bedclothes in search of anything to tether herself to solid ground.

"When . . ." she gasped. "When did you decide I had nothing to do with it?"

His mouth was hot and soft against her belly. "When I met you in Frome," he murmured.

"Because I . . ." She lost her train of thought as his fingers ran up her leg, curving gently under her knee and easing her legs apart. "Was it because I introduced you to Scott?"

"No." He was laughing at her, she could tell from his voice, but only a small part of her brain registered it. And it was much too small a thing to protest now, when his teeth nipped at the tender flesh of her inner thigh. "Stop thinking about it, please."

"Because I allowed you to come along on my tour at the ironworks?" she persisted.

"No." His fingertip ran down the furrow between her legs, and her eyes rolled back in her head.

"Because . . . Because I . . ." She sucked in her breath in a long, aching gasp as his tongue flicked over the same path his fingers had just taken.

"Tessa," he said, looking up at her through the disheveled waves of his hair, falling over his brow. He was the most beautiful man she had ever seen, braced on his elbows, his arms forcing her legs apart, leaving her wantonly exposed to his eyes and his lips and his tongue and whatever sinful plans he had for her.

"Yes?" Her voice barely worked for the desire humming through her veins; she could almost hear the roar of it in her ears.

"Stop thinking." He bent his head again, and this time she did.

Chapter 15

Tessa opened her eyes to a strange ceiling and frowned, wondering why it was different today. It took a moment for remembrance to flood back, but it did, in intense, heated waves. Hardly daring to breathe, she darted a look sideways, and saw Charlie, asleep on his stomach, his head pillowed on his arms. His dark hair fell around his temples in rumpled waves, his eyelashes short and dark against his lean cheeks. His wicked, perfect mouth looked softer, less lively but no less dangerous, without its usual grin. If she hadn't been persuaded that he was the handsomest man she'd ever seen, this sight would have done it. Her stomach dropped even as her heart skipped a beat, at the memory of what they had done last night.

Even worse was what she had done. She had gone out at night, alone, in the rain, to the lodging of an unmarried man. She had kissed him and told him to ravish her. She had spent the night in his bed, without any attempt at discretion. And now it was bright out already, leaving no hope that she might creep back into Frome unnoticed. She began to tremble at the ramifications. William would be horrified at her. Louise would disown her in a storm of tears and anguish. Even Eugenie would look at her with pain and regret, kept from fainting only by her wild hopes that this might entice Lord Gresham to offer to marry her.

She darted another glance at Charlie, this time of longing. God have mercy on her, but she no longer felt like protesting Eugenie's hopes. When he laughed at the way she humiliated Richard Wilbur, she had almost burst into tears—she, who never cried. That rash fit of spite had haunted her for nine years. Her family had feared she was unbalanced; at times she thought they still did. Her father had to pay off Richard over his public embarrassment and broken marriage contract. She was neither permitted nor invited to go anywhere for a full year, as everyone they knew whispered about her uncertain temperament. And she'd been so angry, she hadn't even cared for several months.

But the stain lasted longer than her anger at Richard's deception. When her parents had decided to send her away to Great-Aunt Donella in Scotland, she hadn't protested, even though it still galled her that Richard had been judged the wounded party and she was deemed mad. She'd gone off to Scotland, and when she came back a year later, she brought with her a fictitious husband, sadly dead of pneumonia from the Scottish mists. Great-Aunt Donella supported the story—Mr. Neville had been her idea, after all—and Tessa's family accepted it with relief. A widow was allowed to be quiet at home; a widow was permitted to do things spinsters, deranged or not, were never allowed to do.

And most of all a widow was respectable, while a jilt never was.

Tessa had persuaded herself that things had come out well enough, since her disgrace meant her father finally allowed her to take over some of his accounts. Her mother had done it for years, but her health was failing by then; within a year she had passed away and Tessa was running Rushwood. When her father died, William was relieved and pleased for her to continue. If she had to be odd and unpredictable, she might as well make herself useful in some way, reasoned everyone in the family. For almost eight years now, that had been her life: the estate, the accounts, managing William's investments. That suited her, and she had thought it always would. Only now did she admit how lonely it was at times, or how wonderful it was to have that moment of feeling appreciated, admired, understood by someone else. By Charlie.

But that was all wrong. She knew better than anyone else how dangerous it was to give in to strong emotions. This could end as badly as her affair with Richard had.

She inhaled a deep breath for courage, and wriggled carefully from the bed, not wanting to wake him. She slipped back into her shift, stiff and wrinkled from a night on the floor, and had a moment of panic when she couldn't find her dress. She couldn't remember exactly when Charlie had peeled it off her. On the stairs? Outside the door? Tessa pressed her hands to her mouth as more memories unfurled across her mind's eye. Goodness; she had no idea.

Stay calm, she told herself. She had been wearing the dress, as well as a cloak, when she arrived; therefore, they must both still be in the house. Somewhere. With a little cautious searching, she located a silk wrapping gown and pulled it on. It was luxuriously soft, and it smelled of Charlie, coffee and brandy and tobacco. Tessa couldn't resist the urge to press her nose to the collar and breathe deeply. How had she never noticed before how heavenly a man could smell?

She tiptoed across the room and eased open the door. When she first glanced out, the corridor was clear, so she stepped out, stopping to close the door as quietly as possible. Then she turned toward the stairs and nearly screamed when she found a man standing in front of her.

"Good morning, madam," he said with a bow. He held a steaming pitcher in one hand, and a spotless towel was draped over his arm. "May I offer my assistance?"

"Oh—ah—well, perhaps," she said, clutching the banyan closed at her neck. "Have you found a dress, by any chance?" Her face burned as she realized what the servant must be thinking—and that it was all true.

"Indeed, madam, I did." His face didn't betray the slightest scorn or contempt. "I took the liberty of hanging it up to dry, and then sponging the mud off the hem. I shall have it ironed and returned as soon as possible."

Tessa cleared her throat. "Oh, really, that's not necessary, to iron it . . . Could you just bring it now?"

He looked at her, but bowed again. "As you wish." He stepped past her and went into the bedroom she had just left. Tessa hesitated, but without her dress she wasn't going anywhere. Standing in the hall, where she could be discovered by all the other servants, wearing Charlie's dressing gown . . . She edged back into the bedroom doorway.

"There you are." His voice made her freeze. Her eyes flew to the bed. Charlie lay on his back now, arms folded behind his head, smiling his lazy, seductive smile at her.

Tessa fought down the sudden urge to throw off the dressing gown and leap back into bed with him. She glanced at the servant, who had set down his pitcher and towel and was tidying up the room. She blushed at the disarray of the room, which gave every indication that two people had torn each other's clothes off and spent the night in sinful debauchery. "Yes."

"Come here." He crooked his fingers at her. "Barnes is going to make a pot of coffee—real coffee, not the swill they have in Frome."

"No, I—I think I should return home." She cast another awkward glance at the servant. "Thank you for taking me in last night, when I became lost in the rain."

Charlie met her gaze evenly. He knew as well as she did that Barnes, of all people, wouldn't believe that tale. "Barnes would never breathe a word of anything improper he might witness in my employ."

"Absolutely not, my lord," said the valet promptly. "Not that I ever see anything improper in your household."

"Precisely. And what sort of host would I be if I let a woman who caught a chill in the rain last night walk over a mile into Frome this morning?"

Tessa bit her lip, and Charlie sat up. "Barnes makes very good coffee. Not quite as superb as my chef in London, but highly palatable."

"I do my best, my lord," murmured the valet.

"Go to it, then," he said, watching Tessa. She looked scrumptious, wearing his dressing gown with her hair streaming down her back in wild waves. If she'd stop watching Barnes as though the man were a constable come to arrest her, Charlie was sure he could get her back into bed for a proper morning greeting. And then there would be coffee. "Make it strong, and bring some treacle with it."

Barnes slipped silently from the room. Tessa edged away from the door to let him out, but then didn't come any closer. Charlie threw back the blankets and got out of bed to fetch her. "Were you planning to sneak out on me?" he asked, closing the door with one hand and reaching for her with the other.

"Yes," she said, staring in fascination at his chest.

"Ah." He took her hand and pressed his lips to her knuckles, then to her palm. "Why?"

"Charlie, you're naked . . ."

"Yes." He kissed the fluttering pulse on the inside of her wrist. "Do you find that objectionable?"

Her gaze dropped lower. He loved the way her face stilled in open desire when she looked at him. "No."

He smiled. "Then come back to bed."

"Eugenie will be worried," she said, letting him lead her.

"So she will be." He left her beside the bed and went to a writing table across the room, coming back with a pen, a bottle of ink, and a sheet of paper. "Lie down."

"Why?"

"So I can write her a note, easing all her fears," he explained reasonably, tugging her hands away from where she still clutched the dressing gown closed. "You could be more cooperative. Remember this is for Mrs. Bates's peace of mind."

"I don't think this is the most efficient way to write a letter," she said, but she let him lead her to the bed.

"How your mind works," he exclaimed, divesting her of the dressing gown and then the shift. "Who said I must be efficient about it?"

She was trying not to smile as he pressed her back until she lay on the bed, her hair fanned across the discarded dressing gown like a mermaid's, caught out of water. "I don't think this is a *decent* way to write a letter."

"Hold still, or my penmanship will be deplorable." He laid the paper on the flat plane of her belly and set the ink between her breasts.

"Charlie," she said, before her voice dissolved into a long sigh as he leaned over her to swirl his tongue over one nipple.

"Yes?" He continued as he was, and she even cupped her hand behind his head as he sucked lightly on her flesh.

"You're going to spill the ink," she gasped as he moved to her other breast.

"Indeed," he murmured, groping for the pen. With a magnificent effort, he sat back on his heels and surveyed her, spread out before him like a pagan sacrifice. "Very well, if you insist . . ."

He nudged her knees apart and moved between them. She shifted to allow him, and even linked her ankles behind his back. "Now I can begin." He uncapped the ink and dipped his pen, settling his elbows comfortably astride her thighs. "'Dear Mrs. Bates,'" he read aloud as he wrote, "'have no fear for Tessa. She is safe with me.'"

She laughed.

"Be still," he scolded her. "You'll smear the ink."

"It tickles," she protested.

"Good." He lowered his head to kiss the middle of her belly. "You ought to be tickled more."

"With an ink pen?"

"Then let me finish." He dipped the pen again. "'After wandering out in the rain, she happened by my cottage, and I took her in so she wouldn't catch pneumonia,'" he wrote. He'd have to seal this letter before Tessa saw it, for his handwriting was a misshapen scrawl at best. His eyes were drawn more to her pert breasts, cradling the ink pot, and to the easy, almost dreamy look on her face as she stared at the ceiling and idly twirled a lock of hair between her fingers. She looked so happy—with him. She was also lying naked on his bed, partially wrapped in his dressing gown, which was sinfully seductive. He needed to finish this letter immediately. "'As soon as I am satisfied she is in no danger, I will return her to you in Frome,'" he added to the letter, ignoring the splatter of ink on the last word and signing his name with a flourish.

"In no danger." There was a smile in her voice as she twisted her head to look at him. "With you?"

"You are in very great danger of being thoroughly ravished before you have coffee," he told her, capping the ink and removing paper and pen to the floor behind him. "I didn't think it prudent to say that to Mrs. Bates, though."

Her smile bloomed, mysterious and coy. "I didn't even ask for coffee."

"Good." His answering grin felt wolfish. "Barnes takes a long time to prepare it."

He bent over her again, no paper or ink in the way. This time he was in no rush. Today, in the bright light of day, he had all the time he wanted to explore her skin, as smooth and fine as fresh milk. He found the small mole on her right knee, and kissed it until she laughed. He studied the lofty arch of her foot, and how her toes curled when his fingers brushed them. He was entranced by the hollow of her navel, the delicate lines of her ribs, the plump curves of her breasts.

He supposed he spoke, effortless mindless words that spilled out of him, not to seduce or impress but only to marvel at her. At times she murmured replies, although he was too lost in a haze of desire to distinguish the words; all he recognized was the tone, the meaning. She liked what he did. She was every bit as lost in him as he was lost in her. For once, there was no argument from her lips. Everything he whispered, he did, and she responded to it like straw to a flame.

It was almost ironic, really; the most idle rake in London found himself undone by a woman who knew no artifice, who practiced no seductions, who told the truth even when it was the foolish thing to do. She opened her eyes, her pupils so wide with arousal her startling eyes were almost black, and Charlie knew that any chance he'd had of letting her go was gone.

"Do you want me?" he breathed. "Here?" His fingers ran up her thigh, into the dark curls there, until she convulsed with a gasp.

"Yes." Her nails dug into his wrist as she tried to pull him closer.

"Now?"

She nodded, a feverish flush overtaking her face. "Yes!"

Sweat broke out on his brow. He was in real danger of coming right now, his erection so hard it hurt. But he loved hearing her voice, breathless and throbbing with need. Tessa, so in control, so poised, so sure of herself, melted into a puddle of the same incoherent lust that was drowning him. He didn't want to blink and miss a moment of it.

He pushed two fingers inside her, flicking with his thumb. She made a strangled squeak, and then her own hands covered his. Rocking her hips back and forth, she guided his hand, showing him how to touch her, inside and out. His vision narrowed down to that sight, and he almost stopped breathing.

"Now," he growled, yanking his hand free. With one arm he swept her up, toppling her over onto her hands and knees. So eager his hand shook, he pressed the head of his cock against the soft, wet entrance to her body. "My God," he choked, sliding deep. "Tessa . . ."

"Yes," she sighed, bowing her spine, driving her hips against his. He held her still a moment, just to get himself back under control, and then he didn't, holding her by the waist as he stroked into her. When she dropped her head and her shoulders dipped, he paused only long enough to roll her onto her back. He wanted to see her face when she reached completion—he could see it coming, from the way her breath shifted and her arms tensed—

And then her eyes squeezed shut and she threw back her head, her lips parting in a sensual, soundless cry of release. Charlie barely had time to catch his breath before the convulsion of her body pitched him right over the edge into his own release.

For a while he thought it had killed him. There was a buzzing in his ears and his lungs seemed to have stopped. When he finally dragged in a full breath, it was Tessa he inhaled—the passion-damp scent of her skin, the faint hint of rosemary in her hair, the fresh bite of rainwater. Her head was turned away from him, but he could see her profile when he forced his eyes open, sated and content and even blissful. Warmth bubbled up inside him, bringing a smile to his lips. He relaxed, brushing a light kiss on the pulse at the side of her throat.

Even God couldn't help him now. He was absolutely lost.

Chapter 16

By the time Barnes brought the tray with coffee, Charlie had dragged the blankets back over them. Tessa wasn't sure she would ever move again, but she jumped like a startled deer when the valet knocked lightly at the door. Charlie only grinned as she grabbed for the covers and sank still lower beneath them when the valet came in bearing a tray covered with dishes and a pot whose fragrance made her poke out her nose like a hound on the scent of a fox.

"What sort of coffee is that?" she asked after Barnes had set the tray down and bowed out of the room.

"The best sort," Charlie replied, getting out of bed and going to the tray. "Not merely palatable, but delectable. Do you like it sweet?"

"A little."

He gave her a raffish grin. "Excellent. Prepare to be overwhelmed by ecstasies of delight."

Tessa laughed as she sank back into the pillows. She already had been overwhelmed by ecstasies of delight, and they had nothing to do with coffee of any kind. She watched Charlie, still naked, pour and prepare two cups of coffee. He was beautiful, long-limbed, strong and lean, his skin golden in the morning light. His dark hair fell in rumpled waves around his neck, sliding forward to hide his face as he poured milk into the cups. Helplessly her eyes feasted on his arm, how the muscles moved as he stirred, how his fingers gave a little tap to the spoon before setting it down. He twisted, reaching for something else on the tray, and her gaze slid down the strong lines of his back. She admired his legs, strong and muscled from years of riding, and thought of how those legs felt tangled with her own. How his feet, so much bigger than her own and yet elegant as well, gently batted hers under the covers. He stooped to collect the coffee, and she almost leered at his backside, as firm and perfect as the rest of him. It made her blush to think how she was lying here ogling him, until he cast a simmering look over his shoulder.

"Are you enjoying this, madam?"

"Yes," she said. "It's not every morning a gentleman makes me coffee."

He turned fully around, as aware of his beauty as she was. "Your passion for coffee must exceed my own, judging from the look on your face."

She blushed hotter. "It isn't every morning a handsome, naked gentleman prepares my coffee. I find I like it exceedingly."

He laughed. "And you haven't even tasted the coffee!"

For the way he looked at her, and the way he settled back in bed so comfortably beside her, drawing her close to his side with one arm, Tessa thought he could serve her water drawn straight from the Thames and she would enjoy it. He handed her a steaming cup, and she smiled, raising it to her lips for a sip.

"Well?" prodded Charlie a moment later, watching her from beneath lazy eyelids with a knowing smile.

"It is divine," she sighed, sipping more. "More than divine. I've never tasted the like!"

"Good," he murmured, raising his own cup.

"How did you learn to make this?" She inhaled over the cup before taking another long, rapturous sip. "I could drink the whole pot!"

"Now I have spotted your weakness," he said. "Ah, yes, Barnes did rather well today. Almost as well as Gilbert, my London chef."

"Your chef makes better coffee?" she exclaimed. "Good heavens, how?"

"I have no idea, but I pay him a fortune to continue making it." Charlie leaned his head back against the wall and sighed, feeling exceptionally pleased with the world today. Tessa, curled warm and soft, against his side, moaned with sensual pleasure every few minutes as she sipped his mixture of coffee, treacle, and whipped milk. Barnes was a clever man, to bring everything ready in separate pots so he could have the glory of mixing it himself for her. Charlie rather liked that look of incredulous admiration on her face, as if he'd hung the moon and stars for her.

She finished her coffee and looked into the empty cup with a sad sigh. "You really are the most wicked fellow."

"Ah, but you seem to enjoy this bit of wickedness."

"I do," she admitted readily.

"You also seemed quite pleased last night."

"Vanity," she accused him with a smile and a faint blush. "You know I was."

"I like making you happy."

Her smile turned dreamy. "You do."

His heart constricted. He looked at her lying easy and relaxed in his bed, her hair wild around her bare shoulders and her eyes soft and glowing—at him. She looked at him not with coquetry and calculation, not as an earl, heir to a wealthy dukedom, but with warm, open affection. And the realization that she cared for him, not for his title, struck him like a blow to the chest. He wanted to make her happy forever. He wanted to see her look at him this way for the rest of his life. She saw him as he was, and admired him all the same. When he was with Tessa, he wanted to be a better man, even as he wanted to make her laugh and make her sigh in pleasure and hold her next to him every minute of the day.

"I must return to Frome," she said, although without the stiff, uneasy tone she'd used the last time she said it. This time it sounded more like regret. "Eugenie will be wild with worry."

Charlie took a deep breath. Barnes had sent off his letter to Mrs. Bates, who—he hoped—would understand its real meaning. And whatever damage was done by Tessa's overnight stay at Mill Cottage would hardly be undone by her return to town now. "I was hoping you'd stay. I would like your help."

Her eyes opened, bright and curious. "With what?"

He smiled grimly. "Exposing Hiram Scott."

"Is this all?" She surveyed the stack of cursed marriage registers with a distinct lack of apprehension. By the time the coffee was gone and they ate breakfast, Barnes had produced her frock, looking quite as good as new. Charlie offered to help her dress, but his true motives must have been plain; she batted his hand away, laughing that he would spend the entire day in bed when there was work to be done. It was shocking, the effect her attitude had on him. Once he explained what he had to do, Tessa was ready to get down to it, and strangely enough, Charlie even found himself filled with renewed determination.

He flipped one journal open. He had explained everything to her, about the clues his father left and the progress Gerard had made, the role they suspected Scott had played in their disgrace, and how he needed proof to establish his right to the dukedom. He would have told her everything anyway, but it had struck him that of all the people he knew, Tessa was the most likely to be able to help. She had a logical mind and the diligent patience he lacked. Even the full revelation about Scott only made her mouth tighten and her eyes flash, though the man had done her almost as great a harm. And as he should have expected, she was ready to tackle the problem at once, which was what brought them out into the sunshine and the little table where he'd first offered her lemonade, ready to face the wedding registers—but this time together. And it didn't seem so ominous anymore. "They are sixty years old or more, faded from age and half ruined with damp. What I'm looking for may not be in them at all. So you see it's really not as simple as finding an entry for new stockings in the household accounts."

"But there are only eight, and you've already scoured three. Does Mr. Scott know about these?" She took the chair he pulled out for her.

"I've no idea." Charlie looked at the registers again and remembered his brother's tale of discovering them buried in a stable in a remote country village. "I believe he does not."

"Excellent." She gave a rather vindictive smile as she picked up one register and opened it. "Then he will have no suspicion we're about to trap him."

"If he has any indication of it, he's hidden it remarkably well."

"Snakes never have telling expressions."

He chuckled in spite of himself. "You've taken his actions remarkably in stride."

She calmly turned the pages and settled back to read. "Why do you think I'm helping you ruin him?"

Charlie stared at her a moment, then burst out laughing again. "God help me if I ever cross you!"

"As if you haven't already done so, many times!" she exclaimed in apparent affront, but he could see the smile lurking at the corners of her mouth.

"Ah yes. I arrived in Bath. A grievous sin, indeed." He grinned at her stern glare. "And then I was kind to Mrs. Bates."

"You beguiled her with sherry."

"An *excellent* sherry," he noted. "I only beguile with the best temptations."

"Scoundrel," she said under her breath, but the word trembled with laughter.

"It was all merely a ploy to make your acquaintance," he added.

She glanced up at him, a thin frown on her brows, as if she couldn't decide whether he was teasing or not. "You didn't know who I was."

"I knew Hiram Scott had left you a letter, and that you were anxiously awaiting it," Charlie replied. "That was enough for me."

"You could have simply asked about him." With a roll of her eyes she went back to scrutinizing the page in front of her.

Charlie leaned forward. He loved the way she bit her lower lip when concentrating. He loved the little furrow between her brows. "Where's the challenge in that?"

Tessa raised her brows at him. She waved one hand at the dingy marriage registers on the table. "Haven't you got enough challenges at the moment?"

Charlie's grin faded. "Yes." He had forgotten that he was running out of time, with no more proof of his legitimacy than when he left London. He couldn't decipher Scott's actions. He hadn't located Dorothy, nor found any clue of where to search for her. He'd barely made his way through three of the eight marriage registers. At any day, word could arrive from Edward that he must return to London to face the Committee for Privileges as they decided whether he was the rightful duke. His only choice now was to confront Scott and hope he could break the man's thus-far-unshakable composure. If he couldn't, he would have nothing to prove beyond all doubt that he was his father's legitimate heir. Without proof, he could still be stripped of his title and expectations, and now, more than ever before, he found that thought intolerable.

For a long while they worked in silence, supplied with tea and scones by Barnes. Charlie finally reached the end of his register, tossing it onto the far side of the table with a muttered curse. "I beg your pardon," he said when Tessa's head came up sharply. "Very ill-mannered of me."

"Not ducal at all." Her clear green eyes danced.

He smiled faintly. "Unworthy of the title, am I? Unfortunately, darling, I've no other choice. I can't think of anything else I could be."

"Not a lawyer," she said. "Or a bookkeeper." Charlie shuddered, exaggerated for effect but fully in accord with his sentiments regarding those two occupations. "Hmm." She tilted her head, looking amused now. "What could a gentleman be?"

"I fear to think what you will recommend." He picked up another register and made a show of opening it. "I feel miraculously energized for the search, now that you have clarified my alternatives."

"You could do whatever you wished to," she said.

He laughed a little bitterly. "I have it on good authority that being a gentleman of leisure, but without title or fortune, is a rather hard life."

"Well, you might not be able to continue at leisure," she conceded. "But there is nothing wrong with making something of yourself. Even titled gentlemen have done it. The Duke of Bridgewater began the mania for canals by conceiving the idea and carrying it through. That is a skill as much as being able to design and build one."

"He had his title and fortune to fall back upon, should his canal have failed," observed Charlie. "To say nothing of some coal mines. And I thought we were done speaking of canals. God knows I've heard enough of them."

"It was merely the first instance that came to my mind. I believe too often gentlemen are encouraged to think they need do nothing more than indulge in idleness and revelry. As if being born to wealth entitles one to do nothing with it!" She shook her head, that little frown line back between her brows. "It's such a waste."

"How revolutionary you are."

"Oh! Not really. I just think it's a shame for men of education and breeding, sent on Grand Tours to burnish their minds and possessed of enough wealth that they needn't go hungry or cold, to spend their time gambling and drinking and chasing other men's wives. These are the men who should be engaged in scientific pursuits, who can afford to ponder great difficulties and questions and who are best suited to discover new ideas." Tessa lifted one shoulder as Charlie looked at her in astonishment. "They ought to leave something to the world other than the numeral after their name."

"There is a great responsibility with that numeral," he replied, wincing at her words. What would anyone remember about him, beyond his rank as the eighteenth Duke of Durham? Assuming he did in fact become the Duke of Durham.

"Enormous," she agreed, reading again. "My brother is a viscount, you know."

"Some would say it is all-encompassing. A duke

must sit in Parliament, influence the government, manage his estates . . . When should one embark on these enduring contributions to the world?"

She looked up. "Stand for something in Parliament other than higher tariffs on corn. Women have been too long excluded from most arenas; the only way a woman may own property of her own is to be a widow or a spinster of advanced age, and then it still depends on the permission and tolerance of men."

"Yes," he said, struck by her words. Of course she was right. Hadn't he bristled on her behalf at the way Sir Gregory Attwood treated her? Hadn't he seen how Mr. Scott slighted her in favor of him, even though Tessa knew far more about the canal than he did? It really was not fair that an intelligent, capable woman was dismissed and overlooked merely because of her sex. "I could support that," he added softly, almost to himself.

"You could?" She looked up, her eyes wide.

"Did you speak in jest?"

"No, but . . ." A slow smile dawned over her face, delighted and confident at once. "Of course you could. You're a very decent man."

He grinned. "Why, thank you, madam! Now let us buckle down, so that I might have some influence to wield and not be left a pig farmer."

Tessa laughed. "It looks like you've already begun! Behold the pig on that journal."

"Is there?" He turned it over. All the registers had suffered some degree of water damage, and this one bore a dark stain in the rough shape of a pig. He chuckled. "So I have! You may address me as Charles, Farmer of Pigs."

"I'm sure you'd be quite good at it, if you decided to make a go of it." With these matter-of-fact words, she bent her head over her own register and went quiet.

"Yes, ma'am." Still grinning, he followed suit, wondering how on earth he could find so much enjoyment in this task, simply because she was here, when it had seemed the grossest abomination just a few days earlier when he faced it alone.

It was just over an hour later that he found it. A faint grin still curving his lips, Charlie stole another look at Tessa—radiant in the sunlight, and more beautiful than ever with that expression of focused concentration on her face—and turned another page. When he looked down, his father's name leaped off the paper at him, faded and small but undeniably familiar. For a moment he stared in disbelief; the signature below was different than he remembered, but of course his father had been Durham Charlie's whole life, not Mr. Francis de Lacey, as he had been when he signed this register in 1752.

"Tessa," he said quietly. He couldn't take his eyes off the record. He could hardly breathe for a moment. Here, in faded ink, was the key to his fate, the proof that his father really had stood beside a high-tempered actress in a Ludgate pub— he flipped to the front of the register to determine that—and married her, for better and for much, much worse. *Joined in Matrimony this 12th day of June, Francis Lacey, bachelor, and Miss Dorothy Cope, spinster.* "I've found it."

She was at his side in a moment. "Oh, my," she whispered. "There's why you couldn't find her." In the register, the bride's name had been originally written as Dorothy Cope, as his father had remembered. But then someone had drawn a line through the name Cope and written, in tiny, cramped letters, the name Swynne above it. The woman's signature below it, in a small round hand, clearly read Dorothy Swynne.

"Swynne, not Cope," Charlie murmured. "I wonder who changed it, and when."

"It only matters what happened to her," said Tessa, practical as ever. "At least you can look for the right person now."

Charlie shook off the daze that had fallen over him at the sight of his father's signature, so strong and youthful, dashed off in a fit of reckless love, never guessing how it would cloud his life for decades to come. "Yes," he said. "And I know where to start."

Chapter 17

The next morning Charlie dressed like a duke. His usual sartorial standards had relaxed in the country, but now he returned not only to his best London form, but exceeded it. Barnes was in raptures, shaving him with unusual care and bringing out a box of jeweled pins and watch fobs. By the time Charlie surveyed the result in the cheval glass, he impressed even himself.

He drove into Mells and found Scott in his offices at the foundry, all too pleased to see him. "Come in, my lord, come in." Scott rushed to pull a chair forward. "May I offer you a refreshment?"

Charlie waved it aside. From the corner of his eye, hanging just outside the window, he could see the carved wooden sign: SCOTT & SWYNNE, IRON MANUFACTORS. "No, today I've come to do business."

"Excellent!" Scott's smile brightened and his gaze sharpened. "I'm delighted to hear it."

"I thought you might be," murmured Charlie. "Tell me about your foundry. Is it a family business?"

"Indeed, sir. Three generations. My grandfather started it."

"Scott, or Swynne?" asked Charlie on impulse.

Scott blinked, but only in mild surprise. "Swynne, actually. My mother's father. My father joined the foundry when he married her, and took it over when my grandfather died."

Charlie nodded, putting things together in his mind. At last the connection emerged. "And now it is yours."

The other man looked a bit perplexed. "Yes. My father is rather elderly, and stepped aside some years ago."

"Hmm." Charlie took a turn around the room, thinking hard. "Very good."

"Have you any other questions?" asked Scott after a moment. "If you would care to see the complete account books, brought from Poole by Mr. Tallboys, I would be happy—"

"What of the locks?" asked Charlie abruptly.

Scott seemed to freeze for a moment. "What of them, sir?"

"I heard of only one trial," Charlie replied. He finally took the seat Scott had pulled out earlier. "Were more done?"

Slowly Scott sank into the chair opposite him. "Yes, partial trials, primarily to refine the design of the gates."

"I presume you are satisfied with how the designs work." He paused, and repeated something else he'd learned from Tessa. "There is a rather large drop over the course of this canal, so efficient locks are vital to its success. You must understand my concern."

"Of course. I assure you, the locks will be ready to perform as expected, my lord." Scott's smile was a bit stiff at the corners. He was lying.

It gave Charlie a moment's pause. If he could tell Scott was lying now, what did that mean about the other times he'd tried to trip up the man about the blackmail? Or was it obvious now merely because he knew it was a lie, thanks to Mr. Lester?

Charlie shook off the doubt. Scott had posted those blackmail letters, and one way or another, he meant to make the man squirm until he confessed or exonerated himself.

"May I put you down on our list of shareholders?" Scott asked at his silence. He pulled a bound book from a drawer and looked up, his polished smile back in place. "If you've no other questions, that is."

Charlie inclined his head and moved in for the kill. "By all means." He watched Scott uncap his ink and dip the nib into it, waiting just until Scott set the pen to the paper. "I suppose you had better use my new title. Now that my father has died, I shall soon become the Duke of Durham."

Scott looked up, raw astonishment stamped on his face. "The Duke of Durham? Why—Your Grace—I'd no idea!"

"No?" Charlie's smile was thin and cool. "I thought you might have suspected."

"Indeed not, sir!" exclaimed Scott. "How could I have?"

Charlie watched him closely. Scott was obviously taken by surprise, but displayed no sign of panic or guilt. That made no sense. Either Scott had known all along who he really was, and thus had plenty of time to prepare for this confrontation; or only just this moment discovered the subject of his blackmail had turned the tables on him, meaning he should, presumably, be in a state of some alarm. Instead Hiram Scott appeared merely disconcerted, a little embarrassed, even a little delighted. Nothing at all like the subtle unease he'd shown over the locks. "There was mention of it in the papers."

"Ah—yes, yes, I did see something about the name, now that you mention it . . ." Scott cleared his throat. "I'd no idea you were the heir, my lord— Your Grace."

"In fact I am." Charlie paused. "You may have heard of some uproar attached to the title." Something flickered over Scott's face—but still not alarm. It was infuriating. Charlie wanted him to writhe like a worm on the hook, to know he'd been caught and was about to face retribution. "Rest assured it won't affect my decisions today."

"Why, how should it? I'm sure I didn't presume so," burst out the other man in surprise too obvious to be feigned. "I don't follow London gossip out here in Somerset. And either way, I'm a businessman; as long as a man has honest coin to invest, I'll deal with him, no matter what his personal troubles. Who hasn't had a spot of trouble over a woman or a hand of cards now and then?" He chuckled, giving Charlie a knowing look.

"Quite so. You looked concerned. I merely wished to allay any fears you might have about my 'honest coin.'"

Scott chuckled, apparently at ease again. "From the Duke of Durham? No, I think not. Your

Grace's estates and position is well-known, even in these rustic parts." He leaned forward with an ingratiating smile and lowered his voice. "In fact, I feel some small connection to Your Grace. It's an old family story, and I daresay has gathered some embellishment over the years, but it might amuse you. My mother once was acquainted with your father."

Charlie kept his face impassive even though he'd just been thoroughly shocked. Was Scott about to carry on his blackmail demands *now*, face-to-face? The man had to be the most brazen—or inept—criminal in the history of Britain. "Indeed," he said, falling back on his lofty, bored tone. "How so?"

"Well, I daresay it wasn't the most refined connection." Scott chuckled again. "I understand they met in London when your father was a young man and my mother was a beautiful young girl, and . . . well. She remembered him quite fondly. I was just a boy when she died, but I remember her laughing in delight when she discovered he'd inherited a dukedom. 'I might have been a duchess,' she used to say. 'I almost landed myself a duke.'" He beamed. "Isn't it odd we should meet all these years later, and come to do business together?"

Charlie didn't move a muscle. If he so much as shifted his weight, he was sure he'd not be able to stop moving until he pounded in Scott's smug face. How dare the scoundrel laugh and make light of Durham's clandestine marriage, as if his father's folly was one grand joke. How dare he send blackmail letters threatening to ruin his and his brothers' lives, and then sit there grinning like a cat in the cream. "Your mother was Dorothy Swynne," he said.

"Well—why, yes, she was!" Scott smiled in pleased surprise. "Dare I hope your father remembered her? It would have gratified her immensely if he had."

"Yes, Mr. Scott, he remembered her. All too well." Charlie drew the first blackmail letter from his pocket and laid it on the table, letting it fall open. The cursed words were still sharp and clear: *I know about Dorothy Cope.* "As you ensured he would."

The other man's face was comically blank as he looked at the letter. "I beg your pardon, sir—what do you mean? Who is Dorothy Cope?"

Charlie drew out the second hateful letter and put it on top of the first. *Your secret will be exposed.* "She signed the register as Dorothy Swynne, but my father knew her as Dorothy Cope. The postal clerk in Bath remembered you. He gave my brother your name after your recent visit to that city. We haven't tracked down a postal clerk in London who will swear you sent the other letters, but the writing is the same." He added the third and fourth letters to the stack, never once taking his gaze from Hiram Scott. He left these folded, but knew every word by now. *Five thousand pounds in gold coin will buy my silence, left at the grave of James Addison Fletcher, St. Martin's churchyard. The past is never forgotten; I will ruin you.* "I do believe blackmail is illegal," he added.

The color drained from Scott's face as he looked at them. "My lord—Your Grace—I—I don't know what you mean," he stammered. "Blackmail? I *never*—not under *any* circumstances—"

"Perhaps you've forgotten what was in the letters? By all means, read them again. Consider their import carefully." Charlie clasped his hands around the head of his walking stick.

Scott wet his lips. He had recoiled in his chair when Charlie brought out the letters, but now slowly reached out and chose one at random. He flipped open the broken seal and read the single line within. "I didn't write this," he said, breathing hard. He snatched up another. "Nor this one." He seized the other two and read them all again. "Your Grace, I swear to you, I didn't write these letters!"

"But you sent them." Charlie pasted a studious frown on his face and tilted his head back. "If you didn't write them, who did?"

Scott dropped the letters and put his hands down flat on the table, as if grappling for balance. He looked as if he might cast up his breakfast all over the table. "His Lordship," he croaked. "He's the only person . . ."

"His Lordship," Charlie said scornfully, although his heart sank at the words. There was someone else—of course . . . But the question of whom wiped away any elation at the prospect of discovering the truth. Charlie had a bad feeling he knew what name Scott would say; he'd heard it in Bath, although only in passing, and he'd brushed it aside, telling himself it was too incredible, merely a coincidence. Perhaps he'd been wrong all along . . .

But he kept his attention focused on Scott. "This sounds like evasion. You sent someone else's letters, and yet knew nothing of their purpose?"

"No, no, I did it purely as a favor." Scott eyed

the letters with dismay. "If I'd know—if I'd had any idea what he wrote, I never would have sent them!"

"I find that very hard to believe. You're not the soul of honesty, are you? Telling Mrs. Neville you've got a full slate of subscribers when you're actually scraping for funds and calling for more capital from current investors. Trying to extract an investment from me, knowing full well your primary investors are beginning to demand their money back because the locks are proving too expensive and difficult to build. You're a swindler, Mr. Scott, and swindlers go to prison."

Scott jerked his gaze up. His initial dismay heated into anger. "Are you calling me a liar?"

"And a blackmailer," agreed Charlie.

"Who told you the locks are failing? We've had a few troubles, but with some time—"

"I don't care about the canal," said Charlie curtly. "Only these letters."

"I didn't write them! I had no idea what was in those letters, or I should never have sent them! How dare you call me a swindler—"

"I dare because this *threat* you sent my father has caused a bloody lot of trouble!" In the blink of an eye Charlie lost his poise and shot out of his chair, slapping his hands down on the table and leaning toward Scott with murder in his heart. "When did your mother die?" There was still a chance this could come out right. Scott said he'd been a child, and the man was probably a good decade older than him. As long as Dorothy had died before April of 1774, Durham's marriage to his duchess would be legal and binding; Charlie and his brothers would be his indisputably legitimate heirs. It all hinged on the date . . .

"How dare you—" began Scott furiously, but Charlie cut him off.

"I can ruin you," he promised in a low, hard tone. "I can, and I wouldn't lose a minute of sleep regretting it. When did your mother die?"

" 'Seventy-three!" shouted Scott. "In November of 'seventy-three. She caught a chill in the first frost."

Seventeen seventy-three. Charlie inhaled a ragged breath. The date sounded like an amen to a long, desperate prayer. His shoulders slumped and he hung his head as the pulsing fury inside him bled out; 1773. "Thank God," he muttered.

Scott shoved back his chair and lurched to his feet. "I regret my participation, however unwitting, in your troubles, but you have gone too far, sir!"

Charlie took a deep breath. "Allow me to explain. You are not my adversary, it seems." He took his seat again. He found he wanted to know the entire story, and now that he knew what happened to Dorothy Cope, there was no reason to keep it silent. "Your mother did not merely know my father; it was not merely an affair. For a few weeks in 1752, they were married."

Scott had been eyeing him with a mixture of distrust and dislike, but now his jaw dropped open. "What?"

"She didn't mention that? Perhaps not, if she had also married again." Charlie shrugged. "It was a Fleet marriage. All I know of the matter is what my father wrote on his deathbed, begging pardon for keeping it secret for so long."

Scott flushed. "You have proof of this, of course."

"I have my father's letter detailing their marriage and parting, and the register recording their names, signed by their own hands. You may see it if you wish."

"Merciful heaven." The man had gone gray. "But then—that makes my mother a bigamist," he said slowly. "And my brother and I . . ."

Charlie gave him a level look. "Bastards? Yes, I understand that's what it means." All too well, in fact; until this moment, Charlie had feared, deep down, that it would come out the other way, that he, Gerard, and Edward would be the ones proven bastards, cut out of the succession and disinherited from their father's wealth. He didn't know what he would have done had Scott named a date after 1774 for his mother's death, but now it didn't matter—thanks be to all the saints in Heaven. It allowed him to feel some sympathy for the man across the table from him. He inclined his head. "I apologize for any roughness of my manner, in the heat of anger."

"Good God," whispered Scott, looking thoroughly stunned. "She never told us . . ."

The words of his father's confessional letter echoed in Charlie's mind. "My father considered the marriage dissolved, and possibly invalid from the beginning. Still, he resolved not to marry again, and nearly didn't; only when he inherited his titles was it borne in on him that he might still be married to her in the eyes of the law, if not in his eyes or in hers. He made an effort to locate her, but failed." He paused. Perhaps Dorothy had wished to forget the marriage as much as Durham did. If Scott's story was true, by the time Charlie's father became Durham, she had a new husband and a family to think of. If either of them could be accused of bigamy, surely it was Dorothy more than Durham. Oddly enough, Durham probably could have secured a divorce because of her remarriage, if he'd known of it, and spared them all this trouble. "What did she tell you of her time in London?"

As if rousing himself from a stupor, Scott shuddered. "She told us she had gone to the city when she was young," he said in a numb voice. "For adventure. Mells is rather quiet and dull, certainly for so bright a creature as my mother. She wanted more . . . but she only found work as a seamstress, and came home two years later."

"My father said she was an actress when he met her."

The older man flinched but didn't protest. "She said she met the fellow who became the Duke of Durham and remembered him fondly. I understood, between the winks and nods, that he'd courted her, or at least been very friendly. She teased my father that she might have been a duchess, if only she hadn't come home to Somerset and married him. I don't believe anyone thought she meant it, but . . . my mother was enchanting. My father claimed he was bewitched from the first moment he saw her. As a boy, I suppose I thought that if my mother had set her heart on charming a fellow, no man could resist her, be he a duke or a chimney sweep." He ran one hand over his face and for a moment it looked as though he would put down his head and weep.

Charlie knew how he must feel. A few weeks ago he'd had the same grief for his own mother, fearing her memory would be tarnished, no longer the beloved and lamented Duchess of Durham, but the bigamous wife who never knew the infamy her husband had exposed her to.

"I would prefer not to speak of this ever again," he said a touch more kindly, "as I'm sure you also prefer. But I must have proof of her death."

Scott raised his gaze, hollow and bleak. "My lord—Your Grace—I did not know. I heard a few rumors of a challenge to the Durham title, but never dreamed my mother had any part in it. I did not even know you were the duke! And I swear to you, by all I hold sacred, *I did not write those letters.*"

For a long moment Charlie said nothing. No longer smooth and confident, Scott looked like a man who'd been taken off guard and attacked, horrified and angry and defensive all at once. "Mr. Scott, I have no interest in dragging your mother's name through the mud. I have no interest in challenging the validity of her marriage to your father—quite the contrary. If I could prove she was never married to my father at all, I would. But should the court decide to uphold their marriage— conducted in a tavern near the Fleet, by the by, under the blessing of a dubious minister who never held a parish—should they declare that marriage binding, I must show Dorothy Swynne died before my father married again."

"So you can inherit," muttered Scott. "So you can be legitimate."

Charlie inclined his head. "As you say. And I

would very much appreciate your assistance." He paused, then repeated, "*Very* much."

The older man seemed to grasp his meaning; he took a deep breath and nodded. If he wished to, Charlie could cast serious doubt on Hiram Scott's own heritage. Who knew how much that would matter away from the rarefied air of the haut ton, where lineage was everything, but it would cause a stir in this part of Somerset, and that was the last thing Scott needed as he tried to save his business and entice investors into the canal project. And that didn't even touch on the emotional anguish it would cause his family to learn about their beloved mother's secret, scandalous past.

He could also bring the canal scheme down around Scott's ears. The books had been altered to show a rosy picture, but a few questions, a few indiscreet remarks, or even a call for an investigation in Parliament, would shred that picture. The canal would probably fail, eventually, but Charlie could make it happen overnight.

But if Scott cooperated . . . he would have earned the gratitude of a duke. And he knew it.

"Go to the church in Nunney," said Scott softly. "The curate there will be able to show you; she was married there"—he winced at the word—"and is buried in the churchyard. Her name was Hester Dorothy Swynne before she married my father. I never heard anyone call her other than Hester, but I suppose she used her second name in London to keep her actions quiet."

"Of course." Charlie gathered up the letters. He already suspected he knew the answer to his last question, but had to ask it anyway. "You say you sent these letters as a favor for someone. Who?"

Hiram Scott swallowed. "One of our largest investors. I told him my mother's story in a moment of boasting; there is no other word for it. I may have . . . implied a certain connection to the late duke. But he was very amused by the story, saying he had an old acquaintance with His Grace but hadn't spoken to him in years. He asked me to send the letters when I would depart for Bath or Bristol, since the post is unreliable and infrequent in the wilds of Somerset. He invested quite generously in the canal and lent his support in Parliament, and I was delighted to do him that small favor . . ." His voice trailed off as he stared at the letters in revulsion, as if realizing he had unknowingly tied his own noose.

"And his name?" prodded Charlie, steeling himself. Every word had sent another prickle of dread down his spine.

Scott looked up, and gave the answer Charlie had feared. "The Earl of Worley, sir."

Chapter 18

The village church of Nunney was small and ancient, with a crenulated gray tower rising above the neat gardens around it. Charlie opened the gate and led Tessa inside, up the path, and through the stout wooden doors. It was cool inside the church. Tessa had the feeling of stepping back in time as they walked up the nave, the stained-glass windows casting multicolored light across the weathered stone floor. Off to one side she glimpsed effigies in full armor lying in close quarters, right up to the windowsill as if they still guarded the church from invaders. It was hushed and peaceful and her chest hurt with how much she wanted Charlie to find the answers he sought here.

They reached the carved oak screen on the altar. No one came out to meet them. Charlie cleared his throat. "Good day," he called, his voice echoing off the arched ceiling. "Is there anyone here?"

Silence was the only reply. Tessa glanced up at him. She could feel the tension in him through his grip on her hand. "We could go look in the graveyard ourselves," she suggested.

He looked around the church once more. "Yes."

They went back out into the churchyard, skirting around the building. The graveyard was neat and well-tended, with lines of graves winding along the edges of a narrow path. It wasn't a large graveyard, and they were looking for a stone of some vintage, so it didn't take very long.

"Here," he said, stopping abruptly. Tessa looked down at the stone in front of them. Weathered and leaning to one side, it was at the head of a well-tended grave. Cowslip grew amidst the grass waving gently in the breeze.

HESTER DOROTHY, WIFE OF JEREMIAH SCOTT
AGED 40 YEARS
BURIED THIS 7TH DAY OF DECEMBER 1773

Here was the proof.

She felt the silent shudder that went through Charlie. His fingers eased around hers, just a little, but enough to make her realize she'd been holding her breath and could let it out.

"May I help you?" Tessa started and turned at the pleasant voice behind them. A middle-aged man in vicar's garb stood on the path, smiling at them. "I am Edgar Thomas, the curate."

She curtsied. "Thank you, sir. This is Lord Gresham, and I am Mrs. Neville."

"I'm delighted to make your acquaintance. Are you seeking a particular grave?"

"Yes," said Charlie. "This one. Have you had this curacy for long, Mr. Thomas?"

"Oh, my, nearly twenty-five years," he said with a smile. "The gentleman I replaced was here for over forty!" He glanced at the stone behind them. "Are you a relation of the Scott family?"

"We are acquainted with Mr. Hiram Scott of Mells," Charlie said. "He directed us to you. Might we speak inside?"

"Yes, of course." Mr. Thomas led the way to the nearby cottage, where he sent his serving girl for some refreshments. "Now, how can I help you?" he asked again when they were seated.

Charlie explained, in circumspect terms, what he needed, and gave Mr. Thomas the letter Hiram Scott had written, asking his help. When the tea arrived, Tessa poured it in silence and listened.

After Charlie found the marriage lines in the register, she had gone back to Frome feeling almost as though an idyll had ended. She knew he'd gone to see Scott the previous morning; he had called in Frome afterward and asked if she would come with him to Nunney to find Dorothy's grave. But he had been somber and preoccupied, and told her about his visit to Scott without any of the emotion she'd expected to see.

And then he conspicuously avoided her questions about the true blackmailer, Lord Worley. Aside from a vague recollection of Mr. Scott mentioning him the night of the awful dinner, Tessa had never heard of the man, but when she wondered aloud why he would send threatening letters to the duke, Charlie changed the subject. She wasn't much of a liar herself, but she certainly recognized that he didn't want to tell her, for some reason. She let the question fade away, unanswered, but it planted a seed of worry in her heart that Charlie's troubles weren't ended by the discovery of Dorothy Cope.

"Well, my goodness, that is a delicate problem," said Mr. Thomas when Charlie was done. "Of course I shall be glad to testify to the facts of when Mrs. Scott died, only I do hope it might be done without undue imposition on the family. Mr. Jeremiah Scott and his younger son are still parishioners here, and I hesitate to cause them pain or public censure. These events happened decades ago."

"I assure you, I don't wish public notoriety on any of them," Charlie replied. "I don't plan to mention the lady's name except to establish that she died before my parents married, relieving any need to examine her clandestine marriage to my father, and thus sparing her family further distress. Hiram Scott agreed that his family would not wish to imperil my rightful claim to my title."

"Very good, my lord." The curate got to his feet. "I shall be glad to provide a letter, if you'll excuse me for a few minutes."

After he left, Tessa looked uncertainly at Charlie. He was still distracted and tense, his hand resting on his knee in a fist. "Isn't this all you need?" she finally ventured to ask. "Is there something else that would make your petition absolutely unquestionable?" He had let her read all the documents sent by his brother, including the legal petition filed in London with the Home Office. Tessa was no lawyer, but she couldn't see anything except this clandestine marriage standing between Charlie and the dukedom.

He started at her voice, as if he'd been deep in reverie. "No, I don't think there's anything else I need produce for the lawyers."

"Is something else wrong?" She almost feared the answer. Something clearly was wrong, and she had no idea what.

He didn't answer for several minutes. "Nothing that isn't my own fault."

She didn't like the sound of that at all. She lowered her gaze to her cup and turned it around and around on the saucer. Neither of them spoke again until Mr. Thomas came back into the room, bearing a letter.

"Here you are, sir." He handed it to Charlie. "I shall be glad to seal it, after you've read it."

"Thank you." Charlie read it and handed it back. "You have been most helpful. I shan't forget it."

"Thank you, Your Grace." Mr. Thomas bowed and hurried to seal the letter. "If there is anything else I might do, you have only to ask."

"I will. Good day."

They drove back to Frome in silence, Charlie still consumed with his own thoughts, and Tessa caught off guard by her own. There was no way to describe Charlie's behavior in Nunney except haughty. He wasn't her laughing, charming lover, but a regal duke with an air of lofty restraint. How silly she felt, after all the times she had reproved him for not being serious, for wishing now that he would revert to his usual irreverent self.

But perhaps that was her mistake. He wasn't hers at all, and perhaps this was his usual self, not the other.

By the time they reached Mill Cottage, she could stand it no longer. "What happened with Mr. Scott?" she blurted out as he helped her down from the carriage. "Why would Lord Worley blackmail your father? I thought this would please you, but I can tell it hasn't. What's wrong, Charlie?"

Without a word he took her by the hand, striding off so rapidly she almost stumbled and fell before getting her balance. Away from the house he led her, around the stable and across the grassy lawn where they had shared lemonade only a few days ago. Tessa clapped one hand to her head to keep her bonnet from falling off as he towed her down the crumbling stone steps to the old mill.

"What is wrong?" she demanded again, breathlessly, as he finally stopped on the far side of the building, in the shadow of the slip where the wheel had once turned.

"Nothing at all," he said, and kissed her, bearing her back against the wall. Her eyes fell shut as she succumbed at once to the spell of his kiss, ruthless and demanding. With one hand he held her nape, tipping her head just so as he plundered her mouth, and with the other he stroked her back, her waist, and finally her hip, drawing her firmly against his erection.

"Charlie," she gasped when he broke off the kiss. Her heart galloped inside her chest and she clutched at his sleeve, her head spinning and her breath ragged.

"Shh." He plucked her hand off his arm and stripped off her glove. "We'll talk later." He brought her hand to his groin, drawing her palm down his length. "Part your legs for me."

"Here?" She gaped at him, startled out of the fog of desire he had conjured around her.

"Do it," he said in the same wicked, velvet voice.

Tessa's throat closed up. They were out of doors

. . . although very sheltered from view. She moved her right foot over a few inches.

His eyes were pure black now. "More," he growled. He brought her hand up and then down again, showing her how aroused he was.

Tessa jerked her chin higher. Now she was aroused, too, curse him. Defiantly she lifted her foot and raised her knee, curling her leg around his and flexing her foot to pull him closer.

"Yes," he muttered, ducking his head for another scorching kiss.

She shook off his grip on her hand and began stroking him at her own pace. Her other arm she flung around his neck for balance. As he made love to her mouth, his tongue plunging deep then tangling with hers, he was hiking up her skirts between them. His fingers slipped over the slick folds between her legs, then pushed high inside her. Tessa moaned as a thousand sparks of lightning shot through her. His thumb circled lightly, then firmly, over that deliciously sensitive flesh. His fingers pushed deep and then withdrew, only to do it again. Tessa could hardly breathe; with one hand she yanked at the buttons of his trousers. Charlie did nothing to help her, just continued his maddening assault on her senses, pushing her toward delirium.

The last button came free as she felt her muscles tensing up in anticipation. Tessa was almost gasping for air as she slid her hand inside his trousers and finally took him in her bare hand. His chest tensed up as he sucked in a sharp breath, and then he seized her wrist, forcing her to guide him between her thighs before he pulled her hand away and thrust deep into her.

She must have made a startled noise; he paused for a heartbeat, his eyes sweeping over her face. She managed a nod. A shiver seemed to ripple through him, and he pressed closer, then surprised her by boosting her up off her feet. Tessa tightened her grip on his shoulders, hazily fearing they would fall, but that was the last thought she had. Charlie leaned her back against the wall, his hands curved under her hips, and rode her with a hard, driving rhythm. He didn't stop even when she clutched at him and gave a little scream and almost bucked him off in the throes of climax. Only as she went limp in his arms did he clasp her tighter, leaning his weight on her as he shuddered in his own ecstasy.

"Darling." His kiss was gentle, even though his arms trembled and his chest heaved with every breath.

Eyes still closed, Tessa reached for him, holding him close as she rested her cheek on his shoulder, her face pressed against the crumpled linen of his cravat. *Darling.* He was more than dear to her, more than just a lover. She had known Charlie was dangerous from the moment she first saw him, although she hadn't guessed how thoroughly she would succumb to it. He had invaded her life, earned her respect, utterly enslaved her body, and now stolen her heart as well.

Immolation, indeed. She felt like a straw, liable to burst into flames every time he touched her.

He took a deep breath and gently let her down. It took a few moments to disentangle from each other; Tessa realized with a start that she had been wrapped around him, arms and legs, and her clothes had snagged on the buttons of his coat. Charlie grinned as he freed his buttons from the trim of her pelisse, and her heart jumped and bounded at the sight. She smiled back rather helplessly, letting him help her set her skirts to rights and then smoothing his cravat into some semblance of rectitude. Folding her arm snugly around his, Charlie led her back around the mill, toward the table and chairs. Tessa blushed at the sight of fresh lemonade and glasses, set out by a silent, invisible servant. What Barnes must think of them for running around the mill and then reappearing like this.

She sat down and poured two glasses, but Charlie remained on his feet. The lighter, peaceful look faded from his face as he drew out the letter from the Nunney curate and looked at it.

Tessa waited, but he said nothing. She sipped her lemonade. She shifted in her chair, trying to think what had made him somber again. "Do you still hold your father in contempt?" He glanced up, his eyes puzzled. "For the scandal," she clarified. "For all the trouble you had to go through."

He gave a deep sigh. "Contempt . . . No." He hesitated, then put the letter back in his jacket pocket. "I have to make a short trip."

"Oh." Tessa blinked. Perhaps he meant to see his brother. "To Bath?"

"No."

"To—To London?" she asked uncertainly. He did have to go to London, to present the curate's letter and settle his title and put a final end to the uncertainty. But it wasn't a short visit to London, and once he went, there was no reason for him to return to Frome.

"Not to London, either." He wasn't looking at her but staring toward the road, his eyes shadowed.

She wet her lips. "To see Lord Worley?"

His nod was barely perceptible.

"Oh." She sipped her lemonade some more. He hadn't touched his. Quietly she set her glass down and pushed it away. "What will you do?"

"I owe him an apology," he said, an odd note in his voice. "And he owes me an explanation."

He was not here with her, but somewhere else, far distant in his mind. Tessa felt a renewed tremor of apprehension. "Will it be . . . ?" She hesitated, not sure how to ask. Would it be dangerous? What did he plan to do to Lord Worley? Why did he say he owed the man an apology? And why must he go at all? Surely Charlie's discovery of Dorothy's grave had unstrung Worley's poisonous bow. Somehow she couldn't bring herself to ask again why Worley would blackmail him about his father's marriage.

"I imagine it will be quite cold and civil."

"Civil?" she exclaimed. "*Civil?* When he was blackmailing your father?"

"I don't think my father had much to do with it, in the end," he said after a moment.

That only made her more nervous. She rubbed her hands together, wishing she hadn't drunk the lemonade. There was a bitter taste in the back of her throat. "Why do you say that?"

He sighed. He sat down in the other chair and scrubbed his hands over his face. "When we first met," he began, not quite looking at her, "what did you think of me?"

"I was all wrong," she said quickly.

"But what was your first impression?"

Tessa bit her lip. "A wealthy, conceited, indolent rogue. A—A scoundrel, I suppose."

He nodded. "Precisely. You wouldn't be the first to call me so, with good reason."

An awful feeling bloomed in her chest. "How did you offend Lord Worley?"

"Do you recall," he said, more slowly than ever, "the other night, when you said your family sent you away to recover your nerves and your dignity?" Tessa gave a wary nod. "You were fortunate. I . . . I also had an ill-fated love affair in my youth. She was beautiful and coy, and I was young and impatient. My father disapproved and prevented the marriage, and in response I stormed off to London, vowing never to speak to him again." His mouth bent bitterly, sadly. "What an arrogant little coxcomb I was."

Tessa sat in mute anxiety, unable to open her mouth.

"I refused to see that he had valid reasons for stopping it. I refused to see anything but my own wounded pride, with the unfortunate result that I never stopped thinking I had been unfairly divided from my true love."

She licked her lips and made a guess. "Lady Worley."

He hesitated, then gave a slight nod.

And then she didn't want to know any more. Something else he'd murmured stuck in her mind— about giving up married women—and she didn't want to hear anything about the ravishingly beautiful Lady Worley who had been his first love, and almost his ruination. She rubbed her hands on her skirt and jumped to her feet.

"Well, then, you must let Lord Worley know he wasted his efforts," she said in a loud, too-bright voice. "With Mr. Thomas's letter, you have nothing to fear from him."

He rose, too. "I'll be back in a few days."

"You will?" She dared a quick glance at him.

He seemed to become himself again. He gave her a sideways glance and a rueful smile. "Did you fear I wouldn't?"

"You didn't say," she pointed out, not wanting to admit that yes, she did fear he wouldn't come back to her. Here in this provincial town, she could ignore the fact that he was, or very soon would be, a duke. Here in the quiet of a Somerset cottage, she didn't have to think about his intentions, as yet unstated and unclear. Here she could pretend that things would go on as they were, without the interference of family or the demands of a title or the allure of a more sophisticated woman he'd been in love with for years.

"I'll come back," he said. "Will you wait for me?"

She still had her doubts, but something inside her melted as always when he looked at her that way. "Yes," she said, shoving aside the doubts. "I will."

Chapter 19

Uppercombe, the seat of the Earls of Worley, was a rambling estate from the time of the Tudors set deep in the Somerset hills above Kilmersdon. Charlie gave a cursory look for any signs of neglect as he rode up the winding drive, but there were none. He didn't really expect to see any. If Worley had sent the letters, it wasn't because of money, nor any other reason connected to Durham or even to Edward and Gerard.

It was because Charlie had had an affair with Lady Worley.

He had never forgotten how deeply it cut when Maria Gronow refused his frantic proposal to elope. She'd left him, bereft, standing on that little bridge in the woods near Lastings, after telling him she loved him desperately . . . but not desperately enough to defy his father and run away with him. When she'd married the Earl of Worley less than two months later, it had seemed his life was permanently blighted, forever robbed of the woman he loved through his father's callous interference. For years he'd nursed a smoldering fury that his father had refused to bless the match, blaming Durham for his loss of Maria. He'd gone to London hell-bent on putting his thumb in the duke's eye at every turn to repay some of the pain his father had caused him.

But after a year or two he had stopped thinking of Maria so much. A variety of other pleasures filled his hours. The Worleys didn't spend much time in town, remaining in the country most of the year. Periodically Charlie would hear gossip that Lady Worley had borne another child, filling up the nursery at Uppercombe, and he told himself she must be blissfully happy. She must have fallen in love with Worley and become a devoted wife and mother, no longer the bewitching young siren who dreamed of being the toast of London on his arm. He told himself he was glad she was happy, and over time the scar across his heart ceased to ache when he thought of her.

If only he'd been wise enough to leave it that way.

He pulled up his horse in front of the house but remained in the saddle. Perhaps he should turn around and ride away. He'd found the marriage record, found Dorothy's grave, and secured the proof he needed that his father had legally and legitimately wed his mother. His inheritance and title would be secure, and nothing Worley or anyone else did could change that. What was there to gain by stirring up old hurts and past mistakes?

Slowly, Charlie dismounted his horse. A servant came running up to take the reins, and he handed them over. He owed his brothers a full explanation, including any apology due for his own actions. He had earned whatever retribution was coming. And, he supposed, he should be man enough to face the consequences of his actions, whatever they might be.

The butler was waiting when he reached the door. "Tell Lord Worley I've come about his letters," Charlie told the man, placing one of his father's calling cards on the butler's salver. They were inarguably his now, embossed with the title *Duke of Durham* in elegant script above the ducal coat of arms. Edward had put them in with the rest of the duke's papers, where Charlie found them after emptying the satchel.

He wasn't left waiting long. The butler showed him into the library, where Lord Worley stood with one elbow propped on the mantel. He didn't say a word until the butler had closed the door behind him. "Lord Gresham," he said then, a trace of malice in his voice. "To what do I owe the pleasure of your visit?"

"You may call me Durham," replied Charlie. Neither man made any pretense of a bow.

Worley's brow arched. "Precipitous, by the rumors one hears."

Charlie just smiled. "You shouldn't listen to rumors, sir."

The earl's lips curled into an expression every bit as sardonic as Charlie's own. "Oh, but the pleasure they afford! The foibles of our fellow man are better than a farce on the stage. Surely you agree."

"Of course. And one should credit them with as much truth as a farce on the stage. There is often more fiction at work in gossip than in the finest drama."

"And yet, like some of those dramas, gossip is often based so closely on truth."

Worley was enjoying this, Charlie could tell. "Or supposition, in your case," he said, tired of prevarication. "An old story, fleshed out with threats and blackmail demands."

"Well." The other man rocked back on his heels, looking rather pleased with himself. "One doesn't want to be ignored or overlooked."

"And yet you didn't sign your name. I daresay you would have received an immediate response if you hadn't taken pains to conceal yourself."

Worley gave a faint chuckle. "Do you think I didn't want to be caught out? Do you think I didn't want you to know I sent them? You're as foolish and oblivious as gossip says, if so." He leaned forward, his humor vanishing in a sudden glitter of hatred. "I wanted you to know, whelp," he said savagely. "I didn't think it would take even you this long to work it out, but I never planned to conceal it from *you*."

"You shouldn't have sent them to my father, in that case," Charlie shot back. "He told no one for over a year. If you relished the thought of the agony you were causing me, know that it only began when he died and we discovered the letters in his effects."

Worley's eyes narrowed. "Yes, that was a miscalculation. I expected your brother Edward would open them and drag the entire affair into the light, demanding answers. I would have been delighted to see your own father enact my vengeance."

"You underestimated my father and my brother. My brothers and I are all, in our own ways, very much Durham's sons." Charlie opened his arms wide in a gesture of defenselessness. "For instance, you can see I have no hesitation in confronting a man. I don't ask unknowing and uninvolved people to send libelous blackmail letters for me."

Worley's smile was poisonous. "Ah, poor Mr. Scott. He finally told you."

"I worked it out on my own," replied Charlie evenly. "How did you know Hester Swynne was really Dorothy Cope?" That was the only link missing in the chain, as far as he could see.

The other man raised his eyebrows. "Oh, really—surely you wouldn't have believed your father paid court to a lowly wench from Mells. It was only a guess, I admit, but it seemed to me there was more to it. I sent a chap out to ask some questions, and he found old Jeremiah Scott—and lo, the vein was even richer than expected. The man's gone barmy with age, but a bottle of strong port loosened his lips remarkably, even to the point of confessing himself a bigamous husband. I expect it was a relief for him to tell the tale, after keeping it secret for so long. Durham actually married the tart! Isn't it shocking what men will do to get a woman to open her legs?"

Charlie's hands were in fists, and he took a deep breath, forcing his fingers to uncurl. Worley was savoring every bloody moment of this, and Charlie wanted to shake that damned triumph off his face. He dropped his hands. "Undoubtedly—which brings me to the reason for my visit. I was wrong to dally with Lady Worley."

At her name, the earl flinched and his expression darkened. Then his mouth twisted, but this time in rage. "You were sick with love for her your whole life, weren't you? Both of you were just waiting for me to cock up my toes, all these years. And the widowed Lady Worley would have become the next Duchess of Durham, as she wanted to be all along. I always wondered if you were truly enslaved by her, as she often claimed. I know she was a virgin when I married her, which can only mean she made you dance to her tune as she made me."

Charlie was stunned almost speechless. "I never saw her," he replied, just as harshly. "Yes, I wanted to marry her once, years ago. But she refused me. From the time she refused to elope with me in spite of my father's wishes, I never saw her. She went to Bath and married you, and I never spoke to her again until . . ." He stopped.

When Worley looked at him again, his face no longer held any fury, but a sort of stony acceptance. "Until that night? I can almost believe it."

That night. That one cursed night three years ago, when he'd encountered Maria at a ball in London. When he'd fallen, half drunk and feeling reckless, back into his old burning passion for her. He'd only meant to flirt outrageously with her, both as a sop to the echoes of his wounded youthful pride and to torment her with what might have been. By then he fully appreciated what it meant to be the handsome heir to a wealthy dukedom; at least a half-dozen ladies in the ballroom that night would have eloped with him on a moment's notice, if he'd asked them. But Maria, the one girl who'd refused him, was all he could see, as he crossed the ballroom. She was still beautiful, still tapping her toe in time with the music as she watched, but when he swept a bow in front of her, she gasped in astonishment.

"Is it really you?" she'd asked, sounding almost fearful before a joyous smile blazed across her face. "It is—oh, thank the heavens above, it *is*!"

The rest of the night had passed in a blur. She was miserable in her marriage. After four daughters and three miscarriages, Worley was displeased with her as a wife. He kept her virtually a prisoner at Uppercombe, only bringing her to London for brief trips every other year. He was abrupt with her and made shocking, even cruel demands of her in his quest for a son. She confessed to Charlie, in a voice choking with sobs, that she bitterly regretted refusing him; that she hadn't known a moment of happiness since that day; and that she had never stopped loving him, even as she was forced to give herself to her cold and abusive husband. It was a tale of loneliness and despair, and Charlie, still under the influence of that remembered adoration as well as a large quantity of drink, believed every word.

As the hours passed and the wine flowed, Maria poured out all her troubles and laments into his too-sympathetic ear. When she exclaimed at the lateness of the hour, he took her hand and pulled her into a dark corner to kiss her. He declared he wanted to protect her, to save her from her tragic lot. And when she clasped his hand and told him to come home with her, that Worley was away for the night and her heart might break forever if Charlie didn't make love to her just once, he went without a second thought.

It was the next morning when he realized the stupidity of his actions. From the moment he opened his eyes and saw that he was in another man's bed, with a wife not his own, he repented of the reckless decision to come home with her. He didn't know Lord Worley personally, but the man's reputation was not the forgiving and forgetting sort. Charlie's scandals to that point had been mere trifles compared to carrying on an affair with a jealous man's wife. When Maria awoke and began murmuring about seeing him again, even hinting that Charlie might help her divorce her husband, he knew he'd made a horrifying mistake.

By the time he extricated himself from her tears and arms, he felt he'd made the narrowest escape of his life. He had gone to bed with her because he'd spent too much of his life dreaming of doing it, but it hadn't changed anything. She was still married to someone else, and he was surprised to find he didn't want her as badly as he had once thought. In the clear light of morning he realized he no longer loved her. And the thought of being drawn into a criminal conversation suit for adultery with Lady Worley was simply unthinkable. It was enough to make him swear off ever bedding another married woman again, let alone Maria Worley, and breathe a sigh of relief that it hadn't been worse.

But now it was clear he hadn't completely escaped. Somehow Lord Worley had discovered his wife's infidelity and focused his vengeance on him, even though it happened almost three years ago and Charlie hadn't seen Maria since. It seemed an extreme reaction to one night's sin. Blackmailers went to prison, and if Durham had discovered him in time, Worley would have suffered a great deal worse. If Worley truly wanted to punish Charlie, a suit for criminal damages would have done it very

well, socially and financially. He understood the
source of Worley's anger, but not its methods.

"It was only one night," he said, "undertaken in
a rash moment and swiftly regretted. I've not seen
her since."

Worley's grim expression faded, and suddenly he
looked old. "I hated you for years," he said softly,
almost to himself. "Everything I did she compared
to you, and I was always found wanting." He
turned and moved slowly across the room. "I lived
with that; I lived with the knowledge she would
have left me for you at any moment. Every time I
denied her anything, she flung it in my face that I
was her second choice, that fate had stolen her true
love from her. And because I was a fool, I accepted
it and told myself she was mine and always would
be, no matter what she said in anger." He pulled
the bell for the servant. "But this went too far."

A servant tapped at the door almost at once.
"Bring Lord Cranston," Worley told the maid,
who curtsied and disappeared.

"What did you hope to gain?" Charlie demanded, struggling to hold his temper in check.
He had sinned with the man's wife—he admitted
it—but he had done what he could to mitigate it.
He would have understood if Worley had called
him out, or demanded some other form of direct
retribution, but this cowardly blackmail scheme
had upset his brothers' lives and ruined his father's
final months on earth and, perversely, left his own
life relatively unscathed. The intentional cruelty to
his family left him furious. "There was no scandal
of that night. She left London and I never saw her
again. If your honor required satisfaction, why not

challenge me to a duel? Why torment my father on his deathbed? If you'd done any investigation you would have realized there was no basis for your threats. Dorothy Cope died decades ago. My mother's marriage was valid. What did you gain?"

The earl's eyes flashed. "Gain?" He gave a harsh bark of laughter. "As much as I longed to put a bullet into you, it wasn't worth the trouble. Why should I subject myself to any danger? It wasn't my intent to roil Durham's last days, but his secret marriage was the perfect opportunity. What could hurt Charles de Lacey, reprobate rake and useless fop, more than losing his inheritance and being declared a bastard? I don't care if it's true or not. I don't care if it upset your brothers' pampered lives a little, or sent Durham to his grave thinking his lies had caught up to him at last. You had to be punished, no matter what the cost."

Charlie drew breath in fury, but before he could respond the door opened. The maid had returned, and with her was a dark-haired toddler, who pulled loose of the maid's hand and ran across the room to Worley. "Papa!" cried the little boy. "Papa!"

All trace of anger and venom left the earl's face in an instant, and his expression transformed. He now wore a fond smile, his eyes bright with affection. He caught the child up in his arms and embraced him for a moment. "Here I am, Albert! What have you got today?"

"Rocks, Papa." The boy opened his chubby fist and displayed some pebbles. "From th' garden."

"I see." Worley shot Charlie a defiant look, then bent to set his son down. The little boy wobbled, then sat down hard, his skirts puffing up around him. Worley helped the child back to his feet. "Albert, make your bow to His Grace the Duke of Durham."

The boy turned round blue eyes to him, then gave a careful bow. He clutched Worley's hand the whole while.

"Your Grace," said Worley, with a hard edge to his voice, "this is my son, Albert."

Charlie gave a slight bow. "How do you do, Albert."

The boy hid his face. Barely keeping his own expression impassive, Charlie looked to Worley. Now he knew why. "A very handsome child."

Worley's jaw twitched. "He is. Go back to the nursery now, son."

The boy ran to his waiting nurse with only a nervous glance at Charlie, who watched him go. He was glad for the respite. Holy God. The boy was the right age—and Maria's other children were all daughters. He turned back to Worley when the child had gone, feeling sick to his stomach.

"He is my heir," said the earl. He put back his shoulders and glared at Charlie. "My only son."

His mouth was dry. "Is he?" Charlie managed to ask. He wanted to run after the child and inspect his face, to look for any sign of de Lacey features in him. The boy looked like Maria, with her coloring and eyes, not like Worley at all—but nor did Charlie see himself in the child. Was that his child, the product of his night with Maria? Did he have a son he could never claim? "Or is he mine?"

Worley was breathing so hard he shuddered with each exhalation. "He is *mine*," he said violently. "Whether I sired him or not."

"Don't you know?" exclaimed Charlie, suffering

some strong emotion of his own. "Did you blackmail my father because of a bloody *possibility*?"

"She told me," bit out Worley. "She told me he was probably yours. My son—my beloved, only son—not mine but *yours*." It was the furious wail of a lamed animal. "I didn't know she'd been with you until she threw the truth in my face during an argument a year ago. And now—to know my son and heir might be a cuckoo in my nest—"

Charlie's fists were shaking. "Do you mean to cast the boy aside?" he managed to ask. "Or his mother?"

"Never," Worley snarled. "I will never surrender my son. Under the law he is mine. I pray every night he is mine in truth." He took a breath and calmed a bit. "As for his mother, she is also mine—my Delilah, my Judith, but mine. I don't give up what is mine."

After a moment Charlie jerked his head once; he understood. Worley knew his wife had betrayed him, but there was no way to know beyond a doubt who had fathered her child. Worley loved his son, but was consumed by the doubt. Maria was probably suffering under that doubt, but Worley appeared to want her as well, in some tragic way. They had each trapped themselves; Maria had deceived her husband in hopes of escaping her marriage, but he wanted her too much to set her free. Charlie had been the only one not suffering, and that, Worley could not bear. Gerard had been right, nearly: the only purpose behind the blackmail had been to torment, not all three Durham sons, but Charlie alone. He had been the cause of all of it, because of his reckless infatuation with Maria.

Good God, his father had been utterly right to try to save him from his own foolishness. Without a word he turned to go.

"If I ever hear word of you so much as making a bow to my wife again, or setting foot within a hundred yards of my son, I'll kill you myself," Worley added as he reached the door.

Charlie turned his head to look at the earl. Worley's eyes glittered with hatred, and his voice was ice cold. He meant every word, and Charlie believed him. "I never meant to see your wife again," he said quietly. "And I never knew your son existed until today."

"I know I cannot touch you, legally," said Worley. "But I won't hesitate to kill you if you cross me again."

Slowly, Charlie shook his head. "No, I won't." He hesitated a moment longer. "Be good to the boy. He bears no blame, either way."

The earl glared at him. "Get off my property. And don't speak of my son again."

Charlie nodded once, and let himself out.

Chapter 20

Thankfully the butler was waiting nearby when Charlie stepped into the corridor. He wasn't sure he could have found his way out of the house unassisted. He followed the servant almost blindly, grappling with the new knowledge Worley had flung at him. Could it be his son?

No. Even if the child had Charlie's blood in his veins, he would never be his son; the law gave that to Worley. He had rarely thought of being a father, and he'd never gotten a woman with child, for just this reason. He hadn't been as careful with Tessa, but then . . . he didn't recoil in alarm from the thought of Tessa bearing his child. He could almost see and hear her, in fact, cuddling a green-eyed child in her arms, patiently explaining how to keep neat and accurate account books. He would have the cleverest, most capable heir of any duke in England, with Tessa as the child's mother. The thought made him smile.

"Gresham . . ."

The faint sound of his name made Charlie stop. Maria stood at the foot of the stairs, still as beautiful as ever, her face alight with dawning hope and joy. She pressed one hand to her bosom and wet her lips. The butler tactfully faded away, to Charlie's consternation. The last thing he wanted was to see Maria in any semblance of privacy.

"You came for me," she whispered. "Finally. Oh, Gresham . . ."

He held up his hands unsteadily as she rushed toward him. "No. Maria, *no*."

She reached for his hands, clasping them despite his effort to avoid it. "I knew you would come, I knew it—oh, darling, you've no idea how desperately I've longed for you these last interminable years . . ."

"I've just seen Worley."

"Oh—but of course you must!" She stepped closer, her smile blinding. "He'll have to file a suit, naturally—it will be dreadful, but in the end we can be together—oh, Gresham, you are the best of men to endure it for me!"

He couldn't bear to let her go on deceiving herself. He couldn't stand to hear any more of her wild hopes and plans, so he moved to end them now, once and for all. "He told me about Albert. I saw the boy."

She paused, then laughed lightly, but not before he caught the flicker of unease in her eyes. "Of course he would. A son and heir! Nothing else matters to him. Albert is paraded around like a prize-winning colt."

"He told me you claimed the boy was mine."

Her chin quivered at his tone. "I was angry—Worley knows I don't mean a word I say in anger. We were quarreling—these things happen between husbands and wives . . ."

"Maria, is he my child?" His question stopped her nervous chatter. She regarded him with disappointment, her expressive eyes shadowed. "Because if you're not certain beyond all doubt that he is," Charlie went on, finally losing some grip on his temper, "how dare you say such a thing to your husband? How dare you impugn your son's lineage?"

She shrugged one shoulder. Her mouth twisted. "Impugn! Nothing can keep Albert from inheriting Worley's title."

"That hardly matters to your husband!" He inhaled deeply to master his anger. "Is it true? Is he my child?"

She hesitated, her expression wary. "I don't know. Truly, I don't."

Charlie swallowed a string of curses. "How could you?"

"How could I?" She shook her head, tears glimmering in those magnificent eyes. "How could I want one moment of happiness, with the man I had loved for years? How could I crave one night of bliss out of the years of misery? Can you even ask?"

"How could you risk this? You had to know your husband wouldn't look the other way. He says he loves the child now, but who knows if his feelings will change as the boy grows? And I—" He had to pause for a moment. "If he is my son, you've forever deprived me of him. How could you do that to all of us?"

Her lip trembled but she put up her chin. "I wasn't thinking of that. I was only thinking of how unhappy I was, and how desperately I longed for you."

Charlie longed to shake her even as he pitied her. It was a risk he'd run by going to her bed at all, and he did believe she was unhappy. But he couldn't forgive her actions since. Even if he was as much to blame, even if Worley had earned her scorn, she had forever poisoned her son's future. Worley would be eternally on guard for any sign of him in the boy. Charlie prayed Albert was not his child, for the boy's own sake. Worley might be a kind father now, but as the lad grew and became rebellious or independent or anything other than Worley wanted him to be . . .

"And Albert most likely is Worley's own child," Maria went on as he said nothing. "Worley never spent more than a week away from my bed before he was born; he was there the very night after you left me. The more I think of it, the more I think he must be Worley's. He's such a strange child, nothing at all like you. A handful of rocks amuses him for hours."

"I was wrong to spend that night with you," he said quietly. "I wish I hadn't done it." Shock flashed over her face, but he felt no urge to soften his words. For too long he had let his youthful infatuation with her color his life. "We were both wrong, in fact. You knew Worley wouldn't look the other way, and I . . ." He sighed. "I didn't speak to my father for more than ten years because of you."

"You didn't?" She looked at him, lips parted in amazement, and he had the feeling she was somehow pleased that she'd had this much power over him.

"Because I was a dashed fool," he said bluntly.

"A young idiot, too stupid to see how right my father was to keep us apart."

"Oh, no!" she burst out hysterically, reaching for him. "Don't say that! It was my fault, my mistake—when you said we should run away, I was a fool to say no! I was too young, too silly, too afraid! But I love you; all these years, it's only been you!"

He looked at her gravely. She was still beautiful, still as vibrant and alluring as she'd been years ago. Standing before him now, her hands clasped in supplication, her large eyes pleading, she was just as he had dreamed . . . and he felt nothing. Pity, perhaps, for her bitter unhappiness, and regret for all the little ways he might have encouraged her hopes, unwittingly or not. But the wild desperation to have her was gone. For the first time in his life, Charlie fully appreciated what his father had feared. His love for Maria—perhaps like Durham's for Dorothy—was the wild passion of youth, the giddy defiance of authority, the obsession of first love. If he had eloped with her a decade ago, he doubted they would have been happy for a year, even had they had Durham's blessing.

"You don't love me," he said at last. "Don't lie to yourself that you do. And I don't love you. I cannot interfere in your marriage. I'm not here to take you away. I don't expect to see you again, in fact."

"How can you say that?" she cried, tears beginning to leak from her eyes. "Didn't you come to see me? I don't understand!"

"I haven't come to save you from an unhappy marriage," he said. "You wouldn't be happy anyway. All your desire to run away with me now is only a wish to escape."

"Yes! Yes, it is!" She dashed the tears from her cheeks. "If you had any idea of the hell I've endured these ten years—"

"As Countess of Worley?" he asked. "As a celebrated beauty? As a wealthy lady? Wasn't that what you wanted?"

She drew in an unsteady breath. "You're angry at me—because I didn't wish to be poor. Neither did you! We were young and foolish but if only we had waited a bit, thought it over, we should have been happy enough together to endure it. But it's not too late for us, it isn't!"

"It is. It always was." He shook his head. "Could you really leave your children? Could you really stand to drag your name through the mud for a divorce?"

"But as your duchess, none of that would matter," she whispered, even though her already pale face grew deathly white at his query. "People would forget . . ."

"You know they wouldn't. And you would soon hate me as much as you hate him." He made a very formal, deliberate bow. "Good-bye, Lady Worley."

"Wait!" She lunged for his arm as he started to turn. "He'll kill me! He's tried to many times already, when he's angry over something. I beg you, even if you no longer want me, take me away from here! I shall die here, Gresham, I know I will, if you leave me!"

Charlie hesitated. Worley was a coldhearted man, no doubt about it, and his fury at his wife's infidelity ran deep. He knew he couldn't take Maria with him, but neither could he abandon her to cruelty. "If you ever feel in peril of your life, or in fear for your children's lives, my brother Edward will do all in his power to aid you. But it would only make things worse if you came to me. Worley will forever despise me because of his doubts about your son. Whatever the truth may be, he'll kill us both if he thinks there's anything between us. For your own sake, Maria—for your son's sake—don't run after me."

Her grip on him slackened and fell away. For a moment her face registered such desolate despair he wondered if she truly feared for her life. "You never loved me, did you?" she whispered, anger touching her voice for the first time. "If you did, you would never be so callous."

A faint, sad smile bent his mouth. If she only knew. Three years ago—even three months ago, perhaps—he would have insisted he had, once upon a time. But now he knew better. What he felt for her had been a sort of love—a young man's reckless, impetuous passion, fueled by frustrated lust for her and impotent fury at his father, thriving off the very obstacles that thwarted it. "Once, I did," he told her softly. "But it was not the sort of love that can last."

"How do you know?"

He knew because of Tessa. Because while he'd wanted Maria, he'd never needed her. She had never challenged him to be a better man, as Tessa did. She had never made him furious and aroused and amused, all at the same time, as Tessa could do so effortlessly. She never stood up to him when he was foolish, or turned to him in a moment of need. If it had been Maria by his side when it seemed he would lose his title and all its trappings, he was rather certain she would have abandoned him, not stood by him and declared it made no difference to her whether he was a duke or a gentleman scholar. She definitely wouldn't have told him he would make a good pig farmer.

"Did you ever love me?" he asked instead. "Or was it only my title and fortune that caught your eye?"

She paused, tilting her head in the coy way he remembered too well, and it struck him that her look was almost calculating. "I did love you. You know I did. I still do."

"Your father asked my father for money."

She blinked. "Well—perhaps he did—we were rather poor—"

Charlie shook his head. "Never mind. It doesn't matter. Good-bye, Lady Worley. Remember what I said about Edward."

He went out of the house and took the reins of his horse. As he swung into the saddle he caught sight of Maria, who had followed him to the doorway and stood watching with one hand at her lips. He just gave her a level look before raising his eyes, scanning the rest of the windows, wondering if Worley watched him go as well. For a moment he thought of the little boy again, of his innocent blue gaze, and then he closed his mind to it. There was nothing he could do in any event. Under the law, the boy was Worley's, and Maria—the only person who might know the truth—claimed she didn't know who had fathered him. He prayed

Worley never held that doubt against the boy. He prayed the boy grew up to look like Worley. And most of all he prayed for forgiveness.

He turned his horse away and rode off without looking back.

Chapter 21

The hours seem to stretch to last an eternity once Charlie left. Tessa longed to know what he was doing, and she worried about Lord Worley's reaction. She wished she could forget his intimations about his devotion to Lady Worley, even though it drove her wild with curiosity and uncertainty. Did he still love the lady? Would Lord Worley call him out? Would he call Worley out? Images of Charlie, shot for any reason at all, tormented her at all hours. And the resulting heartache made her castigate herself for not telling him how deeply she cared for him before he left.

To occupy her time she walked. It didn't matter where she went, or with whom. Eugenie strolled about Frome with her the first day, but then begged off. Tessa apologized—she knew she was tense and restless—but Eugenie just smiled.

"I quite understand why, dear, *quite* understand," she said with a sympathetic pat on the hand. "I was once young and bedeviled by a young man."

Tessa laughed uncomfortably at that. "Bedeviled! I'm sure you had Mr. Bates sorted out in no time. You're a sly one, Eugenie, for all you protest it."

"Sly!" Eugenie blushed and looked prim. "I'm sure I don't know what you mean." But she gave herself away with an impish smile. "But my Henry did require a *bit* of encouragement!"

It was on her walk two days later that she gave in to temptation and let her steps stray past Mill Cottage. Just walking past would calm her, and, why, if Barnes happened to be out, and happened to spy her, he might mention any word he'd had from his master. It was unlikely Charlie would write to his valet, especially when he planned to be gone only a few days, but Tessa shoved aside those annoyingly rational points. She missed him, and only that mattered to her.

She was quite shocked to see a large coach on the gravel drive beside the cottage. Imposing, lacquered in black with bright red-trimmed wheels, it was as out of place in Frome as the King and Queen would have been. Tessa stopped in her tracks, openmouthed, and then caught sight of the crest on the door. It was the same crest she'd seen across the Duke of Durham's papers, which meant this was Charlie's town coach. Of course—he must have gone through Bath after all and decided to travel back in comfort. She distinctly remembered his grand arrival at the York Hotel in just such a coach.

As she stood on the road, daring to hope he might have just returned, she saw him. He sat out in the sunshine as he'd done that first day she ventured this way, his dark head bent over as he read. Tessa's heart skipped, jumped, and soared. Impulsively, she turned across the grass and hurried his way. The sun was behind him, and she squinted as she got closer, close enough to see the light glint off his signet ring and to see that he had cut his hair. She liked it longer, she decided, although this made him look very ducal.

She slipped her arms around his shoulders and rested her cheek against his temple. "You're back," she whispered. "I missed you."

He went utterly still at her touch. "Have you?" he said after a pause.

Tessa blinked, then leaped back in horror. It wasn't Charlie, but a different man, rising from his seat and turning to face her. He looked like Charlie—the same fine, long nose, the same arched brows—but his eyes were gray, and there was no mischief in his expression. He was also a bit leaner, and his hands were definitely different. Her brain seemed to be cataloging differences all on its own as she stood and gawked at him like a lunatic.

"I thought you were Charlie," she said inanely. "I—I apologize most humbly, sir."

He smiled. Now he looked even more like his brother, because of course this had to be another de Lacey. "So I gathered. I am Edward de Lacey, his brother."

Flushing to the roots of her hair, Tessa dipped a curtsy and mumbled something polite.

"He is not at home at present," said Lord Edward, watching her. "No one seems to know precisely when he will return."

She had to wet her lips. "No. He did not say, before he left."

"Ah." He tilted his head. Tessa had to clamp her jaw tight to keep from scowling at him; she didn't like being studied so brazenly. "Do you know where he has gone?"

"No." She kept her head up. Instinctively she thought Charlie would want privacy, and she had no business telling anyone what he had confided in her. "Don't you?"

Lord Edward's brow creased thoughtfully. "No."

Tessa hesitated, but he seemed in no hurry to speak. She deeply regretted coming over; even if it had been Charlie, back from his private mission, she should have waited for him to seek her out. Had she learned nothing from Louise? "I should be going," she announced. "I am sure he'll return soon, and be delighted to see you."

"Will he be?" Lord Edward had a way of looking at people as if he knew what they meant to say, regardless of what they did say. "I daresay he won't be very glad. I have come to bring him back to London."

Her heart seized up. "Have you?" she said, striving for disinterest. "I believe he was about to return to town anyway."

He nodded, growing grave. "That is fortunate, for he must come now, whether he wills it or not."

She shouldn't say anything, but Tessa suddenly remembered that he would have the same vital interest in Mr. Thomas's letter that Charlie himself had. "He found it," she blurted out. "The proof he was looking for, about Dorothy Cope."

Lord Edward's eyes blazed and he tensed. "Proof?" he demanded. "Legal proof?"

She nodded. "A record of death from the church at Nunney. We saw her gravestone." She noticed then what he'd been reading: those impenetrable marriage registers. "Look in the one with the stain shaped like a pig," she said with a nod toward the registers. "About one-third of the way through. Her true name was Dorothy Swynne, and she was buried in the Nunney churchyard in December of 1773."

Lord Edward regarded her with narrowed eyes. "We," he repeated with emphasis.

Tessa nodded even though her face warmed again. "I offered my assistance. It was a tedious job, but Ch—Lord Gresham would not be deterred."

He stared at her for a long moment. "Thank you," he said finally. "I am deeply grateful for your assistance. That is excellent news for my family."

Tessa bowed her head in acknowledgment. She hadn't done anything for him or his family, excepting one member. "I really should be going," she said for the second time. "And I do apologize for my ill manners."

"On the contrary," he replied with a ghost of a smile. "It was a pleasure, Mrs. . . . ?"

"Neville," she said. "Teresa Neville." She bobbed a quick curtsy. "Good day, my lord."

"Good day, Mrs. Neville," Edward de Lacey murmured, watching her hurry away without looking back, her hands in fists at her sides. What an intriguing visit that had been, he thought. "Who is that woman, Barnes?" he asked the valet, who had come out with the paper, pen, and ink he'd requested.

Barnes looked after the departing visitor. "Mrs. Neville," he said after a pause. "A widowed lady."

"Indeed." She'd called him Charlie. She'd thrown her arms around him and all but kissed him when she thought he was Charlie. "Has she visited often?" Edward asked.

"I couldn't say, sir." The valet's face was blank.

"I see. Did my brother by any chance meet her in Bath, before he came to Frome?"

Barnes hesitated again. "I believe she and her companion were staying in Bath at the same hotel as His Lordship, sir."

"Ah." Edward recalled the curious story his brother Gerard had told him, about Charlie's fascination with a woman who allegedly despised him. "That will be all, Barnes."

He settled himself at the table once more, picking up the register Mrs. Neville had indicated, the one with a large watermark in the shape of a pig. Edward regarded it for a moment with a small smile. "And Charlie laughed at *me* for falling in love," he murmured. "Oh, how fate has repaid him!"

Tessa had a stitch in her side by the time she reached The Golden Hind, walking as fast as one could walk without breaking into a run. "Eugenie," she called as she hurried into their rooms. "Eugenie!"

"What is it, dear?" Eugenie came out of her room, little bits of thread on her skirt from her embroidery. "Is something wrong?"

"Why would you think that?" Tessa took off her bonnet and inhaled a deep breath. "We leave for London tomorrow. Mary, finish packing," she said to the maid who popped out of the other room. Mary nodded and disappeared again.

"Tomorrow!" Eugenie's mouth dropped open.

Tessa nodded. "We've delayed too long as it is.

Louise is expecting us, and it's wrong of me to dally. Your packing is almost finished, isn't it?"

"Well, yes, nearly, but Tessa dear . . ." Eugenie wrung her hands. "What about Lord Gresham?" To say Eugenie's hopes regarding Lord Gresham's intentions had risen was an understatement. After Tessa returned from her overnight escapade, swathed in blankets to bolster the lie that she'd taken ill in the rain, Eugenie had fussed over her as much as if she had been sick, but with such a bright, knowing smile that Tessa wondered if she'd already sent a wedding notice to the newspapers.

"Well, it's interesting you mention him." Tessa smiled brightly. "He's also going to London soon. On my walk I happened to meet his brother, who's come to fetch him back to town." That was literally true.

What Tessa didn't say was what she had thought about after leaving Mill Cottage. Lord Edward had asked if they'd found legal proof; he had been in charge of the legal filings regarding Durham, and now said Charlie must come back to London whether he wished to or not. Tessa thought that probably meant the Committee for Privileges was about to consider the case, including the contesting claim from Charlie's cousin. In her mind, that led to three inescapable conclusions.

First, that Charlie would be occupied for some time in London with this hearing. He had the proof he needed, but there was no way to know how easily or quickly the committee would accept it.

Second, that meant he would have little time for her. How could he, when he must fight for his birthright and everything he'd been raised to become? Tessa wouldn't have wanted to distract him even though her heart quailed from facing it. And then he would be a duke, blessed by God and the King, and much too high above the likes of her.

So thirdly, she should go to London now. She was only delaying the inevitable by lingering. As hard as it was to leave without a farewell, she preferred it this way. If she left before he returned to Frome, there would be no need for promises that might be regretted later. There would also be no chance that he would return only to tell her he was still in love with Lady Worley, or regretted taking up with her, or had just remembered that he was a duke and would be expected to marry a proper duchess once he reached London. There would be no unpleasant scene of any sort. And what had she expected, anyway? That he would escort her and Eugenie to London? She remembered the shiny black coach at Mill Cottage, and almost shook her head at her foolishness.

She told herself this was the best way. If by some chance he wished to see her again, she would be in London, too. If he didn't wish to see her again, well, London was a large place. They had parted on good terms, with no trace of scandal or unseemly behavior, for which Tessa was deeply grateful. This way, she couldn't possibly make a fool of herself again.

But Eugenie was looking at her with stricken eyes, and it took real effort to keep her smile fixed in place. "Come," Tessa said to encourage her companion, "we knew we would go to London. As you said, it is likely we will meet him there, if we're meant to meet again."

"Are you running away from him, Tessa?" asked Eugenie sadly. "Oh, my dear, it's because of *that vile man*, isn't it?"

She took a deep breath. Richard had never once crossed her mind. "It has nothing to do with Mr. Wilbur. I am not running away. I am keeping to my plan, which I told you weeks ago in Wiltshire. The travel chaise is engaged, and I hope to leave in the morning."

And so they did. Eugenie went and supervised Mary's packing, but with a somber air that strained Tessa's forced cheer. By the morning both moods had all worn away, though. After a sleepless night, Tessa admitted to herself that she was running away. She was glad she'd already arranged for the chaise; if there had been any delay she might have lost her head and run back to Mill Cottage, because . . . because she was in love with him, and her heart was breaking because she didn't know if she would see him again.

Would Charlie come to her in London? She had worried at that question for most of the night, staring up at the lines in the plaster ceiling. There was a chance, she granted. But there was also a chance, a very good one, that he would wonder what he'd ever seen in her, once he was back among the glittering elegance of town. How could she compete with the woman he'd been in love with for years? How would she look compared to the beautiful and sophisticated ladies of London? Not well, Tessa thought—or rather, she would look like what she was, a country woman of no great wealth or fashion, who was nearing thirty years old.

She had weathered her first broken heart because

she'd been filled with rage. Richard had lied to her, taken advantage of her, and seduced her, and she couldn't think of any fate too cruel for him. She couldn't hate Charlie for anything, though. She didn't know how she would ever forget him, nor how she would ever think of him without wanting to weep.

Eugenie, on the other hand, had recovered hope by the morning. She took one look at Tessa's expression at breakfast and said in her comforting way, "It shall be such a pleasure to see Lady Woodall again, and the children! And Lord and Lady Marchmont will be there as well. You are right to return to your family, dear, and I am certain Lord Gresham will waste no time in calling upon us."

Tessa managed only a thin smile. "Perhaps you are right, Eugenie."

They reached London late in the afternoon after two long, dusty days of travel. For once Eugenie hadn't said a word of complaint during the journey, not that Tessa would have heard her anyway. She was sunk too deep in her own gloomy thoughts to be companionable, and Eugenie seemed to realize it. "He'll call," she'd said confidently at random intervals. "I know he will, Tessa dear."

She didn't know what to say to that. Perhaps? That he might come, if he had time to spare? Should she laugh and say she hoped he would come but they mustn't get their hopes up? Or should she just agree with Eugenie and let it go at that, with no mention of all the reasons he might well never come to see them?

Her head ached by the time they reached St. James's Square, where Louise had taken a house.

Eugenie murmured something about how pleasant the square itself was, but Tessa didn't even look. She climbed down from the carriage, as exhausted and sore as if she'd walked from Frome.

Louise was in high spirits when they went inside the house. "I've been expecting you for days now," she cried, pressing her cheek to Tessa's and then embracing Eugenie. "Well, my dears, haven't we got a very pretty arrangement here? I'm so glad to have you both, now it feels like home!"

Tessa managed a lackluster smile as she pulled loose the ribbons on her bonnet and handed it to the waiting footman. "Thank you, Louise. It is good to be here at last." But it wasn't. She would much rather have stayed in Frome, or even better, hidden away at Mill Cottage for another few decades, with Charlie all to herself. Even Rushwood would have been better.

Louise frowned, inspecting her. "What's wrong? You don't look well. Good heavens, Tessa, have you caught some wretched canal-worker illness? I told you it was foolishness—"

"Louise dear, how are the children?" Eugenie asked quickly. "I've missed them! I'm sure they've grown so in the last month, I shall hardly recognize them."

"They're perfectly well. I can't think why they aren't down here already," Louise said, still watching Tessa sharply. "I'm sure they heard you arrive . . ." Even as she spoke, there came the sound of running feet, and with a chorus of happy cries, Louise's children burst into the hall.

Tessa turned at once to embrace her nieces, Pippa and Helen, and greet her nephew Thomas, now taller than she was. She was unquestionably glad to see them; her nieces and nephew were lovely children and she adored them all. As they chattered excitedly about their trip to London, and Pippa's finger getting smashed in the carriage door and the goose that chased Thomas and the very elegant people who lived all around them now, Tessa dimly heard Louise scolding Eugenie. The older lady's reply was too soft to hear, but Tessa knew from her sister's gasp what Eugenie had told her. A gentleman. An attachment. An indiscretion. But no betrothal. Poor, poor Tessa.

She resisted the urge to turn around and dispute it. She was a grown woman, supposedly a widow, and her life was her own. She had never expected a proposal from Charlie. It was nothing like when she'd been so foolish over Richard Wilbur. Even before she knew about the dukedom, Tessa had known Charlie wouldn't marry someone like her. She might be a viscount's daughter, but her papa was a countrified, rather ordinary viscount, more at home walking his fields with the dogs than in a drawing room. Her mother had been a banker's granddaughter, with the dowry and head for business to make the family comfortable but certainly not fashionable. Louise was the closest member of the family to good society, and even that was rather tenuous; Viscount Woodall had hardly moved in the first circles. The Marchmonts were simply not good ton, and Tessa was well aware that her family's lack of status was only the first of her personal deficiencies.

Her affair with Charlie had been a pleasant diversion, nothing more; once he was back among his own set, he'd wonder what he ever saw in her. And if by some chance he did care to see her again, he would have to seek her out. Even she knew ladies in London didn't chase after gentlemen, no matter how well acquainted they were. She could hardly explain to everyone that he was her lover, or that she had utterly lost her heart to him. The first would scandalize her family, and the second . . . the second was no one's concern but her own.

As soon as the housekeeper offered to show her to her room, Tessa said she was tired and wanted to rest, hurrying upstairs to the room prepared for her. She even turned the key in the lock, but it was no match for Louise. Her sister knocked and knocked and threatened to send for a physician if Tessa didn't let her in, so finally she opened the door.

"What happened in Frome?" Louise demanded at once. "Eugenie said something occurred."

"Yes," said Tessa without looking at her. "The canal was a sad disappointment. William will have to find another investment, for I wouldn't let him send ten shillings to Mr. Scott. The man's a charlatan."

"Pooh on the canal," said Louise crossly. "You know I don't care about that. What else?"

Tessa steeled herself. "Eugenie made the acquaintance of a gentleman, Lord Gresham. Did she not tell you? It was the crowning glory of her trip."

Louise's eyes narrowed. "Lord Gresham," she repeated. "Lord Gresham, the heir to the Duke of Durham, who was the most eligible man in all England until a few months ago, when the greatest scandal in living memory engulfed him?"

"In living memory?" Tessa said, striving for disinterest. "I thought that fuss over the Duke of

York and Mrs. Clarke selling army commissions was only last year . . ."

"You know what I mean." Louise waved her hand impatiently. "What happened in Frome? And how on earth does it involve the Earl of Gresham?"

Tessa went to the window and stared out. The lovely green of St. James's Square was visible, barely, if she looked far to the right. Through the ripples of the glass, it had an unreal, fairy look about it, a distant oasis of lush, peaceful green. She thought of the refuge behind Mill Cottage, where the willows grew in the ruined old mill and the brook ran past and where Charlie had called her darling, then had to close her eyes for a moment. "Lord Gresham was there to look at the canal. He called on me and Eugenie a few times, which was very kind of him; Frome is possibly the quietest town on earth, Louise. It was terribly inconsiderate of you to make Eugenie go along just because you wanted her out of your way."

Louise put her hands on her hips. "Tessa, tell me now," she said through her teeth. She made no effort at all to deny the charge about Eugenie, which indicated how serious she was.

Tessa took a deep breath and exhaled slowly. "Eugenie thought he paid me some interest," she said at last. "But I am convinced he meant nothing by it." Her heart hurt as she said it, even though she told herself it was factually correct. The only sort of interest Louise would be interested in was a proposal of marriage, and Charlie hadn't made one.

"The new Duke of Durham paid you attention," said Louise as if she couldn't believe her ears. "The Duke of Durham."

"Well, he isn't the duke," Tessa pointed out. "He is still Lord Gresham. Eugenie and I didn't even know about the Durham Dilemma until . . . later."

"When did you know?" Louise caught her hesitation. "After what?"

After he kissed her. After he made love to her. After he made her feel justified for her actions to Richard Wilbur, not like a half-mad betrayed spinster. After she lost her heart to him. "After we knew him a bit," she said. "You know I never pay attention to gossip."

"Never pay . . . ?" Louise gaped at her. "Tessa! The Durham Dilemma? How could you not remark that? *Everyone* is talking of it!"

"Eugenie didn't know of it, either," Tessa defended herself. "No one in Frome was speaking of it, I assure you."

Louise put her fingertips to her temples. "Very well," she said, her voice gone higher with strain. "You didn't know. With you, it might be true. But then—" She inhaled and exhaled loudly. "Then how acquainted were you with him?"

Tessa turned back to the window. "He was there to see the canal," she said quietly. "That's what he told us. He assisted Eugenie when she felt unwell, and then he continued his kindness. He drove me to see Mr. Scott once or twice, as he also had business with the man." She gave a slight shrug. "Then he left to return to London."

"Yes," said Louise. "He must come back to London for the trial before Parliament on whether he shall inherit or not!"

"It's not a trial," said Tessa without thinking. "It's a hearing before a committee."

"You knew!" Louise screeched in triumph. "I knew you knew more than you let on! How well did you become acquainted? My heavens, Tessa, he's the most talked about man in England! Do you realize what this could mean for us? Assuming he wins this trial or whatever it is, he'll be the *Duke of Durham*! Do you understand what that means, Tessa?"

It meant he could have his pick of all the women in England. Charlie would have been hard for any woman to refuse even as a penniless scoundrel with no assets but his charm and his looks; possessed of an ancient, illustrious title and all the wealth that went with it . . . He would forget her name within a week. Tessa laid her palms against the cold windowpanes and bit down hard on her lip, trying not to betray any sign of her feelings.

"We must be delicate about this," Louise was saying, although her voice brimmed with joy. She started pacing, wringing her hands. "We must arrange a public meeting, where he can acknowledge you—oh, I'm so glad you've come to town, dear, darling Tessa! This will establish us in the very best circles! And once we're publicly acquainted, we shall invite him to dine—"

"No," Tessa said harshly, rounding on her sister. "You will not. If you try to push me into his path, I will leave London and never return, even if I have to walk all the way to Rushwood."

Louise blinked in astonishment. "What happened, dear?" Comprehension finally seemed to be emerging from the haze of delight over the prospect of a ducal acquaintance. "Did he lead you on?"

Her breath seemed to have caught on something in her chest. It hurt to inhale, and her throat burned. "No."

Her sister frowned. "Did he trifle with you?"

"No."

"Then what happened?" cried Louise, frenzied with curiosity.

Tessa opened her mouth to reply, but no words would come. *I fell in love,* she wanted to say. *I fell in love with him but even if he loved me, it's not meant to be.* But her throat tightened up and she snapped her mouth shut.

Louise's face changed. "Oh, my dear." She looked as though she might burst into tears, and then she opened her arms. Louise loved nothing more than a tragic drama, Tessa told herself, but somehow she went into her older sister's arms and took the comfort they offered.

Chapter 22

Charlie left Uppercombe in a somber but turbulent mood. He rode aimlessly at first, needing some peace to absorb the news. Eventually he realized he had wandered far from the road home, too far to return that day. A small inn provided a perfect haven as he tried to think of what he should do next. It was a hard blow to learn he might have a son who would always belong to another man— and a man like Worley at that. He didn't get much sleep, kept awake by that thought and by remembrances of his own father. Durham had been stern and demanding, but Charlie had known he cared for all three of his children. He'd been exacting, but never cruel. Charlie hadn't always thought the duke's punishments were merited, but he also acknowledged that he got into the most trouble of the Durham boys. And of course, his father's greatest sin—denying him Maria—turned out to be no sin at all, but a mercy.

There was something very humbling in the realization that his father had been more like him than he knew. Charlie wondered how he would have reacted if Durham had confided in him, when he was deep in the throes of his passion for Maria, about Dorothy. If that admission of weakness and foolishness would have knocked some sense into him, and at least kept him from succumbing to momentary madness three years ago with Maria. It could have prevented all this scandal and upheaval, and allowed his father to die in peace. He had been as impulsive and shortsighted as any young man, and even more so under the influence of infatuation, but there was no question that his father's heavy-handed discipline had also spurred him to rebellion many times, before and after Maria. It was uncomfortable to peer into his own juvenile mind and examine his motives. How many of his actions had been driven purely by the desire to prove himself independent of his father's whim?

He delayed an extra day at the inn, excoriating himself for being petulant and obstinate. If he had only humbled himself to return home, even years after the break, to ask his father for an explanation, this all might have been avoided. It was lowering to admit he had been just as bad as his father in clinging to his pride, each determined not to concede to the other. Charlie realized he had no trouble doing this before other people; in fact, he had deprecated himself many times in his pursuit of Tessa, and not found it galling at all. Edward always insisted their father was fair-minded, and he'd explicitly told him that Durham wished to see him. It was the hardest realization of all: that his father might have wished to remedy the breach, to apologize or at least to explain, and he had ignored it. What was the discomfort of traveling with a broken leg, after all, compared to the reconciliation and peace he might have granted his father at the end? He could barely stand to think of how Edward had said the duke called for him in his last hours.

And what would Tessa think of him now? The whole scandal had been his fault, because of his recklessness. Gerard was liable to punch him in the face, and Edward would castigate him for being so idiotic, and he would deserve both. But if Tessa looked at him with disgust and loathing when she heard the full story . . . he didn't know how he would bear it.

He reached Mill Cottage late in the day, dismounting and handing his horse to the boy who came running. He trudged toward the house, his heart and mind still heavy with the results of his journey. He had to tell his brothers that everything had been his fault, however unintentionally. He had to tell Tessa—God above, he needed to see Tessa. He told himself she would understand. Everything else seemed to make more sense after he talked it over with her, and he hoped desperately this would be the same.

"Welcome home, my lord," said Barnes, waiting for him in the doorway.

Charlie nodded absently. "Yes, yes. Draw a bath and bring a bottle of wine." As much as he needed to see Tessa, he needed to clean up first.

"Yes, sir." Barnes took his coat and hat. "Lord Edward has arrived, my lord."

Charlie's head jerked up. "Damn." For some reason, it made him think of Gerard's reaction to his own arrival in Bath. The de Lacey brothers, who'd gone months without a single letter ex-

changed, were now popping in for visits to each
other at the most inconvenient moments. "Where
is he?"

"In the back parlor, sir."

Edward looked up when Charlie opened the
door. He had a stack of papers in front of him, as
usual. "Always hard at work," said Charlie. "How
are you, Edward?"

His brother rose and shook his hand. "Well
enough."

"And your wife? I trust you left her well?"

There was no mistaking the light that came into
Edward's eyes. "Splendidly well."

Charlie nodded. "I thought as much." He didn't
ask what had brought Edward all the way into
Somerset. He didn't have to.

"I hope you've been half as well," Edward said.
"I wondered, and Gerard did, too, but we had no
word." Charlie made no effort to deny the implicit
accusation. "In fact, I had the devil of a time finding you," Edward went on, "given that Gerard
only knew you were leaving Bath in pursuit of
Hiram Scott. After you left town, he was able to
discover Mr. Scott's ironworks in Mells, which is
where I went initially. When you weren't there, I
asked after the lady you followed, Mrs. Neville,
and traced you to Frome."

"How is Gerard?" asked Charlie. "He wasn't
pleased to see me when I arrived in response to his
summons, in your place."

Edward smiled. "He's decided to buy a house
in Bath. I believe his bride took a liking to the
town, and they intend to stay." Charlie nodded.
His brother eyed him expectantly. "What have you

learned, Charlie?" Edward finally asked bluntly. "I came because the hearing has been scheduled. Cousin Augustus's contesting petition will be heard, and you must defend your claim—*our* claim."

Charlie turned and walked away, out of the house. Edward followed, but neither spoke until they reached the path along the brook, rushing past the old mill. "Dorothy is long dead," Charlie said at last. "I have a letter from the curate of the parish where she's buried, testifying to her date of death five months before Durham wed our mother. Unless Durham had another secret marriage that comes to light, there is no question of our legitimacy."

Edward nodded. "And have you dealt with Scott?"

Charlie squinted at the sunlight flashing off the water. "Yes."

"Will anyone find the body?" Charlie glared at him. Edward just raised his brows. "I presume you put an end to him for blackmailing Father."

He heaved a sigh. "Scott wasn't much to blame. He posted the letters, but he didn't write them." He paused. "Dorothy Cope—or Dorothy Swynne, as she was born—was his mother. Her youthful escapades in London were quiet family lore; when Father inherited Durham, she remarked that she might have been a duchess, and wasn't that a grand joke? Scott was a boy, but he remembered. He thought she'd only had an affair with Father, or been courted by him; he had no idea they'd actually married. Although it seems clear she never thought the marriage was real, since she came back to Somerset and had a new husband and family by the time Father inherited Durham."

"And you found proof of all this?"

He nodded. "Somehow Gerard unearthed the minister—if one could truly call him such—and got hold of his registers, including the one recording the marriage of Francis Lacey to Dorothy Swynne Cope. It also recorded the marriages of whores and children and people so poor they had to pay the minister on credit. Good God, Edward, can you imagine Father being married in a tavern by a charlatan of a minister?"

"No. But I daresay we are all fools for love, in our own ways."

Charlie gave a huff of bitter laughter, thinking of Maria. "You've got the right of that."

"Mrs. Neville doesn't seem a fool," remarked Edward. "I daresay she'll pull you out of it. I wish you very happy, Charlie."

His head whipped around. "When did you meet her?"

Edward grinned like a cat that had just cornered a mouse. "Two days ago. She . . . mistook me for you, for a moment." His grin grew wider at Charlie's expression. "I quite understood why you hadn't written us, after meeting her."

"I was busy," said Charlie through his teeth, "hunting down a blackmailer and trying to save our inheritance."

"And I commend you for it," replied his brother gravely. "She told me she helped you."

"Dash it all," grumbled Charlie. "She's brilliant, Ned—cleverer than you and far more beautiful."

"Yes, I believe she will make a fine addition to the family." Edward turned and started back toward the house. "I enjoy this much more when you are the fool, sick in love," he called back. "I shall go write to my wife and tell her to plan a dinner in honor of her future sister."

Charlie replied in vulgar terms, and listened to his brother laugh all the way to the house. A fool, sick in love; had he teased Edward so badly over his precipitous plunge into love and matrimony? Edward had almost married the wrong woman as well, before the damned Durham Dilemma upended the betrothal. Perhaps they were all the same: Durham, Edward, and now he himself, all sure of their own judgment and determination, all learning humbling lessons about love.

Of course, it would be hard to regret anything if he ended as happily as Edward had.

He went back into the house and up the stairs, where Barnes had a steaming bath waiting. On impulse he opened the satchel of documents Edward had given him all those weeks ago, digging through the papers until he found the letter. He had read it before, when his brothers arrived in London to break the news of Durham's clandestine first marriage, but was in such a rage at his father then that he'd only gleaned the basic facts. Now he carried it to the table where Barnes had left the wine waiting, and stripped off his dusty, dirty riding clothes. When the heat of the bath had begun to soothe his sore muscles and he'd fortified himself with a glass of burgundy, Charlie unfolded his father's last letter and read.

My dear sons—
　I write this with a heart made heavy by regret for the actions detailed below. Of all the sins in

my long life, this is the one I shall most bitterly lament, for the sin itself and for my inability to remedy it through my own efforts and repentance. For leaving this burden on you all, I am most humbly sorry.

The source of my troubles was my own fiery nature. In my youth, long before Durham descended to me, I was a young man of some small fortune and no responsibility, and as such, took myself off to London, endeavoring to spend as much time as possible on all manner of frivolity. In the spring of 1751 or 1752, I met a young woman by the name of Dorothy Cope, called Dolly. She was a beauty, with wit and spirit and a welcome willingness to share my revels.

Had I been older and wiser, or more sober, or simply more hesitant, I might have avoided all this trouble. Instead I soon thought myself passionately in love with Dolly, and devoted myself to winning her. She was trying to make her way on the stage, and in my vanity I thought she would surely see the benefit of my protection. Instead she spurned me as a boy not yet in possession of his fortune. It was entirely true; my father was still living, and made me a handsome but not excessive allowance. I was grand-nephew to the Duke of Durham, but had no expectation of succeeding to the title. Had I but taken her rejection with cold, clear-eyed calm, or even set myself to brooding in magnificent dudgeon, none of the following would have happened.

When she would not become my mistress, I declared I was different from her other suitors; when she asked how, I said I would marry her. This she *also refused with a laugh, which only inflamed me. I said it again and again until she finally consented. You, my sons, will note how foolhardy I was in pursuing a woman who did not want me, who had to be bullied into marriage. I was by no means an ineligible husband, being a gentleman of good birth and family connections with a comfortable income, even if it was not entirely my own then. You will also exclaim in shock at the manner of our union: in a tavern near the prison, by a knavish fellow in a parson's robe, with only a half-drunk dockworker and the parson's clerk for witness.*

I have endeavored to recall every detail about that ceremony. We both swore that we were aged 21, although Dolly had not yet reached that age, and that we both resided in London, although my home was properly in Sussex. The parson was one Rev. William Ogilvie—I recall that distinctly, as some merriment was made over the name sounding like the call of a bird—of Somerset. The dockworker was an illiterate fellow, paid two shillings to make his mark as witness. The clerk's name I do not recall at all, if I ever knew it. The parson recorded the marriage in his register book and both Dolly and I signed our names. We all celebrated with a drink in the tavern, and Dolly and I took our leave of the Reverend.

My folly was apparent in short order. My eyes had seen only so far as making Dolly my own; I had never imagined a life with her. We were both possessed of the same hot temper, and within weeks we were quarreling over the slightest thing. When she declared her intention of returning to her theater company and traveling the country with them, I insisted she would not. A terrible argument followed, in the course of which she said it would be better if we had not married, and in a fit of fury, I burned our marriage certificate, such as it was. Upon that, she proclaimed herself well-satisfied that we were no longer husband and wife, and I agreed, telling her to get out of my lodging. She packed her things and left, after heaping more scorn and abuse on my head, and I, to my shame, reviled her in turn.

After this I returned to my old life—quite easily, as the few friends of mine who knew I pursued her believed her to be merely my mistress, even during our brief attempt at living together. When she left, they assumed it was nothing more than a woman turning her sights on a wealthier man, and I endured their teasing in silence. Bad enough to be left by a mistress of a fickle or mercenary disposition; worse still to have foolishly married her and been deserted by a wife of low class. Within a few weeks the affair was mostly forgotten. Only the landlady of our lodging had thought us married, and in those days it was not uncommon for a couple to claim a marriage where none in fact existed, or the only "union" between the two was a spoken promise.

I did see Dolly once more. It was months after we parted, and our tempers had cooled by then. She had done well with her theater company and embraced the life; I heard from others that she had a wealthy protector, and indeed she was in fine trim when I encountered her by chance. Feeling some residual duty to her, I inquired if she

*were well and if she needed anything from me (by
which I meant money); she smiled and said no,
she had everything she wanted at the moment.
We mutually agreed again that we had no connection, and that was for the best, and then we
parted. I never saw or spoke or wrote to her ever
again.*

*For almost twenty years I did as I pleased,
thinking little about her. It was a youthful mistake, best forgotten. I was never tempted to
throw myself so rashly after a woman again, and
never had the urge to marry. Not until Durham
descended to me, quite suddenly and unexpectedly, did I dredge up more than a passing thought
of Dolly. But a duke must marry; he must have
heirs; and they must be legitimate. I confess I half
expected Dolly to come forth upon my inheritance. To reject a gentleman of modest fortune
was one thing, but to lay claim to the title Duchess of Durham might tempt even the most alien-
ated woman. I waited, but she did not appear.
As I turned my thoughts to marriage—I was then
forty years old, and had little time to waste—I
made efforts to locate her, which all failed. After
twenty years of absence and two attempts to find
her in order to secure a full and legal divorce, I
persuaded myself she must have died, or left England, or fallen into such a life that I had nothing to fear from her. In time I took a wife—your
beloved mother—and she filled her role to perfection, not the least in giving me you three, my
dear sons. Decades marched on, and Dolly faded
almost entirely from my memory.*

The first wretched letter arrived last summer,

after I had fallen ill. It was short and shocking: someone claimed to know about Dolly. At once I sent out investigators to search for her again, to no more success than before. Another letter arrived, threatening denunciation, and then another demanding a large sum of money. Each letter taunted me for my unpardonable complacency over the years. I alternated between fury and despair; Edward, no doubt, remarked my agitation, but I kept the cause from him, and Charles and Gerard were mercifully away from home. Do not blame Mr. Pierce for not revealing it. I forbade him to tell you anything, even as I pressed him ever harder to search. It was all for naught. As I write this, I have found neither Dolly nor the man who claimed to know of her, and now it is too late for me to undo what I have done.

Forgive me, my dearest lads. I have been betrayed by a young man's foolishness and an old man's pride. A better man would have confessed his dark secret at once, so that you might at least have had the chance to question me about it. I have waited too long; my time grows too short. The shame of leaving Durham to you under such a cloud overwhelms me. I have remade my will to secure as many benefits as I may to each of you, but am consumed by anguish for what you could lose if this vile blackmailer exposes me. I leave you everything I have that might possibly expose this villainy, and exhort you to finish what I could not. Durham was a prize I never expected to hold, but it has been my purpose in life these forty years. Fight for it; it is your birth-

*right now, and each of you are more worthy of it
than I ever was.*

   *I beg your forgiveness, though I do not deserve
it, and remain ever your devoted father.*

                                    Francis de Lacey

Charlie laid the letter aside. Yes, he could forgive his father, finally, if only because he had been
every bit as big a fool. Of all the misery that had
sprung from his father's ill-fated love affair, Durham's had been greatest. He, Gerard, and Edward,
though—once the initial blow faded—had come
out better for it all. If not for the scandal, Edward
would have married his first fiancée, and never met
the fiery Francesca who bewitched him and cap-
tured his heart. Gerard would still be fighting the
French, not setting up house for his wealthy bride,
Kate, whom he'd married as a hedge against disin-
heritance, but with whom he'd fallen madly in love
since. And he . . .

He would never have been forced out into the
desolate hills of Somerset, where a blunt-spoken,
green-eyed temptress would call him indolent, talk
to him of canals, and manage to invade his heart so
thoroughly he couldn't fathom living without her.

And for the first time since he left Uppercombe,
Charlie smiled.

Chapter 23

The next day did not begin well. Despite the need for haste, Edward made no complaint when Charlie said he must pay a call in Frome before leaving for London. He was grateful to his brother, but it turned out to be a pointless concession. Tessa and Mrs. Bates had left by the time he arrived at The Golden Hind, and there was only the briefest message left for him.

We are departing in such a rush, my lord, wrote Eugenie Bates. *Tessa explained it all to me, and I perfectly understand, but I do hope we will have the pleasure of seeing you in London! I am sure I'm not the only person who would be very glad to receive you.*

"Troubles?" inquired Edward mildly, watching him read.

"I believe I've been rebuffed." Charlie stuffed the letter into his coat pocket and tried not to show how bereft he felt. He had hoped to see Tessa before the long journey to London, and she had promised to wait for him. He knew that once he left Frome, there were be little time for anything other than settling the damned Durham Dilemma, and he'd so wanted one last blissful reprieve with her, even for a quarter hour. But now she was gone, with only a note from her companion, nothing at all of farewell from Tessa herself. What had happened? What, exactly, had Tessa explained to Mrs. Bates? Why hadn't she waited? "They've already left for London."

Edward raised one eyebrow. "Ah."

Charlie glared at him. "What does that mean?"

His brother rose from his seat in the inn's parlor and gestured at the servant to bring his hat. "It means I recommend we start for London at once, before it is too late."

"Too late for what?"

Edward put on his hat and took his walking stick, his expression serene but his eyes twinkling with glee. "For you to win her back, of course."

Charlie muttered a rude reply and strode out to the waiting carriage, very tempted to leave his brother behind.

During the long drive, he had to tell Edward about Worley and Maria. It was a painful confession, but Charlie spared himself nothing. In the end, Edward was more understanding than anticipated. "I am hardly in a position to cast stones," was his response. "I came far closer than you did to marrying the wrong woman—with Father's approval, no less. Ironic, isn't it, how the scandal has been almost a blessing in some ways?"

"I thank God for it." Charlie nodded at his brother's raised eyebrows. "We all should, I suppose. Without it, we three would have gone on just as we were, never shaken from our paths. I cannot speak for you or Gerard, but I shudder to think what I would have missed, if that had happened."

"I had arrived at much the same conclusion," Edward murmured after a few minutes. "Although it is easier to admit it now that you've solved the dilemma entirely—as I knew you would." Charlie glanced at him in surprise. Edward nodded. "You're a great deal like him, Charlie. Nothing sets either of you off like a challenge, the harsher the better. Father would be devilishly pleased that you were the one who saved Durham."

"Astounded, you mean."

"No, pleased." Edward grinned. "And only mildly astounded."

"There you go," said Charlie at once. "I wasn't sure we were speaking of the same man."

Once they reached London, as expected, it was a frenzy. Every newspaper and gossip sheet was full of the Durham Dilemma, with excited descriptions of the dueling heirs, as one rag labeled Charlie and his cousin Augustus, who had also petitioned the Crown for the dukedom. The lawyers were practically living in Durham House, and they fell on Reverend Ogilvie's register and Mr. Thomas's letter like a horde of locusts. Every day, the barrister, Sir Richard Chalmers, came to prepare the case, with the supervision and insight of the attorney, Sir James Wittiers, and Charlie spent hours closeted with them, reviewing every word of his petition to the Crown. It was already facing intense scrutiny, and a single mistake in the lineage exposition now could undo all the good of Mr. Thomas's letter. In addition, a steady stream of callers passed through the drawing room—from genuine friends come to offer support, to rabid curiosity seekers come in search of spectacle—and Charlie had to receive them all with the austere composure of a duke. At this stage, he knew that nothing must be left to chance, and presenting the image of a duke, calm and utterly assured of his right to the title, would reinforce the hard evidence he had for the committee.

But worst of all, he couldn't visit Tessa. To call on her now would mean turning the blazing glare of public attention on her, and he couldn't do that. He struggled to put his thoughts into a letter, but found no way to write what his heart felt. He wondered how she was, if she had grown any fonder of London. He wondered if she'd ever found a good source of coffee, and if she liked it better than what he made for her. He wondered if she really had left him, preferring that their affair remain a secret, fleeting thing. He didn't think about that possibility for long, though; as more and more of his honors and responsibilities settled upon him, the more certain he became that he wanted Tessa at his side to share them. Every time the lawyers raised an argument, he wished he could puzzle it out with her. Every night when he watched Edward head to his own suite, arm in arm with his own wife, Charlie wished he had Tessa's hand in his. He missed her more than he'd ever thought possible.

Finally, in desperation, he turned to his Aunt Margaret, Lady Dowling, running down the stairs to stop her when he learned she had just called on Francesca, Edward's wife. Aunt Margaret was his father's younger sister, but nothing like Durham. From the moment she learned of his break with Durham eleven years ago, Margaret had opened her home and her arms to him. Of all his family, she alone seemed to understand him, and Charlie hoped this would be no exception.

"I need a favor," he said bluntly, deeply relieved to catch her without her friend Lady Eccleston. Lady Eccleston was a charming woman, and very amusing when one wanted to trade gossip, but Charlie thought he'd rather publish his intentions in the gossip papers than tell her. Lady Eccleston never could keep a secret.

"Anything," his aunt said at once. "Shall I send for Dowling?"

"No, I ask it of you." He hesitated. "There is a lady . . . Well, I haven't had a moment to spare since arriving in London, but I want to know . . . Well, I want to know if she's well," he finished lamely. "Would you call on her and send my compliments?"

"I am to be an emissary," she said in some surprise. "Who, pray, is this lady?"

"She's not like London ladies," he said, fixing a stern look on his aunt. "And I prefer her that way. If you alarm her on any count, I shall never forgive you."

"Go on." Margaret looked highly intrigued now.

"The moment I can call on her, I will," he went on. "If I went now, it would draw an unseemly amount of attention to her, and I don't want to expose her to that."

"Consolation to every woman's heart," his aunt murmured.

He flexed his hands, which he'd curled into fists. "So you think I ought to go, no matter what? Hang it all, I should. I'll tell Chalmers and Wittiers to bugger themselves for an hour—"

Margaret laughed. "No! Of course I will go to her. But you must tell me who she is."

Charlie gave a shame-faced grin. "Oh, right. Tessa Neville. The woman I hope to marry."

The commotion began not long after Tessa returned from her morning walk. Louise wasn't keeping a carriage or horses in town, so the main exercise available was walking. After a couple of days, Tessa began to miss the wild hills around Frome more than she ever would have expected. There was no peace in London; everywhere she walked, at every hour, there were hundreds of people about. She felt oppressed by the tall, close houses with the long windows that seemed to peer down upon her as she paced the pavements around Pall Mall. The parks were better, but then Louise fretted that she was so far from home, and might get lost or set upon by footpads, or even worse, miss a caller at home. A compromise was finally brokered by Eugenie, where Tessa would take two turns around St. James's Park with Mary in tow and then content herself at home for the rest of the day.

The truth was, Tessa didn't care when or where she walked; she only wanted to leave London. She knew Charlie had arrived—all the newspapers were full of it, reporting in breathless, overwrought detail about his demeanor and activities and the upcoming hearing about his title—but he hadn't come to see her. Not even a note had arrived in St. James's Square. She told herself he was much too busy, as she'd known he would be, but that didn't offer any comfort at all. Even Eugenie had quit mentioning his name, and if Eugenie gave up hope, Tessa knew it might as well have become an impossibility.

Tessa wasn't good at wrestling with her emotions. Normally she considered her options, practically and rationally, and then acted. Being caught in this half-life, desperately longing to see him yet afraid of what he might say if they met, wishing she could flee to Rushwood as much as she wanted to stay in London where there was still a chance he might visit, was shredding her nerves and paralyzing her from any action at all, which was utterly foreign and demoralizing. In addition, there were no accounts for her to mind in London, no problems to solve, no organization to oversee, nothing at all to distract her from her misery. Louise wanted her to attend soirees and pay calls on people she didn't know and sit in the parlor, sedately embroidering. Tessa began to think she really would go mad, and then that it wouldn't be so bad, as a bout of madness would persuade Louise that she must go home with William.

She was staring blindly at the pages of one of Eugenie's novels when the uproar broke out below. Uproars were not uncommon in Louise's house—William had removed himself to a hotel after a violent tempest over some dresses made up too snugly to fit—and Tessa had long since decided her best course was to avoid them entirely. But that was scotched when Eugenie knocked on her door and barged in, bright pink and out of breath.

"Oh my dear," she gasped, "oh, *my dear!*"

"What is it?" Tessa asked in genuine concern.

She put aside her book and got up to urge Eugenie into a chair. "Has something happened?"

Eugenie nodded, fanning herself with her handkerchief. "Oh, yes—or is about to—oh, I don't know! But I wanted to warn you—"

"Of what?" Tessa could barely speak; her heart leaped into her throat. Had Charlie come? She didn't even dare ask the question.

"Not Lord Gresham," said Eugenie, sending her heart back down with a thud. "But almost as incredible—oh, dear, you must prepare yourself—"

"For what?" Tessa began to panic. She ran to the window and craned her neck to peer out. A town coach stood in the street below, but she couldn't see any identifying marks. "What, Eugenie?" she demanded, whirling back around.

Before Eugenie could find breath to reply, there was another furious knock on the door and Louise burst in. "Oh my stars!" her sister cried in a whisper. "The Countess of Dowling is below, asking to see you!"

Lady Dowling was Charlie's aunt. A slow burning knot of hope ignited in Tessa's chest. "Now?" she asked stupidly.

Louise rounded on her, white-faced and determined. "Yes, now! Fix your hair!" She seized the bell and nearly tore it off the wall. "Tell Mary to find a decent dress. Pinch your cheeks. Eugenie, you're also wanted." The older lady's mouth dropped open, and the pink drained from her face. "I've never met a more elegant lady—her dress! Heavens above, if only she had called a week ago, when I might have changed my order for that sapphire riding habit to have such a collar! And her manner—so elegant! I daresay that drawing room has never held such a noble personage in all its history!" Louise advanced on Tessa, her rapture turning into fierce admonition. "Tessa, if you bear me any sisterly love at all, be gracious and polite. Lady Dowling is bosom bows with Lady Eccleston, who is nearly the hub of all gossip in London. They move in the highest circles. I have no idea why she's come to see you, of all people, but please, please, *please* impress her!"

"I know who she is, Louise." Tessa ignored the rest of her sister's plea. "She is Lord Gresham's aunt."

Louise froze, her eyes perfectly round. "His aunt," she whispered numbly. "His aunt."

"Am I really wanted?" asked Eugenie in a small, stunned voice.

"Yes," said Louise in the same blank tone.

Tessa inhaled deeply. She had no idea why Charlie's aunt might have come to see her, but she wasn't going into the parlor alone. "Yes, Eugenie, you must come with me. We mustn't keep the countess waiting."

They went downstairs together, Eugenie wringing her hands, Tessa pale and rigid with nerves. At the drawing room door, she smoothed her hands down her skirt, took a deep breath, and went in. "Good day, Lady Dowling."

A handsome older woman turned at her voice and smiled. Her silver hair was arranged simply but elegantly, and her dress was the same, a dark blue pelisse that Tessa would have liked to own herself. Her blue eyes twinkled kindly. "Mrs. Neville, Mrs. Bates. Do forgive me for imposing on you."

"Not at all." Tessa came forward and dipped her curtsy. "It's a pleasure to make your acquaintance."

"Oh my, yes, indeed, my lady," added Eugenie, hovering close to Tessa's side. "A *pleasure*."

"Not half so great a pleasure as I feel, to meet you," replied the lady. Her sharp gaze touched Tessa's face a moment before moving to Eugenie. "I've been told we have much in common, Mrs. Bates. My nephew has told me about his meeting with you. I do hope he wasn't impertinent."

"Oh, no, my lady, he was decorum and charm itself!" cried Eugenie, blushing pink again. "The model of a gentleman!"

Lady Dowling laughed. "I am relieved to hear it! He's as dear to me as my own son is. Indeed, I would never presume to call upon you if he had not assured me you wouldn't think it too much amiss."

"Not at all," said Tessa, wishing she could simply ask why Lady Dowling had come. "I hope—I hope he is well," she couldn't resist saying.

The countess's expression softened at the longing in her words. "He is in very fine health," she replied. "But I think in another way, he is rather unwell."

Tessa was frozen. She wished she dared look at Eugenie for help. "Oh," she murmured, not knowing what else to say.

"He is quite miserable that the lawyers have taken up every moment of his time," Lady Dowling went on. "He bade me call upon you and bring his compliments." She paused, tilting her head thoughtfully. "I realize I am a poor substitute for him, but he does hope to call on you himself soon, if he is welcome."

"Of course," Tessa said immediately, then blushed hotly. "That is, you are very welcome, and not a poor substitute at all."

Lady Dowling laughed again, her face gentle with understanding. "My dear, you have nothing to fear from me. If anything, I must be the nervous party; one false word and I shall be disowned by my own blood."

"Charlie would never—that is—I'm sure you have nothing to fear." Tessa wanted to smack her own forehead. She sounded like an idiot.

"Don't be so certain. The Durham men are quite implacable once their minds are set. The affections of an aunt would count for very little if I were to spoil his name with you."

Tessa sat mute from tension and uncertainty and hope. Did that mean . . . ?

"Mrs. Neville . . ." Lady Dowling hesitated. "If I may be so bold, I would like to offer an old lady's advice to a young lady: give Charles a chance. He is in earnest."

Tessa wet her lips. "About what, my lady?"

She smiled. "I will leave it to him to tell you— and if he dithers about it, ask him directly. I suspect you prefer it that way."

Blushing, Tessa managed to duck her head. "Yes, ma'am."

"Very good." Lady Dowling beamed at them. "Is this your first visit to London, Mrs. Bates?"

"Oh, yes, my lady," said Eugenie with an anxious glance at Tessa.

"I hope you will be able to see all the sights. London was quite overwhelming when I first came here, and now it is even more so. Have you viewed the Bridgewater Collection? My nephew Edward tells me it is not to be missed."

Tessa sat, half attending to the conversation be-

tween her companion and the countess. She recognized the same light, effortless charm Charlie
possessed in Lady Dowling, and she watched Eugenie's face light up as it had all those weeks ago
at the York Hotel. It made her yearn for him even
as it made her fear his visit. He was in earnest, the
countess had said; that did not sound like something one said about an affair, and Tessa was quite
sure London gentlemen didn't conduct affairs via
family proxy. But then that would mean he meant
marriage, a prospect both thrilling and terrifying
to her. The poised, elegant way Lady Dowling held
herself made Tessa feel dowdy and clumsy; the
easy, gracious way she spoke made her feel curt
and rude. She could never call on a stranger and be
as warm and amiable as Lady Dowling. It stirred
a sort of panic within her, that Charlie must have
his aunt in mind when he pictured a duchess, and
Tessa knew she could never be that way.

When Lady Dowling took her leave, Tessa almost
wilted in relief. Louise appeared in the doorway as
soon as the countess was gone, though, dashing all
hope of being alone with her thoughts.

"Well?" she demanded. "What happened?"

"Oh, my dears!" Eugenie's head was on a pivot,
turning to beam at first one and then the other. "Isn't
she the most gracious lady? So elegant, and so kind,
and so very *delightful*! And the cut of her pelisse—"

"Yes," said Louise rudely, waving one hand.
"Why did she call on Tessa?"

Eugenie stopped speaking and smiled proudly
at Tessa. "Why, she came to give Tessa His Lordship's compliments. I daresay we shall see him in
this drawing room soon!"

Louise sank onto a chair. "In my drawing room," she repeated with awe. "The Duke of Durham."

Eugenie nodded. "And what's more, Her Ladyship says he is in earn—"

"Eugenie," cried Tessa. "That's enough."

"Yes, dear," said her companion without a trace of penitence. "*Quite* enough!"

"Tessa." Louise looked at her with tears in her eyes—tears of joy, proven by the wide smile that split her face. "Tessa, you darling girl. You shall be the making of us! The Duke of Durham!"

Tessa shot to her feet. She couldn't bear another minute. "I'm going for a walk," she said, even though she had just returned from a walk an hour ago. Louise was so enraptured she made no mention of the fact that this violated their agreement, and Tessa was out the door as quickly as she could tie on her bonnet and summon Mary, who came running down the stairs in confusion.

This time she headed straight for Green Park, not caring how far from home she went. She cast a nervous eye over the elegant mansions that lined the western edge of the park, the pillars and cornices rising high above the lush gardens that surrounded them. The particularly elegant building faced in Portland stone was Earl Spencer's house, she knew; Eugenie had read about the perfection of its design in one of her guidebooks. Charlie's home must be a good deal more elegant, for he was a duke. Tessa thought of the rambling Tudor house at Rushwood, comfortable rather than beautiful. That was where she fit, in the unfashionable country house, while Charlie fit in the marble-tiled mansions of Mayfair.

Her head recognized all this, but her heart
fought back. She loved him; did that count for
nothing? And if he loved her, was that not enough
to outweigh all the difficulties? She tried to imagine life with Charlie, from the bliss of sharing his
bed and waking to his smile every morning, to the
agonies of attending balls and soirees and fearing
she would humiliate him with her outspoken ways.
She thought of the heartbreaking but safe choice
of continuing as she was, a supposed widow under
her brother's protection, compared to the dangerous, exhilarating leap of marrying a duke, where
so much would be expected of her in return for the
joy of being Charlie's wife.

She walked the park until the shadows grew
long and Mary pleaded to go home. The answer
was still not apparent to her as they walked back
through the streets to St. James's Square, but Tessa
knew one thing with painful certainty: she had no
confidence which choice would make her happy.

Charlie all but ran from the room, leaving behind
a startled barrister in mid-word, when he caught the
sound of Aunt Margaret's voice downstairs. "Did you
see her?" he demanded. "Is she well? Am I welcome?"

Margaret waved away the footman. "I saw her.
I must say, dear, she's not at all like the women you
carry on with."

"I'm done with them," he said. "What did she say?"

"Not much. I believe I surprised the young lady
greatly, and her companion. I felt quite gauche,
calling on perfect strangers."

"Aunt," he said through his teeth, and she smiled.

"She is well, and I believe you will be welcome. Although . . ." She paused. "Why didn't you tell her? The poor girl looked drawn and tense. Women do not presume, you know; a man must make plain his love, or we are dreadfully uncertain. And I believe this is a lady who likes to be certain."

He sighed. "She does. I would have told her, Aunt, but by the time I realized it . . . she had already left."

"Then I suggest you waste no time in assuring her. Her sister, Lady Woodall, made some mention of family leaving for Wiltshire. You'll have a harder task ahead of you if you must go all the way to Wiltshire to court her."

Charlie nodded. "The committee meets tomorrow, but the day after, nothing shall keep me from St. James's Square." On impulse he leaned down and kissed her cheek. "Thank you, Aunt."

"It was my pleasure." She turned to go, then turned back. "Do you know," she said quietly, studying him with perceptive blue eyes, "I believe your father would be very proud of you—of all three of you, but of you in particular."

"Don't—" he tried to say, but she put one finger on his lips.

"He would be," she said again. "I knew him longer than you, and I had the advantage of not being his child. Francis could be as stubborn as a goat, but it was always in defense of what he thought was right. And when he was wrong, he admitted it and tried to atone for it."

"I can't atone for what I've done."

"Nor can your father," she whispered. "You must forgive him, Charlie."

He was quiet for a minute. "I do."

She smiled. "That is all he would ask of you. He never gave quarter, but neither did he ask it for himself. I promise you, he blamed himself for your estrangement more than he ever blamed you. Just because he never humbled himself to beg your pardon doesn't mean he didn't feel the breach every bit as keenly as you did." She stepped back and pulled on her gloves. "Now repay him by learning from his mistake. Go marry that girl at once. Your father, and your mother, would heartily approve."

Charlie stared at her, then began to laugh. "I intend to, Aunt Margaret."

Chapter 24

The next day and a half seemed to last an eternity. The hearing passed in a long, mind-numbing blur. Charlie was thankful he had missed the first few meetings and motions on the petition and counter-petition. Sir Richard Chalmers, his barrister, laid out the claim in a droning voice that would have put the worst professor to shame, but driving each salient point relentlessly home. He swept aside every counterpoint raised by Augustus's counsel, while Augustus sat in the gallery across from Charlie looking more and more annoyed. Even Charlie could tell his petition was based on rumor and greed more than any solid footing, but he had duly received his hearing. The presentation of Reverend Ogilvie's register produced a jolt to the committee, and then the letter from Mr. Thomas another, opposing, jolt. When the committee's decision was finally read aloud, there was no great surprise, but an enormous relief just the same.

"Resolved, that it is the opinion of this committee that the claimant hath every right to the titles, honors, and dignities claimed by his petition . . ."

Charlie didn't hear the rest as men leaned over to congratulate him. From across the room, Augustus gave him a tight-lipped nod before disappearing into a crowd of his own supporters.

"Well done, Durham," murmured his Uncle Dowling, clapping him on the shoulder. "Well done indeed."

"Thank you, sir," was all he managed to say before being surrounded by well-wishers. There was more to it, of course, as the committee's decision must still be sent up to the full House and then on to the Crown, but that was a formality now. And with the dukedom decided, Charlie was besieged by peers maneuvering for another vote in favor of their projects. Under his father's gimlet eye, he hadn't been at liberty to indulge in politics, which made him a complete blank slate now.

But finally, he was free. When he went to bed long after midnight, it was with a sense of satisfaction. Durham would be his. And tomorrow, hopefully, so would Tessa.

By the time his carriage stopped in front of a neat town house just off St. James's Square, his heart had sped up and an irrepressible smile had fixed itself on his lips. It had been over a fortnight since he'd seen her—too bloody long—and he all but jumped out of the carriage, not even waiting for his footman to open the door.

The butler opened the door as he reached the step. He took one glance at the Durham town coach behind Charlie and swept the door all the way open, bowing low. "Yes, sir?"

"I've come to see Lord Marchmont." Charlie handed over one of his new calling cards, no longer his father's but his, engraved simply, DURHAM.

"Yes, sir, indeed." The butler showed him into an elegant parlor and vanished with inelegant speed. Too impatient to sit, Charlie circled the room, oblivious to his surroundings.

Had she read the papers? Did she know everything had been settled? He remembered her reaction to the news that it was a dukedom he would inherit, and his smile grew wider. That led to a recollection of what followed, and by the time the butler came hurrying back, Charlie had almost forgotten why he ought to see her brother first, instead of just demanding the butler fetch Tessa herself down.

"This way, Your Grace," said the butler, sounding a bit winded. "His Lordship will see you."

Lord Marchmont was waiting in the main drawing room. He had a genial, pleasant face, with Tessa's coloring but none of her direct boldness. In fact, he looked a bit worried as he bowed. "Your Grace, what an honor."

"How do you do, sir?" Charlie returned the greeting. "I beg your pardon for calling at this hour, but I have something of a most urgent nature to discuss with you, and I confess, I could not wait."

Marchmont blinked nervously. "I see. No trouble at all, none whatsoever. Won't you be seated?"

Before they could sit down, there was a minor racket outside, then the door was opened by a very lovely woman. She had to be Tessa's sister, Charlie realized; they looked quite similar, although Lady Woodall's hair was dark blond and she was a few inches shorter than Tessa. And her eyes were a normal, ordinary shade of green, not the clear lustrous peridot that sparkled in Tessa's face. Lady Woodall raised one hand to her bosom at the sight of them in patently false surprise. "Oh! Forgive me, I did not know anyone was in here." She turned a blinding smile on Charlie as she came forward, not sparing a second glance at her brother. "I am Marchmont's sister."

"How utterly delightful to make your acquaintance." Charlie bowed and raised her hand to his lips.

Marchmont cleared his throat. "Your Grace, this is my sister, Lady Woodall. Louise, His Grace the Duke of Durham."

"It is an honor," she said, sinking into a deep curtsy. If her eyelashes fluttered any faster, there would have been a breeze. "I hope I haven't interrupted anything."

"Er . . ." Eyebrows raised, Marchmont looked at Charlie, who smiled.

"Not at all, madam. In fact, I've come hoping to see your sister, Mrs. Neville."

"Tessa," said Lady Woodall, as if she hardly dared to believe it. "You've come to see Tessa?"

Charlie bowed his head. "I have indeed."

Marchmont cleared his throat again. "Ah, yes. She's not at home at present—"

"She'll be home at any moment," Lady Woodall said quickly, shooting him a severe look. "May I send for refreshment? Some tea? Some breakfast? Or even a brandy?"

He smiled at her eagerness. "Thank you, no." He hesitated, then decided he didn't care about propriety very much right now. "I've come to court your sister, Marchmont."

"Er . . . yes." The viscount looked anxious. Lady Woodall made a happy chirp.

"I daresay it's no surprise to you that I've

become very fond of her, since our chance meeting in Bath." Charlie wasn't sure what she had told them, but he was quite certain Mrs. Bates would have related every detail of his time with them.

"Oh yes, Mrs. Bates has told us so much of your kindness to her and Tessa in Bath, and later in Frome," gushed Lady Woodall in confirmation. "Let me add my thanks, Your Grace, for our entire family. We do worry so much about her, gadding about on her own—"

"Louise," said Marchmont firmly, and his sister closed her mouth at once, although a bit sulkily. "I'm sure it won't surprise you, Your Grace, to hear that my opinion of your suit matters very little," he said to Charlie. "My sister knows her own mind, and if she's opposed, there is nothing I can do to help you."

Charlie raised one eyebrow. "Do you think my cause is doomed?"

"No, no, no!" burst out Lady Woodall. "Heavens, the very thought!"

"I don't know," said Marchmont, frowning at her. "You will have to ask Tessa."

"I'm sure she will be so conscious of the honor you do her," began Lady Woodall, at which Charlie laughed.

"Indeed, madam. I know exactly how honored your sister will feel." He winked at her. "I'm hoping to persuade her anyway."

Marchmont's face eased. "Well, perhaps you've got a chance then."

"Splendid!" Lady Woodall beamed at them both. "Shall we sit down and have some tea while we wait?"

Fortunately, Charlie was spared a reply by the

sound of the door below opening and closing. He caught the excited treble of Eugenie Bates's voice, and his heart jumped a pace. Tessa must be with her. Marchmont knew it, too; he was already turning toward the door when it opened and Mrs. Bates came in.

"Lord Gresham!" she cried, her face wreathed in smiles. "Oh, no—forgive me," she said hastily, blushing pink. "You are Your Grace now." And she started to curtsy.

"None of that between old friends," said Charlie, striding forward to take her hands. "It's a pleasure to see you again, Mrs. Bates."

"A very *great* pleasure, indeed." She paused and glanced over her shoulder. "But I suspect you'd rather see someone else. Tessa was right beside me, where did she go?"

At that cue, she stepped into the room. Charlie's grin faded away and for a second he was lost, drowned in those crystal clear green eyes that saw right through him. She stood just inside the door, poised and composed, her hands clasped before her, and in that moment no one else existed in the whole world.

Marchmont cleared his throat. "You've a caller, Tessa," he said unnecessarily.

"Yes, I see." Without taking her eyes from his, she dipped a curtsy. "Your Grace."

"Well," said Lady Woodall after a moment. "Come in, Tessa, come in."

"Louise dear, would you come assist me in the dining room?" said Mrs. Bates. "I saw the most cunning way of arranging flowers in Bond Street, I must show you at once before I forget it." With surprising speed, she bustled across the room and towed Lady Woodall out before that lady could make more than an incoherent protest.

Marchmont cleared his throat once more. "Yes, well, ring if you require anything." And he followed the ladies.

Tessa barely stirred as her family left, but as her brother closed the door behind him, a flush brightened her cheek. "You've settled everything, then."

"With the title," he said. "Yes."

She nodded once. "Good. I was glad to see it in the newspaper this morning."

"Were you? Why?"

She opened her mouth, then closed it and frowned. "You wanted the title, now you have it. Are you not pleased?"

"Oh, yes—about that."

She swallowed. "And—And your visit to Lord Worley?"

He drew a deep breath; yes, it was best to tell her now and get it over. "He sent the letters because I had an affair with Lady Worley." The flush faded from her face, but her expression didn't change. "It was years ago," Charlie said. "I regretted it at once."

"You wanted to marry her," she said softly.

"A very long time ago," he agreed. "I was young; foolish."

"I know how that feels," she murmured.

He nodded, steeling himself to tell her the worst. "My father prevented the match, but he couldn't order me to be sensible. I succumbed to that youthful infatuation when I met her again as Lady Worley, three years ago. I had too much to drink and she said she still loved me, and I . . ." He paused again to take a breath. " . . . and I was still a fool. Too late I saw that she was merely miserable with her husband, and I was conveniently at hand. I went away and didn't see her again, and vowed never to carry on with another married woman. And if that had been the end of it, I suspect Worley wouldn't have cared much, but . . . she had a child. Worley's heir."

Now she was as pale as snow. "Is it your son?" she whispered.

"There is no way to know. Worley believed the child his for a year, and quite possibly he's correct."

Tessa swallowed. "What do you believe?"

He hesitated. "I do not know," he confessed at last, "but I devoutly hope the child is Worley's own." She didn't say anything. "Can you forgive me?" he asked. "It is a hard thing for anyone to overlook."

"So is mad, deranged behavior in church," she said. A bit of color came back into her face. "Worley still ought not to have done what he did."

"It would have been much more sporting for him to shoot me."

"Don't say that!" she exclaimed, and Charlie felt hope—and relief—surge in his heart.

"It would have been more honest," he said. "And I've come to value forthright honesty very highly."

She smiled, but it faded quickly. "Are you still in love with her?"

"With Lady Worley?" Charlie shook his head. "I don't believe I ever was—not truly. But I never really understood that until I met you."

She darted him a wary look before her gaze dropped, veering from side to side. "Is there anything else you wanted, Your Grace?"

"Want? Yes," he said. "I want you to call me Charlie again, not 'Your Grace' as if you're a housemaid."

"It wouldn't be proper," she said after a pause. "This is London, not a country village."

"Ah. And we're very proper here in London, are we?" He crossed the room as he said it, hoping this change in her was due to her sister, the last fortnight's separation, the shock of his confession . . . anything other than a change in her affections. "Where is the woman who called me a lazy, arrogant, ass?" he cajoled. "I've missed her."

She glanced up, the familiar fire in her eyes, and he kissed her. His hands cupped her cheeks, and without a word she melted against him. Charlie's heart leaped as that feeling of connection sizzled through him again, the sense that now he was complete. He gathered her close and took his time, making up for all the kisses he had lost over the last few weeks apart from her.

"I missed you," he breathed, his lips whispering against her throat, her neck, the delicate skin of her eyelids. "Desperately. Tessa, darling, can you overlook my many faults and marry me before I go mad without you?"

Tessa felt an almost physical thump as she came back to her senses. As usual, all her sense and hard-thought decisions went up in smoke when he touched her. She took a step backward, to clear her head. "I—I'm sorry," she said quietly. "I don't think I should."

He grew very still. "I cannot change what I did, Tessa, but—"

"Oh!" Her face felt hot. "Neither can I! It would

be unfair for me to hold it against you, when I have been guilty of deeds every bit as unwise. No, I . . . I fear I would be an embarrassment to you," she tried to explain as logically as her aching heart would allow. "Sooner or later, just as I was during that dinner in Frome. I didn't understand what the gentlemen were about; I said the wrong thing and made a fool of myself." She paused, then forced out the next painful admission. "I do that quite a lot, you see. I speak my mind and perplex everyone around me. My family has been mystified by me for years, but they're loving and kind and they can overlook it now." That point had helped persuade her this was the right choice; if even her blood relations found her odd, it would only be a matter of time before Charlie did, too.

"You don't mystify me," he said. "Not beyond what I can bear, or find fascinating."

"But it would matter to you if I were your duchess. You need someone who can throw grand parties and be a model of elegance and I can't do it." Her voice trailed off to a whisper at the end.

He looked at her for a moment. "Are you truly afraid?"

She managed to give a tiny nod. "Yes." She hated confessing it, but it was true. It was better to make the cut now, when she would have only happy memories of him, than to watch his understanding turn to impatience and then disgust. She had never regretted not marrying Richard Wilbur, and in time, surely, she would cease regretting this.

"Are you afraid of being a duchess, or of marrying me?"

"They are the same," she tried to say, but he made a dismissive sound.

"No. You talk of grand parties and elegance, but nothing of love."

Her heart jumped at the word. "It must be obvious that I love you."

He assumed a comically astonished expression. "Obvious? You just refused to marry me."

Tessa scowled at him. "Because it makes no sense for you to marry me, Charlie! We had . . . an affair, discreet and brief."

"If all I wanted was an affair," he said, "I wouldn't have begged my aunt to call upon you when I could not. I wouldn't have come to ask your brother's permission, very properly, to marry you. I wouldn't be standing here arguing with you about my fitness as a husband—"

"You'll make a splendid husband," she said quickly. "I—I fear I won't make a good wife."

He stared at her in obvious bemusement. Tessa kept her chin up. Her reasons were very logical, and he would understand eventually. That was why they would never suit, not really. Abruptly his dark eyes softened and one corner of his mouth curled up. Instinctively she backed up a step, recognizing the danger. She found it impossible to resist Charlie when he looked at her this way.

"But I need your help," he said in a compelling, reasonable tone. Oh dear; she could steel herself against charm and even kisses, but if he intended to *reason* with her . . . "Now that I've got the dukedom, I've got to run it. Eight large estates, all over England and Scotland. Well over three hundred thousand acres. My brother Edward has done all the work for the last eight years, so I haven't the first idea where to begin. Ah—and wait." He held up one hand as she pursed her lips. "I forgot to mention I must give up two of the estates. My father wanted me to deed one to each of my brothers. The entail ended with me, you see; Father inherited from his great-uncle, rather unexpectedly, so the tails were not renewed. Naturally he chose two of the prettier estates for Edward and Gerard, which means I shall lose at least forty thousand acres, with nearly twenty-two thousand pounds a year income."

"What is your income now?" asked Tessa before she could stop herself.

"After deeding those estates away, I shall have only eighty-six thousand a year."

Her jaw dropped. William was a wealthy man, and his income barely topped eight thousand. "Only!"

He nodded somberly. "You see my difficulties. How am I ever to scrape by on such a pittance? I hoped you might advise me on investments, how to manage the remaining estates, and so on."

"Hire an estate manager," she said unsteadily. "It's easier to get a new one if the first isn't satisfactory."

That wicked grin was back, in full force. "I've already got an estate manager; probably more than one. What I haven't got is a wife, and I want you. You satisfy me very much. I want you poring over my books, telling me when the underbutler is siphoning off funds meant for coal. I want you telling me what bonds and shares to purchase, but quietly, so my brother will think I've become a financial genius overnight. I want you beneath me in bed at night, telling me when to ride you harder and digging your nails into my shoulders. I even want you looking at me as you're doing now, as if I've lost my mind and you must be especially gentle and kind to me. Your gentle kindness makes my heart race."

"Duchesses are supposed to be elegant and polished," she said, ignoring the blush burning her face. "They have charitable causes and art salons and spend their evenings at the opera, dressed in silk and diamonds."

Charlie nodded thoughtfully. "I don't believe my mother ever went to the opera. My strongest memories of her, in fact, are of her wearing a plain linen dress with dirt on her hem, working in the gardens. She loved her gardens, and her roses. She cut dozens of stars from paper and hung them from my ceiling to cheer me when I had measles. She taught me and Edward how to swim in the pond at Lastings, with nary a diamond in sight. She set a pack of puppies loose in my father's study when she thought he was growing too irate with a visiting gentleman." He spread his hands. "She was the last Duchess of Durham. And I think she would be enormously fond of you."

Tessa bit her lip. "I don't like London much."

He winked at her. "Perhaps you haven't seen the right parts."

"You're not being sensible," she burst out, fighting back a smile. How did he *do* that, make her smile when she really felt something else entirely? It was that damnable charm of his, always aimed at her weakest point, always worming its way into her heart and turning it inside out, stripped of logic and sense and only aware of him.

"Of course not!" He caught her in his arms and pulled her close. "I'm a man in love, trying to persuade a confounding, infuriating, beautiful, brilliant, wonderful woman that she's bewitched me and I can't live without her."

She couldn't help laughing. "Flummery."

"No, it makes perfect sense." He tucked her against his chest, his forehead against hers. "First, I need someone to keep my indolent ways in check; you have had greater success than my father and all my tutors combined, so you are my best hope. Second, you need someone to make you laugh even when the accounts are off by a shilling and fourpence, and as you assured me, I have far too much humor for one person, so I am the best choice for you. Third, we both take great pleasure in each other's company, even when reading rotting marriage registers or discussing the dullest canal project known to mankind. Fourth, when we argue—which I have no doubt will happen—I plan to end the argument by taking you to bed until we forget why we argued, which both of us will find highly satisfactory in all ways. Fifth, I love you to distraction, far more than I could ever care for someone polished and elegant who would never go visit a canal works herself because she might lose her diamonds in the dirt." He paused. "Do I need more reasons?"

Tessa took a deep breath and surrendered. "No."

"And you'll marry me, in spite of all the trials it will entail?"

She blushed. "If you'll have me, despite all my inadequacies."

"They are my favorite parts of you," he said, making her laugh.

"As long as you know what you want."

His arms tightened around her. "I know exactly what I want. My brother once told me a man never appreciates something unless he has to work for it. He meant Durham, but you mean more to me than any rolling hills and old manor houses." His mouth curled again. "And Lord knows it was far more exciting, pursuing you, than it was Durham."

She smiled. "Yes, I agree." She leaned into him, resting her cheek against his chest and listening to the thump of his heart. Even dressed in the latest London fashions, looking every inch the duke he was, inside he was still her irrepressible Charlie, silver-tongued scoundrel, wickedly magnificent lover, and thoroughly decent man. She was an idiot to think she could give him up, she realized. All her resolve to refuse him and live out her days like a tragic heroine were no match for the pull he exerted on her heart and mind. No matter what she had to learn to be a good duchess, he was worth it. "I love you," she whispered, leaning back to look at him.

"I knew it," he said with a laugh lurking in his voice. "I knew you would have no tolerance for me if your deepest feelings weren't engaged."

She smiled. "The very deepest. But you must stop belittling yourself, or I shall have to tell everyone how determined and insightful you are. How brilliant and clever and daring and kind."

"No one would believe you."

"They will." She grinned. "Everyone knows I am brutally truthful."

"Then know this for brutal truth." He touched her chin, his dark gaze serious. "I love you. Passionately, tenderly, eternally. I love you as you are, not as some mythical duchess you imagine you must become."

"Then I shall try to overlook any sign of pompous ducal behavior you exhibit," she said, and he laughed.

"I knew we were well suited to each other."

"I never would have thought it," she allowed, though with a wide smile, "but we are."

Charlie grinned and closed his arms around her once more—for always. "Inarguably, my darling."

Epilogue

Two years later

He was born to be beloved.

Charlie stood over the cradle and watched his infant son sleep. Dark whorls of hair had escaped the baby's linen cap, giving him the look of a newly tonsured monk, and his tiny mouth puckered up and made sucking motions before opening wide in a yawn. He had gotten one little fist out of his blankets and seemed to be trying to free his other arm.

"He's more active asleep than most people are awake," he said, still mesmerized by his child. "We'll have to hire three nursemaids to keep up with him."

"I knew it," said Tessa, coming up beside him. "I knew it was unusual for a child to move so often."

Charlie put his arm around her. Even though the baby was almost two weeks old, he still hadn't gotten used to the newly slender figure of his wife. He'd forgotten how his arm could fit all the way around her waist. "Aren't you tired?"

"Yes, but I still want to see him." Her voice soft-

ened as she bent over the cradle. "He's beautiful,
Charlie. Even all wrinkled and red."

"He's quite the handsomest child I've ever seen,"
he agreed. "Even Gerard would have to agree that
my son is far handsomer than his daughter."

"Only if you beat it out of him," she replied.
"The very last thing Gerard wants to admit is that
you have surpassed him in any way."

"He needs a name still." Charlie had begun to
worry about this issue, which they still hadn't resolved. "He's to be christened today, you know. We
must tell the curate something."

"He's Gresham," she said. "I have very fond
memories of that name."

"He needs a proper name."

Tessa sighed. "We could call him Charles."

"No, not Charles," he argued, as usual. "It's
pompous. Charles is always the villain, the prosy
bore no one wants to be seated next to, the jilted,
unlamented, unwanted suitor."

"I shall ban Eugenie from the house if she con-
tinues to bring those novels." She spoiled her stern
words by grinning. Charlie winked back. Eugenie
had come to stay with them during Tessa's confine-
ment, bringing with her a large stock of novels. He
had begun reading them aloud as entertainment
since Tessa couldn't do much else in the evenings.
It wasn't very ducal, perhaps, to act out certain
scenes, nor to embellish his voice to suit the characters and action, but it made her laugh until she
cried. Even after two years of marriage, he loved to
make her laugh. "I like the name Charlie."

He chuckled. "He needs his own name, darling."

The baby stirred some more, wrestling his

second arm free of his wrappings. His face wrinkled and he let out a fretful whimper. Crooning softly, Tessa picked up her son and cradled him against her shoulder. She rested her cheek against the baby's soft head, and his little hand groped blindly, then clasped onto a fold of her dressing gown. With a sigh, the baby's squirming ceased and he snuggled under her chin.

Charlie knew how his son felt. He, too, was more at peace with Tessa in his arm. It still caught him off guard at times, how strong an effect she had on him. Far from being a disaster as a duchess, he thought she'd done better by her role than he'd done by his. As expected, she had taken him at his word and learned how to run the dukedom from the ground up—and even more surprisingly, she had taught him much of it as well. What first began as a simple desire to be with her had grown into a partnership. He was the one who signed his name to documents and gave orders to the stewards and bankers, but it was after frank discussion with her. For the first time in his life, Charlie thought he might actually have fulfilled his destiny and lived up to his father's expectations.

There was a timid knock on the door. "Come in," called Tessa.

Eugenie Bates peered cautiously around the door. "Oh, my dears, I don't wish to intrude! Tessa dear, should you be out of bed?"

"Come in," Charlie urged her. "As you can see, she is perfectly well, and woe to the man who says otherwise."

Tessa scowled at him. She had handled her pregnancy very well, while Charlie had been on constant edge, urging her to sit down, or rest her feet, or eat something every hour. That all changed when her labor began. The first scream she uttered seemed to shake him into a state of steadiness while she lost all grip on reason and raved madly at him for being so calm.

Eugenie came into the room, a small wrapped package in her hand. "I just had a trifling gift for young Lord Gresham. Of course he'll wear the Durham christening gown, but I wanted to add some *small* thing from the Marchmont side of the family."

"How very kind of you," exclaimed Tessa. "I'm sure it's not trifling at all." She made to place the baby back in the cradle, but Charlie put out his arms. The baby yawned and puckered up his face again, until Charlie began a soft patting on his back.

"How beautiful," said Tessa, holding up the delicate tatted cap she had unwrapped. "Eugenie, it's lovely. Thank you."

Eugenie's cheeks flushed pink with pride. "Thank you, dear. I did try to make it masculine, with the Durham crest worked in . . ."

"It's exquisite," Charlie told her. "You're too kind to take such trouble." She flushed brighter pink and beamed at him. "Perhaps you can help us choose a name," he said on impulse. "Tessa and I cannot agree."

"I suggested Charles, for his father," Tessa said, pursing her lips at him.

"Oh, very good," said Eugenie warmly. "I feel certain he'll grow up to be a great man, just like his father."

"No," said Charlie at once. Not that. No boy

deserved that burden, that expectation. The dukedom would be weighty enough. His son would be a boy who caused trouble and got into scrapes and vexed his parents, but who always knew he was loved. He would make mistakes like any man, and Charlie told himself he would be understanding when it happened, and never try to impose his will without explanation. He hoped his son would be a great man, but not because it was imposed upon him from birth.

He hoped all boys everywhere were so beloved.

"Alexander," he said, gazing into his tiny son's face. His father's eyes had been the same dark blue, and even though everyone assured him the color would change, somehow Charlie knew it wouldn't. "His name will be Alexander Francis Charles."

"A marvelous name!" cried Eugenie Bates, clasping her hands together. "So strong, so bold, so masculine."

Charlie looked at his wife. "Do you agree, my dear?"

She slid her arm around his waist. "It's everything Eugenie said. And it suits him." She looked down at their son. "Alex," she cooed, and the baby blinked his eyes at her. Gently, Charlie laid him back in the cradle.

"He'll need a brother. Perhaps two." He winked at Tessa. "Every boy needs a brother."

"Or a sister," she said tartly. "My brother would have been lost without his sisters."

"Oh, if we can give him a sister, so much the better for him," said Charlie at once. "Especially if she's like her mother."

Tessa smiled and laid her cheek against his

shoulder. "Managing and opinionated, headstrong and outspoken . . ."

"With superior intelligence, wit, and devotion," he finished, tipping up her chin to kiss her softly on the mouth. "And so breathtakingly beautiful it makes my eyes burn." He kissed her again, until both quite forgot they were standing over the baby's cradle, with Eugenie watching.

"I take it back," Charlie murmured to his wife. "He might need a sister and a brother."

K.I.S.S. and Teal: Avon Books and the Ovarian Cancer National Alliance Urge Women to Know the Important Signs and Symptoms

September is National Ovarian Cancer Awareness month, and Avon Books is joining forces with the Ovarian Cancer National Alliance to urge women to start talking, and help us spread the **K.I.S.S. and Teal** message: **K**now the **I**mportant **S**igns and **S**ymptoms.

Ovarian cancer was long thought to be a silent killer, but now we know it isn't silent at all. The Ovarian Cancer National Alliance works to spread a life-affirming message that this disease doesn't have to be fatal if we all take the time to learn the symptoms.

The **K.I.S.S. and Teal** program urges women to help promote awareness among friends and family members. Avon authors are actively taking part in this mission, creating public service announcements and speaking with readers and media across the country to break the silence. Please log on to *www.kissandteal.com* to hear what they have to share, and to learn how you can further help the cause and donate.

You can lend your support to the Ovarian Cancer National Alliance by making a donation at:
www.ovariancancer.org/donate.
Your donation benefits all the women in our lives.

KT1 0912

**Break the Silence:
The following authors are taking
part in the K.I.S.S. and Teal
campaign, in support of the**

Ovarian Cancer National Alliance:

THE UGLY DUCHESS
Eloisa James

NIGHTWATCHER
Wendy Corsi Staub

THE LOOK OF LOVE
Mary Jane Clark

A LADY BY MIDNIGHT
Tessa Dare

THE WAY TO A DUKE'S HEART
Caroline Linden

CHOSEN
Sable Grace

SINS OF A VIRGIN
Anna Randol

For more information, log on to: **www.kissandteal.com**

A V O N

An imprint of HarperCollins*Publishers*

www.ovariancancer.org
www.avonromance.com • *www.facebook.com/avonromance*

KT2 0912

This September,
the Ovarian
Cancer National
Alliance and Avon
Books urge you to
K.I.S.S. and Teal:

Know the
Important
Signs and
Symptoms

Ovarian cancer is the deadliest gynecologic cancer and a leading cause of cancer deaths for women.

There is no early detection test, but women with the disease have the following symptoms:

- **Bloating**
- **Pelvic and abdominal pain**
- **Difficulty eating or feeling full quickly**
- **Urinary symptoms (urgency or frequency)**

Learn the symptoms and tell other women about them!

Teal is the color of ovarian cancer awareness—help us K.I.S.S. and Teal today!

Log on to **www.kissandteal.com** to learn more about the symptoms and risk factors associated with ovarian cancer, and donate to support women with the disease.

The Ovarian Cancer National Alliance is the foremost advocate for women with ovarian cancer in the United States.

Learn more at www.ovariancancer.org

KT3 0912

At Avon Books, we know your passion for romance—once you finish one of our novels, you find yourself wanting more.

May we tempt you with . . .

- **Excerpts** from our upcoming releases.
- Entertaining **extras**, including authors' personal photo albums and book lists.
- Behind-the-scenes **scoop** on your favorite characters and series.
- **Sweepstakes** for the chance to win free books, romantic getaways, and other fun prizes.
- Writing **tips** from our authors and editors.
- **Blog** with our authors and find out why they love to write romance.
- **Exclusive content** that's not contained within the pages of our novels.

Join us at
www.avonbooks.com

AVON *An Imprint of* HarperCollins*Publishers*
www.avonromance.com

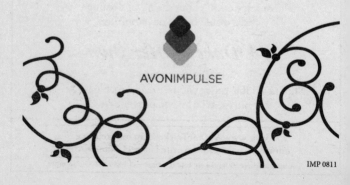